COLONY ONE

BOOK ONE

TARAH BENNER

ALSO BY TARAH BENNER

Recon

Exposure

Outbreak

Lockdown

Annihilation

Lawless

Lifeless

Ruthless

Dauntless

Bound in Blood

The Defectors

Enemy Inside

The Last Uprising

To my husband — for helping me fight the good fight.

"The trouble is not what robots will do to humans, but what humans will do with robots."

— Benjamin Blum

1

JONAH

Somebody's gotta exterminate the bad guys. I guess it might as well be us.

We're deep in the bowels of frigid Siberia, holed up in a portion of the Trans Siberian Tunnel. On the surface, Siberia is just the flip side of hell — twenty-five degrees below zero at noon. On a bad day in January, it can get even colder than Mars.

Venture outside and you might lose your nose. But underground the air is warm. We're deep in some Russian-made death trap fifty feet beneath the permafrost. It's a network of tunnels that stretch for miles, where American intel only goes so far.

There's a saying in the army: hurry up and wait. That's how we live our lives.

We're sitting across from each other with our backs against the tunnel: me and Rogers, Jefferson and Lovingood. The other guys are talking and smoking — it's all you can do when you're waiting to kill.

A rumpled cigarette is smoldering between Jefferson's lips as he doles out the cards. He's got these long brown fingers that seem to move at the speed of light. He's quick with his hands and even faster with his mouth. He'll steal the Skittles out of your MRE if you're not watching.

"What you got?" asks Rogers.

I look up. "Three. You?"

"Three."

"We'll go six," I say to Lovingood.

He writes down our bid on a crumpled scrap of paper.

"What d'you have?" Jefferson asks his partner.

Lovingood takes his sweet-ass time, rumpling his baby face as he scrutinizes his cards. "I got four. You?"

"Three." Jefferson raises his eyebrows. "Well, lock it up, then. Shit."

Jefferson is a hustler at cards. He started playing with his granny when he was six years old, but he tends to screw himself when he opens his mouth. That's why I'd rather partner with Rogers.

Rogers is smart, quiet, and dependable. He wants to be a surgeon.

I throw down a three of hearts, and Lovingood tosses in a five. Rogers puts down an ace with a look of triumph, but Jefferson slaps down a four of spades.

Me and Rogers swear.

"Eat shit, motha fuckaaas!"

Lovingood grins.

"Asshole," Rogers mumbles.

I shake my head, but before I can say a word, I get an alert on my Optix. It's timed — I don't get a signal here. I just have to hope that the other team is in position.

Jefferson's smart-ass expression disappears instantly, and the rest of the team falls silent. It's go time.

They stub out their cigarettes, and we throw our cards into the middle. Jefferson scoops them into his pack, and I grab my headlamp tacked up on the ceiling to make sure that the whole team is ready.

We all trained with the green berets in close-quarters combat, but our unit has one specific purpose: We're pursuing a node of the Bureau for Chaos that's responsible for hijacking a fleet of self-driving cars. They drove into the crowd after the Yankees won the World Series, killing thirty-two people from five thousand miles away.

Before that, the Bureau hacked the blast furnace at an Ohio steel mill. Six workers were killed, and nine were injured. That node was in China, and we took them out.

The Bureau spans the entire globe, but each cell operates independently. No job is too big or small. In their corner of the dark net, all death and destruction is celebrated equally. And yet we still think technology is our friend.

I check one last time to make sure everyone has all their gear. We won't be coming back this way.

I meet Rogers's gaze. We've done this before. "Stay alert, stay alive."

"Stay alive, sarge."

Once I knock out my headlamp, the darkness is absolute. I can feel the rough walls of the tunnel around me, but that sense of groundedness is dangerous, deceptive. It's not uncommon to take a route through the tunnels only to find a branch that's closed off or collapsed.

Stick to the map — that's the first thing they teach you in training for this. Wandering off course is how operatives get lost, and men who take detours rarely surface again.

As we move, I focus on the sound of boots behind me and the tangy stench of sweat. In total darkness, every other sense is amplified. You learn to see with your ears.

We march through the tunnel for what feels like hours, branching off where the map tells us and trying to memorize our route in case the worst should happen. Without the map, they wouldn't have to kill us. We would wander these tunnels until we starved.

I know when we're getting close to the point of contact. The tunnel widens, and the thermal imaging on my Optix detects a body around the corner. He's big and burly, and he's alone.

I flash the beacon attached to my pack to signal my team to stop. There are seven of us, including me. We have to work flawlessly from here on out or risk tipping off the entire node. One tiny screwup and they'll scatter like rats — never to be seen again.

I scuff my feet and watch the guard approach to check out the source of the noise. I'm the closest. I flatten my body against the wall of the tunnel and wait.

When he comes around the corner, I grab him from behind and garrote him with a piece of wire. He struggles — they always struggle — but I dig in my feet and wait for him to die.

The guy is shorter than me but much broader. He's got a wiry black beard that stinks of sweat and hands the size of baseball mitts. He fights me like a dying hog — a mass of meat and hair and limbs.

Finally, the guard goes limp. I lower him quietly onto the ground and signal the rest to follow me down the tunnel.

As we move, I keep my eyes peeled for any sign of warmth and movement. That guy was probably just the lookout. The real muscle will be farther in.

We round the corner. I see the door. My thermal imaging is picking up three bodies on the other side, but there could easily be more. I signal Rogers to go ahead with the battering ram. My heart is pounding, but it's the guiding pulse of this mission.

I grip my rifle and prepare for entry. He breaks down the door, and my team pours into the bunker amid a confusing jumble of voices.

The instant I blaze through the door, I realize our intel was off. Instead of the two or three hackers we were expecting, I'm blinded by the glow of two dozen computer monitors.

The blinking server lights give a starry backdrop to the filth and wires. The computers are resting on old doors laid across stacks of cinder blocks, and at least ten hackers are still sitting in front of their screens. They've been down here for weeks, by the look of things — sleeping on cardboard pallets among the servers bought and paid for by Russian oligarchs.

I yell out commands in Russian, but it's too late. The hackers scatter.

Rogers takes out one of the guards, and Jefferson covers me while I slip to the left. I shoot another guard squarely between the eyes and yell for the hackers to get down on the ground.

Out of the corner of my eye, I see a man raise his rifle. I turn and put a bullet in his brain, but that brief distraction costs me.

A shot meant for me misses by inches, and I turn in time to see the expression of cold shock smack Jefferson across the face as a guard releases a burst of fire.

I watch in slow motion as his brow furrows. I see the pain flash through his eyes before he staggers and falls to the ground.

I shoot at the guard. He goes down. Then a man in a heavy green jacket aims his rifle at Lovingood. I unleash a storm of bullets, but it's already too late.

Lovingood collapses, and I yell for Rogers and the others to go after the hackers. I dive behind one of the servers and take aim at the man who shot Lovingood. He grunts, but it wasn't a kill shot. I shoot him again, and this time he's gone.

I sprint out from my hiding place to get to Lovingood. He's lying in the dirt in the middle of the bunker. The bluish light of the computer screens gives his boyish face a cold, dead look, and blood is pooling beneath his head.

He's gone.

I crawl across the bunker to Jefferson, whose chest is heaving with pain. Blood is spewing from the top of his skinny thigh, and I can see the flicker of desperation in his eyes.

I reach around to grab an Israeli bandage from my pack, but his hand shoots up and grips my wrist. "I'm all right . . . Get the kid."

At first, I don't know what he's talking about. He's *not* all right. He's bleeding to death.

Then I see movement in my periphery. I look up just in time to see a lone figure in a hoodie grab something out of one of the computers. I shout out in Russian, and he makes a break for the tunnel.

I take aim and unload six rounds in his back. The hacker freezes and drops to the ground. Something rumbles just above me, but I barely notice.

When I cross the bunker and flip the body over, blood turns to ice in my veins. Two wide brown eyes are staring up at me in surprise, a thin line of blood trickling from his temple. He's got light-brown hair and a face that's baby smooth. He can't be a day over fourteen.

The distant rumble grows louder, and I feel the quake beneath my knees. I look up and realize the walls are starting to crumble. A flash of fear rips through me, and I open my mouth to call out to my team.

A second later, something heavy pummels me in the back of the head, and then everything goes dark.

I COME BACK to life with a gasp of air.

I choke and cough like a dying man, soaked in my own stale sweat. I blink fast in the blinding daylight and try to place where I am.

I'm not in the Siberian tunnel. I'm back in LA. The bedsheets are tangled around my legs, and I'm not wearing any clothes.

There's a girl perched on the end of my bed who looks as though she just tumbled out of a cologne ad. Her dirty-blond hair is tangled and teased, and her thick nightclub eyeliner is perfectly smudged. She's got her long legs tucked beneath her — black thong, no bra, and one of my T-shirts.

"Are you okay?" she asks, big sooty eyes wide with concern.

"Fine." I sit up and instantly feel as though I'm going to be sick.

"You don't look fine."

"I'm fine."

The dream explains why she's looking at me like that. I sometimes thrash around in my sleep, which tends to freak girls out. It *doesn't* explain my splitting headache, but it isn't the first time I've woken up like this.

I glance around the apartment and see the evidence of last night's escapades. There's an empty bottle of tequila on the coffee table and Styrofoam boxes oozing sweet-and-sour pork.

"You hungry?" asks the girl, whose name I don't remember. "I know a place where we can get —"

"No," I say, pinching the skin between my eyes. There is no way I'm sharing a meal with this girl. "I'm not hungry."

I glance at the clock. It's almost nine fifteen. "Shit."

I throw off the sheets and jump out of bed, nearly knocking her over on my way to the bathroom. I fly through the doorway and turn on the shower. It takes twenty minutes to get hot water in this place, which means I'm going to be taking a cold one.

I slam the door behind me, but it just bounces off the jamb. My apartment complex is one of six they slapped up with machines in less than three months. Everything about them is brand spanking new, but they might as well be made of cardboard and gum.

I glance at my reflection in the mirror. I've got deep circles under my red-rimmed eyes and dark hair sticking up all over the place. The shadow of a beard is creeping in along my jawline, and I'm in serious need of a haircut.

"You need to get to work?" calls the girl.

"Yeah," I yell, grabbing my toothbrush. "I'm late."

I jump into the frigid shower, hoping she'll take the hint and leave. Everything about my apartment is designed to discourage overnight guests. There's no filter on the tap and no food in the fridge. I don't leave clean towels lying around, and I'm always out of toilet paper.

Girls don't like it here, and I keep it that way for a reason.

Just as the water starts to feel warm, I turn off the tap and grab my towel off the floor. I feel scruffy, parched, and out of sorts, but there's no time to shave. Cassandra is going to be pissed.

I fly out of the bathroom and head straight for my hamper. I pull on a plain black T-shirt and a pair of wrinkled athletic pants. My shoes are around here somewhere, and once they're on, she's gone.

I look around. The girl is back in last-night's dress. It's a skimpy black number that barely covers her ass. Progress.

"All right," I say, hoping she'll get the hint. "It was nice to meet you . . ."

For the life of me, I can't remember her name. It might have started with a D, but I really can't be sure.

"We should party again sometime," she says, cracking a flirtatious grin.

Oh no.

"Uh . . . I don't think I'll be partying like that again for a while."

I don't mean to be a dick, but I really want her to leave.

"Well, if you change your mind . . ."

Shit. She's lingering. She's waiting for a hug or cab fare or something, so I do the gentlemanly thing and ping her a car. I charge it to my account and give her a very pointed "See ya later," when what I really mean is "See you never."

"Bye," she says, doing that thing girls do where they look over their shoulder, as if they expect you to ask them to stay.

Not a chance.

Waving her off, I grab a protein shake from the fridge and head out the door. My car is parked in the garage across the street. I hit traffic as soon as I pull onto the main drag. I am so — fucking — late.

I set the destination to work, lean back, and close my eyes. It's been a long time since I've had that dream, and I wish I could gouge that memory out of my brain.

It's been two years, and nobody wants to talk about the cyberterrorist assassinations carried out on the president's orders. It's funny how quickly patriotism can slide into the territory of national embarrassment.

When I enlisted, people were scared. The Bureau was hijacking air-traffic control and derailing passenger trains. It was terrifying because attacks could be carried out anywhere. The terrorists didn't even need to enter the country.

The day I turned eighteen, I walked into an army recruitment office and enlisted with 18X. I was deployed to China when I was twenty-two before being shipped off to Russia. That day, the tunnel collapsed, and the other team had to dig us out. I'm the only one who survived.

I was discharged six months after that extermination gone bad. My reward for eight years of service was a one-way ticket to the army shrink. The doctor diagnosed me with a personality disorder, but what I really had was a temper and too many unanswered questions.

While I got a career-ending diagnosis, the American people got a new lease on life. The new president promised to end the war on cyberterrorism and quietly withdrew our troops from Russia, Turkey, and China.

The conversation turned from national defense to global cooperation, and the American people forgot that we were still entrenched in cyber war.

The attacks didn't stop. If anything, they became more and more frequent. But the Bureau for Chaos quieted down, and corporations began to accept hacks as a necessary cost of doing business.

I get to the gym just a few minutes late and pay six dollars to park on the street. I slide in with a group of young moms, hoping to avoid Cassandra's ire, but there's no sneaking past the eagle-eyed bitch.

"Jonah!"

I freeze, willing myself not to be provoked. I hate every fucking second I spend working for her, but I really, *really* need this job.

"You're — late!"

"And getting later all the time," I remind her, forcing an accommodating smile and pivoting slowly on the spot.

At six foot three, I tower over Cassandra by at least a foot, but she still manages to cut me down to size.

Don't be fooled by her Bowflex body and perky little boobs. Cassandra is a drill sergeant in spandex.

"Your class is waiting," she snaps. "They've been waiting on you for eight whole minutes. Do you realize how unprofessional that is? A few of them already left!"

"I'm sorry."

"Sorry doesn't cut it. Come see me after," she says. A customer just walked in, which is my cue to escape.

ONYX is one of those ultra-trendy gyms in West Hollywood where people go to see and *be* seen. The floors are a shiny polished black, and there are mirrors covering every surface.

I skate through the lobby toward the back activity suite where my class is held Monday through Saturday. It's called Muay Tight, which is one step up from Booty Bootcamp.

I waltz in a good ten minutes late and earn several dirty looks from the women who pay two hundred dollars an hour to be here. I don't know what it is about kickboxing that excites them, but they're here and it's a job.

"All right!" I say, clapping my hands together and striding toward the front of the room. "Let's go to work!"

I ping the sound system to queue up the gym's playlist — some horrible custom EDM mix. We start every class with fast-paced shadowboxing, and twenty stick women start to move with the music.

The gym has rigged lights and lasers to flash with the beat, which gives the impression that we're in a dark club somewhere and these women are fending off unwanted advances. The heavy bass rattles my skull, and I will myself not to puke all over the front row.

I lead them through the warmup, trying to guess how many of them have had work done. I spot six pairs of fake boobs, nine suspected nose jobs, and a whole lot of surgically enhanced lips. Everything in LA is fake.

After warmup, we move to the bags, and I shout out the

ONYX-approved list of positive affirmations: You can do it! Come on, ladies! You are strong! Harder! Faster!

I'm not supposed to correct their technique or give any feedback that could be construed as negative. I learned that lesson the hard way after one edgy model/actress left my class in tears.

As the hour wears on, the music changes to let everyone know we've entered the "hard burn" portion of the workout. I'm supposed to ham it up with extra affirmations. The lights go wild, and my head pounds harder. A few of the women cheer as they pummel the bags.

This is my life now. I'm a professional cheerleader.

Finally, it's time for the cool down. My enthusiasm has tapered off, but they're all too tired to care. The lights come on as I stretch them out, and I get to my feet to let them know the class is over. Time to return to your pathetic lives.

The women start to pack up their duffle bags and pat the sweat off their boobs. One woman wearing just a sports bra and booty shorts makes a beeline through the crowd, and I busy myself with my Optix just in case she tries to talk to me.

She clears her throat and waves a hand to get my attention. Great.

I flip off my Optix and paste on a smile. She asks if I'm a trainer here. I say I'm not. She asks if I give private lessons outside the gym. I know what that means.

I brush her off as nicely as I can, fantasizing about having my way with a big fat burrito the second I get out of here. But the woman follows me across the room, and I freeze just inside the shiny glass doors.

I feel as though I've seen a ghost, and I do a quick mental check to be sure I'm not hallucinating. The woman is babbling on about her glutes. I am definitely still in hell.

Staring back at me from across the gym is someone familiar

and wildly out of place. The man is tall and broad and going bald. He's dressed in jeans and a black bomber jacket, but he wears the army on him like a second skin.

I haven't seen him in almost two years, but in this moment, it feels like yesterday. It's my old captain, Beau Humphrey.

2

MAGGIE

I roll out of bed with the immediate feeling that I've overslept. My heart is pounding against my ribcage, and my brain has been trying to wake my body for several minutes. It's five fifty — I'm already late.

I snatch my glasses off the nightstand and throw myself across the cloud of blankets. I careen into the kitchen, where Kiran is making coffee.

I can see the tops of his chocolatey thighs under his robe, which is more of Kiran than I'd prefer to see on any given day. It's his "gettin' some" robe, which means pocket-square guy must have spent the night again.

"Whoa. Where's the fire? Someone running a sale on tacky T-shirts from the trunk of his car?"

I look down. I'm still wearing my "Pretty Fly for a Jedi" shirt with no bra, but I'm too excited to take offense.

"It's today!" I say in a rush, fumbling with the deadbolt and the three chain locks on our door.

"It's today? Like *today*, today?" All of a sudden, the snark is gone. Kiran knows what this means to me.

"Go!" he shouts, his robe rippling with his enthusiasm. "Go! Go! Go!"

I fly out of the apartment toward the stairs, narrowly missing Mr. Meyers in all his open-robed glory. He's lived in the building since dinosaurs roamed the earth, and he is perennially suspicious of hipsters, iced coffee, and any modern form of communication.

"Morning, Mr. Meyers!" I shout as my bare feet slap down the stairs, picking up a hundred years of dirt and grime as I career toward the lobby.

I'm out of breath by the time I reach the bottom and throw my body against the door. I'm immediately assaulted by a swirl of noises and people — mostly the sporty set out for an early jog with their neon jackets and pale hairy legs. There are club kids still in their torn black tights and a few bums slumped in the shadow of the first stairwell I pass.

Even running down the street barefoot in my cupcake pajama bottoms, I only attract a few alarmed stares. That's the beauty and the curse of New York City — it takes a lot to get people's attention.

By the time I reach the little bodega around the corner, I'm gasping for air. The stitch in my side feels like the blade of a knife, but I am victorious. It's only two minutes past six, which means the papers will still be warm from the presses.

I cast around for the familiar neat stack. I've been writing for the *New York Daily Journal* for more than two years, but today is the first day I'll see my name in print.

"Hey, you," says a voice. "Pajama girl."

I turn.

Raj, the owner, is staring at me with that familiar pucker-lipped disapproval.

"Can't you read?" He points at the front door, which is

15

papered in so many signs that I have no idea which one he's referencing. "No shoes, no service."

I roll my eyes. Not even Raj can get me down today.

"I just need a copy of *The Journal*."

He continues to scowl. "No shoes, no service."

I let out a groan and navigate around the teetering display of sunglasses to the dwindling section of newspapers that are still in print.

I get a shiver as I sweep the first glorious copy off the stack. It's still warm, and the feeling that rolls through me can only be described as orgasmic.

I sigh. The big grabby headline on the cover? "Volkov Is Our Past, Present, and Future." A particularly evil-looking shot of the Russian president fills the cover page, with a smaller subheading referencing the latest Russian cyberattack — a heist on a branch of the US Treasury.

I scan the front page in a frenzy, eyes peeled for the two sweetest words in the English language: Magnolia Barnes. Magnolia Barnes.

Cliff always gets the final say on the headline, but he promised me my byline. Damn him burying me somewhere in the metro section.

I rip open the paper, feeling a little more desperate the farther my eyes travel down the page. My gaze lingers on a feature on one of the New York–based tech startups that's launching a satellite office in space before moving to a profile on the Maverick Enterprises wunderkind Tripp Van de Graaf. Gag.

I get all the way to sports and feel my fury bubbling over. Where the fuck is my piece?

I flip through the whole issue, but I'm not in there. Neither is my story about the city councilman redrawing district lines to sway his party's chances at victory.

"What the hell?" I don't immediately realize I've said this out loud until the bodega falls silent. I look up and realize that an older Hispanic woman is scowling at me from across the counter.

"Get out of ze way," says Raj. "You're blocking my customer."

I narrowly miss the very grabby hand of a Wall Street guy reaching around me for the cooler and elbow him out of the way.

Cliff *promised* me, and he flat-out lied. Two years I've slaved for that man — taking every junk piece he threw at me to fill out the online edition. Hell, I've even been pimping out my integrity for *Topfold* — our parent company's more profitable, clickbait-y publication.

Layla Jones, my sham alter ego, has been raking in the views. But today Cliff promised me a byline as a real honest-to-god journalist. In print — which, as my dad would say, is the only thing that matters.

"This isn't a li-vary," says Raj in annoyance. "Five dollar." His accent clips off the last "s" to make "dollar" sound singular.

"It was four last week."

"Za price just vent up."

My gaze narrows into a glare, and I beam him five bucks from my Optix. What a rip-off.

I shove past Wall Street guy and stumble back to the apartment in shock. I must look as though I'm entrenched in the most hideous walk of shame ever, but I don't even care.

By the time I reach the third floor, I'm completely deflated. I catch Kiran on his way out. He's ditched the porn-star robe for a pair of black Lycra shorts and a studded leather vest, and his bright-purple mohawk is in its full upright-and-locked position.

"Whoa, whoa, whoa," he says, stopping me with a leather-gloved hand before I walk right into his bike tire. "What's wrong?"

I let out a wobbly sigh and hold up the paper. I'm too devastated to tell anyone — even my best friend.

"They misspell your name or something?"

I shake my head, fighting back tears. "He didn't put it in."

"Your article?" he says, his warm brown eyes crinkling in sympathy. "He didn't put it in at all?"

I shake my head again. I'm on the verge of a total meltdown, but Kiran doesn't have time to lend me a shoulder to cry on. His main gig is as a bike messenger, and he's competing with a whole fleet of delivery bots for business.

"I'm fine," I lie. "I'll be fine."

"You're not fine," says Kiran, instantly dropping his breezy smart-ass facade. He knows that this is serious.

"I'm okay," I choke. "You go on. I'm just gonna finish up a Layla piece before my shift."

"Fuck that," says Kiran forcefully. "If I were you, I'd put on some pants" — his eyes flicker down to the dancing cupcakes on my PJs — "march my ass up to *The Journal*, and tear Cliffy a new one."

I let out a heavy sigh. "You think?"

"Abso-fuckin-lutely," says Kiran, that familiar fire in his eyes. "This is bullshit."

"It *is* bullshit."

"Cliff strung you along for two *years*."

"Yeah."

"Posting Layla Jones fluff pieces."

"Yeah!"

"Get mad, girl! Go get in his face!"

"I will."

"Good."

I glance behind him into the apartment. "Pocket-square guy go home?"

Kiran rolls his eyes. "Um, first of all, pocket-square guy has a name. It's Brom. Second of all, that was *one* time. And he went to work."

Wow. Kiran must really like this guy if he's defending pocket squares.

"Well, you better get to work, too, so you can afford an adult-sized robe," I say.

"*You* get to work!"

I laugh. Kiran always has a way of making me feel better about life. He wheels his bike into the hall, belting out a shrill rendition of "R-E-S-P-E-C-T" that's sure to piss off Mr. Meyers.

I slam the door behind him and run into my bedroom before my Kiran high wears off.

The floor is strewn with dirty clothes. I don't even remember the last time I did laundry. I snatch a pair of tangled-up jeans off the floor and pull them on over my ass. It's feeling a little extra juicy these days after late nights fueled by food-truck burritos and the entire Hostess snack line.

I cast around for a clean-ish shirt before realizing that I'm wearing the last clean thing I own.

Screw it.

I snap on a purple zebra bra under my Jedi shirt and grab my green army jacket with all the pockets. I careen into the bathroom and choke on Kiran's lingering cloud of spray-on deodorant.

I look as though I just escaped from a mental hospital. My wild blond curls are a tangled mess, and my bright-green eyes are tinged with red. I splash cold water on my face and smear on some tinted lip gloss. I can't find my sexy librarian glasses, so I'm stuck wearing my gigantic square tortoiseshell ones.

Forget mental hospital escapee — I look like a fortune teller from hell.

I grab my messenger bag off the futon and storm out of the apartment, earning a dirty look from Mr. Meyers down by the mailboxes. Instead of glaring back at him, I force a crazy-eyed smile and throw my weight against the door.

Kiran and I are lucky. We live in a rent-controlled apartment on the Lower East Side that used to belong to his aunt. It's a much better place than we should be able to afford, but every month is still a gamble when it comes time to pay the bills. That's when we find out if it's going to be a takeout month or thirty consecutive days of spaghetti and cereal.

I take the subway to Midtown to talk to Cliff, flipping through my feed to find where he buried my article.

It isn't there.

The entire digital edition looks different. It still reads *New York Daily Journal* at the top, but underneath is a line of tiny text that says "Part of the Futurewise Media Network."

I frown. Futurewise Media owns *The Journal* and *Topfold*, but they haven't been very public about it until now. I glance through the technicolor projection from my Optix at the people shuffling on and off the subway car. Most of them are commuters with their brains buried in *Topfold*.

I should be grateful. A few thousand people spending ten to twenty seconds in one of my stories will earn me a cup of coffee or half of a kung pao combination plate. But it just makes me feel like more of a fraud.

I get out at my stop, and my heart starts to pound in my chest. People blaze by in a blur of noise, and I can hear the steady beep of construction machines outside. A load of tourists bump past me in their rush to board the subway, and I push through the crowd with determination.

I will *not* take no for an answer.

I zone out on the short walk to the Futurewise Media building. It's a towering silver skyscraper just a block from Times Square. *The Journal* offices are on the forty-fifth floor, and they share the building with at least a hundred other publications.

I shove around a small fleet of delivery bots filled with the staff's coffee orders from across the street. They're glorified coolers on wheels equipped with cameras, sensors, and GPS, but they deliver on the cheap. I pretend to trip and kick one over on my way to the elevator. Take that, robots trying to put Kiran out of work.

Everyone in the elevator is immersed in their feeds. It's easy to tell the businesspeople from the content creators. The finance and ad people are all in suits — fresh and glowy from morning spin class and artisan avocado toast. The content creators are sloppy, jumbled, and exhausted. Most of them are in jeans and T-shirts like me.

They're deeply entrenched in their own stories, making minor corrections and refreshing their views. Some of them are even dictating replies to comments in low rapid voices. Engagement is the name of the game in immersive journalism, so rapid-fire responses are key.

The elevator dings, and I almost lose my nerve. I don't want to talk to Cliff, but it's that or stew in silent misery.

A guy with a Jesus beard and a frizzy black ponytail pushes past me, and I resist the urge to kick him in the seat of his skinny jeans. I've never met him, but I've watched his stuff. He's a tech journalist for *Topfold* whose job is to review the latest gadgets and patches. He thinks he's God in scraggly coffee-breathed form.

I grit my teeth and shuffle toward Cliff's office, blinking in the bright light coming through the enormous windows. Every inch of available wall space that isn't glass is covered in screens. They're playing a mix of digital news networks and *Topfold*'s trending stories. One of my own — a Layla Jones piece — flickers on over the water cooler.

Sadly, "Around New York in Eighty Pizzas" is my most viewed story ever. It scored a seventy-eight when we ran the idea through ViralGauge, but even the algorithm underestimated its success.

The story is ten whole minutes of hot cheese goo stretching itself from the pizza to my mouth and greasy pepperonis glistening under red neon lights.

The week I tried eighty pizzas for the story, I gained four pounds and developed a raging case of cystic acne. But that hedonistic masterpiece put Layla Jones on the map and lives on as one of the go-to stories for tourists hoping to get a bite of authentic New York–style pizza.

I reach the glass walls of Cliff's office. At first glance, he seems to be yelling into thin air. He's swimming in a blue cylinder of light beaming from his Optix, but as I look closer, I can just make out the ashen face of another hapless writer.

Cliff wears his Optix as a single titanium stud that looks utterly out of place in his dark thicket of eyebrows. One end projects the image in front of his face and bends the sound of the call toward his ear. The other end is a micro-cam that picks up his image and voice.

Cliff looks like the crotchety high-school principal in every movie ever made. He's got greasy olive skin, thick sausage-y fingers, and a ring of curly black hair that looks like pubes. He's always got stains on his wrinkly button-downs, and he's always spitting and sweating.

I knock. Cliff keeps talking but waves me in, and the tiny camera swirling from his Optix recalibrates to capture his movement. His office smells like fast-food grease and old gym socks.

As I slink in and slide the door shut, I am hyperaware of the fact that Cliff manages dozens — if not *hundreds* — of writers. I'm barely a blip on his radar.

He finishes his rant and disconnects the call.

"Good morning," I say, momentarily forgetting my resolve to be cold, sharp, and demanding.

"Is it?" says Cliff. "If I get one more call from some jack-off defending Lisa Strauss's fashion choice at the MTV video music awards, I'm going to kill myself." He lets out a sigh and slams back into his rolling chair. "What can I do for you, Maggie?"

Suddenly, every shred of anger and disappointment I felt this morning rises up in my throat. It comes on suddenly like a flash of inspiration, only it's bitter, heated, and out of control. I reach into my bag, pull out the paper, and slap it down on Cliff's desk.

"You didn't put it in," I say.

Cliff gives me a blank look.

"My redistricting piece," I add, suddenly flustered. "The scandal — a full-on middle finger to the democratic process." I rip open the paper to Tripp Van de Graaf's smug face. "Instead it's full of this shit."

Cliff is still staring at me as though he thinks he might have me confused with someone else. It's as if he doesn't even remember the piece.

"You *said* it would be in today's issue," I press, working to keep the waver out of my voice. "What the hell happened?"

Suddenly, he groans and puts a hand to his forehead. "Oh, no . . . Not this again."

"What?"

"Look," he says, thrusting his head forward like a matter-of-fact rooster. "It was out of my hands."

"What was out of your hands?"

"The decision came from up top. And it wasn't just you."

"What wasn't?"

He sighs. "You know how hard it is to hawk an actual print newspaper this day and age?" He lets out a dark guffaw. "It's 2075, for cryin' out loud. People don't read anymore. They're only consuming immersive content."

"But this is important," I growl.

"Believe me, I know. But the boys upstairs are lookin' to cut costs. You know Futurewise just got bought by Maverick Enterprises?"

"No."

"Of course you don't. You're a 'creative.'" He puts the most condescending air quotes around the word. "I don't get that luxury. It's my job to deal with this mess, and I just got word from our new corporate overlords that we're not takin' any more freelance content for *The Journal*. From now on, all the news copy is gonna be AI-generated."

"*What?*"

"The algos already tell us what people want to read . . . This just streamlines the process. The program A/B tests hundreds of ideas, gathers up all the little tidbits it needs from the web, and generates the text — all in a few minutes."

"That's not reporting," I say, shaking with rage. "That's a term paper — and not a very good one."

"What can I say, kid? If it bleeds, it leads. People will consume whatever the *Topfold* algorithms slap in front of their stupid faces. If we want our paper to be part of the conversation, the stories have gotta be just as sexy."

"But this is the *news!*" I scream. "Not 'Who wore it better?' We're the fourth fucking estate!"

It occurs to me at this moment that Cliff's office isn't exactly soundproof. I can sense people watching me from the other side of the glass, but I don't care.

"Keep your shirt on, kid. They still need more Layla for

Topfold. You're raking in the views with that food porn. Keep it comin'."

"This is bullshit," I say, my voice low and deadly. "You already gave my story the green light. You said if I killed it, you'd give me a byline."

"Well, I guess you didn't kill it," says Cliff with a shrug. "Take it up with billing. We're done here."

Cliff settles in and touches his Optix. This is his way of saying he's done with me — finished, problem solved, on to the next thing.

I can't believe it. He's dismissing me. After all the work I've done for him — all the blood, sweat, and tears I've poured into my articles over the last two years — he still treats me like a piece of shit.

"Are you fucking kidding me?"

"Keep your voice down."

"No!" I shout. "I'm one of the few *real* journalists you've got left, and you treat me like garbage!"

"Oh, you're a real journalist now?" he says. "Tell me. What the fuck is this all about?" He gestures down at my T-shirt and wrinkled jeans. "Is that the look of a true professional? Or are you just so full of integrity that you can't be bothered to put on real clothes?"

I open my mouth to form some snarky reply, but no words come out.

"Listen. Unless you want to be writing Layla Jones clickbait for the rest of your life, you'd better clean up your act and show some goddamned respect."

I fall silent. It's not the moment of silence before the clap of thunder or the I'm-gonna-get-you kind of silence. It's full of shame and sadness, and I have to get out.

I turn and shove my way out of Cliff's office before the

waterworks start. I can feel the humiliation scorching my face — the heat of failure burning me from the inside out.

People are staring. I hate them all. I will not give them the satisfaction of a show. I will get to the elevator before I completely lose my shit.

On the way down to the ground level, I focus on my breathing. It's low and shallow, and it's the only thing keeping me tethered to the earth.

I reach the lobby in a daze and stride purposefully toward the door. The delivery bot I kicked is still there, turtled in a pool of somebody's cold coffee.

I get an idea. It's the surge of clarity after the storm, fueled by rage and the manic energy of someone who's got nothing to lose.

I take a deep breath to stave off my tears and click my Optix to record. It's Layla Jones live — and it is a *doozy*.

3

MAGGIE

Three hours later, I'm sitting behind the counter at Revolutionary Café, wondering what the hell I've done.

In a blind rage, I streamed a live rant from Layla Jones about Futurewise Media's decision to farm out all of its *Journal* articles to robots without bothering to give notice to staff writers or any of its freelance contributors.

Re-watching the entire thing at the café, I'm stunned by my own vitriol. It's raw, unfiltered, and totally insane. It isn't Layla, but it sure is me.

In my alter ego's profile pic, I'm wearing contacts and my most winning smile. Blond curls fill the frame.

Layla Jones is as sugary as her puns. "Donut Underestimate Me: A Guided Tour of New York's Most Scrumptious Donut Holes-in-the-Wall." Two point five million views. It definitely strikes a different tone than "Futurewise Media's War on Journalism."

Even more shocking is the response. My rant has had more than three hundred thousand views in the past two hours. The comments are lighting up — mostly hate mail directed at Futurewise Media or messages of support for me/Layla.

I don't know what I was thinking. Cliff has most definitely seen this already. I'm just surprised he hasn't pinged my Optix to boot my ass off *Topfold*, too.

I am so screwed.

By the time Kiran rolls into the café, I'm sitting behind the counter torturing myself in the comments section. Revolutionary Café is always slow this time of day. The afternoon rush is over, and the tip meter flashing in the corner of my feed is depressingly low.

Kiran and I have worked here since we first came to New York. It's how we met, and it's how I eat when my Layla Jones stuff is less than lucrative. The coffee shop is one of those grungy far-left cafés with posters of famous revolutionaries plastered all over the walls and ballsy quotes stamped on the cups.

Kiran knows something is up the second he walks in the door. He's nursed me through two breakups and one professional failure after another.

"What happened?" he asks, rolling his bike inside and propping it up against the wall.

I shake my head. I can't even explain what happened this morning. It felt like an out-of-body experience. Even sensible, caffeinated me cannot comprehend how I managed to fuck myself so thoroughly.

"Oh, no," says Kiran. He just caught sight of the half-eaten triple-chocolate Bundt cake in front of me. "What happened?"

I open my mouth and close it again. I think I might throw up.

"Use your words," says Kiran in a cajoling voice. "Suicide by chocolate isn't the answer."

"There are no words," I say. "Though, total nuclear annihilation does come to mind."

Kiran's eyebrows shoot up. "You let Cliff have it? Jesus Christ Superstar."

"It was *bad*."

"How bad?"

"Like I just nuked my whole career bad."

"What did you say?"

I sink back against the counter, wiping my chocolatey fingers on my apron. "It's not what *I* said . . . It's what Layla said."

"Huh?"

"Go to *Topfold*. It's the number-one trending story."

Eyes wide, Kiran flips on his Optix. He doesn't have to scroll at all to find the Layla Jones tirade. I see the reverse image of my face fill his Optix, and I cringe as his expression goes from confused to proud to scandalized — all in the span of about ten seconds.

"Oh, honey . . ."

"I know."

He keeps watching. "Oh . . . Oh, *no*."

"Tell me about it."

He turns it off, eyes as round as coffee cups, and I force a sad smile. "On the plus side, the donut story is getting some nice spillover traffic from this."

"Stop it," says Kiran, coming behind the counter and snatching the rest of the Bundt cake off my plate. "Stop feeling sorry for yourself." He takes an enormous bite.

"Hey!"

"What?" he says around a mouthful of chocolate. "I logged like fifty miles today. I know you didn't pay for this anyway . . . You'll get your break — just not with those ass-clowns."

"It's not about my big break," I say. "I need the money. Cliff is gonna fire me — I mean Layla — and I can't live on what I make here."

Kiran rolls his eyes. "You and Layla will be fine."

"If I don't get sued for libel."

"Well, if you do, I'm sure Rob would give you more hours to cover your lawyer's fees. There's nothing he likes more than sticking it to the man."

I grin despite my best efforts. Kiran's right. Rob, the owner, charges Wall Street guys eight bucks for a Luxemburg latté and ten bucks for a Mandela mocha, but he's got a soft spot for starving artists. For three bucks, writers can come work on their novels and screenplays and drink black coffee all day long.

Suddenly, the little bell over the door dings. Kiran slinks back over to the other side of the counter, waggling his eyebrows as he shoves the last of my Bundt cake into his mouth.

A man and a woman walk in. The man is tall and dressed in a nice gray suit. He's got pockmarked skin and a receding hairline but walks with the confidence of someone who's wildly overpaid. The woman has a cool Nordic beauty: straight blond hair done up in a bun, New York skinny, white funnel-neck coat that probably cost more than my rent.

"Hi," I say, summoning my most friendly barista tone. "What can I get for you?"

The man and the woman exchange a look. Then their gazes swivel back to me. "Magnolia Barnes?"

Shit. I'd been joking about the lawsuit, but maybe I shouldn't have been. These guys are dressed nice enough to be lawyers, though that kind of speed seems fast even for Future-wise Media.

"Sh-she's not here," I stammer.

This isn't the first time I've pissed off the subject of one of my stories, but it is the first time I've had someone hunt me down at the café.

"Maggie's not working today," I add.

The woman purses her lips in what might have been a smirk and then reaches up to the tiny Optix bar on her eyebrow. When she touches it, a life-size image of me fans out around her. It's the photo from my press credentials. I'm even wearing the same stupid glasses.

"Shit," I whisper.

A flicker of confusion flashes across the woman's face, and the man clears his throat.

"My name is Natalie Dubois," says the woman. "This is my colleague, Erik Blain."

I don't say a word. Clearly they already know who I am, and the sort of people who hunt you down by your picture aren't the type you want to exchange pleasantries with.

"Do you think you could knock off early today?" the woman asks. "Get someone to cover for you?"

"Why?" I ask. My throat is suddenly very dry.

"We'd like you to come with us."

At those words, the blood turns to ice in my veins. This is it — every journalist's worst nightmare.

Piss off the owner of a nail salon that's not paying its undocumented workers, and you should probably find someone else to fill your acrylics. Piss off a multibillion-dollar corporation, and you'll need to find another profession. Piss off someone more dangerous than that? Those are the journalists found in bathtubs with lethal doses of heroin in their systems.

I glance across the café at Kiran, who's leaning against the wall pretending to mind his own business. He reads the panic in my eyes and shifts to block the front door. Reaching into the holster around his middle, he produces an expandable baton. It's the kind the police use, and he carries it on his route for self-defense.

"Please, Maggie," says the woman. "Don't be alarmed. We only want to make you an offer."

"What sort of offer?" I ask. *An offer I can't refuse?*

"We want to offer you a job."

I glance over at Kiran once again. "I already have a job."

The woman expels a tiny burst of air through her nose. Is that how she laughs?

"Let's just say that this job does not involve handling hot liquids." She tilts her head forward and gives me a knowing look. "We saw the Layla Jones piece you posted this morning."

I feel the blood drain from my face. "Oh."

She glances over at her silent colleague, whose expression gives nothing away. "Let's just say that the post made an *impression* on my employer."

She sets her purse on the counter and produces a card. It's unlike any business card I've ever seen before. It's clear plastic and heavy, with a frosted white logo but no company name. There's just her name — Natalie Dubois — and an address. The logo is unfamiliar to me — sort of a Celtic knot inside a circle.

I catch Kiran's eye again and give a tiny headshake. I've never heard of hitmen — or hitwomen — handing out business cards.

"Come to the office tomorrow at nine. We'll be able to answer any of your questions."

"Is this a job interview?" I ask, totally stunned.

Natalie gives a playful half shrug. "Call it whatever you like." She picks up her purse as though she's getting ready to leave and then pauses. "And Ms. Barnes?"

I wait.

"Please tell no one about our conversation. This meeting is strictly confidential."

My mouth falls open, but I'm lost for words. Kiran moves aside so that she and her silent goon can leave, and I shoot him a bewildered look. Either I'm a dead girl walking, or I've just been offered the chance of a lifetime.

4

JONAH

"You look like hell."

"Nice to see you, too."

My former captain and I are sitting in a booth at the grimy diner on Sunset Boulevard, and I'm already wishing that I'd ditched Humphrey to get my breakfast burrito alone. He's got this look that tells me he wants something, but after everything he's done for me, I know I owe him one.

"Sure didn't look like you were glad to see me," says Humphrey. "You looked like you wanted to hang yourself on one of those Pilates machines."

"What can I say?" I mutter, choking down some black coffee to try to settle my stomach. "It's a job."

"Whaddya mean it's a job? Of course it's a job. You know how many asses I had to kiss to *get you* that job?"

I don't answer. I don't want to sound ungrateful, and everything I've done up until this point probably makes it seem that way.

"My ex-brother-in-law owns that hellhole. You know how it

makes me look when I recommend someone who comes into work late, hungover, and looking like shit?"

"How do you know I was late?"

"Your buddy Cassaundra told me."

"*Cassandra.*"

"Whatever," he says, grabbing a menu from behind the ketchup. "Kind of a bitch. Nice ass, though."

I let out the breath I've been holding, and Humphrey shakes the menu open.

"So what's good here?"

"No idea."

"You never eat here?"

I shake my head. The diner is one of those places that's been redone to look as though it's from the 1950s. There's a long counter with plush burgundy stools, a couple of narrow booths, and heavy beige coffee cups with ads on them. It's not a place I'd normally go, but it's Humphrey's kind of restaurant.

"I don't know how you live in this city," he gripes. "Everything's quinoa this, kombucha that. When I'm in America, I wanna eat like an American, ya know?"

I nod. It's easier that way.

The waitress breezes by to take our order. Humphrey orders a patty melt with fries. I order biscuits and gravy with a side of bacon.

"Bacon?" says Humphrey. "It's eleven thirty."

"What are you doing here?" I ask, feeling exhausted. The fact that Humphrey is beating around the bush by criticizing me just strengthens my theory that he must want something.

"Is that any way to greet your old friend and mentor?"

I crack a grin and shake my head. "Sorry."

"I came here to offer you a job, actually . . . If you swear that you'll actually show up on time."

I don't say anything because I'm ashamed. I haven't held a job for longer than six months since I was discharged, but Humphrey keeps showing up to save the day. I don't know what he sees in me. Maybe he feels responsible for what happened in Siberia.

"Hello?" says Humphrey. "This is the last time I'm gonna stick my neck out for you, kid. I mean it."

"You don't have to."

"I know I don't have to. I'm not runnin' a charity, dipshit. I'm doing this outta the goodness of my heart."

"Why?"

"If you must know, a friend asked me for a recommendation. Your name was the first that came to mind."

"A recommendation for what?"

Humphrey glances around, as if checking to make sure that no one is eavesdropping. The nearest table is a family of four on their way to see the Walk of Fame. Our waitress is wiping off a table two booths over. No one is paying any attention.

"How would you like to train your own unit?" he asks.

I roll my eyes. "Did you forget that I was discharged from the army?"

"This isn't with the army. It's private-sector work."

"What do they want me for?"

"I told you. Training. Leadership. It's two weeks of officer training plus ten weeks of boot camp, and then you'd be overseeing the operatives you trained. It's a pretty cushy gig, really."

"Who would I be training?"

"I can tell you who you *won't* be training . . . C-list actors and Orange County housewives."

I roll my eyes. "Do they have military experience?"

"Mostly no. These are specialists they want trained for a private military unit — intel eggheads."

I frown. "Why would they want me? I couldn't even land a protection detail with my record."

"You're still the most talented close-quarters fighter I've ever seen. You're no Miss Congeniality, but you get the job done."

"How long is enlistment?"

"Five years. After that, if you keep your nose clean, you can re-enlist or go do something else."

"Five years?"

"The pay is better than you're used to, *and* it comes with a signing bonus."

"And you work for these people?"

Humphrey shakes his head. "Nah, I'm too old. A lieutenant who served under me in Russia is on the recruitment committee. His name's Buford. They're looking for specialists, and he asked for some recommendations."

I frown. Humphrey's offer sounds good, but I can tell by his demeanor that he thinks I'm going to turn him down. "What's the catch?"

He glances around once again to check that we can't be overheard. "It requires a change in locale."

"Where would I be stationed?"

Humphrey glances toward the ceiling, but whether he was making an appeal to God or rolling his eyes, I can't tell.

"What do you know about a company called Maverick Enterprises?"

"The space company?"

He nods. "They're building out a private military presence up there called the Space Force."

"For what?"

"What do you think?"

"Counterintelligence?"

"Nah. They won't ever cop to that. This is supposed to be an all-civilian workforce doing research."

I shoot Humphrey a look. "Come on. It's all over the news. Everyone thinks Maverick is being paid to spy on the Russian military installation up there."

"Well, I don't know anything about that. I'm just telling you what they told me."

I stare at Humphrey for a moment. Humphrey wouldn't lie to me, but he's too smart to believe the words coming out of his own mouth. He knows as well as I do that the Department of Defense has had to get creative with the Bureau for Chaos and freelance Russian hackers siphoning trillions of dollars out of the US economy.

"So you're offering me a job in space?" I say finally.

"Wyatt — you're twenty-eight years old with an administrative discharge on your record. You haven't held a job for more than six months since you got out. Someone offers you an opportunity like this, you take it."

I look away, frustrated by how badly I've fucked up.

"You're not your father, kid. Don't shoot yourself in the foot just because you've had a rough go of it. It's gotta be better than the hellhole you're workin' in now, hasn't it?"

I don't have a chance to answer. Right then, our food appears, and Humphrey shifts his attention to flirting with the waitress. Then he takes an enormous bite of his patty melt and closes his eyes in ecstasy.

Humphrey doesn't have to sell me on it. Hell, I'd take a job in Antarctica if it came with a signing bonus and got me away from Cassandra. ONYX doesn't pay half of what my last job did. I'm up to my ass in credit-card debt, and I'm behind on my car payments.

But that isn't why I have to say yes, and Humphrey knows it.

Once upon a time, the army was my life. When they tossed me out like yesterday's trash, it didn't stop being my life. Unfortunately, there aren't a lot of jobs for ex-army guys with a high-school diploma. There are even fewer jobs for guys who have problems with authority and a so-called personality disorder.

But it doesn't matter. Once you've done what I've done, it's all you know how to do. A soldier is the only thing you want to be — the only thing you *can* be.

5

_____

MAGGIE

It's not until I'm on the subway the next morning that I realize I've officially lost my mind.

I'm wearing my standard interview outfit: gray skirt, blazer, white top with black polka dots. I tug on the hem of my skirt a bit, wishing I'd opted for pants. It's a tad shorter than I remember, but at least I'm wearing hose.

I trace the edge of Natalie's business card in my hand as I barrel through New York's innards. I already performed an exhaustive search on both Natalie and her silent crony, Erik Blaine. Erik is a corporate headhunter, and Natalie's profile listed her as the media director at a big PR firm before she became a digital ghost.

A reverse image search on the strange logo yielded no results, but I was able to take a limited digital tour of the building. It's a swanky high-rise in midtown a few blocks from where I work. Most of the suites are occupied by lawyers, dentists, and insurance brokers. It's certainly an expensive place to kill someone.

"I can't believe you're going," huffs Kiran through my

Optix. I can tell from his feed that he's carving a perilous path through gridlock traffic. A bright-yellow taxi flashes by in the background, and I hear heavy construction noise.

"I just want to know what's going on," I say, tugging on my skirt again. "It's *weird*."

"Yeah, it is. Which is why you shouldn't be going."

"They had my picture," I whisper. "They knew where I worked."

"All the more reason to file a restraining order."

I shake my head. "They could have just sent me a message or gone through Cliff, but they didn't. There's a reason they're being so secretive. This could be my chance . . ."

"Chance to do what?" he huffs, zigzagging around a delivery truck and nearly getting doored in the face. "End up with your body parts scattered in half a dozen dumpsters?"

"At least I won't end up a hood ornament delivering some asshole's meatball sub," I grumble.

"Fuck you," says Kiran. But his heart's not in it. He's genuinely concerned for my safety. Hell, *I'm* concerned for my safety, but I've never let that get in the way of a story.

I end the call and get to my feet, wobbling a little on my wedge heels. It's rush hour, and the streets are crowded.

I shove my way through a jumble of tourists and join the throng of New Yorkers heading to their offices. Most of them have already started their workdays. A few are even trying to chat through an Optix veil as they navigate the crowded sidewalk.

I reach the address on Natalie's card and push my way through the revolving door. It spits me out into a large lobby with gleaming black tile and a wall of windows that stretches twenty feet above my head. Beautiful men and women clack past me on their way to their offices, all of them looking as though they tumbled straight out of a magazine.

Crossing the lobby to the bank of elevators, I'm highly conscious of how I must look lugging around my tattered messenger bag. I don't belong here — wherever "here" is.

I shove my way onto the elevator and punch the button for the twenty-third floor. The elevator stops to let people get on and off, and I catch snippets of several interesting conversations.

One woman is a high-powered attorney handling a multi-million-dollar divorce settlement. Another is a financial advisor urging her client to get into REITs. A man in a lab coat is conversing loudly about his patient's ovarian reserves.

Finally, the elevator stops on my floor. I disembark in a long hallway flanked by a wall of frosted glass. There's no sign indicating that I've reached the correct suite, but I'm guessing Natalie's mystery company occupies the entire floor.

My footsteps echo loudly on the polished white tile, and I find myself regretting my choice of footwear. I can feel two nasty blisters forming on the backs of my heels, but all I can do is grit my teeth and hope that my shoes don't fill with blood before I complete the interview.

Finally, I reach a door. There aren't any letters or numbers — just the same circular logo from the business card imprinted in the frosted coating. I can see through that tiny bit of clear glass to a reception desk in the shape of a trapezoid. I pull the door open and step inside.

"Good morning!"

"Morning," I say, making eye contact with the woman behind the counter. She's wearing a sleek black dress and has her hair pulled up in an elegant twist. Her eyebrows are fashionably bold, and she's got a thin smear of red lipstick painted down the center of her mouth like a geisha.

"I, uh . . . have an appointment. Magnolia Barnes?"

"Of course," she says in a bright voice. "Natalie is expecting you."

I touch my Optix to wake my feed. The time blinking in the corner says that I'm five minutes early.

"If I could just get your approval on this document," says the geisha woman.

I nod, and she produces a tablet with a dense-looking contract pulled up on the screen.

"Standard nondisclosure agreement," she says, waving her hand as if that explains everything. "Just saying that everything Natalie discusses with you is one hundred percent confidential."

"Okay," I say, surreptitiously taking a snapshot of the contract with my Optix as I scroll down to the signature line.

"Oh, you don't need to sign," says the geisha. "We only use three-way biometric authentication."

She swipes to the left, and a box appears to scan my finger-prints. I place my hand over the box, and a friendly beep tells me that my prints have been accepted. Next, I center my image in the facial recognition box, and a computerized voice asks me to speak my name.

Two more friendly beeps tell me I've been authenticated, and the woman takes the tablet back.

"Our security is second to none," she says cheerfully. "And I'm afraid I have to ask you to check your Optix."

"Excuse me?" Outside an interview with a protected source, I've never been asked to take off my Optix. It feels a little like being asked to amputate my arm.

"We don't allow discreet technology past the lobby."

I hesitate. My Optix is protected by facial recognition, but I don't like the idea of handing it over to someone I've never met. Then again, this entire meeting has been so hush-hush that allowing a reporter into the building with a device that can record and broadcast with two clicks does seem pretty stupid.

"Fine," I say, reaching up to detach the Optix from my glasses.

The receptionist produces a white plastic lockbox, and I set it inside. She smiles, snaps the lid shut, and slides it under her desk. She must have hit an unlock button under the counter, because the door to her right beeps and starts to open.

"You can go on through to the conference room," she says. "Natalie will be with you shortly."

Puzzled, I walk through the door and cross the hall to a conference room encased in glass. There is a long white table surrounded with swivel chairs and a single fuchsia orchid sitting in the middle. Natural light is spilling through the wall of windows, and I can see the entire city laid out below. Pedestrians creep by on the sidewalk like a line of ants, and cars meander through intersections at an almost leisurely pace.

"Ms. Barnes," says a voice behind me.

I jerk around so fast that I almost give myself whiplash. Natalie is standing in the doorway dressed in a coral shift dress, black silk scarf, and truly impossible pumps.

"I'm so glad you could come," she says with a warm smile. "Please, sit."

I slide out a corner chair, and the geisha woman reappears in the doorway with a beverage cart.

"Would you like anything to drink?" Natalie asks. "Coffee? Water?"

"Water would be nice," I say.

The geisha woman wheels the cart into the room and sets a tall carafe between me and Natalie. She pours us each a tall glass, and I snatch mine up immediately and take several long glugs.

"Will Erik be joining us?" I ask, setting down my water glass as the geisha woman exits the room.

"I'm afraid he had another appointment," says Natalie. "Erik is an independent contractor we hire to recruit talent. I'll be your point person from here on out."

"What sort of talent are you recruiting?" I ask, glancing around the conference room for some clue as to what the hell this company does.

"All sorts, though Erik specializes in immersive journalists and content creators." She smiles. "He's very good at what he does, so when my employer asked him to vet you and he gave the green light . . ."

"Your employer asked him to vet me?" I ask.

"Yes."

"And who is your employer?"

Natalie smiles. "Erik told me you would have a lot of questions. I work for a company called Maverick Enterprises."

I'm in the process of taking another sip and almost choke on my water. "*Maverick*?" I repeat, utterly dumbfounded. "As in the space company that just bought Futurewise Media?"

"The same," says Natalie, clearly impressed. "Maverick acquired Futurewise Media last week, mainly to scoop up *Topfold*. We plan on rebranding the company as Maverick Media, and given your performance this morning, the timing could not be better."

I feel my face heat up, and I quickly take note of my exits. If I was summoned by the same media overlords I eviscerated in my Layla Jones rant, it can't be good.

"Relax," says Natalie. "We've seen the story. It was Mr. Van de Graaf who requested that we meet with you."

"*Strom* Van de Graaf?"

"No. His son, Tripp."

"Tripp Van de Graaf asked *you* to meet with *me*?" I say,

dumbfounded. "Tripp Van de Graaf . . . Chief Experience Officer at Maverick Enterprises?"

Natalie gives a demure smile. "Correct."

I just stare at her. I have no idea why Tripp Van de Graaf would want anything to do with me, but this is quickly becoming the weirdest meeting I have ever been a part of.

"Why . . ." I shake my head. "I'm sorry, is Mr. Van de Graaf suing me?"

"Quite the contrary. Mr. Van de Graaf was quite impressed with your . . . spunk. And he thinks we may have been too hasty removing the human element from the journalistic process."

"*You think?*"

Natalie is still smiling, but I can tell that she isn't impressed with me.

"As you know," she continues, "Maverick Enterprises is cornering the market on space tourism and galactic living. We're disrupting space travel by making it safe, comfortable, and accessible, but our biggest project over the past five years has been developing the first low-orbit space colony designed to be inhabited by civilians."

"Wow," I say, wishing more than anything that I had my Optix to record this entire conversation. "That's great, but . . . what does this have to do with me?"

"I told you we wanted to make you an offer," says Natalie. "Mr. Van de Graaf would like to invite you — or, rather, Layla Jones — to join our galactic press corps."

"*What?*"

"Maverick Enterprises recently made a sizable investment in BlumBot International, and frankly, we can't afford a full-scale press revolt against the entire robotics workforce at this time."

I shake my head. I don't know which I find more insulting:

the fact that Tripp Van de Graaf wants my airhead alter ego to go to space instead of me, or that his company is trying to hire me to show that they don't have a vendetta against humans.

"You want me to take a job *in space*?"

"That's correct."

I cock my head to the side and smirk. "Thank you, but I'm not interested in being a part of some badly disguised PR maneuver."

"This isn't a PR move," says Natalie. "Trust me. I am head of our PR division, and I strongly recommended that we go another way. But Mr. Van de Graaf insisted on showing his support for human journalism."

I just stare at her.

"Why me?" I ask finally. "I mean Layla. Why not hire some journalist who *hasn't* come after your company?"

Natalie takes a deep breath. I'm guessing she asked Tripp Van de Graaf the same thing. "Our goal is to demystify space," she says. "To show people that living there isn't all that different from living on Earth. It's a luxury adventure with all the comforts of home." She shrugs. "Layla Jones has a loyal following. She's accessible. Her immersive stories are fun, and people like her."

I quirk an eyebrow. "Let me get this straight . . . You want to hire Layla Jones to make space seem more *fun*?"

"Exactly. Elderon is colony one. If we are successful, we'll be constructing a dozen more just like Elderon over the next six years."

"Wow."

"I know," says Natalie. "This is truly a once-in-a-lifetime opportunity."

"Yeah, well . . ."

"It's a five-year contract," Natalie continues in a brisk voice. "That's standard for all of our corporate residents."

TARAH BENNER

"So these are all corporate people?"

"So far more than eighty-six companies have signed on to establish satellite offices on Elderon. Most of these employees work in the STEM fields — tech, healthcare, engineering . . . Of course, they're all relatively young, unattached . . . We're not really equipped for families just yet. This is just a charter mission to show the public that long-term space living is both possible and enjoyable."

"Okay . . ."

"As far as salary, our wages are extremely competitive. We offer a signing bonus of fifty thousand, and of course your travel expenses, food, and lodging would be covered. Our employee medical plan is excellent. Dental and vision come standard. You've already been vetted by our security algorithms, but we will require you to undergo a complete medical evaluation before you can be cleared for launch."

"Security algorithms?"

"We use artificial intelligence to comb through all potential employees' social media posts and vet their personal connections. We run a full-scale criminal background check and flag any suspicious online behavior."

Wow. Talk about creepy.

"So I would be an employee of Maverick Enterprises?" I ask, still processing everything she's thrown at me.

"Technically speaking. We want our journalists to retain their independence, just so long as the stories aren't defamatory or damaging to the company in any way."

"You realize that's not independent journalism, right?"

Natalie lets out an impatient little huff. "Look. The way we see it, we're investing in high-quality *human* journalism. If that helps us diffuse the rumors . . ."

"Like the rumor that Maverick is just a front for secret government espionage?"

"Exactly. We're hoping to distance ourselves from all that nastiness. Maverick Enterprises is a private corporation striving to advance scientific research by bringing the brightest minds together under one roof *and* offering proof of concept for our space colonies. We just acquired BlumBot International and a German logistics firm to make Elderon the most cutting-edge global community anywhere in the galaxy."

"So Maverick *isn't* using Elderon to spy on the Russians?"

Natalie shoots me a cold glare. "As I said, Maverick Enterprises is a private global corporation whose mission is the peaceful advancement of science and technology."

"Right." I pause. My head is spinning from all the corporate doublespeak. "Do you have a pamphlet or something that I can look over?"

"Of course. I already sent you a contract with all the details. All we need is your biometric authentication, and Mira will be in touch to schedule your medical evaluation."

I guess that Mira is the geisha woman.

"I know this is a lot to think about," says Natalie. "But the offer expires in twenty-four hours. The mission begins in just over a month, so if you don't accept, we'll need to find another candidate to fill the position as quickly as possible."

"Okay . . ." Twenty-four hours really doesn't seem like enough time to decide what I'll be doing for the next five years, but what else can I say?

A moment later, Natalie stands up, and I get the impression that the meeting is over. She crosses to the door and offers a cool slender hand for me to shake. "Mira will see you out. I look forward to hearing from you."

6

MAGGIE

Kiran can hardly believe it when I recount my meeting with Natalie. He tells me to do it — integrity be damned. Who cares if I'm working for the man who decided to replace writers with machines? At least I'll be working *in space*.

Part of me can't imagine taking a five-year vacation from my life. The other part of me thinks it's the best thing that's ever fallen into my lap.

I always wanted to live in New York, but in the three years that I've been here, the city has chewed me up and spit me back out. It's time for a fresh start.

It's only a fifty-five-minute train ride to my parents' house in Westfield, New Jersey, but I haven't been back to see them in months. My excuse is always work — one that my dad inherently understands — but I still feel guilty.

The house where I grew up is a Cape Cod–style bungalow built in the 1940s. It's got a covered red-brick porch where my mom likes to host her ladies' Bible group and where I used to make out with Patrick Hanson after debate.

When I get there, I have to steel myself for whatever battle

may ensue once I walk through that door. Dad will be easy —
he's always been easy. Mom is another story.

I open the door, and the scent of burnt casserole and passive
aggression meets my nostrils.

"Hello?" I call, sticking my head inside to get the lay of the
land while I still have an exit.

"Hey, stranger!" comes my dad's booming voice.

I break into a grin and step inside. A second later, he comes
striding into the foyer wearing a pair of threadbare slippers and
his lopsided reading glasses. He's over six feet tall and moves
through the house like a rhinoceros.

"Hey, Dad."

"Good to see you, Maggie Bear!" he says, enveloping me in
a bone-crushing hug.

"You, too."

I pull back. His beard looks grayer than I remember. The
little hair he has left is sticking up in the back, and his eyes are
tired from spending too much time at the ancient Olympia
typewriter he uses. My dad doesn't trust technology.

"How's it going?" I ask.

"Great," he says emphatically. "*Really* great."

"You still working on the new book?"

"Yes! And you know, it's really beginning to take shape. It's
amazing how things change once you start writing. I went into
this pursuing the story of the treasury hack. But I started
digging, and I realized that there are people high up in the
department who should have realized what was happening
—"

"Magnolia? Is that you?"

I suppress a groan. "Yeah, Mom."

I hear her moving around in the kitchen, as though she's
surprised that I'm here after I called, messaged, and called
again to tell her that I was on my way. She sticks her head

around the corner, as if she's *still* not sure who it is. "Oh, you're here!"

"Yeah. Six thirty . . . like I said."

She scoffs and waddles toward me, wiping her hands on her faded apron. Underneath she's wearing a billowy beige sweater, black slacks, and clanky gold earrings.

She hugs me, but it isn't the same as my dad's full-body hug. It's a hug of disappointment. "Good to see you, honey."

"Good to see you, too. Today your day off?" My mother is an ER nurse, and she sometimes works the graveyard shift on Fridays.

"Uh, no. Not today." Something like a secret flickers behind those light-gray eyes, and I instantly get the impression that something is off.

"Anyway," my dad continues. "The story's less about the Russians and more about the dirty officials in our government getting rich off foreign money flowing into this country —"

"Whoo!" says my mother, plastering on one of her "everything's fine" smiles and fluffing her short brown curls. "Haven't we had enough of that? It's almost dinnertime!"

I freeze, trying to throw her a dirty look that my dad won't see. It's a bizarre feat of facial gymnastics that always leaves my face sore after two hours with them.

She's acting as though I'm a guest — as if she has to explain away my dad's behavior. She's always making excuses for the conspiracies he sees as his life's work, but I'm more embarrassed for her than I've ever been for him.

"You can finish telling me in the kitchen," I say quietly, resting my hand on his back and following Mom out of the too-small entryway.

I take a deep breath. I will not kill my mother before I fly off to space.

We go into the kitchen, and I feel as though I'm being suffocated by my childhood. Everything looks exactly the same: dark oak cabinets, hideous bear-shaped cookie jar, and faded plastic magnets that say things like "Home Is Where the Heart Is" and "God Bless This Mess."

Every nook and cranny of the dining room is stuffed with old-fashioned ceramic pitchers, decorative plates, and tiny lamps with red gingham shades.

"Can you grab drinks for everyone?" she asks.

"Sure. You want a beer, Dad?"

"He doesn't need a beer."

I shoot my mom a dirty look.

"Need, no. Want, yes."

I grin and grab him a bottle from the refrigerator. I pour myself some iced tea and get my mom one of those fizzy zero-calorie fruit waters that I can't stand.

She hefts the casserole out of the oven and brings it over to its little potholder pillow on the table. It smells like tuna. She can never remember that I hate tuna. There's also two salads: one green, one fruit.

"Looks great," I say, trying to be nice.

"Well, it's not every day that I get to cook for my daughter."

I suppress a cringe and grab the salad tongs. Whenever I've been gone for more than a few weeks, she resorts to talking about me in the third person.

"Shall we?" she asks once everyone has food on their plates. She's holding out her hands. She wants to say grace.

I force a nod and take her cool, smooth hand and my dad's rough, wrinkly one.

"Heavenly Father, thank you for this food. Thank you for bringing Magnolia safely home . . ." Clawlike squeeze from Mom. "May you bless and keep this family . . . especially Magnolia. Amen."

"Amen," I grunt, yanking my hand out of hers and digging in.

There's a long silence filled with the sound of forks on plates, and I get the same heavy choking feeling I always get in my childhood home.

When I was a kid, I was usually alone. Dad was most often in his office or shut up in the bedroom, and Mom was always, always at work.

"The house looks nice," I say to break the tension.

"Your father repainted. Our realtor says we should remodel, but I don't know . . ."

"Realtor?"

I look at my mom, but she carefully averts her gaze. "We're thinking of putting the house on the market." There's that high-pitched voice again, strained with discomfort.

I stare at her. "Why?"

She shrugs, but she won't look me in the eye. "I just think it might be nice to downsize."

"Downsize?"

"Mmm," she says, taking a tiny bite of salad. "Move into one of those cute condominiums in Plainfield."

"*Plainfield*?"

"Mmhm."

"Why?"

"I just think it might be good to have a change."

I look from my mom to my dad. "Are you guys in trouble?"

"No," says my mother. "Why would you say that?"

"Because you're putting the house on the market and moving to *Plainfield*." I say the word as though it's left a bad taste in my mouth and wait for someone to clue me in.

"It's fine," says my mother.

Dad says nothing.

My parents' money troubles are nothing new. Mom has

54

been pulling grueling twelve-hour shifts for as long as I can remember. My dad has always been a working writer, but he hasn't sold anything since *Kings of Washington*. No publisher would touch him.

My dad's medical bills have always been a burden, and when I was a kid, his spending was, too. Since he was diagnosed, he's only been allowed one credit card with a low limit, but there must be something Mom isn't telling me.

"I may have been laid off," my mother confesses.

"*What?*"

"They're making some . . . *changes* at the hospital."

"What sort of changes?"

My mother goes back to her fruit salad, nervously stabbing a piece of pineapple with her fork. "They've brought on a new fleet of bots," she says. "They do a lot of the things that I used to do, and now they're restructuring the entire staff."

I shake my head. I don't know what to say.

"So, Maggie . . . How is your writing going?" asks my dad, changing the subject so quickly that it nearly gives me whiplash. "Is that editor of yours going to publish your redistricting story?"

I take an enormous glob of tuna casserole into my mouth to buy myself some time. I give a high-pitched grunt and nod. I can't tell them that *The Journal* was taken over by AI software. It would break Dad's heart, and my mother would have a panic attack.

But my dad is still waiting for me to elaborate. His questions are never perfunctory. He wants all the nitty-gritty details.

I know I have to tell them why I really came over, but it seems like sacrilege to tell them that I took a job with Maverick Enterprises. The company that Maverick just bought probably *created* the bots that rendered my mother's position obsolete.

I swallow and take a swig of tea to postpone what I know I have to say.

"Well . . ." he probes. "When is it coming out?"

"Soon," I lie.

"But you're done working on it? It's ready?"

I give a noncommittal nod.

"So what's next? You're always working on something . . ."

This is it. I can't duck the question any longer.

"Actually, I . . . I got offered a job."

"Did you really?" says my father, his eyes lighting up with excitement. "At the paper? Are they going to make you a staff writer?"

"Not exactly . . ."

My dad's eyes widen. "They offered you an editorial position!"

"No," I say. "Nothing like that."

"What do you mean 'nothing like that'?" quips my mother. She's been watching me like a hawk the entire time. Her lips are pursed and her brow is furrowed. She could always spot a lie.

"Well . . . It's with the company that owns the paper, actually."

"What kind of job?" she presses. "I hope it's not another job bartending or whatever it is you do now."

"I'm a barista, Mom. And it's just to help with the bills while I'm freelancing."

"Well, whatever you call it, you aren't working in your field. I keep saying that you should live somewhere cheaper so you don't have to bartend anymore, but you don't listen."

"Still not a bartender," I snap. "And this job *is* in my field."

"What job?" asks my father, anxious to get on with celebrating.

I take a deep breath. I could tell him that I got a job working for Satan himself, and he wouldn't care. As long as I was writing, he'd be proud. My mother is the tougher sell.

"I've been asked to join the press corps for Maverick Enterprises."

There's a long beat of silence.

"The space company?" asks my dad. Now he looks baffled.

"Yes."

"They built that space colony that's been in the news?" he continues.

"Yeah, that's them. They're hiring a team of journalists to report on it, and they offered me a job."

"Does that mean you'll be going to *space*?"

"Yeah," I say, barely able to contain my smile. "Isn't that crazy?"

"Hang on a minute," says my mother.

Here we go.

"Space . . . Like *space* space?"

"Exactly."

"Well done, Maggie Bear!" says my dad, breaking into a grin so huge that I feel bad for not visiting more. "This is just the *best* news."

"And how will you be getting there?" my mother breaks in. I recognize that tone. She's searching for a problem — some reason why it's a bad idea.

"They're flying me up there," I say quickly. "Everything's covered: room and board, travel, and health insurance. They're even giving me a signing bonus! I can help you guys with the house."

"Absolutely not, Magnolia. Your father and I are doing just fine. It's you I'm worried about."

"*Why?*"

"It just sounds awfully dangerous."

"It's not dangerous," says my dad incredulously. He turns to me. "Is it dangerous?"

"No."

"Well, still," says my mother. "It sounds very experimental. What happens in six months when they run out of money and you're out of a job?"

"It's a five-year contract, Mom."

"Five *years*?"

I grimace. Now she's got something to latch on to.

She puts down her silverware. "I'm sorry, sweetheart, but this just doesn't sound like a good idea."

"Don't be ridiculous, Sue. She's going!" He turns back to me. "You're going, aren't you?"

"Yeah. I think so."

"Well, you should," says my dad.

"Don't tell her that," snaps my mother.

"Why the hell not?"

"Five years is a long time, Henry."

"She's only twenty-five years old."

"Exactly. In five years, she'll be thirty. How is she going to meet anybody if she's stuck in space?"

"Whoa!" I say. "Why don't you let me worry about that?"

"Because you never do," says my mother with a snide look. "I know your generation thinks that you can put this off forever. But let me tell you — time is cruel. You only have so many good years left. Ninety percent of your eggs are gone by the time you hit thirty, and —"

"Susie, please," says my dad.

"What? I'm just telling her how it is."

My dad rolls his eyes. "When would you leave?"

"A month."

"A *month*?" He looks surprised, but the pride in his eyes

doesn't falter. I know he's happy for me. He's always happy —
until he isn't.

As a kid, I learned the hard way that an episode of intense
joy is almost always followed by a period of darkness. One day
he'd be on top of the world, and the next he'd retreat to bed for
days at a time, refusing to eat or talk to anyone.

When he landed a publishing deal for *Currency of
Corruption*, things were good for a while. And when he sold his
second book, I thought the bad days were behind us. I
was wrong.

"A month is very soon, Magnolia," says my mom.

"I know."

"Were you even going to ask us how we felt about this? Or
did you just accept without even thinking?"

"I thought about you guys," I murmur. "But I had to accept.
They only gave me a day."

"You shouldn't rush into things like this. If they want you,
they'll wait."

"They had to fill the position, Mom."

"Oh, don't listen to her," says my dad. "These opportunities
don't come twice, and if you don't take them, someone
else will."

My mother rolls her eyes in exasperation. I know she's
heard this all before. My dad's penchant for opportunity-
seizing has made her life a living hell.

"I don't think there's anything wrong with being a little bit
careful," she says. "She's got plenty of time to be a writer."

"Sue, you don't know what you're talking about," says my
dad. I can feel him wavering on the edge of irritation. "Maggie
is a writer, and being a working writer these days is hard. If
you've got their attention, you've got to run with it."

I swallow and look down at my half-finished lump of casserole. I'm just glad my mother has the good sense not to throw my dad's failures in his face.

When *Currency of Corruption* hit the *New York Times* best-seller list, he ran with the attention, all right. He ran straight into a story that would ruin his career.

"I just wish you weren't going to be gone so long, is all," says my mother. I can hear the tears building up in her throat. I don't know what to say.

"Well, we'll keep in touch," says my dad brightly, taking my hand and giving it a squeeze. He still has that familiar twinkle in his eye — the twinkle that says he couldn't be happier. "We'll read every single thing you write."

7

MAGGIE

The loneliness doesn't hit me until I land at LAX — also known as hell on earth. It's the second busiest airport in the country, and everyone from the baggage handlers to the guy working the coffee cart has an "I will stab you" look in their eyes.

I feel naked traveling without my suitcase. I checked my two enormous cargo crates back in New York, so all I have on me is my messenger bag. I'm supposed to be catching a bus that will take me to Vandenberg Air Force Base, where I'll board the shuttle to Elderon and start my new life in space.

It's only nine thirty California time, but it's lunchtime in my stomach. I grab an overpriced burrito from a food-court-style restaurant outside arrivals and flip on my Optix to grab some footage for my journey to the launch site. I'll have to edit out the chewing sounds later, but it's a small price to pay for the gooey queso goodness. I'm sad that my last meal on Earth has to be airport food, but it's better than the bran cereal I choked down in the apartment earlier this morning.

It's a little surreal to be doing something as ordinary as

stuffing my face while I wait for a bus that will take me to board a space shuttle. Natalie told me that my galactic concierge would handle everything, but I still feel that I should be more prepared for the journey. I'm not even wearing my good underwear.

As it turns out, I don't have much time to think about it. My bus pulls up a few minutes later, and I climb aboard. About half the passengers are dressed in dark-blue uniforms that I've never seen before. They don't belong to the US Armed Forces.

The fatigues all have the same black emblem on the front and a country of origin patch on the sleeve. I spy half a dozen American flags on the operatives I pass, but I also spot a couple of Canadians and a German. I pan my Optix over the soldiers, wondering why Natalie never mentioned the privatized military presence on Elderon. One of the female soldiers has a black backpack with the words "Space Force" embroidered in all caps, and I make a mental note to research them later.

The rest of the passengers look as though they stumbled straight out of Silicon Valley or some top-secret government laboratory. The university researchers are all polished and blah: khakis, Oxford shoes, polos — top buttons all securely fastened. The Silicon Valley kids are shamelessly casual and equally blah: jeans, T-shirts, puffer jackets, and ugly neon bubble vests. It makes me miss the unapologetic weirdos that inhabit the Lower East Side.

I find a seat by myself near the back and watch the rest of the passengers board. Most of them are military, but there's one guy in khaki pants and a lime-green button-down who is completely absorbed in his Optix.

I glance to my right and catch the eye of a Space Force guy with very short dark hair. He's tall and well-built and has a steely blue gaze that seems to pierce right through me.

He doesn't smile. He's sitting alone with his legs spread wide, analyzing the passengers as they board.

Unlike the tech workers, who act as though they're catching a commuter jet from San Fran to LA, this guy looks as though he's heading into battle. I get the feeling that his entire body is a coiled ball of energy — just waiting for a threat to materialize.

The bus doors close with a rattle, and we spend the next forty minutes navigating through prime-time LA traffic. I try to enjoy the ride, since I'm about to leave the big blue marble behind, but I find that I'm just annoyed. I'm spending my last hours on Earth crawling through gridlock traffic in what has got to be the dirtiest city in America.

Fortunately, we reach the base in no time at all. The bus stops at a gate, and the driver scans his credentials.

My heart beats faster. I can practically taste the electricity in the air. Even the blasé tech workers seem excited. I can see the endless blue ocean stretching in the distance, and I'm glad that the Pacific will be the last thing I see before we leave the atmosphere.

Winding through the base toward the Maverick Enterprises launch complex, I'm disappointed to see that it looks and feels exactly like an airport. We glide down a one-way road toward the terminal, passing a line of flags from all different countries flapping in the breeze.

The bus pulls up at the terminal, and I disembark with the rest of the nonmilitary personnel. Apparently, the Space Force operates separate from the rest of us.

I walk through the sliding glass doors straight into a sea of people. Most of them are already dressed in their hideous blue jumpsuits, talking excitedly on their Optixes to loved ones before they depart for Elderon.

Enormous screens mounted at each end of the terminal show a perky woman with golden-blond hair and a blinding megawatt smile. She's giving directions to the eager crowd, and I see that the real woman is standing on a raised platform in the terminal, wearing a crisp white dress and a jaunty blue scarf.

"Welcome, welcome!" she says in an electronically magnified voice. "I'm your galactic concierge, Vanessa St. James. I'm here to guide you along your journey to Elderon. Please put on your complimentary flight suit and prepare for check-in. All passengers must pass through security before proceeding to the gate."

I groan and shuffle off to the bathroom to put on my suit, which is crammed into a ball at the bottom of my bag. It's made out of some cheap fuzzy material that snags on my nails, and the thought of enveloping my entire body in the thing makes my skin crawl.

I peel off my jeans and jacket, leaving my underwear and T-shirt on underneath. The jumpsuit is snug in the hips and chest — definitely designed for a man.

When I emerge from the bathroom, Space Flight Barbie is still in the middle of her spiel. "Please have your boarding pass queued for scanning and make your way to the gate for check-in."

I wake my Optix and pull up my boarding pass. It says we board in forty minutes, which seems like a very short layover, considering we're about to leave the planet.

I follow the throng of passengers toward the security checkpoint, and a hostess in white waves me forward. I step into a narrow booth, and the automated doors slide shut behind me.

Once inside, a woman's face appears on the screen in front of me, blinking slowly to create the impression that I'm facing a real person.

"Welcome to Vandenberg Air Force Base," says the woman in a stilted robotic voice. "Please direct your gaze toward the screen and state your full name."

"Magnolia Barnes."

As I speak, a green light appears above me and pans over my entire face. There's a dull ping as the software confirms my identity and runs my name through some big government database.

"Please place your hands on the red circles and answer the following questions."

I flatten my palms on the wall in front of me over two circles the size of bread plates. They're designed to measure my heart rate, blood pressure, and whether my palms are sweating as the woman asks me a series of questions.

They start out normal enough — my age, my address, the city where I was born — but quickly progress to serious.

"Are you a US citizen?"

"Yes."

"Are you carrying any weapons or explosives?"

"No."

"Do you have any illegal drugs in your possession?"

"No."

Each time I answer, the device scans my face and records every microscopic tic. It tracks my eye movement and the timbre of my voice and uses thermal imaging scanners to detect even the smallest hint that I might be lying.

It's over in less than thirty seconds. When it's done, the woman thanks me, and the door slides open to let me through.

"The flight from Earth to Elderon will take around five hours — less than a flight from New York to LA!" booms Vanessa's voice over the speakers. "This *historic* launch is the first of ten that will transport you and your fellow crew members to Elderon, colony one!"

A burst of applause greets this statement, and I see a crowd full of people gathered outside the gate.

"Everyone around you is the best in their field, and you'll be working side by side for the next five years." She winks. "I suggest you use this time to make some introductions."

Right on, Space Flight Barbie. Time to grab some interviews.

I scan the crowd for someone who looks interesting and find my path blocked by a brunette woman in white carrying a tray of what appears to be wheatgrass shots.

"Hostesses will be circulating with complimentary comfort tonics," says Vanessa.

"What's in this?" I ask the hostess, being sure to get a good shot of the viscous green goo.

"It's a tonic derived from cannabis," she says brightly. "High CBD, low THC . . . It's great for anxiety and nausea."

"Mmm," I say, taking one of the shots and tossing it back. Unlike the dirt-and-grass flavor I'd been expecting, the tonic has a pleasant minty taste. It doesn't quite offset the oily consistency, but it's not bad.

"I'll take two," says an elegant Indian woman, elbowing in behind the hostess and grabbing a shot glass with each hand.

"Nervous?" I say, focusing my Optix on her. She's very pretty, but she's wearing an expression that suggests she's about to walk into an amphitheater to fight a tiger.

She rolls her eyes. "My company sent me because I'm the only qualified unmarried woman." She downs the first shot. "I study the long-term effects of simulated gravity on bone-marrow density, but I hate space."

I grin. "What company do you work for?"

"GenMed."

I open my mouth to say I'm with the press, but Vanessa's booming voice cuts me off.

"If you need to use the restroom, there is a facility on board. Please keep in mind that the spacecraft lavatories are modified to function in a microgravity environment. For number one, the big blue hose is where it goes. For number two, seal up your poo!"

The woman takes her second shot, looking as though she's about to pass out. "I took a home enema last night," she says. "No way am I shitting in a bag."

I laugh, but inside I'm filled with panic. Clearly I missed the memo on space shitting.

"We'll begin boarding with our first-class passengers," says Vanessa. "If you purchased our first-class package, you may now board the spacecraft."

"Is it possible that things up there will be exactly like they are down here?" asks the woman with an eye roll.

"Sure seems like it," I say.

I manage to interview a few more people before Vanessa calls the coach passengers.

I line up with the others to get my boarding pass scanned, and Vanessa continues to deliver instructions via the screen behind the counter. She demonstrates the correct way to put on a space suit and how to download the welcome packet to our Optixes.

My heart skips a beat as I'm cleared for boarding and make my way down the jet bridge. It all feels familiar and exciting at the same time.

The door to the shuttle is lower and smaller than the door one would use to board an airplane, and everything has a tell-tale new-spaceship smell.

When I step inside the shuttle, I see seven rows of empty seats equipped with four-point harnesses. Space suits are draped over the cushions, and the helmets are suspended from bungee cords overhead.

Another smiling hostess ushers me onto a lift in the center of the first row and instructs me to wait. I look up.

I'm standing at the bottom of a tall shaft that rises nearly a hundred feet above my head. She fills the lift with six more people and hits a button. We rise slowly through the center of the spacecraft to our designated level. When the lift clicks into place, we pile out, and I look around for my seat.

It's all the way in the back row. I find my number and pick up the suit. I've already forgotten everything Vanessa said about the correct way to put it on, but I remember I need to take off my shoes.

Getting inside is much more difficult than Vanessa made it look. There isn't enough room to sit in my seat and slide my legs in, so I stand in the aisle and shimmy it up my hips.

The suit is lighter than I expected, with rubberized boots, gloves, and a full communication system. There are buttons on the arm for volume, brightness, and climate control — even a help beacon to call a hostess.

Just as I'm preparing to waddle to my seat, another group gets off the lift, and a very attractive, very familiar man sidles toward me down the aisle.

He's only a few years older than me — probably twenty-eight or twenty-nine by the look of him. He's got jet-black hair that falls over his face in wild curls, light-mocha skin, and the sort of do-me eyes that are a hazard to women everywhere.

Oddly, he is not zipped up in the horrible blue onesie. He's wearing low-slung jeans and a tight gray T-shirt that shows off his tan, muscular arms.

"Is this seat taken?" he asks, nodding at the seat beside me.

"Nope," I say, feeling a little less composed than normal. "Are you J11?"

He grins, and a perfect set of dimples appear. "I am."

"You're supposed to wear the jumpsuit," I add, a little annoyed that he thinks he can get away with breaking the rules just because he's so good-looking.

"So they tell me," he murmurs, eyes twinkling with mischief. "How are those things, anyway?"

"Scratchy. Hot. Whatever dumbass designed them is definitely a man."

His smile widens. Damn those dimples. "Why do you say that?"

"They don't fit right."

He laughs, though I'm not sure what he finds so funny. He bends down to untie his tennis shoes, and then he does something that makes my jaw drop to the floor. He unbuckles his belt and unzips his jeans.

"What are you doing?" I ask, glancing around at the other passengers. They're all too preoccupied to notice the guy stripping in the aisle, but I have a front-row seat.

"Can't wear jeans in the suit," he says, dropping his pants to his ankles. He's wearing tight black boxer briefs, and I force myself to look away. "The rivets could tear a hole in the thing."

"Uh-huh . . ." I'm not sure what I did to deserve a free flight to space with a cannabis-infused tonic and an underwear model, but I'm not going to question my karma.

He hops into his space suit much the same way I did, and I feel a slight twinge of disappointment once he's all wrapped up. He settles into his seat and secures his harness, and I get a whiff of very expensive cologne.

"I'm Tripp, by the way," he says, turning and offering his gloved hand for me to shake. Up close, I see that his eyes are emerald green — framed by inky-black lashes.

"Maggie Barnes."

A single dimple reappears. "Maggie Barnes . . . a.k.a. Layla Jones?"

I cringe. "Yeah . . . How did you know?"

He shrugs. "It's my job to know."

I study him for a moment, and suddenly I realize why he looks so familiar. "Wait . . . You're Tripp Van de Graaf?"

"Yes . . ."

"CEO of Maverick Enterprises?"

"Uh, no. The CEO would be my father. I'm the CXO — the X stands for 'experience' to minimize confusion. Although . . ." He trails off.

Shit. Maybe I *should* be questioning my karma. I'm sitting next to the man whose company I blasted all over *Topfold*.

Tripp is the son of legendary space architect Strom Van de Graaf. He joined the board of his father's company when he was just twenty-two years old.

"Why are you sitting in coach?" I blurt.

"It's important for me to experience the voyage the way our customers will be experiencing it," he says. "If future charters reach the demand we're anticipating, we're going to have billionaires sitting here." He grins. "Even the cheap seats have to feel like riding in first class."

I blink stupidly at him, wondering if I should thank him for the job or rip him a new one for contributing to the decline of the human race. But before I can decide, a pre-recorded video pops up on my Optix, and Space Flight Barbie is back in all her smiling glory.

"Welcome aboard the Impetus. Please ensure that your flight suit is securely fastened and that your harness is engaged. A hostess will be around shortly to help you with your helmet."

Tripp doesn't wait for the hostess. He reaches up with both hands and pulls the helmet free from its bungee cords. He places it carefully over his head and runs his finger along the neck to activate the seal.

I copy him, and Vanessa's cheery voice is suddenly being piped straight into my ears.

"We have prepared a series of short in-flight films that will help you prepare for your time on Elderon. Once we dock, a series of modules will guide you through a tour of the colony, and the hospitality crew will be standing by to assist you if needed. Elderon is fully equipped with all the comforts of home, but we care about your feedback."

I turn to Tripp, and my comm system automatically pairs with his. "You know, if you wanted to experience the flight the way your customers do, you should have worn the jumpsuit."

"I'll have you know that I *designed* those jumpsuits," he says in a mock-defensive tone, fixing those smiling green eyes back on me.

"I hope you didn't design the spaceship," I mutter.

"I made some tweaks."

My mouth falls open, and I suddenly find myself doubting the efficacy of the so-called comfort tonic.

"Kidding!" he says, leaning over to pat my arm. "Geez, lighten up. Everyone takes this whole space-travel thing so seriously."

I let out a breath of relief, which Tripp seems to find very funny.

"I confess that I did not have any part in designing the spacecraft. But I *did* suggest they do the jumpsuits in blue . . . I look good in blue."

"Noted," I say, taking a few good stills of him with my Optix. "Can I ask you a few questions?"

"Do I have a choice?"

"Hey, it was your idea to pick a seat next to one of the journalists that *you* hired."

"True."

"Why did you ask Natalie to meet with me?"

Tripp seems to hesitate, and I wonder if I'm going to get a straight answer or not. "I liked your style," he says after a moment.

"Come on . . ."

"I did! Well, that and I figured that it would be good to have that biting wit directed at my competitors instead of me."

"A-ha!"

"What?"

"You were scared," I say, feeling a twinge of pride.

"Who wouldn't be?" he murmurs. "You're very scary."

I fight the grin twitching at the corners of my mouth. "What's it like seeing your vision become a reality? Boarding a shuttle with the first civilians to colonize space?"

"It's a bit surreal, to be honest . . . I've never actually been to space."

"You're kidding."

"Nope. My father has, but I never had a chance to go until now."

I raise my eyebrows. "This is a big deal for you, then."

"Oh, yeah."

"Did you get an enema?"

"What?" He lets out a snort of surprised laughter. "Wow. You're not shy."

I shrug. "I'm a journalist . . . and the people want to know."

He shakes his head. "No, I did not get an enema. But I did get a straight-razor shave."

"Interesting . . . So, what's in your cargo bin besides the necessities?"

Tripp doesn't miss a beat, and I get the feeling that he's rehearsed his answer. "A picture of my late mother, a case of Miracle Mousse, and a custom showerhead for my bathroom."

"A custom showerhead?"

"The water pressure is something we never did get quite right."

"Thanks for the heads up," I grumble.

But Tripp is sporting an enormous grin. He's enjoying this.

"What will you miss most about Earth?"

"Surfing . . . and watching the sun set over the ocean."

I do my best to suppress an eye roll. The guy's answers are straight out of the tech executive PR handbook. I pause to think, trying to come up with a good question to wrap up the interview.

"What's your primary emotion today?"

He seems to weigh this for a moment, juggling several possibilities. "I guess I would say hope."

"Oh, come on," I say, unable to hide my derisive expression. "Hope?"

"Yes, hope!" says Tripp in a tone of offense. "We did three test launches this month, and only one of the shuttles blew up."

At those words, I feel all the blood drain from my face. My lungs seize, I can't breathe, and I suddenly feel as though I might upchuck my burrito.

"I'm kidding!" says Tripp, reaching over and squeezing my knee. He lets out a burst of musical laughter, and I have to resist the urge to punch him. "Don't worry so much. I'm sure it'll all be fine."

When I don't relax, he quirks an eyebrow. "Consider this payback for calling my company Big Brother's big brother."

8
———
JONAH

After they herd the last of the nonmilitary personnel off the bus, they dump us off on the other side of the terminal to report to our commanding officers.

The Space Force is bringing me on as a sergeant — one notch below my army rank. It doesn't matter. The signing bonus they offered me was enough to pay off my credit-card debt and put some money back in my pocket.

Three weeks ago, I sold my car, got out of my lease, and packed up everything that would fit in two cargo bins. Everything else went straight in the dumpster. It's not as though I had much anyway. I'm used to starting over. Hell, being on the move feels more natural than staying in one place.

Still, I have that nervous first-day-of-basic feeling as I get off the bus. My uniform still has that scratchy newness, and my leather boots are stiff — never worn.

I line up with the others and wait to check in. The other soldiers are just as keyed up as I am, and I recognize a few from officer training. Several have already coalesced into groups, but I'd rather be alone than glom on to strangers.

When I get to the head of the line, the man sitting behind the folding table raises his head. He gives me a quick once-over but doesn't say hello or even acknowledge my presence. He's got a large square head, thick black eyebrows, and the calculating gaze of an ex-Marine.

The name stitched on his uniform tells me he's my CO, Captain Callaghan. Great.

"Name?"

"Wyatt, sir."

"Service number?"

"85-6827."

He scans through a list on his Optix before coming across my name. "Jonah Wyatt? Former staff sergeant in the army?"

"Yessir."

He shoots me a critical look. "Humphrey says you're a good fighter."

"Glad to hear it, sir."

There's a long accusatory pause.

"Well?" he says roughly. "Do you think you're a good fighter?"

I hesitate, trying to decide how to play this. Some COs like confidence, but most take it as a sign that you need to be knocked down a few pegs.

"It's been a while, sir."

"What kind of answer is that?" he asks, cocking his head to the side. "Your former captain stuck his neck out for you when you've done pretty much everything in your power to get written off as a screwup."

I stare at him in shock, blood pounding in my veins.

"Yeah, I read your file," Callaghan grumbles. "Honestly, I'm not sure what Humphrey sees in you, but I'm gonna have to take his word for it 'til I see what you can do."

"Captain Humphrey's one of the good ones, sir," I say through gritted teeth. "You won't be disappointed."

"We'll see."

I don't say a word. I just stand there grinding my back teeth together, wondering exactly how much direct contact with Callaghan will be required. I already want to kill him.

"Listen up," he says, glaring at me as though I'm some kind of delinquent. "I don't tolerate any bullshit in my company. You give me any reason not to like you, and I won't hesitate to jettison your ass back to Earth like a defective piss valve. Got it?"

I swallow. Callaghan is baiting me. He's hoping that I'll give him a reason to dismiss me right here and now, but it's not going to happen.

"Noted, sir."

He continues to stare. What the fuck is he waiting for?

"Well?" he barks. "Are you going to curtsey or what? Boarding pass!"

I blink furiously and pull up the boarding pass on my Optix. His device registers the barcode, and my seat number pops up.

"L7. Now get your ass on the spacecraft."

"Yessir."

I walk off with the feeling that I've been tossed straight into the viper pit. I knew the Space Force would have access to my service record — I just didn't expect it to bite me in the ass so soon.

By the time I reach the gate, I'm still shaking all over with fury. Callaghan might be the biggest asshole I've ever served under, and that's saying something.

I don't know why he's decided to hate me, but I know I need to watch my back. Guys like Callaghan will push you over the edge if you let them, and pissing one of them off is the fastest way to get your ass court-martialed.

I'm not paying attention when I reach the head of the line, and it takes me a minute to pull up my boarding pass. The hostess rattles off my seat number in an overly cheerful voice, and I storm down the jet bridge to get to the spacecraft.

On my way, I nearly collide with another hot lady in white, but she recovers quickly and ushers me through the door.

My bad attitude is momentarily sidelined as I reach my seat. There's a space suit already waiting for me, and it feels surreal as I pull it on. The woman I almost plowed down on the way to my seat comes over to help me with my helmet. She must be a hostess.

As soon as the helmet suctions down, I can't hear a thing. The inside smells like new plastic, and my view is dimmed by the dark glass.

An instructional video starts to play on my Optix. It features a pretty blond woman with big movie-star hair and an even bigger movie-star smile. She's wearing a short white dress that makes her look like a nurse and one of those old-fashioned blue neck scarves.

"Welcome aboard the Impetus. The Impetus is a wide-bodied commercial spacecraft capable of transporting up to five hundred passengers to low-orbit space. This is the first of ten launches that will be carried out over the next two weeks, transporting passengers roughly three hundred miles from Earth. To ensure your safety, please check that your flight suit is fully zipped and that your harness is securely fastened."

At this moment, an Asian guy comes careening down the aisle. He's sweaty and out of breath, and the patch on his uniform tells me he's a private. He does an awkward sort of tango with the hostess as he attempts to slide around her to his seat, but she picks up the suit for him as though she's going to help him get dressed.

The kid breaks into a huge grin, kicks off his boots, and

starts to unbutton his overshirt. I can't watch. They perform a series of awkward gymnastics to get the kid into his space suit, and by the time he throws himself into his seat, the hostess is clearly traumatized.

The little "fasten harness" light above my seat changes from yellow to green, and the hostess takes one last lap to make sure everyone is ready for takeoff.

All of a sudden, I feel an abrupt cooling sensation spreading inside my suit. It starts around my chest and quickly spreads to my extremities.

I look down. The little blue snowflake icon on my sleeve is illuminated, which means the suit must be trying to cool me down.

I take a deep breath, and another video feed appears on my Optix. I see a man sitting in a cockpit. He's not looking at the camera, but he's speaking with the lazy authority of an airline pilot.

"This is Michael Garrison, pilot in command for your flight aboard the Impetus. Our entire flight today from launch to docking will take around five hours. We are right within our launch window, and we should arrive at Elderon a few minutes ahead of schedule. Hostesses, please prepare the cabin for launch."

Just then, the feed switches, and I'm staring into the helmet of the perky blond woman from the video. "Please remain in your seat with your harness fastened at all times. The spacecraft is pressurized for your safety and comfort, but suits and helmets are required for the entire duration of the flight."

The feed switches, and I'm staring at a map of the spacecraft with a restroom symbol illuminated near the center.

"The lavatories are located on either side of level six. If you need to use the restroom after we exit the Earth's atmosphere, please use the handrails to guide yourself to level six. There is a sanitary hose for urine and solid-waste containment bags available for your convenience. If you require assistance, please illuminate the help beacon, and a hostess will instruct you on proper hygiene procedures."

Suddenly the feed goes dark, and a countdown appears on my Optix. I hear the pilot counting down and grip the armrests for good measure.

"Ten, nine, eight . . ."

I look down to make sure that I'm buckled in. I'm breathing extra hard, and my suit is working overtime to keep me from sweating. I feel the rumble of the main engines lighting — almost as if I'm sitting on the chest of a dragon that's waking up in a furious rage. The shuttle tilts.

"Three . . . two . . . one."

Suddenly, the ground beneath my feet quakes, and the entire spacecraft seems to shudder. Then the rocket boosters ignite, and the force of the blast knocks the wind out of me.

We're thrust violently into the air, and it sounds as though the earth just broke in two. My seat rattles as we leave the launchpad. We've gotta be moving at more than a hundred miles an hour. My stomach clenches, and I grit my teeth to ward off the sudden feeling of motion sickness.

The vibrations grow more intense. The shuttle is shaking us like bugs in a water bottle. My skull is bouncing around on my spine, but I can't move an inch. The force of the acceleration is pulling me deeper and deeper into my seat, and soon I get the feeling that I'm being crushed under a pile of dirt.

Suddenly, I'm back in that Siberian tunnel — buried alive under a mound of rock. I can't move. I can't breathe, and I get the feeling that my ear drums might burst.

I try to tell myself that everything's okay. I'm not trapped underground — I'm up in the air. I tell myself that these feelings are normal — that they were in the welcome packet — but nothing about this experience is normal.

I grip my armrests for dear life, and the sight of my own torso bouncing and shaking with the shuttle's vibrations is enough to make me sick. I'm amazed the human body can withstand such an assault.

Then the pressure changes. The engines ratchet down, and then they're back in full force. The high-pitched whistle of the slipstream reaches my ears — almost like the whistle of a tea kettle.

A flash of light bursts in my periphery, and I know the boosters have separated from the shuttle.

I close my eyes, willing it all to be over. And then, suddenly, it is.

The immense pressure all over my body disappears, and I get the feeling that I've just been thrust into a deep pool. The tension evaporates from my chest, and I suck in a burst of air. I am weightless.

I lie back to enjoy the feeling of floating in the space between my seat and harness when I'm interrupted by the cheerful *ding!* of my Optix.

What the hell? I'm shooting into space, and someone needs to get ahold of me?

A second later, the avatar of a smiling Asian guy appears. It's the guy sitting next to me. He taps on my helmet, and I jerk around. This kid is unbelievable.

Resisting the urge to deck him, I reach up to answer the call. The feed from inside the guy's helmet fills my Optix — a giant smile and two dark eyes crinkled in amazement.

"Can I help you?" I growl. This guy is shitting all over my space experience.

"You all right, bro?" he asks, his California surfer-dude voice immediately grating on my nerves.

"Yeah . . . Fine."

"That was *wild*, man! We lifted off, and you were like —" He rolls his eyes back and mimes a horrified expression. "Pretty sick."

Who the hell is this guy?

"I'm Chao Ping, by the way."

"Sergeant Jonah Wyatt," I grumble.

"Whoa. Officer!" A shadow moves over Chao Ping's face, and I gather that he's trying to salute me. "Right on. You totally stoked for space or what?"

"Yeah," I say, hoping to put a quick end to the conversation.

"This whole mission is *über*-historic. Total once-in-a-lifetime experience. We're gonna go on space walks and experience zero gravity. Plus, it's gotta be like a twenty-four-hour sex marathon up there."

I turn my head to look at him, equal parts intrigued and disturbed.

"Think about it," says Ping excitedly. "They recruited five thousand single, unattached adrenaline junkies in their twenties and thirties to go live in space for *five years*."

"Not everyone's in their twenties and thirties," I say.

"Everyone except for the higher-ups. They want us all young and healthy so we don't, like, drop dead in space or whatever."

"You don't say."

Ping lowers his voice conspiratorially. "I heard they even made all the female crew members get this super intense birth control shot before they came. Don't want 'em to get pregnant from all the crazy *space sex*."

I see movement in my periphery and realize that Ping is thrusting his hips.

I shake my head and hold back a laugh. If anyone's going to

TARAH BENNER

be having crazy space sex, my money says it's not going to be Ping.

"You got your room assignment yet, dude? I mean sarge. No disrespect."

The nickname falls like a badly timed joke. "Don't call me that."

"Sorry." He leans over in his seat and taps a finger on my helmet. I try to jerk my head back, but it's held in place by my headrest. I glare at Ping's gloved finger and see a number and a letter blinking in the upper right-hand corner of my Optix.

"Dude! We're in the same pod!" says Ping excitedly.

Fuck my life.

"What unit are you assigned to?"

"I haven't checked yet."

"Dude . . . Did you read *any* of the stuff they gave you?"

I ignore this and immediately begin scouring my enlistment papers just to make sure I'm not in Ping's unit. *Shit.*

"What's your specialty?"

"Close-quarters combat."

"No way!" says Ping. "So you must be, like, a total ninja."

I hold back a groan. It doesn't look as though I'm going to be able to get rid of Ping.

"I'm what you call an ethical hacker. I used to make my money cashing in on bug bounties, but that racket —"

"You're a hacker?"

"I only use my powers for good," he says quickly.

"So you're the one in charge of hacking Russia to find out if they're going to shoot a missile at us?"

"*Yeah.*"

Now there's a scary thought.

"I mean, it was either this or the NSA . . ." Ping opens his mouth to say something else, but before he can, a pre-recorded video pops up, and the hot blond lady is back.

"Welcome aboard the Impetus. I hope you're enjoying your journey. Soon we'll be docking on Elderon — your home away from home for the next five years."

The woman walks down what looks like a futuristic airport hallway. I can tell she's supposed to be on Elderon, but something about the background makes me think the video was filmed on a green screen.

"The exterior of the space station was constructed using materials interwoven with hydrogenated boron nitride nanotubes to shield the colony from radiation. To simulate the gravitational pull you would experience on Earth, giant solar-powered thrusters rotate the entire colony along its axis."

As she speaks, a computerized graphic shows what looks like a giant three-layered donut rotating in outer space.

"The centripetal force simulates one G, though the colony's rotation will be paused at scheduled intervals so repair bots can perform routine maintenance on the colony's exterior."

The three donut rings separate, and the woman reappears to point out different parts of the space station.

"The colony has three floors — the upper, middle, and lower decks — and is divided into six wings. Within each wing are three sectors containing offices, residential suites, and public spaces. There is also a microgravity chamber located on the middle deck for research and recreational purposes."

The donut graphic splits apart into pie-like slices, revealing the stationary core at the center.

"Our crew has worked tirelessly to equip Elderon with all the amenities you would expect from a luxury resort. Please refer to your Optix map to locate the dining hall, fitness center, infirmary, tech center, and hospitality offices. And don't forget to visit our spa and each of our themed recreational lounges."

I roll my eyes. So far Elderon sounds a lot like Disneyland.

"For your security and convenience, each suite is equipped

with a biometric lock. Your credentials will allow you to access funds in your commerce account. All transactions will be processed in US dollars. You may upgrade your ticket at any time during your stay. Business-class and first-class suites are subject to availability. Please see a hostess for details."

I let out a snort of laughter. What rich asshole gets all the way to space and decides that he should have sprung for the first-class suite?

"Your cargo will be delivered by bot upon arrival, and you'll see a variety of bots at work throughout the space station. Please be advised that all bots are the property of Maverick Enterprises, and tampering with a bot is punishable by law."

I glance over at Ping, who looks as though he's already thinking up ways to tamper with the bots.

"If you have any questions or concerns, please see me or one of your friendly Elderon hostesses for assistance. You'll find our office in Sector E on the upper deck. Thank you, and enjoy your stay."

The screen goes momentarily dark, and Ping's face reappears in my feed.

"Damn! Aren't you excited?"

"So excited," I say, muting my Optix.

It's going to be a *long* trip.

9

MAGGIE

A jolt of excitement flares through me as Elderon comes into view — three thick metal rings stacked one on top of the other, rotating on an axis. We're still too far away to tell, but I imagine it must be whipping around at several hundred miles an hour to recreate the feeling of walking on Earth.

Space Barbie Vanessa reappears as we start to dock, warning us to keep our helmets on until the fasten-harness light turns yellow.

Tripp's leg is jiggling restlessly beside mine, and every once in a while it brushes up against me. This guy is a live wire, but I can't really blame him. None of us can wait to see the colony in person, and his company designed the thing.

Finally, the little light above our seats turns yellow, and I reach up to unseal my helmet. It releases with a snap like a plastic sandwich bag, and I yank it up over my head.

The air inside the shuttle is warm and stale. The heat and perspiration of five hundred bodies has mixed with the aroma of new carpet and upholstery.

I unbuckle my harness and stand up slowly. My butt is

sweaty inside my suit, and my hair is stuck to the back of my neck. I unzip the outer suit and get a pang of embarrassment when I remember what I have on underneath.

Tripp peels off his suit and sits there in his underwear as he retrieves his jeans. Once he's dressed, he runs a hand through his mess of curls, looking just as fresh as he did when he first climbed aboard. Meanwhile, I'm battling a bad case of space-ship hair with my underwear stuck to my ass.

"Well, it was nice to meet you, Maggie Barnes," says Tripp. "Ping me if your suite isn't to your liking . . . You can always come by mine if you feel like stretching out on a California king."

My eyebrows shoot into my hairline, and I don't know whether to feel enraged or flattered. Tripp has this way of making me feel as though I just narrowly avoided being struck by a bus, and it's messing with my verbal skills.

Before I can summon a witty comeback, he's already strut-ting down the aisle toward the lift, and I'm staring dumb-founded in my stupid scratchy onesie.

Shaking my head, I stuff my feet back into my boots and approach the bottleneck of people lining up behind him. When it's my turn, I crowd on with half a dozen others and flip on my Optix to grab footage of Elderon.

We disembark and line up by the jet bridge, and I feel a draft of cool air coming from the space station. I can hear the quiet hum of the air-filtration system overhead, and I get another full-body thrill.

I'm actually in space. I'm about to climb aboard the first-ever civilian colony, where I'll be living for the next five years.

I power walk through the jet bridge toward the door at the end of the tunnel. The doors slide open, and I step into what looks like a mall from the future.

Elderon isn't at all what I was expecting. It's not some dark blue-lit cave with narrow tunnels branching off in every direction. It's open and airy, lit by artsy asymmetrical light fixtures suspended from the ceiling. The walls are made from interlocking white hexagons backlit around the edges, and the floor is covered in white tile speckled with gold.

Little glass plaques positioned near every corner point me toward the restrooms, the mall, and the hospitality office on the upper deck. There's an information desk to my right and a little waiting area with modern white chairs.

Space Barbie Vanessa's tinny voice is echoing through a speaker somewhere above me, quickly followed by a translation in what sounds like Hindi. Voices speaking in French and German join the cacophony, and I stop in my tracks to take in my first glimpse of Elderon.

Passengers are pouring off the shuttle toward the escalators straight ahead. They seem to lead to the mall on the upper deck, but I turn down a hallway to my left to get a more complete tour of the colony.

Immediately I notice two tracks of dotted lines beneath my feet and hear a quiet beeping coming up behind me. I turn around just in time to see a delivery bot barreling behind me, using the dotted lines as a guide.

The bot flashes its lights at me, and I step out of the way to let it pass. It flies down the hallway and cuts hard to the right, zooming toward its preprogrammed destination at twenty miles an hour.

I step off the tracks to avoid another near collision and make my way toward the heart of the colony. Straight ahead is the fitness center, but I hop on another escalator and ride up to the upper deck.

I emerge into what must be the mall — a jumbled maze of shops on risers and bright flashing neon signs. Asymmetrical panels along the ceiling beam down to mimic skylights, and a dizzying spiral staircase winds up toward the ceiling. Shops branch off on their own little levels, and I spot a pharmacy, a coffee kiosk, and a frozen-yogurt stand.

Relieved to know that there's coffee in space, I pull up my orientation packet to locate my pod number and room assignment. Apparently, each pod is like a neighborhood, and mine is in the coach sector.

I take my time on the way back down, getting plenty of footage for my column and trying to identify the smell of the place. It's an odd mix of plastic, new carpet, and biologic cleaners.

Apparently, I have to go through Sector M to get to coach housing, which means I have to walk through the fitness center.

I hop off the escalator and instantly feel a prickle of intimidation. The place is a maze of shiny new ellipticals, treadmills, and weight machines.

I wind along the corridor in the direction of my pod, and the ceiling opens up to the most magnificent neighborhood I've ever seen in my life.

I'm standing in a sort of atrium that most closely resembles a beehive. Five levels of rooms arranged in a honeycomb configuration stretch up toward the ceiling, and a sprawling set of ramps leads to the upper suites.

When I reach my unit number, a tiny pinhole camera scans my face. The door unlocks, I push it open, and a light above my head flickers on.

I step into the room and let out a laugh. I'm standing in a hobbit hole that cannot possibly be my room.

The entire unit is roughly nine feet long and five feet wide, made smaller by the ceiling that slopes to a point. I'm standing on a tiny square platform eighteen inches wide, staring into a child-sized loft. A stack of shelves in front of me doubles as a ladder, and I can see through them to a bed smaller than a twin.

There is no pillow — just a raised bump in the mattress where my head will go. Folded at the foot of the bed is a peculiar-looking cloth bag with a zipper and a thin charcoal blanket that looks more medieval dungeon than space-station chic. A white paper gift bag with a blue ribbon is resting near the head bump, welcoming me to Elderon.

I grab the bag and empty its contents onto the mattress. There's a package of melatonin tablets for sleep, a tiny bottle of the same "comfort tonic" they gave me for space sickness, a bag of chocolate-covered pretzels, and a supergreens granola bar.

I rip open the bag of pretzels, and the nutrition facts pop up on my Optix. I take a handful anyway, and my Optix pans over the tiny bed.

Another pop-up window appears, pointing to a handle just below the mattress. I reach down to give it a tug, and the entire bed — mattress and all — flips up toward the wall. The bed stows away neatly in the cubby, and a desk pops out with a little floating chair.

I pull the bed back down and shake my head. As a New Yorker, I'm used to small spaces, but this is ridiculous.

Dumbfounded, I hang my messenger bag on a hook by the door and flop down onto the bed. It doesn't bounce like a normal mattress. It sinks down with the weight of my body and absorbs the impact like a forgiving cloud. It's ridiculously comfortable.

I kick off my shoes, and one of them hits the opposite wall. A circular hunk of plastic splits open and rotates to reveal a porthole, and I get my first view from Elderon.

Darkness as far as the eye can see stretches out into the endless abyss. The stars are a silvery blur from the spinning space station, and Earth is a wispy blue blob. The motion of the space station combined with the glow of the stars gives my view a twinkling Christmas-light quality, and in this moment, I am struck speechless.

Never in a million years did I think that I would be lying in my space bed looking out at the world from three hundred miles away. It's mesmerizing — unimaginable. This alone is worth the trip.

The blurred glimmers of light look like shooting stars, and it's almost too much for my brain to process. My eyelids slowly begin to droop, and my body sinks deeper into the mattress.

My last thought before falling asleep is that Tripp Van de Graaf is unjustifiably smug. He might have a king-sized bed in space, but his views are the same as mine.

10

JONAH

My alarm blares me awake at oh five hundred sharp. It's dark in the little cubbyhole they assigned me, and I can't find my Optix to save my life. I grope around on the shelf above my bed, and my fingers finally make contact with the stupid thing.

I shut off my alarm and roll over. This place is definitely not what I was expecting.

In the army, my bed was always about as wide as my body and not nearly as long. In basic, it was a bunk bed in the barracks that I shared with twenty other guys. Later, it might have been a cot in some hellhole bunker if I was lucky. The army seemed to operate under the philosophy that the less comfortable the bed, the less time you'd want to spend in it.

This bed is a different story. It's like sleeping on a goddamned cloud. I have a window that looks out into space, but if I stare too hard at the big blue blur that is Earth, I start to feel a little sick.

Rubbing my eyes, I get up and flip the bed into the wall so that I can access the cargo bins stowed under the floor panels.

Both of my bins are only half full. One of them is lined with uniforms, socks, underwear, and a few sets of civilian clothing. The other contains my hygiene kit, a set of electric clippers, a Benchmade knife, my watch, and a worn manila envelope.

I pick up the envelope and pull out the one photo I take everywhere I go: the one of me, my mom, and my brother at Will Rogers beach. It was taken when I was nine or ten years old, just before Ian enlisted. It's the last photo that was taken before he was killed and the very last one of all three of us together.

I stick the photo in a crack above my headboard and grab a clean T-shirt from my bin. I get dressed, lace up my shoes, and head to the lavatory.

It's early enough that I expect to be alone, but someone is already in the shower. He's singing "Hotel California" very loud and off-key, and I try to ignore him as I splash cold water on my face.

The lavatory has six showers, four urinals, and a long row of sinks. Everything is coated in the same charcoal-gray tile, and I'm amazed that the shower stalls actually have doors.

I still have dark circles under my eyes and the start of a five o'clock shadow, but at least I managed to get a decent haircut before coming to Elderon. I stick my head under the faucet to swish some water around in my mouth just as the shower shuts off.

A cloud of steam wafts out from the shower, and a disturbingly familiar face appears behind me in the mirror.

It's Ping.

When he sees me, a huge grin spreads across his face. "Heyya, sarge! Fancy meeting you here!"

"Morning, Ping," I grumble, grabbing a towel from a rack by the sink to dry my face. "Put some clothes on."

Ping grins and wraps a towel around his waist. "You off to get your swole on?"

"What?"

"You goin' to the gym?"

"Uh . . . yeah."

"Well, shit. You need a spotter? 'Cause I'm a real good spotter. Or maybe a sparring partner?" He feigns a few punches at my reflection in the mirror.

"I think I'm good," I say, hoping he'll take the hint and leave me alone.

"Nah. You shouldn't go alone, sarge. Battle buddies!" He gives me an admonishing look. "Hang on one sec. I'll be right back."

He dashes out of the lavatory, leaving a trail of watery footprints behind him. I groan. The *last* thing I need is to have Ping attached to my hip for the next five years.

I toss my towel in the laundry bin and slip out of the lavatory, glancing around to make sure he doesn't see me sneak out.

The barracks are arranged in pods — weird honeycomb modules that stretch five levels high. The officers' barracks are in a different hallway than the privates', but we share a lavatory and a common area.

I slip out of the barracks before he can return and head down the hallway that will take me to the gym. I'm barely a hundred yards away when I hear a familiar voice behind me and the sound of sneakers slapping the floor.

"Hey, sarge! Wait up!"

I keep walking, but Ping catches up. His hair is still damp from the shower, but he's dressed in his workout clothes and ready to go.

"Hey!" he pants. "I told ya to wait!"

"Sorry," I mutter, wishing I'd been a little quicker. "I usually do my workouts solo."

"I get it," says Ping, though I'm ninety-nine percent sure that he doesn't get it. "You're out of shape, and you want a chance to get back in the game before anybody sees."

"No."

"Aw, come on, sarge. I love a good sweat sesh. Wouldn't you rather have a gym bro anyways?"

I roll my eyes, but Ping is oblivious.

"Great! Me too."

I break into a jog — mostly so we don't have to talk — and he runs after me and doesn't shut up.

"You have brothers or sisters?" Ping huffs.

My throat tightens. "No."

"Well, that explains it," says Ping. "Me, I come from a big family — three brothers and a little sis. I'm the oldest. You know I'm the first one in my family to join the armed forces?"

I quicken my pace, but damn if he doesn't keep up.

"Now my little bro wants to join." He chuckles. "My mom cried for days when I told her I was gonna go live in space."

By the time we get to the fitness center, the place is already packed. Most of the people there are nonmilitary personnel, working out on the ellipticals as they check their messages.

I jump on the first treadmill I see to finish warming up. My playlist starts on my Optix, and pretty soon I'm in the zone. Ping falls into pace right next to me, showing no signs of fatigue whatsoever.

I let Ping spot me on the weight bench — a decision I immediately regret. He talks way too much (and too loudly) and sometimes forgets what he's doing. I'm so irritated that I abandon my last set halfway through.

When we switch, Ping spots a woman at the lat pulldown machine, and his arms nearly give out. She's very attractive — dark-haired and ripped — with Middle Eastern features and two prosthetic legs. I have a feeling that I've seen her before, though I can't think for the life of me where.

"Do you know — who that is?" Ping huffs as I help him get the barbell back in the rack.

"Should I?"

He lets out an incredulous laugh. "Uh, *yeah*! That's Ziva Blum!"

I don't say anything. I don't have any idea who that is.

"Former CEO of BlumBot International?" Ping prompts me. "Her company made all the bots in this place!"

"Oh . . ."

"Damn, mama," says Ping, his eyes glazing over as he watches Ziva sweat in her tangerine sports bra.

"She's *old* enough to be your mother," I say as Ping sits up and mops the sweat out of his eyes.

"Mmm. I'd let her spank me if she wanted."

"That's disgusting."

Ping is distracted for the rest of the workout. But the dude keeps at it, and by the time I'm done, his shirt is completely soaked with sweat. He's not lazy — I'll give him that. If he didn't talk so much, he'd almost be tolerable.

He follows me back to the barracks to get cleaned up for our shift, but I manage to lose him between the showers and the dining hall. The first day is all meetings and formalities. I have an officers' briefing at oh seven hundred, which means I don't have much time to eat.

Lucky for me, it doesn't matter. The food looks only border-line edible — and I lived on MREs for close to a year. Breakfast in coach includes a heap of runny eggs, burnt sausage links, and some kind of sugary bread that could be French toast.

But the real spectacle is the things *behind* the serving line: half a dozen humanoid robots like I've never seen before. They have silicone skin, mechanical mouths and eyebrows, and creepy glass eyes that blink and move. They're dressed in the same unisex blue smocks, smiling and scooping as people order their food.

Fortunately, the bots don't have hair — just a bald silicone forehead in the front and a skull made of clear plastic in the back. When the bot nearest me moves its head from side to side, I see a rainbow of wires and mechanical components working behind its eyes.

Feeling queasy, I skip the line altogether and grab a bowl of corn flakes from the cereal bar in the back. Ping joins my table just as I'm finishing up, clearly blown away by the robot lunch ladies.

I say goodbye, dump my tray, and jog down the escalator to the lower deck. I scoot into the briefing room five minutes before the meeting and find my place at the end of the line.

The other officers are around my age. Some are younger; some are older. I recognize most of them from officer training, but we aren't exactly friends.

The other sergeants got recruited straight out of the armed forces. About half of them are American, but there are also recruits from the UK, India, France, and Germany. They were all still completely enmeshed in military life, whereas I've been out of the game for two whole years. While they were stationed overseas or training guys back home, I was busy playing security guard and toning the asses of LA's elite.

Captain Callaghan walks in at oh seven hundred, and the sergeant closest to the door yells to get our attention. We all stand at parade rest, and Callaghan shoots us all a dirty look.

Callaghan might be an asshole, but he's the real deal. According to his profile, he served in Russia about the same time I did and was deployed to Ukraine a few years before that.

"Listen up, people . . . For those of you who don't know, I'm Captain Callaghan. I oversee this company. Squad leaders, meet your COs. Memorize their faces. If you need your hand held, your nose wiped . . . they are your first stop. Any real problems will be passed up to me." He glares down at us, and I feel his eyes linger on me. "If an issue makes it to my desk, God help you."

I glance around at the rest of the squad leaders. They all look as though they'd rather be dead than find themselves at Callaghan's mercy.

"Sergeants, keep your squads in line. I do not tolerate any drama in my company. Troublemakers get a one-way ticket back to Earth — no questions asked."

He looks around accusingly, as if we're already guilty of wasting his time.

"So far we're only at twenty-five percent capacity. Don't anybody panic. Your squads should start to fill out by the middle of the week. By the end of Reception, we'll be at full capacity."

He folds his arms behind his back and starts to pace. "One thing you'll notice about the men and women under your command is that a lot of them wouldn't survive public daycare, much less make it through basic in any branch of the armed forces."

His mouth tightens into a thin line. "Maverick Enterprises and the Department of Defense seem to be laboring under the delusion that the greatest threat we face is a cyberattack from an enemy combatant. That's why they've hired a bunch of eggheads to serve in this company."

There's a brief pause, as if to say that he knows better than Maverick *and* the DoD.

"Personally, it's my belief that we need to be ready to weather *any* sort of attack — not just one that comes in the form of zeroes and ones. I've taken the liberty of reviewing each recruit's file personally. Most of them don't have a lick of combat experience. It's your job to train them up to Space Force standards in ten weeks' time. If you don't, it'll be your ass on the line as well as theirs."

A few officers around me exchange nervous looks. I wonder how much input Captain Callaghan got in the recruitment process. He definitely didn't have any say in recruiting me. He's made it perfectly clear that he'd rather not have me at all.

"Don't think this is gonna be a cake walk just because we're in space," he continues. "I expect you to train your squads as if you were heading into a war zone. The Bureau for Chaos is still at large, but that doesn't mean that an attack won't come in the form of an invasion or a missile."

Callaghan stops pacing and eyes each of us in turn, settling on me for what seems like a very long time.

"Our job is to stay one step ahead of the enemy. Catastrophes can happen when you least expect them."

11

MAGGIE

I wake up suddenly with the immediate feeling that I've overslept. The room is a blur of white and gray, and for a second I completely forget where I am. I've got a cellophane wrapper wedged under my boob, and the mattress is littered with pretzel crumbs — not the first time I've woken up in this position.

I look out the window. The view is pitch black. There's no traffic noise whatsoever — no noise at all except the gentle whir of an air conditioner.

I sit up. Something about my room is different. That's when I remember that I'm no longer in my apartment. I'm in my suite aboard Elderon. I'm living in space.

I grab my glasses and touch my Optix. The time is flashing in the upper right-hand corner, but it looks as though it's still set to Pacific Time. It's a quarter 'til two, which means it's four forty-five back home and a quarter 'til nine on Elderon.

Shit. Double shit.

I must have fallen asleep without setting an alarm. I'm

supposed to meet my new editor for a briefing in fifteen minutes, and I still don't know where the newsroom is.

I swear and roll out of bed, searching in vain for my clothes. All I find is my balled-up jumpsuit and the boots I kicked off last night. Still in my undies, I open my door a tiny crack and peer out into the corridor. My cargo bins are nowhere in sight.

Fuck! The bots were supposed to drop off my stuff by eleven last night, and now I have nothing to wear.

Feeling frantic, I dig down in my messenger bag and shake out my wrinkled pair of jeans. I'm still wearing my "Don't Let the Bastards Grind You Down" T-shirt from the Revolutionary Café. I can't meet my editor looking like this.

Pulling up a map of the colony, I find the hospitality offices. They're located on the upper deck — across the station from my suite.

Not caring that I've got full-on mad-scientist hair, I fly down the stairs to the first floor of my pod, sprint through the fitness center, and jump on the escalator.

It's clogged with about a hundred other people going about their day. Several of them are dressed in lab coats and Dockers. They must be the university researchers. The Silicon Valley people are all in jeans, tennis shoes, and those hideous neon puffer jackets — as though it's *so cold* on the climate-controlled space station.

Squeezing my way between two Brits talking rat DNA, I shoot off the escalator and make a beeline for the clean white counter outside hospitality. There's already a line six or seven deep, and I swear so loudly that several people turn to look in my direction.

"Sorry," I mumble.

I shift anxiously from one foot to the other, watching the minute hand on the clock hanging over the counter. It's five 'til nine — five minutes until I make a horrible first impression by showing up late and unshowered on the first day of work. Great.

I have no idea what this editor is like — only that Alex Brennan was enough of a shark to make it to the galactic press corps. He was the senior associate editor for *The Atlantic* before moving on to *The Times* and getting poached by Maverick Enterprises. He's gotta be Darth Vader with an AP Stylebook.

Suddenly, a smiling woman appears in front of me, and I realize I've reached the front of the line. The woman is wearing the same crisp white dress and blue scarf as Space Barbie Vanessa. She's got light-mocha skin and dark-brown eyes and looks as though she just waltzed out of a skin-care ad.

"Good morning."

"Morning."

"Are you enjoying your stay on Elderon?"

"Uh . . . yeah." There's something weird about this girl. She's looking right at me, and yet I get the distinct impression that she's not *really* listening.

"Wonderful. How can I help you?"

I let out a breath of relief mixed with exasperation. "So I woke up this morning, and my cargo bins are still MIA. I don't have any clothes to wear — or *deodorant* — not to mention my desktop. I haven't eaten breakfast, and I'm supposed to meet my editor in, like, five minutes."

"I am so sorry to hear that," says the woman, offering an apologetic smile. "Let me see what I can find out."

She pushes a little scanner across the counter toward me, and I place my hand over the glass. The scanner reads my fingerprints, and the woman turns her attention to her Optix.

The picture from my press credentials appears in front of her. I see a line of bold red text marching across the page, but I can't read the words in reverse.

"Thank you for your patience, Ms. . . . Barnes. Just give me one moment . . ."

She fiddles around with her Optix for a few seconds, and her cool-as-a-cucumber expression wavers.

"I'm sorry," she says, refocusing on me. "But it seems that your cargo was not delivered to your suite last night."

Well, *duh.* "That's what I just said."

The woman cracks an accommodating smile. "The system is showing me that your cargo is still en route."

"En route to *where*?" I ask impatiently, flinging my body over the counter and trying to read what it says on her Optix.

"Hmm. It appears that there was an error with your delivery information. This bot seems to be headed to a different sector altogether."

"Where's the bot now?"

"The tracking information is telling me that he is somewhere in the defense module . . . Sector Q."

"*He*?" I repeat.

"This particular bot has a masculine designation," she explains. "I can redirect him to your room —"

"No," I say quickly. "There's no time. Can I just find the bot and grab my stuff?"

"If you'd prefer . . . The bot will require your biometric credentials to unload somewhere other than his designated —"

"Fine!" I say, slapping my palms on the desk. "Beam me the location."

She nods, still unfazed by my attitude.

I pull up my Optix, and a little blue dot superimposes itself over my map of the colony. I bump past a guy in a lab coat who's been hovering uncomfortably close behind me for the past two minutes and push my way through the crowd toward the escalator.

I briefly wonder if I'll be able to access the military sector at all, but I walk right in and find myself in a hallway that's as narrow and plain as the ones in my pod.

The doors I pass all have little porthole windows at the top, and I catch a glimpse of a dozen or so meetings with men and women in blue. The Space Force has its own fitness center, and I pass several doors with no windows at all. These rooms bear no numbers or letters — just little scanners off to the side to let official personnel in and keep people like me out.

There are a ton of Space Force operatives milling around — way more of them than the researchers and tech workers I've encountered so far. I'm not sure what use the colony could possibly have for that many soldiers — unless they know something that I don't.

Are they expecting some kind of coup? An attack from the Russian space station? An alien invasion?

My dark train of thought is cut short by the appearance of a little plastic bastard zooming along the dotted lines ahead of me. This bot looks just like the one that nearly ran me over yesterday — just a shiny white box on wheels.

"Hey!" I shout, as if the stupid bot can hear me. "Stop!"

An officer down the hallway freezes at the sound of my voice. He turns, and his annoyed expression morphs into bewilderment as I break into a run and sprint after the bot.

Another soldier — a petite Latina — turns to stare as I close the distance between myself and the bot and throw myself into its path.

"Ex—cuse me," says the bot in a canned British accent. "Please step aside and allow me to pass. Official delivery —"

I cut off the bot and punch the blue button on the front so that it will scan my face and give up my cargo.

There's a low beep, and suddenly the bot seems to reset itself.

"Good morning, Magnolia. Do you wish — to claim — your cargo?"

"Yes," I say in a rush, waiting impatiently for it to unlock the little doors on the sides and free up my bins.

Instead, the bottom of the bot's carrier seems to give out, and it dumps both of my cargo bins onto the ground. I pull the nearest one toward me and rip off the lid.

Ignoring the stares of two passing soldiers, I rifle around under my big ball of underwear to locate a clean pair of pants and a work-appropriate shirt. My awesome first-day-of-work outfit is not in this bin, but I manage to locate a clean burgundy T-shirt and some unwrinkled jeans that do amazing things for my ass.

At the bottom of the bin is a long white cylinder — my desktop. I jiggle the ball in the center of the cylinder, but the device doesn't wake up. The cold temperature in the cargo hold must have killed the battery, which is just perfect, considering I'm going to need to access those files almost immediately.

Stuffing my underwear back into the bin, I growl directions at the bot and try to communicate — unsuccessfully — that I want to resume delivery to my suite. It still wants to drop off my cargo in Sector Q, and I decide that I can deal with that later.

I dash off to the nearest bathroom to change. I'm ten minutes late, my hair is a wreck, and my stomach is eating itself. Feeling frantic, I pull my hair into a messy bun and sprint to the newsroom to catch the briefing.

By the time I get there, I'm twenty minutes late. The desktop with all of my story notes is dead, and I look as though I've been out drinking all night.

The newsroom is a modern-looking office with red walls, charcoal carpeting, and desks arranged in clusters. Everyone is already gathered in the conference room — a big glass box in the very center of the open floor plan.

I slink through the door wearing an apologetic expression, and a dozen pairs of eyes snap on to me. I can practically feel the waves of judgment rolling off the other reporters, and I feel as if my face might catch fire.

Not only am I late, but I'm also the least put together. There's a bored-looking Asian woman dressed in short black overalls and emerald-green heels. The tech asshole from *Topfold* is here, wearing designer jeans, a chocolate blazer, and a bright-orange tie.

I grab a seat next to an elegant blond woman who looks Swedish. She's model thin, six feet tall, and dressed in a smart little pantsuit.

That's when I realize what I've just walked into. This isn't a galactic press corps. This is a five-year convention for the hottest content creators in the world. The people in this room aren't journalists — they're digital celebrities.

The woman presenting can't be more than five foot four. She's built like a pixie and drowning in a black sleeveless shift and the fiercest studded leather boots I've ever seen. Her jet-black hair is piled into a knot at the top of her head and secured with red chopsticks.

She's speaking very fast, pausing only to take the occasional puff from the glowing pink e-cigarette perched between her fingers. She wants ten story ideas from each of us by the end of the day. *That* I can handle.

Suddenly the briefing ends, and I make a mental note to go through her entire presentation the first chance I get. I don't know what her position is here in the press corps, but she seems to be important.

The crowd parts, and the speaker doesn't wait around to take questions. She struts out of the conference room and heads straight for her desk. I watch nervously from across the room as she fields two Optix calls in quick succession and fires up her desktop to review pitches.

The *Topfold* tech asshole accosts her before I can make my move, and so I sidle over like a lost puppy and hover in the wings.

Finally, the woman shoos him off, and her eyes snap on to me. She's wearing black reading glasses with a slice of red along the rims, and when her gaze latches on to me, I feel myself shrink a good two inches.

"Yes?"

"Hi," I say nervously. "I'm Maggie Barnes."

"Oh!" she says, as if this explains everything. "I was wondering where you'd got to."

"I'm so sorry I'm late," I say. "There was a mix-up with my cargo delivery. I swear this is not typical."

She doesn't say a word. She seems to be waiting for me to cut to the chase, so I clear my throat and take another step toward her.

"I'm looking for Alex Brennan."

"You've found her." She quirks an eyebrow and sticks a hand over the desk for me to shake. "Alexandra Brennan."

My mouth falls open. "Oh," I say, feeling my face heat up. I am such an idiot. "I'm sorry."

"Don't be. You're not the only one who expected me to be a balding middle-aged man with food stains on his clothes. Jim's the only one here who fits that description . . ." She nods across the room. "He's just here to upgrade our security software, but he's already had half the staff pitch him stories."

Relief floods through me. Finally an editor with a sense of humor.

"Wow," I say, shaking my head in disbelief. "It is such an honor to meet you. I just read that piece you wrote on AI in healthcare, and I think you really nailed the intangible benefits of human-on-human interactions."

"Thanks. Believe it or not, that story was the last piece of my writing to be published at *The Times*. That was right before we made the transition to immersive, and *god* was that depressing. I was laying off writers left and right, popping half a Xanax with my coffee every morning and pumping my body full of beta blockers." She takes a deep breath. "Anyway, Maverick approached me, and I thought, why not?"

"I know what you mean," I say. "Maverick owns the paper I was working for. Last month my editor told me they wanted bots writing all the stories."

"You're kidding."

"Nope."

Alex frowns and consults her Optix. "I thought you were a *Topfold* girl."

"I am," I say quickly. "I do immersive stories for them under my pen name, Layla Jones. I was writing for the *New York Daily Journal* as Maggie Barnes."

"Gotcha." Alex takes one last quick puff from her e-cig and sticks it down in its little crystal docking station. "I told the doc who did my medical evaluation that I'd quit," she explains, yanking down the neck of her top to show me the nicotine patch below her clavicle. "No smoking in space. Go figure." She shakes her head. "Must be all the oxygen tanks or something."

I raise my eyebrows, not sure that this statement requires any sort of response.

"So . . ." She jostles the glowing ball in front of her to wake her desktop. A digital bulletin board materializes between us, and she swipes to a new blank screen with my name at the top. "What've you got for me?"

"A question."

"Shoot."

TARAH BENNER

"Who would I talk to if I wanted to get my hands on the budget for Elderon?"

Alex scrunches her eyebrows. "Why?"

"Just background," I say smoothly, trying not to make a big deal out of it. I need to confirm my suspicions before I come in and try to pitch such a crazy story.

Alex tilts her chin forward, glaring at me over her glasses as though she knows I'm up to no good. "Maggie . . . I'm your editor. You don't need to worry about me scooping you. What's going on?"

I swallow. I hate showing my hand before I have an idea fully worked out, but I need her to know where I'm headed with this. "I just want to know what portion of Maverick personnel would be classified as military."

Alex frowns, and I can tell that I should've waited until I had something concrete. "Not the sort of pitch I wanted to hear from you this week."

I cringe. I knew it wouldn't be. In truth, I have about two dozen Layla Jones–worthy story ideas sitting on my desktop. The problem is that it's completely dead, and Alex has the uncanny ability to make my mind go blank.

"Wow," she says, still staring at me as though she has x-ray vision. "Not what I was expecting from you at all. The letter of rec from your editor at *Topfold* was *glowing* — verging on creepy." She tilts her head to the side. "Your assessment from Cliff was less glowing but still impressive, considering it was coming from that crusty old dirtbag."

I'm not sure if I want to laugh or cry. On the one hand, this is turning out to be my first-day-of-work worst nightmare. On the other, hearing Alex call Cliff a crusty old dirtbag just made my year.

"Maggie, look. If you're not ready to play with the big girls . . ."

"No!" I say quickly. "I am ready. I am *so* ready. I have a million and one ideas for Layla stories on my desktop right now. The other thing was more of a long-term investigative piece that I wanted to work on."

Alex's eyebrows continue to inch up, and she shakes her head.

"What?"

"I'm sorry . . . Are you on crack?"

"Excuse me?"

"Maggie, you're a smart girl. That is not why Natalie Dubois sent you here. You were sent here to create fluff content to make Maverick Enterprises look good — nothing more. You want my advice? Keep it light. Keep it palatable. Did you take a shit in microgravity? What's it like to shower in space? How's the food? Take our followers on a space walk this week. Use your imagination."

I shake my head. I definitely want to cry, but I cannot afford to humiliate myself any further. "What are you saying?"

"I'm saying that if you want to keep your job, you're going to have to give me *Topfold*-worthy content. Fun. Nice. Light."

I feel my shoulders droop as my body deflates.

"I know, I know," she says. "We all want a chance to play journalist once in a while."

She glances around the newsroom and lowers her voice. "Look, Maggie . . . I get it. And what I'm about to say isn't coming from me . . ."

I perk up. This sounds interesting.

Alex takes a deep breath. "If anybody asks, I told you to kill the piece and bury it out back. But between you and me . . . if you want to work on something like that, I won't stop you. It's just gonna have to be on your own time."

"Yes," I say, nearly collapsing with relief. "Yes! That's no problem. Thank you!"

"Don't thank me," she says, her face utterly devoid of emotion. "Get cracking. I want a Layla story on my desktop by one and another story before you leave today. It'll go out on the feeds first thing in the morning. Hopefully you got plenty of good footage on the way here."

"You got it, boss," I say, practically bubbling over with excitement that she gave me the unofficial go-ahead.

"Maggie," she says, her voice full of warning. "I meant what I said. Officially, all I want is Layla Jones for breakfast, lunch, and dinner."

12

MAGGIE

After I cut together some first-person footage of my voyage to space and my impromptu interview with Tripp Van de Graaf, I overlay my own commentary and send it over to Alex. I close my desktop and head to lunch, following my stomach's desperate hunger gymnastics.

My bot disaster kept me from getting anything for breakfast, and that supergreens granola bar from my gift bag is starting to look marginally edible.

I head to the dining hall in a bleary hunger-induced fugue. I gave up on trying to keep my hair in a bun, and it's back in its usual frizzy blond cloud.

I stumble blindly into the coach line and earn a few strange looks from the polished Space Force operatives around me. I can tell I've got this glazed "give me food" look on my face, and they're probably wondering what the hell I'm doing on Elderon.

When I reach the sneeze guard, I have the briefest thought that I might be hallucinating. The serving line isn't being manned by people, but rather six human-ish abominations.

They're bots, but they aren't like any bots I've seen before. They have skin and eyes and lips, and their faces seem to move into expressions resembling human emotions. Their movements and voices are stilted and jerky, but they've been programmed to blink in an almost human way.

As I draw closer, I see that none of them have hair. Their silicone skin caps stop halfway up their skulls, revealing a grotesque jumble of wires and pistons moving beneath the plastic.

The bots are dressed in plain blue smocks, but subtle curves and peaks beneath the material hint at features verging on feminine. They swivel at the hips to face each person in line, spooning food into plastic trays.

Lunch is some next-level-disgusting beef stroganoff, shriveled green beans, and runny fruit cocktail. I flip on my Optix to capture the weird, disgusting display just as the first bot swivels toward me.

"Would you like — some — stro — ganoff?" it asks in a stilted monotone voice.

"Yes," I say, watching the bot warily.

The bot turns back to its vat of noodles, scoops out a glob, and slaps it onto my tray. Next it fishes a ladle into the congealed brown goo, dumps it over my noodles, and splashes some juice into the other compartments of my tray. The bot doesn't seem to notice the little puddle it created. It just passes my tray to the next bot, which asks if I want fruit cocktail.

By the time I get to the end of the line, the beef juice runoff has fully merged with the sugary fruit syrup, and my hunger has magically disappeared. The last bot tops off my disgusting lunch with a fluffy white roll, and I snatch another one from under the sneeze guard when it's not looking.

I take a detour around a chatty group of engineers and feel a sudden surge of fury. They're chowing down on what looks like fresh chicken parmesan and a crisp green salad that didn't come from a can. They must be in business class.

I slam my tray down at an empty corner table and take a bite of the disgusting stroganoff. It's like chewing on the strap of my bag, and the noodles are some mushy gluten-free rice concoction. I want to cry.

Shoving my tray across the table, I tear off an enormous hunk of my roll and start piecing together my second story for the day. After my blundering show of incompetency earlier, I need to work overtime to salvage Alex's opinion of me.

I crack open the very-berry fruit drink to wash down the bread and hear footsteps coming up behind me.

"Wow," says a familiar voice. "That bad?"

I look up and nearly expel a very-berry snot rocket. Tripp Van de Graaf is standing over my shoulder wearing a pair of perfectly distressed jeans and a long-sleeve cotton shirt rolled up over his beautiful forearms. A slight smirk is playing at the corners of his mouth, which only serves to stoke my ire.

"Is this some kind of joke?" I growl, nodding at my tray of barely touched food. "I'm pretty sure that feeding this to prisoners of war would violate several articles of the Geneva Convention."

An apologetic grin twitches at the corner of his perfect mouth, and he slides uninvited into the chair across from me. "I'm sorry. We're still working out the kinks."

I frown. "There's a sushi bar over in first class."

He cringes. "If it makes you feel any better, it's all imitation crab and cultured tuna."

"It doesn't."

Tripp squirms for a moment in his seat, and when he grins, those damn dimples make an appearance. "Am I going to be watching a scathing review of the food in *Topfold* this evening?"

113

I switch off my Optix and cross my arms over my chest. "If you subscribe to Layla Jones."

"Oh, I do," he says with gusto. "I read and watch everything you do."

I don't know how to respond to that. Some small desperate part of me wants to feel flattered, but he's just trying to butter me up.

"Tell you what," he says, pulling up his Optix and scanning my face. "I'm going to change your meal-ticket status to first class." He cocks his head to the side and waggles both eyebrows. "I can't have the prettiest girl in space starving on my watch."

I open my mouth to protest, but he holds up a hand to cut me off. "Just until we get the food-science lab fully up and running. Right now our fresh produce yields are only high enough to serve our first-class and business-class residents, but in a month or two . . ."

"We'll all be eating shrimp cocktail and Niçoise salad?"

"Exactly," he says. "Not to mention all the fresh fruit your little heart desires."

"Really?" I say, suddenly interested. "That's on the record, you know. I'm gonna hold you to that."

He laughs. "I just sort of assumed that all parts of our conversation were on the record." His eyes flash devilishly. "Unless . . ."

"Unless what?"

"Unless you wanted to come by my suite later for some fun that would be strictly off the record?"

"I think I'll pass," I say coolly. I refuse to be charmed into submission by the heir apparent to a tech dynasty.

"Suit yourself," he says, folding his arms behind his head and leaning back in his chair so that it balances on two legs.

"But . . . I could use your help with something," I say, throwing caution to the wind.

He laughs and runs a hand through his long perfect curls. "Is this a quid pro quo situation?"

"No."

"That's too bad. 'Quid pro quo' always sounds so hot."

I shake this off, wondering when he's going to realize that I'm not interested and give it a rest. "It would be really helpful if I could get my hands on some colony specs."

"Specs?" he repeats.

"You know . . . How much money went into building it. How much Maverick is spending to fund programs like the galactic press corps, the Space Force . . . How much the company has budgeted for very-berry fruit blast."

Tripp quirks one eyebrow, studying me for a moment. "I've gotta say, Mags . . . I've watched every piece you've published on *Topfold* over the last month, and private military spending doesn't strike me as very Layla Jones."

I open my mouth to respond, but no words come out. He's watched every Layla Jones story for the past *month*?

"That's the thing about immersive journalism," I stammer. "The good stuff always looks effortless, but I'll have you know that a lot of work went into that donut piece." I feel my face heat up. "And don't call me Mags."

He laughs. "My apologies. I loved the donut piece. But honestly, I'm more of a big-picture sort of a guy. I leave the very-berry budget to the bean counters."

I let out a huff of disappointment. "But you must have *access* to that sort of information."

He leans forward, and a tantalizing curly tendril falls into his eyes. "Of course I do . . . I'm an all-access kind of guy. But it wouldn't be *nearly* as interesting as an in-depth interview with the man who made it all possible."

I roll my eyes and sit back in my seat. "The guy who made it all possible?" I look up as if I'm wracking my brain to figure out whom he's talking about. "Would that be Miles Lapain the engineer, Cassius Blain the venture capitalist, or your father the space architect?"

"*Ouch!*" He grins in a way that tells me that his ego is not at all damaged by the slight. "I'll have you know that the honeycomb design of the suites was *my* idea."

"So you're the reason I'm living in a hobbit hole."

"The coach suites are a little small . . . But you have to admit that the beds are comfortable."

"They're all right."

"Come on . . . I bet it was the best night's sleep you've ever had."

I don't respond, but he seems to take my silence as tacit agreement.

"Beds are very important to me," he continues. "We spend half our lives in bed."

"I think you mean a *third* of our lives."

"We spend a third of our lives *sleeping*," he corrects. "But I meant what I said."

I roll my eyes, and Tripp shakes his head. "You're a tough girl to impress, Maggie Barnes."

"I'm really not," I say, "once you show me something impressive."

Am I *flirting* with him? What the hell is wrong with me?

"All right. Point taken." There go those dimples again. "Tell you what . . . Why don't you stop by my office tonight around seven-ish — no funny business — and I'll get you whatever documentation you want."

"Really?"

"Yes — on one condition."

I roll my eyes. Here we go. "What's your condition?"

"You let me take you out."

"Take me out?" I repeat. "Out where?"

"Is that a yes?"

"No," I shriek. "No. Dating a source would seriously damage my credibility."

"Oh, come on," he says. "How's it going to damage Layla Jones's credibility if I go out with Maggie Barnes?"

I turn this thought over in my head. I've got to give Tripp credit — the guy can think on his feet.

I take a deep breath. I am in *way* over my head.

"We'll see what you've got," I say. "Then we'll talk."

IT TAKES me a good twenty minutes to shake off the Tripp hypnosis after I leave the dining hall.

Even for someone like me — someone whose job is to cut through the bullshit to see people how they really are — that unshakable confidence is disarming.

Still, Tripp is *so* not my type, and I didn't strap myself into a space shuttle and rocket three hundred miles away from Earth to sleep with some overprivileged tech titan. I came here to make a name for myself, and getting involved with someone like Tripp would be a huge, *huge* mistake.

I finish up my story for Alex and start working on a story for tomorrow. I take a trip to the food-science lab on the upper deck to get some footage and hopefully interview a couple of employees. It's located in Sector D, right across from the mall.

When I reach the sector, I find my path blocked by a set of heavy metal doors with little portholes cut into the top. I can see through them to a long sterile hallway illuminated by long strips of fluorescent lighting.

I pound on the door for several minutes before someone

comes to answer. It's an irate middle-aged man with glasses and a lab coat. He's thin and gray and very pale, and he does *not* look happy to see me.

"Hello!" I say brightly as the double doors swing open.

"Who are you?"

"Magnolia Barnes," I say, sticking out a hand for him to shake. "I'm a member of the press corps, and I'm doing a story on Elderon's food."

"We're very busy," says the man, looking as though he's wishing he never opened those doors.

"I know," I say. "Mr. Van de Graaf told me you would be. But after hearing about the food-science labs from him, I absolutely had to come see for myself."

"Mr. Van de Graaf?" says the man, furrowing his eyebrows.

"Yes."

A-ha! I've said the magic words. It isn't a lie — not exactly. Tripp really *was* bragging about the food labs.

The man studies me for a moment as if he's trying to decide if I'm the real deal. "Very well," he sighs. "Come with me."

I follow the man down the long narrow hallway until we reach the very end. I have no idea what's inside the dozens of rooms we passed, but it all seems very top secret. Everything is quiet and utterly opaque.

A scanner on the door registers the man's face, and he holds it open so I can step inside. The room seems to be some kind of holding area lined with shelves of boxes. The man reaches into one and pulls out a blue smock — the kind that surgeons wear.

"Put this on."

I put it on. I even don the ridiculous paper bonnet, face mask, gloves, and booties.

Once we're both fully scrubbed in, my tour guide scans us through the door on the other side, and we emerge into another world.

I'm standing on a metal catwalk suspended over a two-story warehouse. On either side of me are shelves of plants stretching toward grow lights: tomatoes, strawberries, pole beans, and greens. Each plant seems to be bursting out of a small pallet of soil with tubes carrying water and nutrients straight to the roots. The shelves below us seem to be on solid ground, while the shelves on our level are suspended from cables.

Below us, I see a dozen of the creepy humanoid bots circulating between the aisles, adjusting the nutrient tubes, picking off dead leaves, and harvesting fruit from the more mature plants.

It's fascinating to watch the bots work. Their movements are almost childlike: slow, deliberate, and calculated.

"Growing plants in space has its challenges," says my tour guide. "But we've managed to outsmart Mother Nature."

I'll say. All I can do is stare. I can't believe they've managed to grow all of this stuff in space — or that there will eventually be enough food to feed five thousand people.

The man leads me down the catwalk to a rickety set of stairs, and I follow him down to the lower level. We exit the warehouse from a set of doors on the other end and peel off our scrubs outside.

At first I think that the tour is over, but then he leads me down another hallway past a long line of doors. This hallway is different from the one we were in before.

Instead of numbers, these plaques have words: chicken, pork, tuna, and mutton. We stop at a door with a plaque reading "beef," and he scans us in.

I half expect to find myself in a gigantic freezer, but we're standing in another lab. The room is lit by harsh fluorescent lighting and hemmed in on both sides by solid walls of glass.

There are two rows of stainless-steel tables in the middle,

where men and women in lab coats are busy taking samples from petri dishes and examining them under microscopes.

I pan around the room with my Optix and step up to the glass. On the other side are four enormous steel tankards as tall as a man with a maze of metal tubes and knobs bursting out like tentacles.

"These are our bioreactors," says the man. "We took our satellite cells from live animals on Earth. We feed them our proprietary nutrient serum and allow them to propagate. The bioreactor provides the ideal environment to grow and exercise the cells."

I shake my head in stunned silence and walk around to the window on the other side of the lab. This side contains a solid wall of meat — or, rather, a wall of steel arms holding what appear to be rib-eyes with tiny tubes of red liquid stuck down in the center. The arms are holding the steaks vertically, squeezing and flexing them in a constant gentle rhythm.

"Processed meats are easy for us now," says my guide. "Unprocessed meats are a little trickier . . . They must be individually exercised on scaffolds of artificial bone and flooded with nutrients. These rib-eyes will be served at the welcome banquet at the end of the week."

"Wow," I say, utterly stunned.

"Would you like to try a meatball?" asks my guide, gesturing over to one of the lab techs, who's poking and prodding a lump of beef under a microscope.

"Uh . . . no thanks," I say, trying and failing not to sound disgusted. Suddenly, my freeze-dried beef stroganoff from Earth is sounding much, much tastier.

"We can cook it up for you in a jiffy," he says. "It's no trouble."

"Really, I'm fine," I say. "I, uh . . . just ate, actually."

My tour guide gives me a brief smile and beckons me out of

the lab. "Don't fear the beef," he says, holding the door open for me and leading me back the way we came. "I promise you won't be able to tell the difference."

I'M a little queasy by the time I stumble out of the food-science lab. On the one hand, I got some excellent footage for my story. On the other, I have to relive the entire experience in order to cut the thing together.

I decide to take a quick break and see what became of my cargo. It wasn't in my suite when I stopped by during lunch, so I walk down to Sector E to harass the hospitality people.

When I reach the desk, a different woman is working. She's a perky porcelain-skinned redhead with a freakishly helpful smile. She tells me that my cargo was delivered this morning to a pod in Sector Q, and it takes every ounce of my self-control not to strangle her on the spot.

According to her, the human who handled my cargo must have misread the tag. They punched the destination into the computer as Q325 — not O325. Whatever. All I know is that the bot dropped off my undies with a total stranger, and I am not happy.

Sector Q is part of the defense module, but the pods in the barracks are nearly identical to my own. Still, I feel a little self-conscious as I walk through the pod lounge toward suite Q325. The men and women here are all dressed in Space Force blues, and I stick out like a sore thumb.

I sidle up to the door and take a deep breath, hoping whoever lives here is friendly.

The door flies open after my first knock, and I find myself staring at a hard muscular chest attached to a body in uniform. The insignia near his shoulder tells me that he's some kind of

121

officer, and the name embroidered in bold capital letters says that his last name is "Wyatt."

I follow a row of very straight buttons all the way up to his face and get the immediate sense that I've seen him before. He's tall — well over six feet — and his short brown hair is meticulously trimmed. His pale chiseled face is crinkled in surprise, and he's got the most intense blue eyes that I've ever seen.

"Can I help you?" he asks, clearly wondering what the hell I'm doing here.

I clear my throat. "Yeah," I say, forcing myself to meet his gaze. It's hard — almost like staring into the sun. "I hope so . . . They told me my cargo was delivered to this suite by mistake."

"Oh," he says, though I can't tell whether he's annoyed or relieved. He takes a step back into his room, and I gather that he's inviting me in. "I was wondering when someone was gonna come claim this stuff. The stupid thing tried to drop it off last night, but I refused delivery. Then I came back after PT to change, and here it was."

"Weird," I say, feeling embarrassed.

I look around. I'm standing in the cleanest room I've ever seen. The officer's suite is very similar to mine, except that there are no pretzel wrappers or dirty clothes strewn over his bed. His room looks exactly the way it must have when he first arrived, except that there's a toiletry kit on the bureau and a family photo tucked above the headboard.

He reaches up into the cubby over his bed, and I try not to stare at his magnificent ass. It's hard to do when it's right there in front of me, and I have the urge to give it a smack.

He pulls down my cargo bins one at a time, and my insides squirm at the thought of him opening them. It's bad enough to have a total stranger rifling through my unmentionables. Having Mr. Tidy see that I keep my underwear in a tangled ball of fabric is almost more than I can stand.

"Thanks," I say, bending down to pick up the bins. I have no idea how I'm going to get them all the way back to my suite, but before I even lay hands on them, he swoops down and picks them up — one on top of the other.

"Where to?" he asks.

"You don't have to," I say quickly. "It's bad enough that you had to hold on to these for me. I can take them."

"It's not a problem." His tone is flat — completely neutral. Does he *want* to carry my cargo for me, or is he just doing it because he feels obligated? What are the army values? Duty, honor, selfless service?

"Okay," I say, my throat suddenly very dry. "If you're sure you don't mind."

"I don't."

My heart speeds up, though I have no idea why. Maybe I'm just not used to such chivalry. Maybe it's the thought of having him in such close proximity to my bed.

I lead the way out of his suite, and when we walk into the lounge, every set of eyeballs snaps on to me. I keep my head down and march through the sea of blue. The other Space Force people look astonished, though whether it's my presence or Officer Wyatt that they find disconcerting, I have no idea.

The walk to my suite feels unbearably long, though it's only two sectors over. Officer Wyatt moves in complete silence. I don't even hear him breathing.

"This is me," I say in a weirdly chipper voice. I don't know what it is about him that makes me so uncomfortable, but I'm anxious to be rid of him.

"I can take them inside for you," he says, shifting the bins slightly so he can see me.

"All right."

I scan my way into the room, cringing internally at the state I left things in.

He sets the bins down on the floor, and I sense his eyes scanning the mess.

"Thank you," I say. "Officer —"

"Jonah," he mutters. "My name's Jonah."

"Thanks," I repeat, feeling like a total idiot.

"Don't mention it."

Jonah walks out, and I slam the door behind him as though I'm trying to keep out a horde of zombies.

My skin feels electrified, and my heart is racing. I have no idea what's wrong with me, but at least I have my underwear.

13

MAGGIE

I'm halfway through my Franken-meat story by the time today's shuttle is due to dock. I ate a pitiful supergreens granola dinner at my desk instead of going to the dining hall. After my little field trip to the meat lab, my appetite has been nonexistent.

I can't seem to get Jonah out of my head, which is completely ridiculous. It isn't as though the guy stripped naked and tossed rose petals at my feet. All he did was carry my cargo from one sector to another.

I finally put together why he seemed so familiar. He was the guy I saw on the shuttle to the base — the guy who looked as though he was headed into a war zone.

I'm so absorbed in my thoughts that I almost lose track of time. I glance at the little clock in the corner of my desktop and do a double take when I see that it's a quarter 'til seven. The shuttle will be docking on the lower deck any minute, and I need to be there to see who disembarks.

I shut off my desktop and jog down the escalator to get to the waiting area before the passengers come flooding out. I position myself in one of the uncomfortable white chairs just as one of the perky hostesses opens the door to the jet bridge to let the first wave of passengers disembark.

These people aren't wearing the hideous civilian jumpsuits. They're dressed in Space Force blues and heavy black boots. The men are clean-shaven with short hair and serious faces, and the women all have their hair pulled back in tidy little buns.

I don't have to count the passengers one by one. There's a long pause between each level of the shuttle as passengers disembark, and I count four whole levels of Space Force personnel. A hundred and eighty people plus all the men and women who came in on my shuttle seems excessive for a peaceful colony whose purpose is scientific exploration.

Filled with a fresh dose of resolve, I head up to Maverick's offices to speak to Tripp in person. It's not every day that a reporter captures the attention of a high-powered executive. No matter what Tripp's motives, I would be an idiot not to take advantage of whatever help he's willing to give.

Maverick Enterprises is located in Sector K — the research and technology department. The corridor widens as I approach the offices, and the automatic glass doors swoosh open. I catch a whiff of espresso and pizza — that and the sharp zing of arrogance.

The lounge is decked out in orange, red, and purple furniture. There's ping-pong, foosball tables, and giant screens playing sporting events from Earth. There's even a snack table laden with food and a cooler stocked with energy drinks. I could live here.

A real go-getter appears at my elbow. He's pale and shapeless, and his hair is an anemic whitish blond. He's dressed in tight orange pants and a spectacularly adventurous blue-and-orange paisley shirt.

"Can I help you?" he asks, discreetly tapping his Optix to scan my face.

"Yeah, actually. I'm here to see Tripp Van de Graaf."

"You must be Ms. Barnes," he says, his thin lips stretching into a hollow smile.

"Maggie."

"Welcome. My name is *Porter*, and I'll be your tour guide." He says each word with a delicate emphasis, as though he's picking his way through a patch of mud trying not to get his boat shoes dirty. "Come with me."

I follow Porter through another set of glass doors to a spacious work area with lots of tables. The walls are painted a loud construction-zone orange, and two dozen people are hunched over desktops, deeply entrenched in their work.

Giant screens all around the room flash short messages in different colors. Each message is accompanied by an alphanumeric code, and each statement sounds like a complaint: cold water in shower, escalator too slow, hot in suite.

"We call this area the Workshop," Porter explains. "It's basically the nerve center of the colony."

He gestures around to the screens. "These are all work tickets submitted to hospitality. They get routed straight here, where our software triages them into buckets for emergent, non-urgent, and urgent issues and rates them on a scale from one to ten, according to severity. The severe urgent problems go straight up to the Operating Room. Everything else gets handled by one of these geniuses."

"What's the Operating Room?"

"It's where all our senior programmers work," Porter explains. "They consult directly with Mr. Van de Graaf to fix major bugs."

I nod slowly. It seems to be a big operation for two dozen twentysomethings.

"So, when a ticket is submitted, do your programmers send out someone in maintenance?" I ask. It seems unlikely that one of these nerds would lift a finger to fix the water pressure or repair a squeaky door.

"Oh, no," says Porter. "Pretty much everything around here can be resolved with minor tweaks to the code. A colony this large requires constant fine-tuning, but it's basically one big machine."

"Huh. So can I submit a ticket for the bots?"

"Which bots?"

Porter looks as though he's about to start taking notes, so I hasten to add, "Just a blanket hatred of all of them."

"Oh, absolutely," he says. "I utterly *loathe* the bots. Creepy little things. I swear their eyes follow you around the room no matter where you're standing . . ."

I nod numbly. The orange paint job is giving me a headache. "What's with all the orange?"

"Oh, we're super into colorology around here. Orange stimulates ambition and excitement. It promotes quick decision-making and keeps energy levels high."

"Okay," I say, panning my Optix around the room to get some good footage. "So why do all the complaints go to hospitality first?" I ask. "Why not just send people here?"

Porter lets out a burst of chilly laughter. "Clearly you have not seen any of these beautiful prodigies interact with actual human beings. And you thought the bots were bad!"

I must look confused, because he adds, "Most of us work here because we're better with computers than flesh and blood. The hospitality people deal with people. We deal with problems."

While I'm pondering that philosophical nugget, Porter leads me through another set of doors to a much quieter space that's painted blue. It's filled with offices encased in glass, some of which are frosted to obscure what's going on inside.

"Mr. Van de Graaf believes collaboration only goes so far," Porter explains. "Creatives need privacy to do their best work."

I roll my eyes. As a journalist, I can't afford to be so particular. In fact, I've done some of my best work sandwiched between tourists on the subway.

Tripp's office is located in the very back corner. When we walk inside, I get the immediate impression that a tornado has passed through, leaving a trail of destruction in its wake.

Stacks of papers and vision boards are scattered all over the place: on the desk, on the floor, on the coffee table, and in the futuristic orange chairs situated around the room.

"Can I get you anything?" asks Porter. "Coffee, wine, water?"

"Water would be great," I say.

He gestures to a fancy-looking steel machine built into the wall. "Still or sparkling?"

"Er . . . still," I say.

Porter crosses to the machine and pours some water into a slender glass tumbler.

"Can I take your things?" he asks, setting my glass down on a coaster and holding out his arms for my jacket and bag.

I hesitate. It feels awkward to be treating him like a servant, but it seems rude to refuse. I smile and hand them over.

"All right, then. Mr. Van de Graaf will be with you shortly." He offers me a quick thin-lipped smile. "Please make yourself comfortable, and holler if you need anything."

I nod. Porter closes the door behind him, and a second later, the glass walls frost over automatically.

I take a sip of water and meander around the room, taking in the design ideas all over the vision boards. There are tile samples for the fitness center, sketches of the mall, traffic-flow analyses of the common areas — even a sample menu for a first-class meal.

When I reach Tripp's desk, I notice some papers that look a lot like a line-item budget. Shifting a piece of pasteboard loaded with pictures of high-tech shower heads, I flip on my Optix and quickly snap stills of each page of the budget.

A second later, the office door flies open, and I hurriedly drop the showerhead poster and step away from the desk.

Porter is back, and he's giving me a look that says he knows what I've been up to.

"Mr. Van de Graaf will see you now," he says, a sour edge to his voice.

I get a sudden tingle of panic, but then Tripp swoops in, and I know Porter won't say a word.

Tripp's hair is still perfectly disheveled. He's wearing the same charming smile he had on at lunch, but I can tell from the dip in his shoulders that he's tired or stressed.

"Maggie," he says, squeezing Porter back out into the hallway and shutting the door behind him.

"Thanks for meeting with me," I say, circling around his desk to put as much space between me and the papers as possible.

Tripp's face scrunches up. "So formal, Ms. Barnes. Porter give you the grand tour?"

"Just the Workshop," I say. "I asked if I could lodge a bot complaint."

"You don't like my bots?" he says, sounding genuinely put out.

"*Your* bots?"

"Well, I bought the company that makes them," he says defensively. "That makes them my bots."

"I . . ." I hesitate. I hadn't expected him to feel so personally invested. "Well, they're creepy," I say. "And one of the low-tech ones got lost trying to deliver my cargo. I was late for work, and I'm still wearing yesterday's underwear."

"Oh my," says Tripp, his eyes flashing with mischief. "Well, I will definitely bring this to the programmers' attention. Though, technically, those delivery machines are being rebranded as 'AutoMates' to avoid confusion with our more humanoid bots."

"Whatever," I say, nimbly stepping back as he attempts to close the distance between us. "And while you're at it, you might want to have your programmers recalibrate the bots' scooping vigor."

"Their *what*?" he asks, eyebrows shooting up as he breaks into an infectious laugh.

I blink very fast and try to reorganize my thoughts. "They scoop the food too vigorously, and the juices slosh out into the other tray compartments."

If some douchebag in first class can complain about the water pressure, then I can complain about the meat juice in my fruit cocktail.

"Noted," he says, cracking a sideways grin and snatching the drink out of my hand. "Did Porter serve you *water*?"

"I asked for water."

He rolls his eyes and walks back over to the drink dispenser. "Ms. Barnes, it's happy hour. Red or white?"

"Red."

"Cabernet all right?"

"Perfect."

He sets my tumbler on the counter and pulls out a stemless wine glass. He hits a button on the machine, and a stream of wine dispenses into the glass.

He pours himself one, too, and then sidles back over to me. I take a sip. It's a good cab; I'll give him that. It certainly doesn't taste as though it just came out of a cafeteria milk dispenser.

"So . . ." I say, turning my Optix to record. "You clearly had a big hand in designing this whole place . . . bigger than you let on."

He shrugs, looking charmingly unimpressed by his own abilities. "I may have picked out some carpet samples."

"Don't be modest," I say, pushing some vision boards aside and perching on the edge of his desk. "It doesn't suit you."

He licks his lips, and that devilish grin is back in full force. "Oh no?"

I shake my head. "Come on. Tell me what it was *really* like designing this place."

"What's there to tell? It was a lot of late nights . . . a lot of battles with my father."

"The architect."

"Architect slash engineer," he corrects. "All my father cared about was that the exterior could withstand the G-forces of constant rotation and that the interior was insulated from radiation. He seemed to forget that five thousand people would be making this place their home. He didn't think that it needed to be beautiful or have decent water pressure . . ."

"But you did."

He takes a drink and licks his lips. "I knew people had to be comfortable if we wanted this place to be a success."

"Smart."

"I thought so." He shrugs. "Some of our investors didn't."

"What happened?"

He gives me a sideways look over the top of his glass, as if he doesn't want to go into it but decides to make an exception for me. "We parted ways."

"How did you come up with the money to finish the project?"

"I put up some of my own money," he says, holding my gaze. "Well, some of my shares in the company."

"You sold off some of your shares?"

"A few."

"What did your father think about that?"

He laughs. "You're gonna have to take off your journalist hat if you want to get anything real out of me."

I stare at him for a moment. He's serious. I flip off my Optix and unclip it from my glasses. "Fine," I say. "This can just be on background."

Tripp smiles. He clears off another corner of his desk and sits down next to me, and it's as though his whole body relaxes. "Honestly? I think it might have been the first time my father ever respected me as a man."

"Wow." I have to hand it to Tripp. He's not boring.

"Can I ask you something else?" I murmur, wondering how far I dare push my luck.

He scoots a little closer, and those green eyes twinkle with unrestrained mischief. "Anything."

"What's the deal with the Space Force?"

"What?" Tripp's eyebrows disappear into his curls, and he shakes his head in disbelief. "Ever heard of a transition?"

"I don't like to beat around the bush."

"What *about* the Space Force?"

I give him a cut-the-bullshit sort of look. "I'm not blind. I've seen how many people you've brought on board for your own private military. Something's going on — some threat to the colony that you haven't disclosed."

Tripp is still giving me a weird look, but he isn't angry. He's curious. "This doesn't sound like the sort of interview *Topfold* usually does."

"This isn't an interview," I say quietly. "And you aren't talking to Layla Jones."

He sets down his wine and leans in until his face is just a

few inches from mine. "So this is the *real* Maggie Barnes: whip-smart . . . sexy . . . suspicious to the core."

I snort, and I feel my cheeks heat up. "I've never heard someone describe me that way, but I'll take it."

"How do people usually describe you?"

"Pushy, nosy . . . a nuisance."

"I can't imagine anyone would classify you as a nuisance," he says, edging closer.

I can see where the dark stubble is cutting through his skin, and I'm surrounded by the scent of him: cedar and sandalwood. It isn't hard to guess what's on his mind, and I feel a slight tug of longing deep down in my core.

"The Space Force," I repeat, more for myself than for him.

He closes his eyes and pulls back. "Geez . . . You really have a one-track mind, don't you?"

"I'm afraid that feature comes standard," I say, still feeling off-kilter in a way I don't appreciate.

First Jonah, now Tripp. What the hell is wrong with me?

"Fine." He backs off and rubs the base of his neck with his hand. "The Space Force . . . Well, we are not *unaware* of the fact that Russia has been watching our operations very closely over the past eighteen months."

"How closely?"

"Like, spy satellite closely."

"What are they planning?"

Tripp quirks an eyebrow. "Depends who you ask."

"What does the Department of Defense think Russia is up to?"

He sighs. "You're really not recording this?"

"I'm not even wearing my Optix."

He lets out an exasperated groan and grabs me by the hand. "Maggie, if I tell you this, it has *got* to be off the record. I don't want the biggest story about Elderon to be what the Department of Defense *thinks* Russia might try to do to us."

"You want the biggest story to be that Elderon serves its residents prison food?"

Tripp squeezes my hand and lets out an exasperated groan. He looks as though being in the same room with me is making him question his sanity. I can relate.

"I'm serious," he says. "If the press gets ahold of this, it could ruin everything."

"Why?" I ask in a low voice. "What do you know?"

"Promise me," he says. "This is off the record."

"Fine," I sigh, getting the gut-wrenching feeling that I might be ruining my own chances at the story of a lifetime.

He takes a deep breath and shuts off his desktop, which has been pulsing in sleep mode for the past twenty minutes.

"The Department of Defense thinks that Russia could see this as an opportunity to derail American space development. They think that Russia could launch an attack on Elderon."

My eyebrows shoot up. This is an even juicier confession than I was expecting. "What sort of attack?"

"Nobody knows," says Tripp. "Look, my people spend half their lives fending off cyberattacks from all over the world. We've received threats from people claiming to work with the Bureau for Chaos, some claiming to be Russian hackers . . . I've gotten death threats from North Korea, the American right wing — even some environmental groups. This isn't anything *new* for us, and we don't have any hard evidence that anyone is mounting any attack whatsoever. But my company has a lot riding on Elderon, so we put together the Space Force so that we're prepared to fight whatever we have to."

"Including a physical assault on the colony."

"Missiles, invasions, cyberattacks . . . you name it."

I shake my head. Tripp has already given me *way* more than I bargained for.

"And you're . . ." I clear my throat. "You're confident that the Space Force is prepared to ward off an attack from Russia or the Bureau for Chaos or . . ."

His expression grows serious. "Trust me . . . Nobody does defense like a trillion-dollar tech company."

14

JONAH

The next day I skip the latrine and sneak out of the pod without Ping. It's the first day of Reception, and I need a chance to clear my head before I meet my squad.

I haven't led my own unit in more than two years, and I have this nervous itch — as though I might have forgotten how.

They don't teach leadership in Space Force officer training. Everyone there is already supposed to be a leader. The purpose of those two weeks was to get us acquainted with the Space Force's mission, values, and training procedures. We went over the three stages of basic training that all new recruits will go through and completed a battery of tests.

I passed them all with flying colors, but there's no erasing my record. There's a stink on anyone who's been administratively discharged, and I'm pretty sure the other officers could smell it.

Only my COs can access my personnel file, but it doesn't matter. If anyone in my company lets slip that I was tossed out of the army, I'll lose all credibility with my unit. That's why I can't afford to give anybody a reason to doubt that I belong here.

I do my workout in the civilian fitness center. It's not as though I'm *hiding* my morning fitness regime — I just don't want to draw extra attention to myself. I warm up with a jog on the treadmill and do some shadowboxing on the mats. I bust out fifty push-ups and a hundred sit-ups and then sprint from one end of the gym to the other.

It's oh five hundred, and I have the place to myself.

Once I've sweated out my nerves, I head back to the pod and take a long hot shower. I'm not hungry, but I shovel down a bowl of cereal anyway and chug two glasses of water.

I don't see Ping at all, which is good. I can't shake my first-day jitters, and the last thing I need is his nonstop commentary.

Still, it's a little weird when I make it all the way to the training center without seeing him. The PTC is the only place in Sector R that's large enough to fit the entire company. It's a huge open gymnasium, and for the next eleven weeks, it's entirely devoted to new recruit training.

I step through the double doors, and the familiar stench of Reception hits my nostrils: new uniforms, new boots, and the sweat of anxious recruits. In the army, this would be the day that everybody gets their heads shaved and gear is distributed.

In the Space Force, the recruits already have their gear. They've been inoculated and given full medical clearance. All that's left is for them to take their physical fitness test and get an official initiation into the galactic armed forces.

I cross the room to the huge number thirteen printed on the wall and stand beneath it. This is our squad number, and the four recruits I'm expecting will be looking for it.

I take a deep breath and face the door with my head up, chest out, and arms folded in front of me. I led my own squad once before. I can do it again.

A few more recruits trickle in as the minutes tick by. Most of them disperse to the other squad leaders, but a couple come over to me. One is a tall blundering giant with small eyes and a flabby face. The name on his uniform says Casey, and I remember that his first name is Trevor. Trevor Casey — space weapons expert.

I also get an angry-looking Indian girl with dark frizzy hair and a tall ginger who looks as though a strong breeze would knock him over.

All three recruits are silent and nervous, and they don't have a clue in the world. At least they have respect for authority. They salute me, and I rack my brain to retrieve the other two names: Lee Davis, space comm specialist, and Adra Kholi — former delinquent hacker turned NSA white hat.

Then the doors swing open, and I see Ping bounding toward me. He's wearing his uniform, but it looks all wrong. One of his pant legs isn't tucked into his boots, and he's got too many buttons undone.

"Morning, sarge," he says brightly, giving me the most annoying salute I have ever seen.

I suppress the eye roll that is dying to make an appearance and fix him with a harsh glare instead. "That's Sergeant Wyatt to you, private."

"Yessir," he says, breaking into a grin and wagging his eyebrows at me.

"Don't you grin at me, private!" I yell. "And fix your uniform. Do you think this is a game?"

"No, sir," says Ping, his eyes widening in horror. He bends down to fix his pants, and I want to strangle him.

I can't have my squad thinking that I'm their friend. My authority would be shot.

"Ping!" I yell just as he straightens up.

"Sir!"

"What time is it?"

"Oh six hundred, sir!"

"What time were you supposed to be here?"

Ping glances over at Davis, as though asking whether it's a trick question. "Oh six hundred, sir?"

"Don't answer a question with a question! What time were you supposed to report for Reception?"

"Oh six hundred, sir!" he yells with gusto, clearly enjoying drill sergeant me.

"Wrong!" I yell. "Kholi!"

"Sir?"

"What time were you supposed to report for Reception?"

"Oh six hundred, sir," she says.

"Wrong!" I let that sink in for a moment, watching them all squirm. "The schedule you were issued says oh six hundred, so you need to be here at five fifty-five. Is that understood?"

"Yessir," they say in unison.

"In my squad, early is on time. On time is late. Late is unacceptable. Is that understood?"

"Yessir."

"Now you can all thank your new friend Ping for what's about to happen," I say. "Drop and give me twenty!"

At those words, they all drop to the ground in a flurry of boots and limbs. Kholi the hacker girl is on her knees, and the ginger's ass is way up in the air. Flabby Casey is still struggling to get in position. And Ping . . . Ping's push-ups are out of this world. Of course.

"Davis! What the fuck are you doing?"

"Push-ups, sir," Davis huffs.

"Wrong!" I yell. "Ass down. Casey . . . What is that? Kholi, if you can't do real push-ups, you don't belong here. Start over. As a matter of fact, everyone start over. You'll do this as a team, or you won't do it at all."

Nobody grumbles or says a word, but I sense a general mutinous rush. Davis, Casey, and Kholi struggle through a few pathetic push-ups, and I want to gouge my own eyes out.

"Stop. Stop. On your feet."

All at once, the push-ups stop. Ping jumps up as if he's got springs attached to his boots, and I roll my eyes.

"Six laps around the gym. Let's go!"

Kholi shoots me a filthy look, but Ping jets off and immediately breaks ahead of the pack. Flabby Casey lumbers after him, and the ginger one, Davis, moves like a newborn fawn.

Where did they *find* these people? Is this some kind of joke? Is Callaghan punishing me? This can't be my squad.

But then one of the other sergeants sends her privates limping along after mine, and I hear her grumble under her breath.

"Pathetic."

I turn. The girl has got to be about my age with light-brown skin and delicate features. She's at least a foot shorter than me, but she has the compact build of a track star. I recognize her from officer training. Her name is Maya Walker.

"Yours too?" I say.

She shakes her head. "I don't know what the fuck I'm supposed to do with a bunch of kids who would've washed out of army basic."

"Want to drill them all together for a few hours?" I ask. I've seen recruits step up their game when thrown into a larger unit.

She shrugs. "Can't hurt. I'll see if Jameson and Whitehead want to join."

Jameson and Whitehead are two tall beefy guys that look as though they came from the shallow end of the gene pool. When Walker sidles up to them, I can immediately tell that they're friends. They laugh at some dumb inside joke, and then the tall dark one eyes me from across the room. Immediately his posture changes.

Great. One of them already doesn't like me. Maybe he knows about my record.

They talk for a moment, and then they send their squads to join mine running laps around the training center. They follow Walker back to where I'm standing, and I force my head a little higher and try to suppress my instant hatred.

"All right," says Walker, forcing an awkward half smile and jerking her head over her shoulder at the guys. "They're in."

Jameson frowns but gives a reluctant jerk of his head. The shifty-eyed pale one called Whitehead just stares.

"Let's whip 'em together and make it rain," says Walker.

I grin. Clearly she had a similar boot-camp experience to me. In the army, "rain maker" drill sergeants are the stuff of legend, but I actually had one.

Twice in the middle of summer, my drill sergeant locked us in the gym, shut off the AC, and worked us until we were drowning in sweat. The heat and moisture from too many bodies condensed on the ceiling, and by the end, our own sweat was dripping down on all our heads.

My squad is the first to finish. Casey, the huge one, empties the contents of his stomach in a trash can by the door. Davis looks a little green, too, but he manages to hold it together.

I make them do burpees until the other squads join us. Then we line them up and take turns teaching them basic drill commands for an hour and a half. Every twenty minutes, we run them through another circuit or make them do push-ups.

Basic training hasn't officially begun, but I can see that I'm going to need all the time I can get to whip these losers into shape.

Walker is by far the nastiest drill sergeant I have ever seen. Halfway through another set of burpees, one of her recruits blows chunks right there in the line. Walker doesn't dismiss the kid or stop the exercise; she just yells at him to keep going and makes him drop down in his own puddle of vomit.

I've never been so glad to dismiss my squad for lunch — or what's left of them, anyway. They're a bunch of sweaty, demoralized flesh sacks, and it's still just the first day of Reception.

Whitehead fist-bumps Jameson as they head out the door, but I don't see the close of morning session as anything to celebrate. I see it as a big fucking problem.

I have no idea how I'm supposed to get these people up to Space Force standards in ten weeks' time. I'm not sure a lifetime of training would be enough.

Not one of my recruits has even an ounce of military experience. And Callaghan expects me to turn them into skilled combatants?

Two and a half months of basic training is no substitute for actual military experience. An overseas deployment changes you — hardens you. When you're taken away from all you've ever known and forced to kill for your country, you come back an entirely different person. These kids can't learn that.

One thing's for sure: It's going to be a long ten weeks. I might not be able to turn them into real soldiers, but I can get them into better physical condition and drill them until they follow orders in their sleep.

15

MAGGIE

The story I published on the food aboard Elderon went gangbusters on *Topfold*. It's been live for less than twenty-four hours, and the number of views has already surpassed the traffic on the donut piece.

When I walk into the newsroom Thursday morning, I'm fully expecting to be Alex's new favorite person. At least I hope she doesn't *hate* me. I need her in a good mood for what I'm about to ask.

Since my talk with Tripp on Tuesday, my every waking thought has been consumed by the Space Force. According to the budget that I lifted from his office, *one sixth* of the personnel hired by Maverick Enterprises were brought on board for Elderon's private military.

For the past three days, dozens of men and women in blue have disembarked the shuttle, and for the past two days, I've managed to capture it on film. That level of military preparedness certainly wasn't in any of the press releases Maverick sent out announcing its first "civilian" colony, and it certainly wasn't mentioned in any of the charming interviews that Tripp gave on Earth to drum up publicity for colony one.

I can't publish the information that Tripp shared with me in confidence, but that doesn't mean I can't publish the footage of Space Force personnel piling off the shuttle or ask a rep from Maverick to comment on the hordes of soldiers and intelligence specialists they hired to protect the colony.

When I enter the newsroom after breakfast and sidle up to Alex's desk, I'm greeted by a puff of pink vapor. "I hope you have some stunning space-walk footage for your column," she says, taking a deep drag on her e-cig and squinting at her desktop.

I hesitate. No congratulations on my piece? No "job well done"? It's not as if I need the validation, but I certainly wasn't expecting the cold shoulder.

"I have a space-walk appointment set up next week," I say slowly. "Today I have a piece about microgravity yoga."

"Hmm. All right." Alex still doesn't look up. "But it better be funny. Mr. Van de Graaf did not find the Franken-meat story funny."

"Tripp?"

"His father Strom — chief executive pain in my ass."

I hesitate. "He didn't like it?"

"He didn't like that you were disparaging the food they're serving up here . . . or that we pulled back the curtain to show how the sausage was made. *Literally*."

"That piece got over a million views. That didn't make him happy?"

"Let's just say that it's not the sort of attention Maverick Enterprises was after."

My heart sinks. This is not going the way I'd hoped.

"They're trying to sell luxury space travel to trust-fund kids," Alex continues. "You think people are going to drop millions on a space cruise or spring for a long-term stay in the colony if the food sucks?"

"I was just reporting on my experiences," I mutter. "You've tasted the food . . . Tell me it isn't horrible."

"I'm not arguing with you, Barnes. I'm just relaying a message from our corporate overlords." She finally tears herself away from the projection of her desktop and meets my eyes with a serious gaze. "Tone down the truthiness, okay? We're selling adventure, excitement . . . the next great frontier. Keep it light, for god's sake."

"I wasn't aware that we were 'selling' anything."

"Don't be an idiot," she says in a contemptuous voice. "Of course we are."

"Well, then you're really not going to like this . . ."

"What else is new?" she growls, stabbing her e-cig into its cradle and swiveling her chair around to the coffee maker.

After one day in the newsroom, the coffee station was relocated to a cart just behind her desk. The new location makes it impossible to get a refill without giving Alex a full status update.

"I used to field stories on political corruption, the Bureau for Chaos, and the growing pro-Russian sentiments of China," she grumbles. "But by all means . . . bring on the space toilets and anti-gravity Pilates."

"Yoga."

"Whatever."

"You *told* me to keep it light!" I say in exasperation.

"And I meant it," she says. "Or else it'll be both our asses on the line."

"Well, this isn't microgravity yoga," I say, beaming her the footage of all the Space Force personnel disembarking from the shuttle.

She lets out a huff of impatience. "What am I looking at here?"

"This is footage from Tuesday."

We watch in silence for several minutes, and I can tell that Alex is growing bored. I switch out the clips. "This is Wednesday." Nearly identical footage takes over the screen — more men and women in blue flooding into the colony.

The clip ends, and I can almost *hear* Alex's eye roll. She yawns. "Ugh! Snooze. Where are you going with this?"

"Did you know that more than five hundred troops have already arrived in Elderon and that almost four hundred more are scheduled to be shipped up today and tomorrow?"

"That seems like too many," says Alex around an actual yawn.

"It is," I say, dismissing the videos and pulling up Tripp's budget. "It's more than one sixth of total personnel that's slated to occupy Elderon. More than a *quarter* of non-infrastructure-related spending on the project is going toward military training and supplies."

"How do you know all this?" asks Alex. The woman misses nothing.

I enlarge the budget and zoom in on the lines that I've highlighted. "See for yourself."

Alex scans the budget quickly, her eyes widening with every pass down the page. "Where did you get this?"

"Tripp Van de Graaf."

"He gave it to you?"

"Not exactly."

Alex shoots me a dirty look, but it's not as though she's scandalized. We've all done it. You don't leave important papers lying around when a journalist comes to visit.

"These documents beg a lot of questions, but they aren't enough."

"What do you mean they're not enough?" I cry. "We have a line-item budget *proving* that Elderon isn't what Maverick says it is. You can't be a civilian space colony with nine hundred soldiers on board."

"All you've proven is that we've got a shit ton of private military personnel," says Alex. "The Space Force isn't the army or the navy or the marines. There's nothing in this budget that says 'Russian defense fund' . . . We have no proof that the Bureau is planning an attack or that there's anything fishy going on with the Russian military installation next door."

"I have a source that says the DoD suspects an attack from Russia. *And* they've gotten threats from the Bureau for Chaos."

"When did Mr. Van de Graaf tell you this? During your dirty rubdown alone in his office?"

"It wasn't like that," I say, feeling my face heat up. "I kept it professional."

Alex gives me a dubious look. Clearly Tripp's reputation precedes him.

"It doesn't matter, Barnes. Is he willing to go on record *saying* that his company's trillion-dollar investment has a target on its back?"

"No."

"Then we can't run this — not if that's all you've got."

"Well, obviously I'm going to do more digging," I say. "I just showed you this so that you'd see that there's something to dig into."

"No," says Alex. "Absolutely not."

"Why not?"

"Have you forgotten who signs your paychecks?" she asks. "You think the blowback from your Franken-meat story was bad . . . If we went public with this, they would jettison us back to Earth so fast your head would spin."

"I thought we were supposed to be independent of Maverick."

"Oh, grow up!" Alex snaps, clearly disgusted by my naïveté. "Our job is to make Maverick Enterprises look good — not to shout conspiracy about a program designed for peaceful scientific exploration."

This is *so* not how I imagined Alex's reaction to my pitch. I've been digging into her all week — reading her column in *The Atlantic* and her pieces from *The Times*.

Alex is the real deal — an honest-to-god, get-your-hands-dirty journalist. That Alex wouldn't let fear stop her. That Alex lived to chase a story.

"This is bullshit," I growl.

"It *is* bullshit," says Alex. "But this isn't just about you and me." She lowers her voice and looks around. "Listen. We are only here on the Van de Graafs' good graces. If they feel that they're getting too much heat from the press, they'll send every journalist in this place packing. Then *no one* will be around to report the news when shit really does hit the fan."

I don't say anything. I hadn't thought of it like that.

Alex isn't protecting herself. She's protecting her role as a watchdog.

"What if I got proof?" I whisper. "What if I found undeniable evidence that we are actively defending against an invasion or some kind of attack?"

Alex lets out a heavy sigh. She takes off her glasses and tosses them onto her desk. She's got dark circles under her eyes, and I can tell she is just as frustrated as I am.

"You don't have the clearance to do what you need to do."

"I'll find a way."

There's a long pause as Alex evaluates my resolve and what I'm capable of. I know she must have read up on me, too. She knows I'm a good reporter — even if the biggest pieces I have to my name are about donuts and space meat.

"Don't you want to know what's going on?" I press. "Don't you want to report on this?"

"What I want is for you to do your job," she says with a note of finality. She's giving me a peculiar look, and I know there's more to what she's saying. "Do what you were brought here to do. I want two Layla Jones stories on my desk every day."

I feel my body deflate in disappointment, but Alex keeps talking.

"As long as I get that, I'm not going to question what you're up to in all the other hours of the day," she murmurs. "What you do with your personal time is entirely your business."

My chest swells, and I close my eyes to hide my triumphant expression. This is as much of a green light as I'm going to get from Alex.

"You bring me an airtight story, and I'll do what I can to minimize the blowback if and when we go public."

"Yes!" I resist the urge to jump out of my seat and do a victory dance. I want to leap over the desk and give Alex an enormous hug, but I sense that she isn't the hugging sort.

"But I want someone important who's willing to go on the record saying that an enemy of the state has been meddling in the colony's private affairs or that they have received a credible threat."

"Will do!"

"Just be careful," she says, sitting back in her chair and meeting my gaze with a hawklike expression. "Don't get caught. If you do, even I won't be able to protect you."

16

MAGGIE

I'm so excited after my talk with Alex that I've been lying awake for several hours. My awesome cloud bed should make it easy to go to sleep, but I can't stop thinking about my Space Force story.

I have no idea how I'm going to get insider access to Elderon's private military, but I have to find a way. My gut is telling me that there's something Maverick doesn't want the public to know, and as a journalist, it's my job to drag that truth into the light.

Not long after I doze off, I'm awoken by a loud creak and the odd feeling that the world around me has ground to a halt. I try to ignore it and go back to sleep, but my tired brain is summoned back to life by a loud *ding!* from my Optix.

My bed lurches beneath me, and I suddenly feel sick. I reach up onto the shelf over my head and feel around for my glasses, but they aren't where I left them. My hair is all over the place, and I can't move more than a few inches in any direction.

Earlier today, we received a notice that the bots would be performing routine maintenance on the exterior of the space station. We were instructed to zip ourselves into our bed bags before going to sleep so that we wouldn't float off when they stopped the colony's rotation. The bed bag is basically a thin sleeping bag that fastens to the bed frame. It has a zipper on the inside and room for the scratchy gray blanket.

I unzip the front of my bed bag and immediately feel a swoop of weightlessness in my stomach. I throw up a hand to keep from face-planting into the ceiling and yell out the command for lights.

The light above my bed flickers to life, but I can't see much of anything. My hair is floating around my head like a clump of tangled spaghetti, and the rest of my room is still in shadow.

Yanking my hair tie off my wrist, I gather up my curls and cram them into a bun. I look around. My glasses are floating somewhere near the door, so I kick off from the wall and snatch them out of the air.

I put them on and look out the window. The stars are no longer shooting by in a blur of silver as we spin around the axis of Elderon. We're still orbiting the Earth, of course, but we're moving so slowly that we appear to be standing still.

The star-studded black velvet abyss stretches for infinity in every direction, and I feel an overwhelming sense of calm and insignificance that I haven't experienced before.

I don't know how long I float there staring, but eventually I become aware of a blinking red light in the corner of my Optix. I have an unread message from an unknown sender.

I select the message and read it twice, feeling my sense of inner peace shatter.

I know what you're looking for.

My heart rate ticks up, and all of a sudden I get a swoop of nausea that has nothing to do with free-floating in space. I can't be sure that the sender is referring to my Space Force story, but I don't know what else it could be.

Whoever sent the first message is already typing a second. The instant I read the first message, three blinking dots appeared just below the line of text.

Suddenly, another message appears, and I get a fresh swoop of paranoia.

I can help.

Trying to focus on my breathing, I hurriedly dictate a message of my own: *Who are you?*

There's a longer pause after I send it, and I want to kick myself for spooking the messenger. If the sender wanted me to know who they were, they would have led with their name. They certainly wouldn't have blocked their contact info to send the message anonymously.

But just when I think that I've ruined everything, the blinking blue dots appear, and a third message pops up on my Optix.

Someone who's noticed the same thing you have.

I settle back and float for a moment, thinking hard about the message. I have no idea who this could be or why they would want to help. Of course, they could be fishing to find out what I know, or they could be setting me up.

The sender starts drafting another message, and my breath catches in my throat. I wait, heart thumping violently, and another message appears.

I can get you in.

This time, I don't hesitate. I start to draft a response, thinking that if I want this person's help, I'll eventually have to show my hand.

But before I can send my message, the space station begins to move. I sense it rather than feel it — a great lurching shudder as Elderon begins to spin again.

It's a slow, painful process, and I imagine the sheer amount of energy it must take to move an object of that size. The stars blur as we pick up speed, and Earth is reduced to a smear of blue.

It takes several minutes of turning, but soon I sense that I'm sinking toward the floor. My feet touch down on the platform beside my bed, and I stumble as the craft attempts to stabilize itself.

Just as the sensation of standing starts to feel normal, I get a notification that the mysterious sender is attempting to send me a file. I hurry to block it — thinking it could be a virus — but it's too late. My Optix automatically accepts the file, and it quickly downloads onto my device.

Trembling with anticipation, I select the attachment. I can tell immediately that it's a personnel file. It's typed on Maverick Enterprises' letterhead, and the heading tells me that it came from the Space Force.

There's a photo of a woman in the upper right-hand corner. She's got straight brown hair, a smattering of freckles, and a tiny upturned nose. I can tell from the picture that she's very pretty, but the person who took the photo must have told her not to smile.

The name on the file reads Amelia McDermit, though I have a feeling she isn't the one who's been sending me messages.

According to the file, Amelia is an intelligence specialist who was recruited to join the Space Force. She's exactly my age, and she lives in San Diego.

She's supposed to be docking in Elderon tomorrow.

Just then, I get a notice that my mysterious informant is sending me another file. I don't attempt to block this one. My curiosity is killing me.

It's a copy of Friday's flight plan, and Amelia McDermit isn't on it.

As I scan the document, I get an uncomfortable tightness in the pit of my stomach. I'm *definitely* not supposed to have access to this, and whoever my source is has to be breaking at least a dozen laws to send it.

They must know that this is important.

Moved by a sudden sense of urgency, I flip back to Amelia's personnel file. I'm not sure what I'm supposed to be looking for, but if my informant sent these documents without explanation, they must think that I'll be able to glean something important from them.

I select a box in the upper left-hand corner and scan the file's metadata. The date shows that it was altered last Friday, which seems awfully close to her deployment for anything to have changed.

I scroll down to the bottom. The file is multiple pages long, containing everything from her résumé to her letters of reference. The last page is a copy of her physical, documenting that Amelia was fit for duty. The physician recorded her vital signs, immunization records, and the results of her recent blood test.

In the notes, I see a line of red text that's typed in all caps: *Patient tested positive for pregnancy.*

The realization hits me like a ton of bricks. *That's* why Amelia wasn't on tomorrow's flight plan. The Space Force found out that she was pregnant and cancelled her deployment.

I still don't understand why I've been made privy to Amelia's private medical file, but my wild train of thought is interrupted by a sharp knock at my door.

I freeze.

"Who is it?" I call, scrambling to the door to peer out the peephole.

There's no one there.

The corridor is unusually dark — illuminated only by emergency lighting. In the dim orange glow, I see a stout, bulky shadow looming to the left of my doorway, and my heart skips a beat.

Did someone from Maverick get wind of my story? Did they plant a bomb outside my suite or send an assassin to take me out?

I give myself a mental shake. I'm being crazy. Maverick wouldn't blow up their own station — not when they've invested so much money in making Elderon a success. Plus, an assassin seems like overkill.

I open the door a tiny crack and peer out into the corridor. A bot is waiting patiently to the left of my door, and I almost collapse in relief. It isn't one of the creepy human ones — just one of the delivery bots.

"What do you want?" I ask weakly.

"Package for — Magnolia — Barnes," it says in a stilted robotic voice.

I get another surge of paranoia. According to the Elderon welcome packet, the bots are all equipped with cameras and facial-recognition technology. For all I know, the person who sent me the messages could be watching.

"What's the package?" I ask.

The bot doesn't answer. Instead, it just swivels around to the left, and the light on the side blinks blue. The right side pops open, and a tray slides out. On the tray is a shallow white bin about the size of a shoebox. I take the box with both hands, and the bot immediately speeds off.

I close the door as quick as I can, staring down at the box in my hands.

Taking a deep breath, I slide my finger under the lid and slowly open the box.

Inside is a folded swath of dark-blue fabric. It's a military uniform — smallish — with the name "Jones" embroidered over the chest.

My heart gives an irregular thump, and I feel a swell of confusion. It can't be a coincidence that the last name on the uniform is "Jones." It seems like the sort of sick joke that Kiran would make, but Kiran isn't here.

My mysterious friend beams me another file, and I open it immediately.

My own picture appears in front of my face, and I drop the box on the floor. The photo looks like a mugshot, but it's definitely me. The file is a digital ID card, and the name at the top says Magnolia Jones. All the details match my real ID. Even the weight is scarily accurate.

Everything looks right except for the division. Apparently, Magnolia Jones is a private in the Space Force with low-level security clearance.

A flurry of notifications pop up on my Optix — apparently queued in from a fake account.

Not only have I been assigned a fake identity — I've also been assigned a bunk. I have a summons telling me to check in with my commanding officer tomorrow at nineteen hundred hours.

Suddenly, all the pieces snap together, and a surge of excitement shoots through my veins.

Someone — and I don't know who — just gave me an all-access pass to the Space Force. It's more help than I've ever received on a story, and whoever it is took an enormous risk.

17

MAGGIE

My stomach is in knots the entire next day. I barely notice what I'm eating at breakfast, and by lunchtime, I've chopped together an incoherent piece about the stoppage of simulated gravity last night.

I touch base with a few sources to find out what maintenance was being performed on the colony's exterior, but I'm repeatedly stonewalled with generic PR speak.

Apparently, all the "routine maintenance" is performed by specialized bots, which reduces the need for humans to perform dangerous extravehicular activities. All a person has to do is program the bots and schedule the stoppage in rotation to minimize the risk of equipment loss. Maintenance is completed in the middle of the night to allow activity inside the colony to continue as usual.

But no matter how opaque the hospitality office's explanation of the maintenance seems, I just can't focus. I can't stop thinking about the messages from my mysterious source and my invitation to infiltrate the Space Force as Private Maggie Jones.

Deep down, I know that I should tell Alex what my anonymous helper sent me, but I don't want to. Maybe it's because I know that Alex would never let me follow a breadcrumb trail laid out by someone with top-level access and dubious motives who's concealing his or her identity. She was fine with me digging into the Space Force, but I seriously doubt that this was what she had in mind.

For one thing, I'm fairly certain that falsifying identification and using it to get inside the Space Force is a serious crime. It wouldn't be the *first* crime I've committed in pursuit of a story, but it does seem a little more serious than posing as an administrative assistant to eavesdrop on a city councilman or lying to the police to get out of a minor trespassing rap.

Pretending to be a counterintelligence specialist is definitely crossing a line. But is maintaining my moral high ground more important than uncovering the truth?

My nerves stretch thinner and thinner as the day wears on. I know that this is, without a doubt, the best chance I'll ever get to look inside the Space Force and figure out what's really going on — a chance that expires at seven o'clock tonight.

I eat dinner alone in the dining hall and think about the mysterious messenger. I can feel the uniform burning a hole in my bag, and I start to question not if I *should* do this, but whether or not I'll get caught.

According to my research, the Space Force is at the tail end of its Reception — the period of time where they wait for recruits to arrive, teach basic commands, and get them oriented with the Space Force.

Monday marks the beginning of basic training — a ten-week crash course in Space Force values, hand-to-hand combat, space navigation, weaponry, and military operations both inside and outside the space station. After that, each recruit will be assigned to posts corresponding to their background and their performance in basic.

The question is: Will I have enough time to figure out what's going on inside the Space Force before the ten weeks of basic training are up? Two and a half months seems like a lifetime, but I know from experience that earning people's trust can take a long, long time.

I have every intention of going back to the newsroom to work on my Layla Jones piece — if for no other reason than to distract myself so that I don't put on that uniform.

But instead of cutting through Sector L, I take the escalator down to the lower deck and head straight for the women's restroom outside the waiting area in the docking zone.

The time is eighteen forty, and the shuttle that was supposed to be carrying Amelia McDermit will be docking in twenty minutes.

For a moment, I just stand by the sink, staring at my own reflection. The journalists who really make it are the ones ballsy enough to follow their instincts and take real risks.

What type of journalist do I want to be? One who plays it safe with Layla Jones or the kind who sticks her neck out to get that really great scoop?

"Screw it," I mutter, wedging the doorstop into the crack under the door to keep anyone else from entering the bathroom.

I kick off my boots and peel off my jeans, grabbing the uniform and stuffing my real clothes into my bag. There's a boxy gray T-shirt that goes underneath, androgynous cargo pants with lots of pockets, and a bulky long-sleeve overshirt with my fake name stitched across the chest.

Whoever sent me the messages got the size right, at least. It's a little tight in the butt and hips, but it'll do.

I get all the buttons done up and stare down at my bare

stocking feet. My socks are bright purple, and I don't have the correct shoes. For some reason, my mysterious benefactor didn't bother to include the black combat boots they all wear, but my boots are close enough that I don't think anyone will notice.

I straighten up to examine myself in the mirror and immediately realize I have a problem.

I might look like a Space Force recruit from the shoulders down, but from the neck up I am still one hundred percent Maggie Barnes. My hair seems to have reacted poorly to the gravitational upset last night. My curls are a frizzy mess, and I'm guessing my big tortoiseshell glasses won't be allowed.

I dig around in my bag for the contacts that I never seem to wear. My face looks disturbingly pale and naked without my glasses. I'm suddenly very aware of the bluish circles under my eyes and the stray hairs under my eyebrows that are begging to be plucked.

I gather my hair up into a ponytail and pin my curls into a bun. A few stray tendrils spring loose and curl stubbornly around my face, but I plaster them down with some hair gel to make them behave.

When I'm finished, I look like a completely different person — a person who could use some mascara. I've gotten pretty lazy in the makeup department, but since I can no longer hide behind my glasses, I suddenly feel the need to primp.

What the hell, I think, scrutinizing my face. Whom have I got to impress?

Suddenly, I hear the cheerful garble of Vanessa's voice over the intercom. Passengers must be disembarking from the Impetus. It's showtime.

I kick the doorstop out and hover in a stall until the bathroom door opens. I hear the excited clamor of women pouring in to empty their bladders, and I see several pairs of black Space Force boots. I'm officially in the clear.

I open the door and shuffle out into the crowded lavatory. I catch several looks from my fellow Space Force women as I wash my hands, but they're mostly friendly glances of acknowledgment. Two of them seem to know each other, and I give them each a quick once-over to make sure I'm not missing anything.

Manly uniform? Check. Boring bun? Check. Regulation black combat boots? Working on it.

I hustle out of the bathroom and reach up to get my room assignment from my Optix. I nearly poke myself in the eye instead, and I realize that I'm no longer wearing it.

I head up to the mall and stop by the tech store to buy a new wearable to host my Optix. I purchase one of the Space Force–approved bars that clip onto the skin just outside the eyebrow. I log in and head straight for the Space Force barracks, crossing my fingers that Maggie Barnes's face will get me into my room.

I feel a fresh prickle of discomfort as I slip into the crowd of Space Force personnel flocking toward the defense module. I catch a few strange looks from the people who pass me, but only because I'm staring.

All the Space Force women carry themselves tall and straight. They move with purpose, and I remind myself not to slouch.

Fortunately, I manage to locate my pod without any trouble. I glance around self-consciously before scanning my face, hoping that the biometric lock recognizes me.

To my relief, the scanner beeps in confirmation, and I hear the door click and unlock. I take a deep breath and push it open. Whoever sent me the fake ID clearly knew what they were doing.

I walk into my new suite and am astonished to see a tall

Indian girl sitting on the top bunk. I hadn't realized that I'd have a roommate. Music is blaring from a sound pod on the floor, and her long legs are dangling over the bed in her black combat boots.

"Oh — hi," I choke, staring like a deer caught in the headlights.

She frowns and sits up without saying a word. Clearly she wasn't expecting to share her room either.

"Who the hell are you?" she asks with a frown.

I blink furiously, double-checking the room number listed on my enlistment papers. Yep — I'm definitely in the right place.

"I'm your new roommate, I guess," I say, shrinking under the girl's harsh gaze. "Maggie Ba — Jones. Private Jones."

"No . . ." she says slowly, scrutinizing me as though something is amiss.

I swallow to wet my parched throat. My heart is throbbing, and I don't know what to say. This girl's stare makes me feel as though I'm being x-rayed.

"What happened to McDermit?" she asks. "I was supposed to room with —"

"McDermit was reassigned," I say quickly, relieved to have some legit information.

"Nobody told me."

I shrug as if to say, "You know the Space Force . . ." But this girl isn't buying it.

"Why was she reassigned?"

"It was, uh," I lower my voice, "a medical separation."

At first I feel proud that I managed to remember some military jargon, but my new roommate is still regarding me with suspicion.

"What the fuck does that mean?"

"She got herself knocked up," I say, annoyed by the third

degree. Who is this girl? A private detective? "At least that's what they told me. It was an emergency reassignment. I'm just excited that they brought me on."

The girl is still staring at me as if there *must* be more to the story, but I sense her defenses wavering.

"Adra Kholi," she says.

"Nice to meet you."

I look around. The rooms in the Space Force barracks are even more spartan than my suite. The ceiling is slightly higher to accommodate the bunk beds, but there's no loft and no desk — just two beds stacked one on top of the other, a chest of drawers, and two lockers.

"Your cargo's already here," she says, nodding at the two bins on my bunk. "You can have the bottom drawers. I was saving them for Amelia."

"Thanks," I say, feeling a fresh wave of apprehension.

What the *hell* was I thinking? I'd been expecting to pose as a private during the day and sneak back to the newsroom to work on Layla stories at night.

Having a roommate changes everything. I certainly can't go missing half the nights without arousing her suspicions.

I snap the lids off my cargo bins to have a look inside. There isn't much — just three extra uniforms still in their plastic packaging, six gray T-shirts, a package of underwear, a pack of socks, a mouth guard, a pair of plastic safety goggles, and some shiny black boots.

I hurry to stuff the clothes into my drawers, but Adra stops me.

"Aren't you gonna wash those?"

I hesitate. "They're new . . ."

"They're gonna be wrinkled fresh out of the package," she says. "Wyatt's a real hard-ass. I don't wanna get extra push-ups just 'cause your shit's wrinkled."

"Wyatt?" That name rings a bell. Why does it sound so familiar?

"Sergeant Wyatt?" she repeats. "Our CO?"

Suddenly it hits me how I know the name.

Shit. It's Jonah — the guy who received my cargo by mistake.

"Right. Sergeant Wyatt," I choke. "Uh, sure. I'll send these out with one of the bots to get washed."

I catch a very pronounced side-eye from Adra just as there's another knock at the door.

I throw it open immediately — relieved to have a distraction — but my view of the hallway is instantly blocked by a hard familiar chest.

There's a heavy *thud* behind me as Adra jumps down from her bunk, and I turn just in time to see her snap to attention like the perfect soldier.

I turn back to our guest: clean-cut brown hair, sharp jawline, eyes that could cut glass. I can't see his butt from this angle, but it's him, all right. He's glaring down at me with a severe expression, and I have the immediate urge to slam the door in his face.

Instead, I copy Adra. I straighten up, snap my legs together, suck my stomach in, and thrust my chin up.

Jonah's eyes narrow into slits, and they travel up and down my entire body. It's kind of hot in a dangerous, bad-boy kind of way, but I feel myself start to sweat.

"As you were."

I don't say a word. Jonah is still scrutinizing my face, and I wonder if he recognizes me from when I came to his suite.

"McDermit, I presume?"

I shake my head. "McDermit was reassigned," I choke.

"*What?*" He reaches up to check his Optix, and his eyes move rapidly back and forth as he verifies what I just told him.

His mouth hardens into a thin line, and he looks back to me. "And you are?"

"Private Magnolia Jones."

He just stares at me as if waiting for something else.

"You can call me Maggie," I add. "Sir."

I cringe inwardly. What kind of person tells her commanding officer to call her by her first name? A complete and total idiot; that's who.

Again, I get the sense that Jonah doesn't believe me. He scans my face with his Optix, and I'm both amazed and relieved when I see the reverse image of my mugshot pop up.

"Private Jones," he says, raising both eyebrows. "Counterintelligence."

"Yessir," I choke.

"No prior military experience."

I swallow. This guy is going to be difficult. I can already tell.

Finally, his scowl is downgraded from contemptuous to suspicious. "Welcome to squad thirteen, I guess."

"Thank you, sir."

"Don't thank me," he growls. "Training starts tomorrow at oh six hundred. You're coming in late to the game, which puts you at a disadvantage." He takes a step back as though he's going to leave, and I catch the faintest shadow of a smirk. "Tomorrow's going to be a long day . . . Don't eat a big breakfast."

18

JONAH

The next day when I get to the training center, my entire squad is already waiting — everyone except the new girl. Ping and Davis are stretching. Kholi and Casey just look nervous. I'd been expecting two more new recruits, but after meeting Maggie Jones, I received a notification that my roster was full. It's a good thing, too — I'm going to have my hands full.

When the privates see me, they all jump in line and stand at attention. I give them a quick "as you were" and turn my attention to the large clock hanging over the door.

New Girl runs in a minute before six, and I can tell that she thinks she's late. I let her stew for a moment as she lines up with the others. She seems nervous — almost self-conscious — and she keeps messing with her uniform.

As I watch her, I get this bizarre sense of déjà vu — almost as though I've seen her before. It's something about her eyes, which are this Dead Sea–shade of blue green. They're bright, curious, and full of trouble.

"Jones! You're late," I call, shutting down my own uneasiness with something familiar.

New Girl's eyes widen in horror, and she turns beet red from the sudden attention. She's breathing hard and fast as if she ran here. She's clearly wondering if she got the time wrong.

"Would anyone care to share our policy with Jones?" I ask, glancing down the line.

Davis and Casey exchange nervous looks.

"Anyone?"

Nobody answers.

"Maybe twenty push-ups will help jog your memory," I say savagely. "Go!"

Everyone drops down except for the new girl.

"Drop and give me twenty, Jones!" I yell.

A look of terror flashes across her face, and she throws herself to the ground so fast that I think she might bust her chin on the way down. She props herself up on her hands and feet and shivers down into the most pathetic push-up I've ever seen in my life.

Oh boy. It's like day one all over again.

"Twenty *push-ups*, Jones — not twenty of whatever the hell that is!"

She lets out an exasperated puff of air, and her arms tremble as she struggles down to a ninety-degree angle.

"Jesus," I groan, walking over to her and resting my boot along the center of her back. I apply gentle pressure until she sinks down all the way, and I feel her muscles wobble under the added weight.

"That's one!" I bark.

New Girl pushes herself back up, but I keep my boot firmly in position. She struggles through four push-ups, and when she goes down for number five, I know her arms are about to give out.

"Keep going!" I yell to Ping and Casey, who've already finished their set.

Jones's form really starts to fall apart on push-up number seven, and I call the others off and send them to run laps.

"Get up, private," I mutter, watching her pathetic little arms wobble through push-up number ten. "Go run with the others — six laps."

"Yessir." She gets to her feet but keeps her head down.

She trots off to join the others in their laps around the training center, and I watch her go with a sinking feeling in my gut. She might have a background in counterintelligence, but she's not cut out for this. This girl belongs behind a desk.

By the time they all finish their laps, they're angry, sweaty, and out of breath. At the moment they've focused their rage on me, but the faster they learn that they're only as strong as their weakest link, the faster things will improve.

I spend the rest of the morning reviewing commands with my squad and drilling them on the order of hierarchy in the Space Force. For Jones, this is all new information, but she catches on fast.

The ability to follow instructions and learn new things almost makes up for her pitiful push-ups. Even in the armed forces, being a quick learner is worth something.

"This is it," I say, moving slowly down the line as they recover from another round of push-ups. "Tomorrow is the last day of Reception. You'll each report to the training center at your scheduled time to complete your physical fitness test. The test will be administered by Lieutenant Buford. You'll be asked to run a mile and complete as many push-ups and sit-ups in two minutes as possible. Standards will vary according to your age and gender."

I take a moment to glare at each one of them in turn. "If you fail your initial PFT, you will be held back from basic training and put through a rigorous program to get you up to standards. At the end of next week, you will be given one more chance to pass the PFT. If you fail a second time, you will be sent back to Earth and forfeit your signing bonus. Is that understood?"

"Yessir," huff the recruits.

"I suggest you take this seriously."

My gaze lingers for a moment on Jones, who looks justifiably panicked. I'd be worried, too, if I didn't know the test. The initial fitness test the Space Force developed is a total cakewalk — even for the criminally unfit.

The PFT at the *end* of basic? Not so much.

"For those of you who pass, basic training will commence Monday at oh five hundred. You will complete the day's PT before breakfast and then proceed to the day's scheduled training. I suggest you eat light. Basic is when we separate the men from the boys . . . It is in your best interest to put on a good showing."

I pause for effect. "If you make it through basic, you will be given an assignment on Elderon. That assignment will be based on your professional background *and* how well you conform to Space Force standards. If you don't make it through basic, you will be sent home. You will forfeit your signing bonus and any hopes of a career in the galactic armed forces."

I look around to make sure my message has sunk in. All five of them look slightly nauseous.

"I'll see you back here after lunch."

170

19

MAGGIE

The rest of the day passes in a slow, painful blur. We do push-ups, sit-ups, burpees, and sprints and run through the same progression of eight basic drill commands. We do this until I think I might forget how to do anything else. I'll definitely be right facing and left facing in my dreams.

Jonah's litany of punishments and insults is so repetitive that I begin to wonder if he's a bot. So far his only functions seem to be to yell "Drop and give me twenty!" and "That's the most pathetic (blank) I've ever seen!"

My initial attraction has *definitely* worn off, but at least he doesn't recognize me.

A few times I catch him staring, but I'm pretty sure it's my weak push-ups that have captured his attention. I look dramatically different without my glasses and the full stopping power of my hair, so there's no real reason for him to connect the dots between the girl who came to his suite and the girl who's singlehandedly dragging down his squad's PFT average.

By the time we finish with training for the day, my arms feel like two floppy sandbags attached to a Jell-O body. I hurt in places I've never hurt before. Hell, I hurt in muscle groups I didn't even know I had.

At dinner I grab my tray and sit down at a table alone, and to my immense surprise, I'm joined by the springy Asian kid called "Ping."

"Heyya, Jones! This seat taken?"

I shake my head in stunned silence. After my pathetic showing in Reception, I can't believe anyone wants to sit with me.

Ping throws his tray down on the table and slides into the seat across from me. Even after our grueling workout, he still looks fully energized. He's got the sort of eyebrows that always look friendly and the most persistent smile I've ever seen.

"Sore?" he asks, giving me a sympathetic grimace.

I laugh and instantly wish I hadn't. Even *that* hurts. "Isn't it obvious?"

"Ah, the first day was tough for me, too," he says. "But you'll get used to it."

I open my mouth to say that I don't know if I *want* to get used to being yelled at and berated, but I'm interrupted by a loud huff behind me.

Adra slams her tray down and shoots me the stink eye. "*You're* still here?"

"Down, girl," says Ping.

"I think we did two hundred extra push-ups because of you," she grumbles.

"Sorry," I mutter. "It won't happen again."

"It better not."

"Adra, she's brand new," says Ping in that unperturbed, good-natured way of his. "We were all new — what — three days ago?"

Adra continues to shoot daggers at me from across the table, but she doesn't say anything else. We're joined by Casey, the big burly one, and Davis, the tall freckly redhead who looks about fifteen years old.

They all seem to know each other, and the group dynamics have already begun to take shape. Adra is the bitchy one with the dark wit whom everyone is too scared to cross. Ping is the peppy go-getter incapable of saying a bad word about anyone. Davis strikes me as a shrinking violet who follows Ping and Casey around like a puppy, and Casey . . . Well, Casey is what a homeschooled kid with a genius IQ grows up to be. He talks in a low wheezy voice and picks his nose when he thinks no one is watching, but he's the guy you turn to when you want to build a nuclear reactor out of Popsicle sticks.

After dinner, I change back into my civilian attire and scoot off to the newsroom to finish my Layla story. It's the first in a series about the companies that have established offices on Elderon, and Maverick Enterprises is at the top of my list.

I try to keep the snarkiness to a minimum as I cut together the footage from the Workshop and overlay commentary from my discussion with Porter. I include a quip about my cargo-bot delivery saga, but Alex cuts it to avoid annoying Strom.

She sends me off with a buttload of edits, and I get the feeling that I'm being punished. Making her changes will take me *hours*, and it's already almost nine.

Alex doesn't care. She doesn't know that I've taken on another full-time job, and she doesn't *need* to know. I don't want to tell her what I'm up to until I have tangible evidence that the Space Force is preparing for something big.

It's nearly midnight by the time I upload my finished story and trundle off to the barracks. I change back into my Space Force fatigues before heading down to the lower deck. I can't risk muddying my two worlds and having someone figure out that I'm pretending to be someone I'm not.

Fortunately, Adra is already snoring by the time I reach our suite. I take out my contacts and fall into bed, wishing more than anything that I could take a nice long bath. My shoulders ache, I can't feel my arms, and it feels as though Jonah took a sledgehammer to my back.

Story or no story, I'm going to be in fantastic shape by the time basic training is over.

20

JONAH

I'm shocked and impressed when I walk into the training center first thing Monday morning. Five recruits are waiting for me in the training center, and they're the same recruits I had at the end of last week.

Their presence here means they must have passed their PFTs, and it means I failed to scare them away during their first week on Elderon.

"Good morning," I say, moving down the line to inspect each one of them in turn. Everyone looks as though they've finally got the hang of arriving on time and standing in line, which means they must have learned *something* last week.

"Glad to see you all made it to basic. This week is when the real fun begins." I stop in front of Kholi, who looks none too happy to be here. "I can see from your smiling faces that you're both surprised and delighted to have me for your drill sergeant." I raise both eyebrows at Kholi, and her face turns white. "Trust me when I say that the feeling is mutual."

I only have an hour allocated to PT this morning, so I can't afford to waste any more time. I send them all on a warm-up jog around the training center, put them through a round of push-ups, sit-ups, and planks, and then line them up and make them run suicides. We won't have access to the weight room until Wednesday morning, so it's good old-fashioned body-weight training and sprints until then.

Davis is the only one who pukes over the course of an hour, which I chalk up to a success.

After breakfast, it's time to issue the rubber ducks. The privates don't even touch a real weapon until week two, so until then they'll be drilling with black rubber rifles to simulate the weight and feel of a real one.

"As far as any of you is concerned," I say, pacing back and forth in the supply room as the squad stands at attention, "this is a real weapon."

I stop and glare at Ping, who's got that infuriatingly pleasant expression on his face that I've come to recognize as his default. "It is an exact replica of the rifles you'll be practicing with in week two and the M500s you'll be issued in week three. It is not a toy. If you drop your weapon, point your weapon at a fellow operative, or mishandle your weapon in any way, you will find yourself on the first shuttle home. Is that understood?"

"Yessir," the squad chants in unison.

I hand each of them one of the rubberized weapons and go through the names for each part of the rifle. I show them how to carry it, and we practice marching from the supply room and back to the training center with rifles in tow.

I put them through a round of push-ups, and then we march back out of the training center toward a room at the very end of the hall.

I throw open the double doors, and I can practically taste the squad's collective nerves. The room is dark. It smells like plastic, and their footsteps echo off the walls.

I hit the light switch, and a dozen strips of fluorescent lights flicker on one by one. They illuminate a room about a quarter of the size of a baseball diamond and an obstacle course designed by the US Army.

The course is not *exactly* like the one that I completed in basic. The obstacles are made out of some high-density plastic, and the controls by the door allow the CO to control the climate and lighting and ratchet up the difficulty with just the push of a button.

I catch a glimpse of Jones's and Davis's terrified expressions as they take in the raised platforms and the apex ladder. The Space Force advises starting privates on the course in week two, but I want to run them through early to get some baseline times.

"You will each complete the course at least twice today," I say. "Once as the operator and once as the coach."

I hear the privates' collective sighs of relief, but their comfort doesn't last.

"It's in your best interest to make sure your partner does well," I say. "Your team will be judged based on your worst score." At this, Jones, Casey, and Davis deflate. "The pair with the best worst score won't have to run suicides after lunch. Everyone else will."

I catch a few calculated glances among my squad members. I can see them sizing each other up, trying to decide who the best partner will be. Nearly everyone's got their eyes on Ping.

"I've already picked teams," I say. "Davis, Casey — you're a team. Jones and Kholi, you're together."

"What about me?" asks Ping hopefully.

"You're your own team," I say.

Ping's shoulders sag in disappointment.

"Davis will coach you on your run, and his score will count as your second score. Got it?"

"Yessir," he says, perking up a little.

I turn to the controls and leave the course on the easiest setting. I keep the temperature on cool and turn back to the squad to see who looks the least prepared. I settle on Casey, whose flabby white face seems even paler than usual.

"Casey, you're up! Davis, on deck. It's your job to help him through the obstacles. You're his eyes. You can offer suggestions, yell, cheer . . . You just can't help him *physically*."

"Yessir," says Davis. He looks nervous.

Casey blunders up to the starting line, and Davis offers him a fist-bump. These two are going to be a shit show, but the allure of competition affects everyone the same.

I start the timer, and Casey takes off at a lumbering sprint. He lunges at the low red wall and somehow manages to heave his enormous body up to the top. He tries to rappel down the other side and falls, and I send him back to do it again.

It takes him three tries to rappel down the wall, and when he makes it, he immediately attacks the line of tires. He gets one of his enormous boat feet caught and trips, and I see his confidence begin to waver.

Next are the vaults. I know before he starts that he wasn't built for this. The recruits who excel at this obstacle are light and speedy, and he moves like a rhinoceros trapped in a vat of peanut butter.

Casey clears the second hurdle with a grimace, and I guess that he twisted his ankle. He keeps at it, though, flopping over the last one as though his life depends on it. He throws himself to the floor at the mouth of the barbed-wire tunnel, and I see his face fall.

This is the place where the big guys struggle most, but lucky for him, the course designer opted for a pit of foam beads instead of hot rancid mud.

Casey digs in his elbows like a champ and pulls himself

through at a glacial pace. He emerges from the tunnel, shoulders heaving, and grabs hold of the climbing rope to hoist himself up.

It's hard to watch. Casey's strong, but his body is heavy. His face turns a horrific shade of purple, and I see the veins in his temples bulge as he gives it everything he's got.

He makes it three-quarters of the way to the top before he starts to slide down.

"What the hell are you doing?" I yell. "Finish it!"

I can practically see the hopelessness in his face as he turns his eyes to the ceiling. He is spent, and I know from experience that that last five feet can feel like a mile.

Finally he makes it to the top, his giant feet propelling him the entire way. He slides down and lurches over to the balance bridge, where he wobbles dangerously for about five seconds. He shoots across as fast as he can, falling twice and doubling back to the start of the obstacle. He leaps down to the narrow platform, and I see his life flash before his eyes.

Finally, Casey jumps down and lands on the lowest platform. He climbs up the apex ladder and bonks his head on the way down. I look up. He did the whole thing in just under eight minutes, which is pretty good, considering the shape he's in.

Davis and Kholi both complete the course in about six minutes. Then it's Ping's turn.

Ping scrabbles up the wall like he's got flypaper on his hands and springs through the line of tires as though his feet are on fire. He pulls himself up the rope in twenty seconds flat, trots across the balance bridge, and slithers down the apex ladder. He does the entire course in just under four minutes.

I don't know what else to do — I clap. The others turn to stare at me as though I've just sprouted two heads. Ping thrusts out his chest and beams.

It doesn't matter that the guy annoys the shit out of me. That was the most impressive first run I have ever seen.

Unfortunately, New Girl is next in line, and I have a feeling that her performance is going to kill my good mood. She's pale and sweaty and looks as though she might blow chunks. This is not gonna end well.

When she comes down the line, I think she's going to run straight into the wall she's supposed to scale — flat like a pancake. Instead, she stops short and gives a bizarre sort of hop to catch her fingers along the top of the wall.

She slams face-first into the side of the structure and flails around as she struggles to pull herself up. She walks her feet up until she gets to the top and drags her torso over with her arms and shoulders. She flops the rest of her body around and nearly falls off the wall when she misses the rope.

She makes up some time on the tires, but it all falls apart when she reaches the hurdles. Kholi runs alongside her yelling and screaming, and New Girl looks as though she's on the brink of collapse.

Finally she face-plants at the mouth of the tunnel and drags herself through like a zombie crawling out of a grave. Her hair is spilling out of its careful bun, and she's gasping for air.

All I can hear is the sound of Kholi's screams. She's yelling in a way that makes me think she'd be a damn good drill sergeant, but it definitely isn't helping Jones. She's slowly drowning in the squishy foam beads, and I think she's got some in her mouth.

Finally she emerges, and the rest of the squad cheers.

At least that part of my plan is working. The competition is bringing out their animal instincts, but it's also making them a team.

The climbing rope is next, and I know before she even starts that she's gonna have problems. New Girl can barely get through ten push-ups, let alone pull herself up a twenty-foot rope.

Sure enough, Jones moves like a squirrel trying to climb up a greasy flagpole — maybe the worst I've ever seen. Her shiny blond hair is tumbling out of its bun, she's gritting her teeth, and her lip is bleeding.

By now, Kholi's voice is hoarse from yelling. I'm half convinced that she might tear Jones to pieces if she slides down the rope one more time.

Halfway up, New Girl emits a whimper and slides down all over again. I've seen enough.

"Stop! Stop!" I call, walking across the course to make sure she heard me. One more slide like that, and she'll have rope burn so bad she won't be able to hold a rifle for a month.

"Stop!" I repeat.

Now they hear me. Kholi whips her head around with such ferocity that I briefly wonder if she's gone all *Exorcist* on me.

"Time's up!" I yell.

"What?" snaps Kholi.

"You heard me."

"She was almost *finished*!"

"It's been ten minutes," I say. "Time's up."

New Girl slides wordlessly down the rope. Her face is red, and her lip is trembling.

Shit. I know that look. She's breathing hard and fast, her mouth is slack, and I sense that she's about to unravel.

She brushes the hair out of her eyes and stalks off the mats, but not before I see she's got tears in her eyes.

"*Christ,*" I groan, watching her go. I don't know what the hell I'm supposed to do with that. I know she's upset, but damn — watching her on that rope was painful for everyone.

I clear my throat and try to salvage the exercise, but the damage is already done. I march them back to the training center and let them run laps, but the rest of the morning is a total shit show.

Everyone is quiet and subdued, but I can feel the waves of animosity pouring off them. The obstacle course had the effect I intended. I managed to get them operating as a team, but they've united in their hatred for me.

I don't know what I'm going to do. Four of my privates are truly terrible. I'm going to have to push them to their limits to get them in shape, but the harder I push, the more they resist.

The real thorn in my side is Maggie Jones. Something about her seems off, but I can't figure out what it is. One thing's for sure: She needs to toughen up.

When I dismiss them to go to lunch, I yell for Jones to hang back and talk. She freezes. Her lips are pressed together in a hard line, and she won't quite meet my gaze.

"Sir?" Her voice is cold and icy.

"I saw your effort out there on the course, but I'm gonna need you to step it up moving forward."

"Yessir."

"I'm not trying to make you feel bad. There are standards on the PFT that you're gonna have to meet."

"Yessir."

I grit my teeth, inexplicably annoyed. "You're gonna have to work twice as hard as everyone else to get to where you need to be. That means extra time in the gym — giving a hundred and fifty percent in training. It's gonna be tough, and if you can't handle it —"

"I can handle it," she growls, snapping her eyes on to mine.

I nod slowly, glad to have gotten a rise out of her.

"You want to tell me why you're here?" I ask, glancing around the training center. The place is completely deserted.

"*Excuse* me?"

"Come on . . . You aren't cut out for the Space Force. You're an intelligence geek. Tell me why you're really here."

Jones looks momentarily startled — panicked, even. It happens so quickly that I wonder if I imagined it, because a second later, she just looks offended.

"I told you," she says through gritted teeth. "Amelia McDermit had a medical issue. They assigned me to go in her place."

"That's not what I asked," I growl, taking a step toward her so that we're barely six inches apart.

The closer I get, the more I'm convinced that my hunch is dead-on. Jones isn't the military type. She's wearing mascara, for crying out loud. She's too soft, too sensitive, and seriously lacking in upper-body strength.

"Why did you come here?" I murmur. "You have an impressive résumé. You could have applied to work in any other department on Elderon. What could *possibly* have motivated you to join the Space Force?"

"I'm here for the same reason as everyone else," she says with a shrug. "I wanted to make a difference."

"Cut the bullshit, Jones. Why are you really here?"

"What do you want from me?" she snaps.

"I want you to tell me the truth."

"I am," she says, losing all her composure in the blink of an eye. "Why are *you* here?" she growls. "Shouldn't you be interrogating members of the Bureau for Chaos in some army black site? Clearly you get off on torturing people . . ."

A jolt of rage flares through my system, and I can tell at once that Jones knows she's overstepped. She shrinks under my harsh gaze, and I resist the impulse to tear her a new one. I'm shaking all over with fury, but I need to keep it together if I hope to make my point.

"Look," I growl, trying to keep my voice steady. "I don't

know why you're really here, and I don't care. You're on my squad now, and you better get your shit together. Otherwise, I'm gonna have to talk to the captain and let him know you don't belong here."

By now, I'm so close to her that I can detect the faintest hint of freckles skirting across her nose. They're doing something strange to my insides, but I ignore the feeling and keep my scowl firmly in place.

"The captain?" she says in a fake impressed voice. "*Wow.*"

The way her lips form the word, I know she's fucking with me. A ghost of a smile flickers across her face, but I can detect the undercurrent of panic in her eyes.

"You're dismissed," I growl. "Get out of my gym."

Jones doesn't need telling twice. She skitters off to join the others for lunch, and in this moment, I know I'm right.

There's something off about Maggie Jones. I just can't put my finger on it.

21

MAGGIE

I stumble out of the training center in a daze, shaken and unnerved by Jonah's assessment. He suspects something — I can tell.

Who can blame him? I'm clearly not cut out for this. I'm going to have to step up my game. Otherwise I might get kicked out of the Space Force before I have a chance to do what I came here to do.

I hightail it to the dining hall, running a hand over the top of my head to smash down the curls trying to escape from my bun. I keep my head down while I wait in line, hoping I don't see anyone I know. If Tripp or someone from the press corps sees me, my cover will be blown.

The bots serve me a steaming slab of veggie lasagna with dried globs of cheese and the most pitiful bowl of iceberg lettuce I have ever seen. I can't exactly take advantage of Tripp's first-class dining ticket — even when there's a steaming bowl of lobster trotolle with my name on it.

I grab a drink at the end of the line and look around for an empty table. I can't exactly go sit with my squad — not after I earned Adra a grueling round of suicides.

"Hey, Jones!" yells a voice to my left.

Davis is sitting at a table with Ping, Casey, and Adra. He and Casey seem to be rehashing Ping's amazing run on the obstacle course, because Ping is bowing from his chair.

Davis waves me over, and I break into a grin. I can't believe they want anything to do with me, but it feels nice to have friends.

I sink down in the corner seat, glancing over at Adra. She's determinedly stabbing her fork into a rubbery brick of lasagna, and she won't meet my gaze.

The guys seem oblivious to the awkwardness between us. They're still laughing about Casey's performance, which was almost as much of a shit show as mine.

Davis mimics Casey sliding down the apex ladder and busting his nose on the lowest rung, and I take a few bites to give myself time to recover from my conversation with Jonah.

"Better eat up," Davis says to me after a moment.

"Yeah," says Casey, shoving a hunk of bread in his mouth. "Otherwise Wyatt might come over here . . ."

Davis scrunches his face into a surly expression. "Time's up! No lunch for you!"

They both double over in a fit of laughter, and I force myself to smile. I'm glad *someone* found the incident funny.

Ping lets out a nervous burst of laughter, and Adra shakes her head. "Asshole."

"That wasn't cool, man," Ping agrees. "You were almost to the end."

I let out a breath of relief. So they *don't* hate me for being terrible.

"Wyatt's such a dick," says Adra.

"Careful," says Davis, jerking his head at the table of officers behind us.

"I don't care if they hear me," Adra snaps. "They probably think the exact same thing."

"Jonah's not a dick," says Ping.

"Oh, you're on a first-name basis with him?" scoffs Adra.

"Jonah's cool once you get to know him," says Ping. "His CO must be riding him to make sure we can pass our PFTs." He glances around conspiratorially. "Anyway, the other sergeants are worse."

"I'm surprised you noticed with your head so far up Wyatt's ass," Adra mumbles.

I look back to Ping, expecting him to look angry, but he just laughs it off.

"For real, though," says Davis, "I heard the PFT is brutal. Buford administers them at the end of basic, and if you don't pass . . . I guess they send you right back to Earth."

"I don't believe it," Casey mumbles. "That would cost a fortune."

Davis shrugs. "I think they do."

"It doesn't matter," says Adra. "Wyatt's been riding her since she got here. And he cornered her back there."

"What did he say?" asks Ping.

I feel my face heat up as everyone turns their attention to me. "Basically that I better get my shit together," I mumble.

"Screw him," says Adra. "He is such an asshole."

"Yeah . . ."

"You should report him to Buford."

"No."

"Why not?" Adra presses. "Tell me you don't think he deserves it!"

"No, you're right," I say. "Wyatt is an assho —" I break off. Adra is shaking her head, her eyes bugging out in panic.

"Go ahead, Jones," says a cold voice behind me. "Finish that thought."

An icy wave of dread rushes through my body, numbing me from the inside out. I turn slowly, face to the floor, and my eyes land on a pair of shiny black boots. They travel up a pair of strong, solid legs, past Jonah's magnificent ass, to a wide muscular chest.

By the time they reach Jonah's face, I am completely frozen with shock. He's clutching an empty tray in his hands, and his knuckles are as white as a bone.

"What did you call me?" he asks, his eyes full of malice.

"Nothing, sir," I mumble, hoping his glare doesn't vaporize me on the spot.

Jonah doesn't move. I sense his gaze panning over the others and feel a cold nervous sweat bead up under my arms.

"If you're all done *bitching* that your lives are so hard, grab your mouth guards and get your asses back to the training center. *Now*."

Nobody needs telling twice. There's a loud scrape of chairs as Ping, Davis, and Casey get up to dump their trays. Adra moves at a much more leisurely pace, but I nearly trip over my own feet in my rush to get away from Jonah.

I glance over at him as I dump my tray and catch him staring at me from across the dining hall. The waves of dread keep crashing over me, making it nearly impossible to breathe. If Jonah didn't have it out for me before, he most definitely does now.

"Dude," says Adra. "That was *brutal*."

"You could have warned me," I snap.

"I tried! He literally came out of nowhere. What was I supposed to do?"

"Nothing," I say weakly. "It's not your f —"

I break off and stop dead in my tracks. Striding into the

dining hall looking fierce as hell is . . . Alex. She's dressed in a dark-green metallic pantsuit with enormous shoulder pads, and she's staring directly at me.

Her expression registers brief confusion, followed immediately by rage. She gives an infinitesimal shake of her head, her jaw locked in an expression of fury.

I swallow and lengthen my stride to catch up with Adra, tearing my gaze away from Alex.

To her credit, Alex doesn't say a word. I can feel her eyes burning a hole in the back of my neck, but she doesn't blow my cover.

I try to breathe normally, but I'm having a hard time. It feels as though an elephant is sitting on my chest. My hands are shaking, and I'm sweating all over.

In less than twenty minutes, I managed to piss off my fake CO *and* my real boss. I am so incredibly screwed.

BY THE TIME we reach the training center, Jonah is already waiting under the enormous number thirteen.

His expression is cold, unreadable. He has something horrible planned. Maybe we'll be spending the afternoon scrubbing toilets with our toothbrushes, or maybe he plans to throw us out into space and watch while we asphyxiate.

Once we're all assembled in a line, he orders us to follow him and leads us out of the training center. We walk down the same narrow hallway, and for one horrible moment I think he's taking us back to the obstacle course.

Instead, he stops halfway down the hall and scans us into another room. We file in one by one, and I can practically taste the tension.

We're standing in a room filled with hanging punching bags

that smells like bleach, sweat, and pain. The floor and walls are covered in thick foam mats, and suddenly I realize what Jonah has in mind.

Along one wall is a window that looks in on the gym from a smaller observation area. Maybe that's where the officers gather to watch privates beat the shit out of each other.

"Grab some gloves and partner up!" Jonah barks. "No talking."

I follow the others to a bin of black boxing gloves in the corner of the room. I select the pair that looks the smallest and turn to Adra to be my partner.

To my dismay, Adra's expression doesn't match my level of dread. She looks *ready* to punch someone.

"Today we begin your close-quarters combat training," says Jonah, stuffing his own hands into a pair of boxing gloves and thumping his fists together. "Most of you look like you can't take a punch. We're gonna fix that or die trying."

I swallow. This is *not* what I signed up for.

"Now, your first defense against any attack is your stance," says Jonah. "Chin down, hands up, feet shoulder-width apart. Keep your weight on the balls of your feet. You need to keep moving, but you also need to be able to strike from any position."

He demonstrates the boxer stance and makes eye contact with each of us one by one. "Never, *ever* cross your feet, and never let anyone get you on your heels." He beats his gloves along the sides of his head. "Protect yourself. That means hands up. Got it?"

There's a general murmur of assent, but my head is spinning as I try to copy Jonah's stance. Chin down and hands up makes sense, but walking around on my tiptoes feels incredibly stupid.

Jonah spends the next few minutes coming around and

correcting our posture. When he gets to me, he rests his glove on the top of my head and forces my chin down until my shoulders meet my ears. He raises my gloved hands so that my face is protected, and I catch a glimpse of those probing blue eyes.

He's still angry with me — I can tell — but he seems to be putting his resentment aside. Right now, he's focused and attentive — or maybe he's just anxious for me to get my ass beat.

"All right," he says, smacking his gloves together again. "Now it's time for footwork."

The next drill is deceptively tricky. Jonah has us all line up and practice moving in a boxing stance. It should be simple: left-right to take a step forward, right-left to go backwards, left-right to move to the left, right-left to move to the right. The idea is to move each foot the exact same distance and avoid crossing one foot over the other, but the execution is surprisingly difficult.

Once he's convinced that we can move backwards, forwards, and side to side, he teaches us how to throw a jab and a cross. We add the strikes to our bizarre square dance, and I start to wonder how this could possibly help us win a fight.

As if Jonah read my mind, he claps his gloves together again, and I get a now familiar swoop of dread. "Okay. Find your partner. You look like you're ready to hit each other."

BY THE TIME Jonah dismisses us for dinner, I'm ready to fight someone for real.

We spent the afternoon learning how to slip and parry punches, and Adra got her chance to sock me in the face repeatedly.

The idea was to throw soft, slow punches at our partners to

give them a chance to defend, but apparently "soft" and "slow" are two words that aren't in Adra's vocabulary.

After dinner, I change in a bathroom on the middle deck and slink back to the newsroom with my tail between my legs.

"What — the fuck — were you — thinking?" yells Alex the second I walk through the door.

The douchebag tech guy from *Topfold* and the fancy Swedish chick both turn to look in my direction. I sigh. I'm sweaty and bruised and in desperate need of a shower. I am *not* in the mood for this shit.

"Alex, before you say anything —"

But Alex is apoplectic with rage. Her hair is tumbling out of its careful knot, and it looks as though she already sweated through her blazer.

"Conference room — now!"

I don't have the energy to argue. I just march into the big glass cage, preparing to put on a show for the nosy assholes hanging around the newsroom.

Alex stalks in behind me and slams the door. Or, rather, she tries to slam it, but the rubberized coating along the edges of the glass dampens the sound.

I take a seat at the far end of the table, immediately wishing that I'd stayed on my toes and practiced Jonah's boxing stance.

"What — were you — thinking?" Alex yells, leaning over the desk and positively quivering with rage. "Posing as a member of the Space Force? Pretending to be a soldier so you can — what? Prove that there's a story there?"

"I know how this looks," I mutter. "But I —"

"Save your excuses, Maggie. You are finished. I mean it."

"You don't understand."

"Oh, I understand."

"I had help," I say quickly, standing up and glancing out into the newsroom. Douchebag tech guy and the sultry blonde are still staring at me with interest. Rationally I know they can't hear through the walls, but I'm still paranoid that they could be spying on me.

"What are you talking about?" Alex cries. She looks as though she's about to break down in tears, and for a moment, I feel a twinge of guilt that my actions could blow back on her.

I lower my voice and turn my back on our audience so there's no chance of someone reading my lips. "I mean someone knows I'm working on the story," I say. "They reached out in the middle of the night last week and offered to help."

"How would someone know you were working on this?" Alex growls.

"I don't know."

"Did you tell anyone?"

"No. I swear."

She shakes her head, justifiably confused. "And what do you mean they're *helping* you?"

"I mean they reached out with a fake military ID and a position in the Space Force. It's a long story. The point is I've taken the place of a girl whose assignment got scrubbed. They think I'm one of them, and I have ten weeks of basic to —"

"No!" says Alex, looking as though she wants to leap over the desk and strangle me. "No, no, no! Absolutely not."

My heart sinks. She's going to yank me off this story. I'm going to be stuck writing about donuts and Franken-meat for the rest of my life — or worse.

Alex shakes her head again, big enamel earrings clanking. "Do you have *any* idea what will happen when you're caught?"

"I know," I say quickly. "And if they send me home —"

"Send you home?" She lets out a deranged burst of laughter. "No. Oh, no. They aren't going to just send you home and forget about this."

Alex's eyes bulge so big that I'm slightly concerned that

they're going to pop out of her head. "Your career will be *over*," she says. "No publication will want to touch you. You'll be lucky if you're not brought up on criminal charges."

I let out a groan of frustration and turn away from her. I knew she wouldn't understand. This was why I was so determined to get something tangible before I went and revealed my methods.

"There's a story here," I say slowly. "I *know* there is."

"There might be!" says Alex. "It doesn't matter."

I turn back around. Alex looks just as frustrated as I am, but I have a feeling that we're exasperated for very different reasons.

"You can't just pretend to be a member of the Space Force," she says. "If you get caught —"

"I'm not going to get caught," I say roughly. I glance around again and take a step forward, lowering my voice to make sure we're not overheard. "Listen. Whoever is helping me . . . They're *really* high up." I touch my Optix and pull up my fake ID, beaming it to her so she can see it for herself.

"Whoever did this . . . They know I'm onto something."

"But you don't know who might be helping you!"

"I know."

There's a brief moment of silence as Alex scrutinizes the fake ID. That familiar feeling of failure and disappointment is worming its way back into my gut.

She's going to tell me that I'm off the story — or that I'm out of the press corps. I don't have the luxury of taking a stand. I need this job more than I'd like to admit.

"Wow," says Alex after a moment, flipping off her Optix.

I freeze, not sure I heard her correctly. I certainly wasn't expecting *that*.

"This is good," she says after a moment. "You were right."

Wait. What? She can't be saying what I think she's saying.

"Whoever sent you this is the real deal. We are in way over our heads."

I open my mouth, but no words come out. Did Alex just use the word "we"?

"I'm going to regret this," she says with a sigh. "I just know it."

"Regret what?" I croak. She's going to fire me. I can feel it in my bones.

"Regret allowing you to keep going with this," she says. "Clearly there's a story here, and whoever sent you this . . . I think they're your source."

"You think it's someone in the Space Force who knows what's going on?"

Alex shrugs. "I have no idea, but that's what you need to find out."

I hesitate. Surely she can't be saying what I *think* she's saying.

"Does that mean I'm not fired?"

"You're on probation," says Alex with a glare. "Get to the bottom of this — just do it fast. And don't come crying to me if you get caught."

22

JONAH

"Throw out that jab! Throw out that jab! Keep her off you, Jones! Jesus!"

Kholi is walking Jones around the ring, and Jones seems incapable of defending herself. Kholi's still one of the worst fighters I've ever seen — all flailing elbows and sloppy T-rex hooks — but even she can get Jones on the ropes.

Jones peeks up from behind the cover of her gloves and throws out a desperate Hail-Mary cross, but she sticks out her chin and leaves herself open, and Kholi takes her shot.

Jones staggers backward, reeling from shock, and I see the faintest hint of crazy in her eyes. She charges Kholi with a one-two punch, but she gets too close, and Kholi bops her on the nose.

"Time!" I shout, calling an end to the round. I can't watch any more of this.

Kholi immediately snaps out of her trance, shocked and horrified by what she's done. Jones is still standing in the corner of our improvised ring, and blood is gushing from her nose.

"Jesus!" I growl, peeling off my own gloves and tossing them to the ground. "What the hell was that?"

"I'm sorry!" says Kholi. "I didn't mean to!"

"It's okay," says Jones, still trying to stem the flow of blood leaking from her nose.

"It's not okay!" I yell. "Kholi — control! The idea of practice is not to beat the shit out of each other. Jones —" I shake my head, completely lost for words.

Well, not completely. Useless. Terrible. Blind baby deer running headlong into a rock. Those are the words that come to mind, but instead of adding insult to injury, I take a deep breath and try to edit my frustration.

"Keep — your chin — down. Hold your position, and throw out that jab."

Jones looks as though she's about to cry. Blood is gushing from her glove onto the mat. What a fucking mess.

"You can't go into the ring timid like that," I say. "Make her scared to come to you."

I drop my glare and let out a sigh. "Jones, go to the bathroom and clean yourself up. Casey, mop up that blood. Kholi, you're benched. Ping and Davis, you're up next."

Unfortunately, the guys are even more of a shit show than Jones and Kholi. Davis is beside himself with nerves and seems reluctant to hit *anyone*, while Ping is a coiled spring of misguided energy. He bounces around the ring like a kangaroo on steroids and occasionally manages to whop someone so hard that I have to make him sit out.

This is *not* going the way I'd planned.

Two and a half weeks into basic, and my squad is still terrible. The five of them are in marginally better physical shape, but none of them can block a punch, land a kick, or hit a target with a rifle to save their lives.

After Ping chases Davis around the ring for a solid twenty

minutes, I call an end to the sparring session and dismiss them all for dinner. The privates are exhausted, and I need to regroup.

I head to the civilian fitness center to blow off some steam, but before I'm even out of the sector, I hear someone calling my name.

I stop in my tracks and close my eyes. I swear to god if it's Ping . . .

I turn. It isn't Ping. It's my CO, Lieutenant Buford. Buford's a few inches shorter than me with thinning brown hair, a baby-smooth face, and the over-friendly smile of an annoying neighbor.

Compared to Callaghan, Buford is a cakewalk. He doesn't seem overly concerned with my privates passing their PFTs. He pretty much stays out of my way and lets me train my squad.

I give him a quick salute, which he returns with a jaunty little snap.

"Sergeant Wyatt . . . Good to see you."

"Sir."

"I saw your private run out of the combat gym with a bloody nose." He raises his eyebrows and lets out a hiss. "Rough day?"

"My squad has been a little slow to pick up the basics of hand-to-hand," I admit. "But I'll get them there. I just need more time."

"Hmm. Yes, well . . ." Buford trails off, glancing behind me as if to make sure there's no one else there. "Some soldiers pick things up quicker than others."

"Yessir."

"You know I'm here to help if there are areas where you're struggling . . ."

"Thank you, sir. But I think my squad just needs more time to train."

Buford studies me for a moment, and I get the feeling that he's trying to decide whether or not I'm up to the challenge. "Walk with me."

I hesitate. The last thing I want is for Buford to appoint himself my personal babysitter. It's hard enough training my squad without someone constantly looking over my shoulder. But something in his expression tells me it isn't a request, so I follow him back down the hallway.

He scans us into the room attached to the combat gym. It looks almost like an interrogation room, and I've never really understood its purpose. There's a table with four chairs in the middle of the room, a single strip of fluorescent lighting, and a long window on one wall looking out into the gym.

"I've been watching your squad closely since the beginning of basic," he says, turning toward a set of cabinets built into the wall. "And I have to say . . . You've got your work cut out for you."

"Yes, sir."

I'm not sure why he brought me in here, but I'm getting an itch to leave. Nothing good ever comes from an extended one-on-one with your CO. These conversations usually end with an ultimatum.

But Buford seems oddly casual as he opens up a cabinet and pulls out a shallow white box. It's about the size of a small sheet cake with a biometric scanner on one side.

"Trust me when I tell you that the amount of work these recruits require is not lost on us. Neither Captain Callaghan nor any of the people under his command had much of a say in the recruitment process."

"Who did have a say in recruitment?"

"Maverick Enterprises worked with private recruiters to select for a few very specific skill sets," says Buford.

It sounds as though he's choosing his words carefully so as not to give too much away.

"What sort of skill sets?" I press.

"Space weaponry. Intelligence. Cryptography and cyber-security . . ."

"Meaning?"

"Meaning that the people in your squad will be very helpful in defending this colony against any long-range attack from our adversaries. Close-quarter combat is where they struggle. I can help with that."

Buford presses his thumb against the biometric scanner, and the box pops open with a slight *pfft* of air.

"Captain Callaghan has given the lieutenants access to some proprietary technology designed by a subsidiary of Maverick Enterprises. They developed this technology in an effort to simulate more humanlike movement in their bots, but they discovered other applications for it as well."

He opens the box. Inside are two identical devices unlike anything I've ever seen before. Each has a tiny bronze shell and a dozen or so wires sticking out in different directions.

"What is this?"

"It's called a SPIDER," he says. "It stands for Simulated Procedural Memory Intake Decoding and Encoding Receptor. The acronym should really be SPMIDER or something, but I guess they thought SPIDER was catchier."

He chuckles a little at his own joke, and I meet his gaze, utterly confused.

"What do you do with it?"

Buford smirks. "It'll make more sense when you see for yourself."

Buford taps his Optix to ping someone, and a second later, a man picks up. "Kelso, do you copy?"

There's a moment of silence as the man on the other end responds.

"Can you come down here, please? I'm in the combat lab. Over."

Buford ends the call and raises his eyebrows. "I think you'll be very impressed when you see what it can do."

We wait in silence for several minutes, and I take the opportunity to study the device up close. The shell is contoured to fit something round, and each of the SPIDER's wires has tiny claws at the ends.

Suddenly the door clicks open, and a tall sergeant walks in. I recognize him from officer training, but I didn't know his name until now. Kelso has a thick mat of greasy black hair, a large nose, and an expression that isn't exactly friendly.

"Thanks, Kelso," says Buford. "I want to show Wyatt here what the SPIDER can do."

I glance at Kelso. He doesn't seem at all confused by this request.

As I watch, Buford peels one of the SPIDERs out of its protective foam packaging and presses a tiny button on the underside of the shell. A blue light comes on somewhere underneath, illuminating the metallic elements and giving it the appearance of an alien creature come to life.

Kelso sits down, and Buford slowly places the device along the back of his head. I cringe as I imagine the creepy little appendages brushing the back of my scalp, and then, suddenly, the metal arms begin to move.

Kelso blinks twice very fast, and I get the feeling that the arms are digging into the back of his head. Buford removes his hand, and I see that the SPIDER has suctioned itself to Kelso's skull like a creepy many-armed starfish.

"What now?" I ask. The SPIDER doesn't seem to be doing anything, but maybe I just don't see it.

"Now I want you to forget that the device is even there," he says. "Your file says that you're an excellent fighter, sergeant."

I don't confirm or deny that statement. It's a lose-lose proposition. Tell someone you're great, and they want to knock you off your high horse. Tell someone you're just all right, and they'll hate you for being modest.

"How's your jiu-jitsu?"

"Not great."

That *isn't* me being modest. I've always been a stronger stand-up fighter, which has its disadvantages.

"Kelso here is a black belt in BJJ."

Kelso looks embarrassed to have the lieutenant bragging on his behalf, and I wonder where the hell Buford is going with this.

The lieutenant grins. "Why don't you get in there and roll a few rounds?" He nods through the window to the combat gym, and I get a tiny prickle of unease.

Callaghan must have sent Buford and Kelso to teach me some kind of lesson. Good fighter or not, I don't stand a chance against someone with a black belt in Brazilian jiu-jitsu. It's like bringing a knife to a gun fight.

"Feel free to start standing up," says Buford, the edge of a smirk in his tone.

I shoot Buford a dirty look, nod at Kelso, and head for the door. I don't care if I'm about to get my ass handed to me. You don't pass up the chance to roll with someone who's got a significantly better ground game. There's no way to walk away from that without learning a thing or two.

Kelso's got this look that says he's about to kick my ass, but it's not cockiness I'm sensing. It's almost as though he's resigned himself to being Buford's gun for hire, and he doesn't enjoy it one bit.

We head out into the gym, and the stench of new mats and

bleach washes over me. I pull off my boots, socks, and over-shirt, and the sensation of cool foam under my feet puts me at ease. I'm back at home in the ring.

We each find corners along one of the tape rings on the mat, and a yellow light starts to blink above the window separating us from Lieutenant Buford. There are three low beeps, and the light turns green.

I face off against Kelso and raise my hands. The first thing I notice is all the ways Kelso's stance is different from mine.

In the army, my instructors were ex-boxers, black belts in taekwondo, and experts in Israeli self-defense. Striking is my game.

Kelso, on the other hand, wants to get me to the ground as quickly as possible. His stance is lower — feet splayed wide, torso bent forward in a lunge. His hands aren't curled into fists or raised to eye level to parry a strike. They're down at his chest and slightly open, as if he's preparing to grab me.

We circle each other slowly and deliberately. He's waiting for me to throw the first punch. I'm waiting for him to shoot in for a takedown.

But Kelso seems to be keeping his distance. He's a patient fighter, which makes him dangerous.

I throw a few jabs to test my range, and Kelso slips them expertly. He doesn't need his hands to parry; his head movement is excellent.

I throw out a combo, and Kelso counters. I barely avoid his cross and catch half a hook to my temple. It's been too long since I've really sparred, and my nerves are on full display. I'm too eager to get some strikes in, and it's making me sloppy.

But as the round stretches out, I start to loosen up. My tried-and-true combos return like old friends, and my movements begin to sharpen.

Then I throw out a kick, and my mistake is immediately

apparent. Kelso shoots in, and I feel my legs fly out from under me. We hit the ground in a clash of limbs, and I roll to secure a better position.

It's no use. Rolling with Kelso is like wrestling a bear — I don't stand half a chance. His movements are fluid, precise, and effortless. His body barely ripples, but a second later I'm flat on my back with Kelso in my guard. It's an awkward position for any stand-up fighter to have another dude between his legs, but the guard is where jiu-jitsu guys thrive.

It seems that Kelso knows what I'm going to do before I do. He anticipates my every move and passes my guard in less than a minute.

With Kelso's legs pinning me on either side and his weight pressing down on my chest, I feel as though I'm slowly suffocating in a python's grip. I try every trick in the book to topple him, but he only seems to strengthen his position.

The round ends with Kelso's legs wrapped around my neck, though I have no memory of how he got there. I tap out, and he relinquishes his hold and graciously helps me to my feet.

"Nice," I pant, though it doesn't feel nice. It feels like I just had my ass handed to me, and I'm not quite sure how it happened.

"Again," calls Buford's voice from the intercom.

I sigh.

We go another two rounds, and both times Kelso gets me to tap before the bell rings. Each time, he gives me a good two minutes of stand-up fighting so I don't feel like a chump, but each time he takes me down and forces me to submit.

On the second round, Kelso gets me in an armlock from side control. On the third, he puts me in a triangle choke before I ever have a chance to pass his guard.

After Kelso chokes me out in a humiliating fashion, Buford sounds the bell and calls us back in.

"All right, Wyatt?" asks Buford.

I'm glad he's enjoying this. I'm heaving as though I just sprinted up six flights of stairs.

"Fine," I huff, wiping my brow.

"You don't look fine."

I shoot him a dirty look. I'd like to see *him* try to beat Kelso in a hand-to-hand fight. Buford would shit his pants.

Kelso is determined to avoid my gaze. I think he feels bad about kicking my ass, whereas Buford is amused. He's messing around with the instant replay on his Optix. At least I think that's what he's doing.

Finally he seems satisfied, and the SPIDER sitting in the box lights up on its own.

"This'll make you feel better," says Buford. "Take a seat."

I continue to glare at Buford but sit. I have this strange feeling deep in my gut, and Buford's smirk isn't helping. I make a mental note to grab a workout with Kelso and see if he'll teach me a few ground sequences.

Buford picks up the glowing SPIDER from the box and takes a step toward me. He slides the shell down along the back of my head, and every muscle in my body tightens.

I don't like the feeling of its creepy little appendages, and I cringe as the metal legs twist and bend. The shell feels warm — as though I've been holding it in my hands — and its thin spider legs seem to be trying to burrow through my skin.

"It can be a bit uncomfortable the first time," says Buford.

That's an understatement.

Once it's in position, the SPIDER starts to vibrate. I don't notice it at first. I just feel a slight tingle at the top of my spine. I have the urge to scratch the itch, but then the vibrations grow more intense.

I hear a faint humming in my ears, and my body detects a faint pattern to the vibrations. They're pulsating through my skin and making every hair on the back of my neck stand on end. Soon the pattern is strong enough to vibrate my bones until it feels as though my whole body is attuned to the rhythm.

Kelso is watching me out of the corner of his eye. At first I'm barely aware of anyone else, but once I come back to the present, there's something in his expression that sets me on edge.

A second later, a notification pops up on Buford's Optix, and he claps his hands together. "All right. Let's go."

At first I'm not sure what he means, and then I realize he wants us to roll again.

Buford turns his attention to Kelso. "Just like before. Don't throw any new material at him. Just give him a chance to defend."

"Yessir," Kelso mutters.

I hold back a groan. I really must have looked pathetic if Buford is telling Kelso to go easy on me.

I give myself a mental slap and prepare my body to commit Kelso's moves to memory. If I'm going to be tossed around like a wrestling dummy, I at least want to learn something I can use.

Kelso and I head back into the ring, and I wait for the light above the window to turn green.

This time, Kelso doesn't mess around or give me a chance to throw my strikes. He shoots in almost immediately, going for a double-leg takedown.

Instead of resisting, something in my brain tells me to let him. We fly toward the mat in a tangle of limbs, but this time my body is ready to react.

We twist in midair, and I manage to slide my body into a better position. We hit the mat, and I slip effortlessly out from under his body and get him locked in side control.

He seems to anticipate me going for the armlock, which I had no idea how to execute just moments ago. When he shrimps out from under me and gets to his feet, I drop him to the mat in a beautiful single-leg takedown.

Kelso grunts, and for the first time I get the feeling that we could be equally matched. I don't know how that's possible, but I'm not going to question it.

He gets impatient and tries to put me in a triangle, but my body seems to know what to do. Unlike last time, I can sense what Kelso's attempting each time he repositions, and my body moves expertly to avoid being trapped.

I counter each of Kelso's submissions, completely baffled by my new ability.

Frustration is pouring off of Kelso in waves, but I'm riding the high of my newfound power.

A second later, I hear a low beep. The light above the window flashes red. The round is over.

We break apart, and Kelso doesn't help me to my feet. He's sweating through his T-shirt, and he won't look me in the eye.

I'm speechless. I think I just had an out-of-body experience. My temple is throbbing dully, but I don't even care.

"How —" I break off, trying to wrap my head around what just happened. I stare down at my hands, which look the same as they did before. I'm still *me*, which doesn't explain how I just did what I did.

Buford calls us back in, and I feel a headache coming on. I remember the piece of equipment fused to my skull, and I get a shiver of paranoia.

"What the hell was that?" I ask, striding across the room. "What is this thing?"

"That," says Buford, "was the SPIDER."

I turn to Kelso in bewilderment, but he won't look me in the eye. His jaw is tight and his brows are drawn — almost as though he feels cheated.

"How — is that — possible?"

"Oh, believe me," says Buford. "I was just as skeptical as you are. But this technology is the future of training. It is absolutely extraordinary."

I rub my head, still unable to process what just happened. My headache has morphed into an intense throbbing in both my temples, and I can't seem to think straight.

I reach up behind my head to yank the device off, but Buford stops me and releases it remotely. I'm guessing these little things are very expensive, and he doesn't want me to break one.

The second Buford swipes his Optix, I feel the SPIDER's appendages loosen. I pry the thing out of my hair and drop it in the box, where it nestles itself into the foam like a creepy little animal.

"What the fuck *was* that?" I choke.

"Simulated motor-memory encoding," says Buford.

"Fake muscle memory," Kelso translates, taking off his device and shoving it into the box next to mine.

"See these things?" says Buford, picking up Kelso's SPIDER and flipping it over. "Each of these appendages is an electrode. Kelso wore it for the first three rounds, and the SPIDER recorded the sequence of firing in his motor networks. The SPIDER can transmit the firing sequence to any paired device — in this case yours — and then the sequence essentially plays on repeat."

"What does that mean?"

"By firing that sequence a hundred times a minute, it allows the appropriate synaptic connections to form in your brain without you ever having to learn those sequences manually."

"Does that mean it taught me what Kelso already knows?"

"In a way."

"In a way?" I repeat.

"It's not the same as training," Kelso mutters.

"Correct," says Buford. "Because the sequences fire so rapidly in such a condensed period of time, you likely won't remember those submissions tomorrow. Now, if we spaced out the repetitions and extended your sessions, you could learn them in a fraction of the time it would take in training."

I sit back. I can still feel a dull ache of pain in my temples. "So, you're saying that anybody can learn to fight without actually needing to train?"

"Not just fight," says Buford. "Anything that relies on muscle memory. Someone who has never touched a piano could learn to play a song like a master in just a few sessions."

"Exactly," says Kelso irritably. "One song."

I glance from Kelso to Buford, utterly confused.

"You can't become a master," says Kelso. "You can just learn pieces of what they know."

"Yes, exactly," says Buford, seemingly oblivious to Kelso's sour attitude. "The limitations of the technology are such that you can only learn the precise movements and sequences that the master brain performs."

"Master brain?"

"The instructor — or the user where the original synaptic connections formed. The SPIDER can only send very specific recorded signals to the mimicking brain."

I shake my head. "Why are you telling me all this?"

"You said your squad was falling behind," says Buford. "This should help you get them up to speed."

There's a long moment of silence as I try to process what he's telling me.

"You want me to *program* them with this SPIDER thing?"

"I want you to use the device as a tool in your training," says Buford.

I open my mouth to protest, but Buford cuts me off.

"I've seen your squad in action, Wyatt. You might be able to get them into decent physical shape, but their hand-to-hand skills are seriously lacking." He holds up the SPIDER. "This is the solution."

I shake my head. "But you said yourself . . . This doesn't actually teach someone to fight."

"You're right," says Buford. "That's *your* job. The SPIDER is only a tool."

I open my mouth again, but I'm almost too shocked to speak. Is Buford really asking what I think he is? He wants me to use a piece of unproven technology to fake teach my squad a few martial arts tricks?

"With all due respect, sir, I think this is a mistake." I glance at Kelso, who is still avoiding my gaze. "The device . . . It makes you *feel* as though you've learned something, but the effects are only temporary. You said yourself —"

"This isn't a discussion, Wyatt," says Buford, his tone suddenly icy. He places the SPIDER back in its case and closes the lid with a snap. "This is the future of the Space Force. I want every underperforming squad using it to get up to speed. Consider that an order."

23

MAGGIE

I jerk awake with the feeling that I've forgotten something important. I'm sitting at the desk in my old suite, and there's a big puddle of drool soaking through the printouts in front of me.

I've spent hours poring over my notes from the Space Force, but none of it makes any sense. I've introduced myself to well over a hundred privates outside my squad, noting their names, their specialties, and their professional backgrounds.

If my sample is representative of the entire Space Force recruit pool, nearly half of them are intelligence specialists. Ten percent are linguists and communication experts, ten percent work in cybersecurity, and almost fifteen percent are hackers. There are a handful of astronomical engineers, space-weapons specialists, and cryptologists in the bunch, and the rest wouldn't tell me what the hell they did before they were recruited.

We have recruits who speak Russian, Tatar, Chechen, Mandarin, Farsi, Arabic, and Korean, but no one seems to know why they were recruited in the first place.

I can't get any officer higher than a sergeant to say more than two words to me, but I can't push too hard and risk raising a red flag. All the information I've gathered so far has come to me under the guise of sheer friendliness, and no private is *that* friendly with a higher-ranking officer.

I glance at the clock and almost fall out of my chair. It's four thirty. I was asleep for almost two and a half hours.

I grab my uniform and run to the latrine. My newly formed muscles are stiff and achy, but I'm used to it. Jonah has been working us like animals for the past three weeks, and I've actually started to form triceps.

Luckily, I'm the only one awake this early in the civilian pod. I don't even have time to wait for the water to get warm. I just rinse off the cookie crumbs and energy-drink residue, climb back into yesterday's uniform, and twist my wet hair into a bun. I have to be in the training center in less than ten minutes.

Grabbing a granola bar from the stash in my suite, I jet over to the training center. I sneaked out of the barracks as soon as Adra fell asleep, which means that the couple hours at my desk was the *only* shuteye I got. I can feel my body rebelling. I am in desperate need of coffee.

Halfway there, I realize that I forgot my fake rifle. I double back to the barracks to grab it, and Adra is already gone.

PT starts in four minutes. I am so screwed.

I arrive at the training center with less than a minute to spare and find my place in line. Adra shifts beside me, and I feel her gaze flicker up and down.

"Where were you last night?" she hisses.

"What?"

"I woke up and you were gone."

My tired brain starts and stutters. My mind goes blank, and every good excuse I've ever formulated seems to evaporate in an instant. "Uh . . . I wasn't feeling very well," I lie.

Adra doesn't say a word. She seems to be waiting for a more complete explanation.

"I spent the night on the bathroom floor," I add.

"I didn't see you when I got up to piss."

"Are you serious?" I say, turning my head forty-five degrees in her direction. "We had, like, an entire conversation."

Adra looks suspicious and then confused. "Wait. What? We did?"

"*Yeah,*" I say. "Don't you remember?"

"No."

I shake my head. "Maybe you were sleepwalking . . . sleep pissing."

"Maybe. Fuck. Am I gonna catch this shit?"

I shake my head. "I don't think so — not unless you got sushi from the market after dinner."

"Damn," she says. "No wonder you look like hell."

"Gee, thanks."

Just then, the rustle of whispers around me stops. The sergeants must be filing in. I see Jonah in my periphery and snap my head around to the front. He's got this grouchy look on his face. Well, it's grouchier than his default, at least.

I don't have the energy for extra push-ups, so I shut my mouth and straighten my back. He looks as though he's got something on his mind, which doesn't bode well for any of us. If Jonah's CO has been giving him a hard time, he's definitely going to take it out on us.

Physical training starts just as it normally does. Jonah runs us through circuits of push-ups, sit-ups, burpees, pull-ups, and sprints. My pull-ups are still weak, but my push-ups have improved.

He doesn't say a word to me the entire morning, which seems like a stroke of luck. In fact, he barely yells at anyone. Even when we move on to target shooting after breakfast,

Jonah is eerily calm — as though our sergeant has been body-snatched.

When the morning's training session is over, he dismisses us for lunch, and I hurry to get away from Adra. It seems as though she bought my lie, but I'm treading on thin ice.

I can't let her catch me out of my bunk again, but I need to get to work on my story. Alex is growing impatient, and I need to find *something* to give her.

We file back in to the training center afterward, and Jonah is waiting for us in our squad's area. His mouth is drawn into a thin angry line, and I get an immediate swoop of panic. Jonah never beats us to the training center, and part of me wonders if we're going to be punished.

"Listen up!" he says as we fall into line. "For the rest of this week and next, you'll be training with Sergeant Walker's squad in the afternoons. I'll be working with a few of you individually to get you up to speed on what we've been doing." His gaze lingers on me for what seems like forever, and I feel my face heat up.

"Ping, Kholi, Davis, Casey — fall in with squad fourteen. Jones, you're with me."

My heart sinks. That feeling of dread is back in full force. How is it that I'm stuck training with Sergeant Sunshine on today of all days? Am I being punished for sneaking out of the barracks? How could he possibly know?

My overtired brain won't stop dreaming up horrible scenarios as I follow Jonah out of the training center. He leads me down the hallway toward the combat gym, and my sense of foreboding grows.

Nothing good ever happens here.

"Grab some gloves," he says. "You're on the heavy bag."

I do as I'm told, and Jonah runs me through the series of combos we worked on yesterday. The sound of my gloves hitting the bag is strangely gratifying, and pretty soon I'm sweating through my shirt.

My lungs are burning. My arms are on fire, and each breath comes like a knife to the chest, but I keep striking. I know better than to stop with Jonah hovering a foot behind me.

Every time I ease up a little, he yells at me to hit harder, faster, cleaner. I'm not sure what I did to deserve this personal hell, but it feels as though it will never end.

Just when I think my arms might completely detach from my body, he tells me to stop and take five.

I drag my sorry ass over to the drinking fountain, trying and failing to catch my breath. I suck down a few gulps of water between heaving gulps of air and focus on calming my heart rate.

Jonah isn't facing me, but I sense his eyes following me around the gym. I have a question burning inside me, but I seriously doubt that I'll get a straight answer.

Finally my breathing returns to normal, and I pad back across the gym.

"Sir?" I ask, my voice fading to a whisper before the syllable has even left my mouth.

"What is it, Jones?"

"Can I ask you something?"

Jonah turns to me and scowls. I can tell that small talk isn't his thing, but he doesn't refuse.

"Why . . . Why am I here?" My real question is "Why are you torturing me?" but "Why am I here?" sounds less combative.

Jonah stares at me for several seconds, and I feel as though I might combust. Looking at Jonah really is like staring into the sun, but I hold my head high and force myself to meet his gaze.

He sighs. "Look, I'm going to be honest with you . . . The entire squad is behind in training. Kholi, Davis, Casey, and Ping

. . . They're slow, but they're getting there. You . . ." He shakes his head. "Half the time it's like you aren't even here."

My face burns with shame. Am I *really* worse than Davis?

"If you don't work hard," Jonah continues, "and I mean at least *twice* as hard as everyone else, you are not going to make it here."

My humiliation and defeat must show on my face, because he adds, "I'm not trying to be a dick. It's just a fact."

I nod, trying not to show how much his words bother me. This might not be my real job, but my pride is still wounded. No one wants to hear that they suck.

"But if you're willing to put in the work, I'll help you."

For the first time, his voice isn't rude or condescending. It's actually kind of nice.

"Fine," I say, filled with a sudden determination to be the best fake private here. "What can I do to improve?"

"You can *listen*," he says, raising an eyebrow. "Do what I tell you. No back talk — just do it."

"*Okay*," I say, completely taken aback.

Jonah doesn't say anything else after that. He goes over to the bin and digs out some headgear and a padded vest. He also grabs some gloves for himself, and I get another swoop of apprehension.

He tosses me the vest and the headgear.

"Put those on," he says. "We're gonna spar."

Great.

"Are you serious?" I groan, forgetting for a moment that he's my sergeant and I just agreed to do as he says.

"I know you're tired," he adds. "We won't go hard."

I hesitate. I'm sweaty and exhausted, and my arms are killing me. The last thing I want to do is stand here and let Jonah beat me to a pulp.

"You can quit if you want," he says nonchalantly. "The door's right there. No one is forcing you to be here, Jones."

I grit my teeth and wriggle into the vest. It smells like straight-up ass and smooshes my boobs uncomfortably.

Fuck him. This fight is bigger than me — bigger than my story on the Space Force. This fight is for weak-armed nerd girls everywhere.

Jonah the dickwad can't make me surrender. He's gonna have to *kick* my ass out of here.

"Let's go," I say, pushing the headgear down over my bun.

Jonah fixes me with a peculiar expression, and I catch a glimmer of amused satisfaction in his eyes. He walks over to the plexiglass window and lets himself into the room on the other side.

By the time Jonah emerges again, my nerves are stretched to the breaking point. I'm padded up like a human marshmallow, while he's stripped down to his T-shirt.

Jonah pulls on a pair of gloves and secures the straps with his teeth.

"All right," he says, pounding his fists together. "Let's go."

I take a deep breath and raise my guard. My entire body feels as though it's made of rubber bands stretched to their breaking point.

We start to circle, and Jonah meets my gaze. "I'm not going to counter. I'm just going to defend your strikes."

I swallow. I am frozen with nerves.

"Any time now . . ." says Jonah. His voice isn't condescending, but it is impatient.

I throw out a jab. It's really just a slow grope through the air, and Jonah dodges it easily. I try another jab, and he bats my glove away like a cat pawing at a ball of string.

I throw out a double jab and a cross, stepping in for the last strike. Jonah deflects every punch effortlessly, but I feel myself relax.

We move around the ring in a slow circle — me throwing every strike I've learned at Jonah, and him defending me expertly. Eventually, one of my crosses slips through, and it glances off the side of his jaw.

Jonah lifts his eyebrows as though he's impressed, but I'm not convinced he didn't give me that on purpose.

Soon I'm a panting mess of nerves and defeat, and Jonah isn't even breaking a sweat.

"Time," he says, lowering his guard and going back into the little room with the window. I catch a glimpse of something shiny embedded in his hair, but I don't have a chance to ask him about it.

He motions for me to follow, and I trail after him with a huff.

What the hell was that all about? What was the point in letting me throw a bunch of sloppy punches if he wasn't even going to counter my strikes?

I peel off my headgear and catch a glimpse of my reflection in the glass. My hair is falling out of its bun, and my curls are plastered to my forehead with sweat. I look like a hot mess.

I follow him into the room, where I see a shallow plastic box sitting on a table. Jonah opens it. Inside is a piece of metal with long wire protrusions sticking out in all directions.

"What's that?" I ask.

He hesitates, and I realize suddenly that the thing in the box is identical to the piece of metal he's got clipped to the back of his head.

"Look, Jones," he says, pressing his fingers against the edge of the table. "I don't know why you're here —"

I get a sudden jolt of apprehension.

"And they haven't shared any particulars of our mission with me . . ."

I sigh. There goes Jonah's potential as a source. Does nobody know why the Space Force is here?

"Since no one is going to let me in on the joke," he continues, "I need to make sure you aren't a liability to my squad."

Ouch.

"With a little extra work, I think you'll pass the PFT. Where you're really struggling is close-quarters combat."

He stops talking and looks me up and down, and I get the feeling that I'm being x-rayed by a very judgmental machine.

"That's where this comes in." He nods down at the weird little device in the box. "Lieutenant Buford showed me how it works, and I've been training with it the past couple of days to put some of my own data into the system."

"What kind of data?" I ask. "What is this thing?"

Jonah hesitates, and I reach up on the pretense of scratching an itch to flip on my Optix.

"It's hard to explain," he says. "Honestly, you won't believe me until you see it for yourself."

He reaches down into the box and carefully extracts the weird device.

"This is part of a set." He turns his head to the side so that I can see the one he's got clipped to his skull. "I'm wearing its mate. Once I activate yours, they'll be able to talk to each other."

"What will they say?" I mutter, unable to keep the smart-ass tone out of my voice.

"You just have to trust me."

For a moment, we just stare at each other. His expression says that he's letting me in on something that's supposed to be secret, but I have no idea why he'd be entrusting me with this information.

Feeling impatient, I reach down for the device, but his hand shoots out and snatches it up.

"Let me," he says gruffly.

I let out a huff of annoyance and turn around so that he can attach the thing to the back of my head. I run a hand along my neck to catch any stray hairs, and I get a shiver as Jonah's fingers brush against my skin.

As soon as the metal touches my head, that warm tingly feeling is replaced by panic. A dozen tiny claws are digging into my skull, suctioning to my head like an alien that's about to eat my brain.

I wince, and the thing seems to adjust itself until it's only exerting a dull pressure along the back of my head. A slight tingling sensation dances over my scalp, and the device starts to vibrate.

I meet Jonah's gaze with an expression of panic. I'm not enjoying this at all.

"Don't worry," he says. "It'll be over soon."

"What will?" I squeak. "What's it doing?"

"Just relax."

I open my mouth and stare incredulously. How the hell am I supposed to relax? I want to rip the thing off my head, but then the uncomfortable vibrations stop, and the sudden lack of motion gives me a feeling of unease.

"All right," says Jonah, maneuvering around the table and leading me back into the gym. "Let's go again."

"Are you *serious*?"

My arms feel as though they've been filled with molten lead, and my legs are dangerously wobbly. I didn't finish my lunch, and my body is running on empty.

Jonah ignores my misgivings. "This time, I'm going to throw some strikes at you. I don't want you to worry about hitting me back. Your only job is to defend yourself."

I groan. I feel as though I'm going to be sick. Jonah wants to punch me now?

"You can wear your headgear if it makes you feel better," he says.

Steeling myself for the worst, I cram the headgear back on over the creepy device and secure the Velcro straps.

We square off in the ring, and Jonah gives me a reassuring nod.

"It's going to be better this time," he says. "Just . . . trust yourself."

I let out a derisive laugh. *Trust myself*? I've been at this for less than three weeks. How the hell am I supposed to trust myself?

Still, it seems as though I don't have a choice. Jonah's not letting me leave here with my pride intact.

I raise my hands and tuck my chin, bracing myself for a punch.

"You have to keep your eyes open," he says, his voice rough with irritation.

"I know," I say. I force myself not to squint, but it's tough when every one of my muscles is locked in a full-body cringe.

A second later, Jonah throws out a jab, and miraculously my head slips to the side. It isn't one of my clumsy ducks. My head only moves a couple of inches, and I feel his glove breeze past my face.

I reposition my feet, and he throws a double jab followed by a cross. My feet move without consulting my brain, and my glove shoots up to parry the cross as though I'd been expecting it.

We move around the ring in a slow circle, my arms and legs firing in perfect synchronicity. I block a punch, slip a jab — even counter a kick meant to take out my front leg.

I manage to avoid every single one of his strikes. My mind is officially blown.

Jonah ramps up the intensity, and I don't have time to think. He fakes a cross and aims a kick at my head, and my left hand shoots up to grab the leg that's airborne.

I take his other leg out from under him. He hits the mat with a surprising *thud* and springs back up before I have a chance to process what just happened. I shoot in with a combination of my own, and I feel a strange electricity moving through my body.

Jonah told me to focus on defending, but I have an urge to counter him. It's as though an invisible actor has taken up residence inside my body. It's weird and kind of creepy, but I don't fight the sensation.

Jonah deflects my first two strikes as though he'd been expecting them, but the third is too quick. My uppercut catches him right under the chin, and he staggers back in a daze.

I try another combo, but this time, he's ready. He dips to the side to avoid my cross and comes in with a hard hit to the body. I throw an elbow down to protect my ribs, but I still feel his fist dig into the padding of my vest.

At the moment of contact, Jonah seems to come to his senses. He backs up — his expression apologetic — but the damage is already done.

I don't think. I just act. A new energy is thrumming inside of me, egging me on and overriding my senses. I turn over my shoulder and swing my body counterclockwise — elbow poised to do real damage.

I spin my body around in a full three-sixty, bashing him cleanly in the mouth. Jonah backs away, and I know I got him good.

His lip is bloody. He's doubled over, and I feel a surge of triumph followed by regret.

"I'm sorry!" I blurt, backing away.

What the hell did I just do?

"It's okay," he grunts, visibly stunned but trying to play it off.

"I'm sorry," I repeat, horrified by what I've done.

Jonah's got blood on his teeth. His lip is cut, and it's already swelling.

"Don't be."

I open my mouth to say something else, but then my guilt starts to morph into anger.

That wasn't me. I would never do something like that. It has got to be this thing that's attached itself to my skull, but I don't know how that's possible.

I peel off my gloves, throw my headgear to the ground, and fumble around the back of my head.

"Don't —" Jonah blurts.

But it's too late. I yank the device away from my skull, and I feel the little wire legs catch in my hair. It's almost like an alien parasite desperately clinging to its host, and I want nothing to do with it.

I yank the thing out, and a few strands of hair separate from my scalp. I throw it to the ground and step back in revolt.

"What the *hell* is that thing?" I growl, glaring at Jonah with unrestrained fury.

"The Space Force's newest toy," he grumbles, spitting out a glob of blood and wiping his mouth on his arm. "A gift from Maverick designed to expedite training."

"What does that mean?"

"It's called a SPIDER," he explains. "It uses simulated motor-memory encoding to help people learn faster."

"Are you saying . . ." My head is throbbing dully, making it difficult to think. "Are you saying that that thing was *teaching* me?"

Jonah shrugs. "In a way. Really, *I* was teaching you. You just didn't know it."

"What's *that* supposed to mean?" It sounds as though he's saying that he — Jonah — was in my head pulling the strings. But that's too creepy to be real.

"It can only teach you things the master brain has recorded," he says, teeth still bloody. "It sends the signal to your brain hundreds of times a minute. I've been sparring with it for the past few days, but I hadn't tried it with its pair until now."

"So you used me as your *guinea pig*?" I snap. "Thanks a lot."

He laughs, and I want to deck him. I am absolutely livid. That *thing* was burrowing into my brain, which is the definition of invasive.

"You could have warned me!" I cry. "I had no idea what was going to happen."

"I did," says Jonah. "Well, not *everything* that was going to happen . . ."

"I could have really hurt you!"

"No, you couldn't have."

"Why not? You were basically sparring with yourself."

He shrugs. "Basically."

"That's a little narcissistic, don't you think?"

Jonah chuckles, and I find the sound simultaneously infectious and infuriating. The throbbing in my temples has morphed into a splitting headache, and the pain seems to be stoking my anger.

I cross my arms over my chest. "You couldn't defend that last move, though."

"That move can't be defended," he says matter-of-factly. "No one ever sees it coming."

I roll my eyes. "God, you *are* full of yourself."

"Hey, it worked," he says, crossing over from indulgent to annoyed. "In three minutes you learned to execute moves I couldn't teach you in three weeks. A little gratitude would be nice."

"*Gratitude*?" I snarl, not caring that I'm dancing on the edge of insubordination. "Are you fucking kidding me?"

"Watch yourself, Jones . . ."

But I am past the point of no return. I point at the device on the ground, which is still glowing in an otherworldly sort of way. "That *thing* hacked my brain!" I screech. "It got inside my head and made me do things that I . . ."

"That you'd otherwise be incapable of?" Jonah finishes.

I shake my head. He is the worst. I'm glad that I busted his lip.

But Jonah's expression is growing stormy. "Listen," he growls, clearly done with his version of Mr. Nice Guy. "I don't have *time* to deal with your feelings. I have five privates to train, and you are by far the most behind. If you want to learn — if you want to survive here — this *thing* is the answer. If you can't or *won't* work with me, I will personally escort you to the captain to request a discharge. Is that understood?"

I just stare at him, stewing in my own tangled mess of emotions.

I want to tell Jonah to go fuck himself. I want to waltz out of that gym, slam the door behind me, and then storm back in and yell at him some more. I want to slap him and screw him — all at the same time — but you don't mouth off to your sergeant and expect to keep your position.

Taking a deep breath, I school my expression and temper the tone of my voice. "Yes, sir," I growl. "Whatever you say."

24

JONAH

After my training session with Maggie, my head is all messed up. I dismiss her for dinner and head back to my pod to shower. My mind is working overtime thinking about Maverick's creepy simulated learning devices, but it's Maggie that keeps invading my thoughts.

She took to the technology better than I could have hoped, though I'm still not sure that will be enough. It depends how well her brain retains those encoded sequences and builds on what she's already learned.

I grab my hygiene kit from my room and go straight to the latrine. I can't stop thinking about the way she moved.

I don't know what it is about her . . . It was hot. I can't figure her out, which is probably why I find her alluring.

I turn the shower on and step into the hot stream, and suddenly it's as if she's right there with me. She's standing across from me with her guard up, looking as though she'd fight a fucking bear. She's got those springy blond curls falling into her eyes — so much ferocity in such a feminine package.

I don't know if it's the way she moves or the way she smells

. . . All I know is that I've never been enlisted with someone like her.

A surge of heat starts in my chest and travels all the way down to my toes. I feel like a creep for some of the thoughts that flash through my mind: Maggie working out in just a sports bra and a tiny pair of shorts. Maggie on her back, those infuriating curls freed from their bun and splayed out behind her. Maggie naked, pressed up against the shower wall while I —

I shake my head to shut out the images bombarding my brain. The hot water isn't helping, so I switch the tap to cold.

The shower turns icy, and the full-body shiver that rolls through me is enough to dampen my dirty thoughts. I stick my face under the frigid stream and watch the blood from our sparring session wash down the drain in a trail of pink.

Something happened when I put that SPIDER thing on Maggie. I shared a little of myself with her. As we sparred, I could practically see my own thoughts lighting up her neural pathways, tripping her wires and moving her body in a way that I had designed.

Suddenly I'm hit with another storm of filthy thoughts. I plant my feet right under the cold stream of water until my brain is completely frozen.

I step out of the shower and wrap a towel around my waist, but those fierce blue-green eyes are back in my brain. It's like she's standing there mocking me in those big nerdy glasses . . .

Wait. Glasses? Maggie doesn't wear glasses . . .

My brain seizes with the effort of recalling a half-forgotten memory: the girl who came to my room to claim her lost cargo. She was blond with glasses and those same striking eyes.

I stop dead in my tracks. *That's* why she looked so goddamned familiar. I'd seen Maggie Jones before.

Walking back to my room fully clothed, I try to remember

what day she came to my room. It had to have been one of the first days of Reception, but it doesn't make any sense.

"Heyya, sarge!"

I jump at the intrusion and turn slowly on the spot.

"Not now, Ping," I grumble. I can feel my realization slipping away from me, along with the trail of memories I was using to piece it all together.

"Whoa . . . You all right?"

"Fine," I say. I am *not* in the mood.

"You don't look fine."

I slip away from Ping's probing gaze and try to get back to my room.

"What happened?" he asks, jogging along behind me.

That's when I realize he's referring to my busted lip.

"Nothing," I lie. "Just a little sparring session."

"Sweet!" says Ping. "Maggie do that to you?"

At the mention of Maggie, I feel all my walls come up. I'm ashamed by the thoughts that flashed through my mind, but there's something about her presence here that just doesn't feel right.

"You eaten dinner yet, boss?" asks Ping, still brandishing his fists in a mock boxing stance.

"Not yet," I mutter, instantly realizing my mistake.

"Great!" says Ping. "The rest of the privates went without me. No reason two criminally handsome guys like us should eat our dinner alone."

I don't have the heart to tell him no. At least he'll take my mind off *her*.

"Why didn't you eat with the rest of the squad?" I ask.

"I thought I'd get some yoga in before I ate. Gotta stay spry for the ladies."

I press my lips together to hold back a laugh. What *is* it with this kid?

"But the class was cancelled, so . . . here I am."

"Can I ask you something?" I say in a low voice. I know I'm going to regret bringing Ping into the fold, but I don't know anyone else I can ask.

"Anything, sarge."

I hesitate. Ping's a little *too* eager to hear what I have to say, but I have a feeling he'll keep his mouth shut. "This stays between you and me. Understand?"

"Of course."

I take a deep breath. "You notice anything strange about Private Jones?"

"Maggie?"

"Yeah."

Ping's eyebrows shoot up, and he's overcome with a look I know only too well — a look that makes me instantly want to deck him.

"I know she is *fine*." He chuckles. "Is that what you mean?"

"No," I growl, giving him a sharp look. "I mean . . . Have you noticed anything *off* about her? Anything suspicious?"

Ping shakes his head. "Nah. She seems cool."

"Yeah, I know she *seems* cool," I say. "But have you noticed anything that's different about her compared to the others? Does she ever talk about what she did before this? Maybe an old job or her family?"

"Nah. I don't think so. I'll tell you one thing, though . . . She is smokin' hot. She's got this sexy librarian vibe . . ."

I want to smack him upside the head. I don't know why I'm having such a visceral response to Ping's pervy comments, but it's making me think I don't know my own mind.

Luckily, we reach the dining hall before I have a chance to delve too deep into those thoughts. Dinner is a crusty spoonful of mac and cheese and a few soggy chicken tenders, but after my training session with Maggie, I'm hungry enough to eat anything.

A few officers are gathered around one of the long tables near the back, but Ping and I take a seat at an empty table on the other side of the dining hall. I'd rather eat with Ping than Whitehead and Jameson any day.

Bots are roaming between the rows, running a long squeegee down the center of a table to sweep off the crumbs. Ping is absolutely beside himself when we sit down across from each other, and I get a pang of guilt that I haven't been nicer to the kid.

He dashes off to the condiment bar and returns with a bottle of hot sauce. At first I think he's going to use it on his chicken tenders, but then he upends the bottle over his mac and cheese.

"You put that stuff on macaroni?"

"You should try it. It's *amazing*."

"Pass," I say, poking at the stiff lump of noodles with the edge of my fork.

Suddenly, I hear someone hush the loud table full of officers. I turn around. Jameson is standing on his chair, trying to adjust the volume on one of the enormous screens mounted to the wall.

The voice of the reporter gets louder and louder, and then all of the screens in the cafeteria switch to show the forty-something guy standing on a city street. Fires are blazing all around him, and I can see people running and screaming in the background.

Ping stops talking mid-sentence and turns to look at the nearest screen.

The situation here is very frightening. People are fleeing Millennium Park, where there are reports of attacks coming from a group of armed security bots. We don't have any information yet on who might be behind these attacks, but we do know that these are bots made by BlumBot International, a subsidiary of Maverick Enterprises.

The screen switches to a news anchor in the studio — heavily made up and wearing a grave expression. *Thank you, Mike. We do have footage of the first few minutes of this attack, which we are about to show you. Viewer discretion is advised. This footage is disturbing.*

The screen flips to some security-cam footage of Millennium Park in Chicago, where three bots are plowing through the park with their stunners blazing.

I've interacted with these types of bots. The army uses them for bomb disposal, and they were patrolling the airport the last time I flew out of JFK.

They aren't like the bots milling around the cafeteria. They don't have friendly silicone faces designed to look like people or carry squeegees for light cleaning.

These bots have the same humanoid bone structure but none of the bells and whistles. Each of their faces is a clockwork maze of metal, and they're outfitted in solid black armor that's supposed to be bulletproof. They come from the factory equipped with stun guns, but I've heard they can be programmed to shoot rifles, too.

In the video, people are fleeing the scene in terror. The screen switches to another camera, where a seven-foot bot is blazing down the street. It picks up a park bench and hurls it at a moving car. A man engages with a bot whose stunner has been disabled, and the bot tosses him aside like a flimsy rag doll.

The footage ends, and the screen flashes back to the newsroom. The screen is split between the anchor and her guest, apparently some sort of robotics expert. She's questioning him about BlumBot's technology and what it would take to hijack one of the bots. The anchor tells the camera that they have reached out to the manufacturer for comment but haven't received a response.

"Holy shit," says Ping, staring at the screen in disbelief. They're replaying the footage from Millennium Park, where bots are plowing through a crowd of tourists as though they're people made of paper.

"Yeah."

Just then, my Optix dings. I hear a dull echo of dings from all around the room and realize that everyone at the officers' table must have received the same message.

It's a summons from Captain Callaghan. He wants us to report to the training center for an emergency security briefing.

"Gotta go," I say to Ping, picking up my tray.

"What? Where are you going?"

"Emergency briefing . . . officers only."

"Shit," says Ping. "You think it's about this?"

"I have no idea."

"You think it's Russia?"

"How should I know?"

If I'm being honest, it looks and smells a lot like the Bureau for Chaos. Only a few groups have the capability to hack Blum-Bot's system, and it certainly fits their MO. The story the government feeds to the media is that the Bureau is no longer active, but they've just been biding their time.

What's more disturbing is that someone was able to hack the bots at all. BlumBot has always bragged that their security is second to none. They're supposed to be practically incorruptible. But if I learned anything in the special forces, it's that nothing is truly hack-proof.

I glance over at the bots that were wiping down the tables. They seem to have frozen right where they stood. One is bent over the table with its arm locked in position. The other is standing like a store mannequin, staring straight ahead.

By the time I reach the training center, half the officers are already there. Everyone is talking in low anxious voices, and everyone is wondering the exact same thing: Where did the attack come from, and how did they manage to hack the bots?

The higher-ups at Maverick Enterprises have to be shitting bricks. They spent months spouting off to the press about how progressive they are, and now their robotics company is at the forefront of the scandal. Someone is going to take the heat for the attacks, and it's gonna be someone in the colony.

Callaghan rolls in a few minutes later. His face is haggard and serious, and he looks as though he's been putting out fires since the early hours of the morning.

The other officers fall silent as he steps up to the front of the crowd. Everyone edges a little closer to tighten their ranks, and I straighten my back and stand at attention.

"As you were," says Callaghan, his voice low and exhausted. He takes a breath. "I'm sure you've all heard the terrible news . . . I just got off a call with Homeland Security and the FBI. They don't know much more than what's being reported. All we know for sure is that there's been at least one casualty and a dozen people seriously injured. So far six bots have been implicated in the attack — all of them products of BlumBot International."

He pauses for a beat, and a long horrible silence fans out across the room.

"No word yet on where the attack originated, but the FBI suspects Russian involvement. It is highly likely that it came from a Russian cell of the Bureau for Chaos, but we may never know for sure."

He pauses again and looks around. "What I need from each and every one of you is your help and cooperation in securing Elderon. We have temporarily suspended bot service colony-wide as an added precaution until the authorities can identify the malware used and all of our bots have been thoroughly screened. Keep in mind that whoever ordered the bots to carry out this attack has ways of bypassing the technology's defenses. Any suspicious activity should be reported to me *immediately*." He frowns. "We should expect an official visit from Homeland Security, the FBI, and the Department of Defense. All I can say is to be ready for anything. I'll be in touch as soon as I know more."

The captain doesn't thank us or say anything to indicate he's finished speaking. He just turns and exits the training center, and the entire room erupts in chatter.

Everyone is in a panic, and not just about the attack. It didn't even cross my mind that the hackers could target the bots aboard Elderon, but at this point, anything is possible.

Well, that's just fucking great.

We're stuck inside a metal donut floating out in space. We're surrounded by an army of bots, but we don't know if they've been compromised. We have no idea where the attack originated or where the hackers might strike next.

All we know is that these bots can kill, and we are sitting ducks.

25

MAGGIE

I'm sitting outside the frozen yogurt shop in the mall when the news comes on. My sad little bodega meal is staring me in the face: a soggy sandwich, a cup of yogurt, and a very bruised banana.

They shut down the dining-hall serving line at six. I have no idea why. I got there just a few minutes after and had to scrounge a meal from the market. I'm camped out at a table in front of the fro-yo place, watching a live broadcast from Earth.

The screen is playing the broadcast on silent, and I'm reading a ticker along the bottom. Suddenly, I see a burst of flames behind the reporter, and a clump of egg salad falls out of my sandwich.

I touch my Optix to activate the sound, and the reporter's voice starts to play in my ears.

Witnesses say a group of security bots manufactured by BlumBot International plowed through Millennium Park around eleven thirty this morning. One eyewitness says that the bots were functioning normally when one turned and charged at him from the other side of

*the park. Security footage shows the bots firing their Tasers, throwing
benches into parked cars, and attacking pedestrians.*

*The rampage left one person dead and twelve seriously injured.
The Chicago Police Department has issued a statement. The department says that the incident is most likely the result of a cyberattack,
though they are still investigating to determine who is responsible.*

The screen changes to security-cam footage of a team of bots
firing their stunners into a crowd. My heart is pounding in my
throat, and I turn off the sound on my Optix.

Eleven thirty central time . . . That's four thirty our time,
which means the attacks happened less than two hours ago. I
can't believe this. Those bots were made by the same robotics
company that Maverick Enterprises just bought, and now the
executives are cozily sequestered up in space.

Something doesn't smell right.

Just then, a bot passes by my table. It's got two unnaturally
blue eyes bugging out of its silicone flesh mask, and it's
pushing a sweeper across the bottom level of the mall with a
barely audible hum.

I watch it go with a feeling of intense dislike and toss my
banana peel in its path.

I'm not sure what I was expecting. The bot doesn't slip and
fall like a cartoon character. Instead, the peel gets sucked up
into its sweeper, and the motor groans as it struggles to
digest it.

"Traitor," I growl.

Then, all of a sudden, the bot shuts off. It freezes in place in
the middle of the mall, and the sweeper continues to hum.

I freeze. Surely I didn't just stop the bot with the psychic
power of my hatred. Someone else must have had a bad feeling
about being trapped up in space with several hundred
machines programmed for destruction.

I have an itch to do some digging, and I know Alex isn't going to be happy.

Sucking down the rest of my yogurt, I toss the remnants of my meal into the trash and head for my suite. I need to change out of my fatigues.

Checking to make sure the coast is clear, I scan myself into my suite. The place has a musty closed-up smell to it, and everything is exactly how I left it. I change into jeans and an old comfy sweater, let my hair down, and put on my glasses. I grab my bag and head for the newsroom, taking the back way to avoid running into any of the privates who might be congregating in the mall.

By the time I reach the newsroom, the place is buzzing with activity. There's an incessant orchestra of Optix dings in the background. Keyboards are clacking at a frantic pace, and every screen in the room is tuned to Chicago.

In the conference room, I see a face that seems vaguely familiar. She's not a journalist or anyone from Maverick, but I recognize her just the same.

The woman is tall and slim with shoulder-length black hair and serious eyebrows. Her cheekbones are plump like two ripe apples, and she has an angular feminine chin.

But the most notable thing about her is her prosthetic legs. They look oddly masculine and mechanical under her tight pencil skirt, but she's dressed them up with a pair of show-stopping black pumps.

That's when I realize how I know her. She's Ziva Blum — former CEO of BlumBot International and head of robotics at Maverick Enterprises.

As soon as I place her, my brain populates with a surprising amount of information. Her father is Benjamin Blum, founder of the legendary robotics company. Ziva designed her own prosthetic legs after a car accident in her early twenties, and when she patented her design for use on bots, she gave her father's creations the most lifelike gait the world had ever seen.

This innovation added jet fuel to Benjamin Blum's already meteoric success, prompting him to leave the company to her when he died in the late 2060s. Since then, Ziva has earned a place in *Fortune's* 40 Under 40 list and graced the cover of every tech and business magazine in the country.

Right now, she's running through her statement while someone touches up her makeup. The rest of Ziva's people are pacing nervously outside the conference room.

Judging from the backdrop, Ziva is getting ready for a live interview, and the makeup girl is working overtime to blot up her sweat. It's understandable. If I had to go on air an hour after my robots went on a rampage, I'd be nervous, too.

Alex is too busy prepping for Ziva's interview to give me any orders, so I jet over to my desk and call up the one person who might be able to give me more than I could get from anywhere else: an old college friend who writes for *The Tribune*.

Michael doesn't answer the first time I ping him. If it were me, I'd be pounding the pavement interviewing witnesses and then trying to get ahold of someone from the FBI. They're the ones most likely to have the scoop on where the attack originated, and that little bit of information is the missing piece of the puzzle.

Then I get an idea. I may not know who's responsible for the attack, but I do know who's responsible for the bots. I'm looking right at her.

Pivoting my chair to the right, I zoom in on Ziva and send a photo to Michael's Optix. Two seconds later, I'm getting a call.

"What's a girl gotta do to get your attention?" I ask as Michael's face appears in front of mine. He has round wire glasses, pale skin, and a mop of unruly black hair. Right now, he looks exhausted, but I can detect a glimmer of excitement in those sharp analytical eyes.

"Is that Ziva Blum?" he asks, clearly taken aback.

"Yep. I'm sitting about forty feet away from her on Elderon."

"No shit? I didn't know you were up there."

"Maybe you would if you called more."

"Sorry, Mom."

"It's all right," I say. "What have you got so far?"

Michael sighs. "Same as you — a whole lot of nothing."

"Come on," I say in a coaxing voice. Michael and I might be friends, but we're still competitors. I can tell he's holding out on me. "What's going on down there?"

"Absolute fucking chaos. My editor wants to tread lightly on this. No one wants to be the first to call it an act of cyberter-rorism, but that's what it's looking like."

"Russia? Bureau for Chaos?"

Michael rolls his eyes. "Your guess is as good as mine. The method looks like this came from a Russia hacker . . . The tin-foil-hat brigade is saying that it's a cell of the Bureau that we never managed to quash, but it could be a copycat organization or a state-funded hacker."

"What's the FBI saying?"

"Not much. I don't think they've got it figured out yet, but this definitely fits the Bureau's MO. Public space. Middle of the day. Seemingly random. Lots of destruction. What's weird is the low body count. The Bureau for Chaos is a terror group, and whoever pulled this off had to know the bots only had stunning capabilities. The guy who died had a heart condition."

"You got a name yet?"

"Norman Panabaker?" he says, glancing down at his notes. "Sixty-five. He and his wife were in town visiting family."

"Shit," I say, jotting down the name. "P-A-N-A-B-A-K-E-R?"

"Yep."

"Anything else?"

Michael shakes his head. "I'll tell you one thing, though . . . The space-development initiative is about to come under a lot of scrutiny."

"Why's that?"

"Isn't the whole point to spy on Russia and keep stuff like this from happening?"

"We're not a military installation," I say, feeling defensive about Elderon for reasons I don't understand.

Michael gives me one of his signature cut-the-bullshit sort of looks. "You sure about that?"

I don't say a word. I don't have to. Michael isn't stupid. In fact, his gut is usually right.

"I don't know . . ." he says. "Russian robotics aren't that good. Even if they could hack the bots, I don't think they'd have the capabilities to reprogram one of BlumBot's. They'd have to be pretty well-versed in the technology."

I turn that little bit of information over in my head. "You think the Bureau for Chaos has someone on the inside?"

He shrugs. "They might."

I know that look. Michael's terrible at acting nonchalant. If I had to guess, he's digging into Ziva Blum's background as we speak, trying to figure out if she or anyone in her company has ties to the Bureau for Chaos.

"Well, thanks for that," I say. "Keep me posted, will you? I am trapped on a space station with over a hundred of those things."

"*Creepy.*"

"You're telling me."

"Are the bots there acting normal?"

I hesitate. Michael's a good reporter. Give him an inch, and he'll take a mile. Then again, he did give *me* something. I owe him one.

"This is on background," I say quietly. "I don't want my name tied to this in any way."

"Fine."

"They shut the bots down after the story broke."

"No shit?"

I nod. "They're just domestic worker bots, but they all just stopped whatever they were doing."

"Wow," he says. "I guess they realize they've lost control of their technology."

I glance over at Ziva Blum, who's gearing up to go on air. "We'll see."

Michael must have picked up on my change in tone, because he perks up right away. "Maggie . . . What do you know?"

I quirk an eyebrow. "You might want to turn on the news . . . I have a feeling that this is going to be streaming to every major network."

26

MAGGIE

When Ziva goes live, I get up and crowd around the conference room with the others. She's being inter-viewed by Isabelle Larsson, the beautiful Swedish woman who's one of our senior correspondents.

Isabelle is dressed in a smart periwinkle pantsuit that perfectly matches her icy Nordic complexion. Her white-blond hair is pulled back into a sleek ponytail, and she's wearing buff lipstick that makes her look as though she just stumbled off the runway.

Ziva, on the other hand, has let her curly locks run wild. She's wearing pink lipstick and a tangerine blouse, which makes me think she hasn't done this before.

If she had, her PR people would have dressed her in blue and done everything in their power to downplay her looks. Every politician, spokesperson, and media expert knows that blue is the color of trust.

There's no one else in the room besides the cameraman. When the recording light goes on above the conference-room door, Isabelle sits up and gives the camera her most piercing stare.

"Good afternoon. I'm live with Ziva Blum, former CEO of BlumBot International and head of robotics at Maverick Enterprises. Earlier today, a group of six security bots stationed in Chicago attacked a crowd of tourists at Millennium Park. Ms. Blum, your company designed and manufactured those bots. Is that correct?"

Ziva sits up a little straighter in her chair. I can tell that she's nervous but determined to get ahead of this. "Yes, that's correct."

"And it's my understanding that hundreds of these security bots have been stationed all over the country for almost three years. Have any of them ever malfunctioned before?"

"Absolutely not. We have never had any issues with our artificial lifeforms, and these bots in Chicago did not malfunction." Ziva takes a deep breath. "This is not some manufacturing defect, Ms. Larsson. These bots were hacked, and we should be treating this event as an act of cyberterrorism."

Isabelle lets that little statement land and then arranges her face in a look of polite astonishment. "Strong words, Ms. Blum. Tell me . . . Does your company have any information as to who might have tampered with your bots?"

"Not yet," says Ziva. "We are investigating the hack as we speak, and we will be working around the clock until the matter is resolved. My bots are the most secure artificial lifeforms in the world. Only someone with advanced knowledge of the technology could possibly have tampered with them."

"That brings me to my next question," says Isabelle, practically shivering with delight that Ziva gave her such a smooth opening. "There are critics in the industry who doubt your company's ability to conduct an impartial investigation into these alleged hacks. In fact, Lloyd Evans at RoboWorld issued this statement. Take a look: 'We are horrified and saddened by the attacks in Chicago. As responsible stewards of technology, we are appalled by Maverick's negligence. The people at Robo-World have always been strong advocates for the proliferation of bots, but we should all be treating the BlumBot breach as what it is: a threat to humanity as we know it.'"

Isabelle pauses to let that sink in, and I can practically see the fire smoldering behind Ziva's careful expression.

"Those are some pretty inflammatory remarks," says Isabelle. "What is your response to these accusations?"

At those words, Ziva bristles. "My company's security is state of the art. We are not, nor have we ever been, *negligent* with our technology. Lloyd Evans is a fearmonger and frankly should be ashamed for using this tragedy to bolster his company's brand."

"You keep saying your security is second to none," says Isabelle. "If that is the case, could we be looking at an inside job?"

Now I can see that Ziva is truly ruffled. This suggestion seems to offend her to the core. "I would trust my employees with my life. I can assure you that no one from my company was involved. However, I am conducting my own internal investigation, and I am certain that the FBI, the NSA, and the Department of Homeland Security will corroborate my findings."

"So, just to clarify, your company is cooperating with the authorities."

"One hundred percent," says Ziva. "There is no one who wants to get to the bottom of this more than I do."

Isabelle allows herself a thoughtful pause, and her tone changes from hard-lined to sympathetic. "This must be incredibly difficult for you, especially with the attacks coming so close to the anniversary of your father's death." She takes a deep breath. "How do you think he would have responded to this, if he were alive?"

Ziva's mouth stretches into a hard half smile. "My father would have handled this just as he handled everything else: thoroughly, thoughtfully, and methodically — which is how I intend to handle it."

"Mmm." Isabelle's eyes crinkle in a way that's almost human. "Have you spoken to your brother since the attacks?"

"Mordecai and I are in constant communication. He's keeping me updated on our security team's findings."

"And what advice do you have for people who currently have your products integrated into their workforce?" asks Isabelle. "Are your bots still safe to use?"

"As an added precaution, we are asking all administrators to shut down their security bots temporarily . . . just until we can identify the source of the attacks and release a patch to prevent any additional breaches."

Isabelle asks Ziva something else, but I never hear what it is. The newsroom is buzzing with anxious chatter.

I turn over my shoulder to see what all the ruckus is about and see the rest of the press corps gathered around the giant screens.

It's footage from Chicago, but it wasn't captured at Millennium Park. The caption at the top says the video is from Wrigley Field, where it is absolute pandemonium.

People are running out of the stadium, trampling and climbing over each other to escape. The screen changes to a clip from the concourse, where bots are mowing down fans near the concession stand with military precision.

I glance up at the other screens, which show Ziva sitting frozen in her chair. Her eyes flicker to a screen on the left, and I know she's seeing the chaos unfold.

Her dark eyes grow wide, and her face is filled with horror.

Alex is dancing outside the conference room, signaling Isabelle to go to a break, and I see her shift gears to wrap up the segment.

Everyone's eyes are glued to Wrigley Field — everyone's except for mine. I'm watching Ziva, whose face is a portrait of utter devastation. Her mouth is hardened into a thin line, but her eyes are shining with tears.

27

JONAH

It's the middle of the night when I get the message. Callaghan is summoning all officers for another emergency briefing.

It's oh one hundred, but I'm not asleep. No one is.

When I shut myself in my room an hour ago, my entire squad was still gathered in the lounge, their eyes glued to the giant screen. It had been switching back and forth between all the major news networks, playing footage of the cascading bot attacks in Chicago, DC, New York, and LA.

After the Millennium Park rampage, a team of bots handling crowd control at Wrigley Field attacked a group of fans during warmups. The next day in Washington, DC, a labor-movement rally turned deadly when the bots containing the demonstration turned against the peaceful protestors.

Almost simultaneously, a team of bots went berserk in Times Square, and later that evening, they hit the premiere of the *Terminator* reboot at the Dolby Theatre in Hollywood.

Apparently, Maverick had sent out a notice to all of Blum-Bot's customers to do an emergency shutdown on their bots, but several cities and private companies did not heed their warning. I've been watching and re-watching all the footage from my Optix, and it's disturbing to say the least.

The worst attack so far was the Times Square rampage. These bots weren't programed like the ones in Millennium Park. Instead of mowing down bystanders and throwing benches and trash cans, these bots moved like humans trained to kill.

The hackers had tampered with the bots' factory Tasers, resulting in the deaths of nearly three dozen people.

Times Square is one of the most heavily surveilled places in the country, which means that there were hundreds — maybe thousands — of cameras positioned in every direction. Half a million people pass through the square every day, many of them tourists recording on their Optixes.

Seconds after the attack, hundreds of people uploaded videos for the world to comb through and analyze. I've disappeared down a rabbit hole filled with home movies turned deadly.

I keep replaying a clip shot outside a movie theater in the square. It shows a team of three police officers in riot gear attempting to subdue one of the bots.

The thing is moving like no robot I've ever seen. It executes a flawless spinning back kick that catches one officer in the jaw and knocks him out cold. The other officers open fire on the bot, but the bullets don't penetrate the bot's rock-solid armor.

I'm so absorbed that I lose track of time. When a notification pops up reminding me about the briefing, I jump out of bed and sprint to the training center.

I get there just before Callaghan arrives and take my place among the ranks. There's a ripple of blue as he enters the room, and all the officers snap to attention.

"As you were," says Callaghan, his voice hoarse and weak.

He's got heavy lines under his eyes, and his face is a sickly pale gray. If I had to guess, he's been awake all night, and he probably didn't sleep the night before.

"As most of you already know, Maverick Enterprises has ordered an emergency shutdown of all commissioned security bots. The Department of Homeland Security, the FBI, and the NSA are each launching their own separate investigations, and we are expecting representatives from all of these organizations to arrive the day after tomorrow at nineteen hundred hours. They will be questioning employees at every level in this station, and I expect your full cooperation."

"Sir," says a lieutenant from the front. "Any word yet on who orchestrated the attacks?"

Callaghan frowns. "At this moment, we are operating under the assumption that all the attacks were carried out by a single entity. The FBI suspects the hackers are of Russian descent, but the Kremlin is denying any involvement in the attacks. Of course, this has the Bureau for Chaos written all over it — not ruling out a Russian cell — but my sources tell me that these bots are too sophisticated to have been compromised by anyone but a robotics expert." He takes a deep breath. "We can assume that the NSA knows more than they're telling us, but for now, I want all of our resources directed toward uncovering whatever we can about these attacks."

"Sir?" says Lieutenant Buford.

"Yes . . . Buford."

"What is Maverick Enterprises saying?"

"They are saying what companies always say when their technology is compromised . . . They were devastated to learn about the attacks, and they are working around the clock to gather information and resolve the bots' vulnerabilities. As to whether the other bots are compromised, they cannot say." Callaghan raises his voice. "Which is why I have ordered *all bots* within the colony to be shut down until this mess is resolved."

There's a great swell of muttering, but Callaghan silences it all with a glare.

"Unfortunately, this means that the bots will not be performing routine maintenance that was scheduled to begin at oh two hundred. This puts us in a dangerous position. If we cannot monitor the exterior health of the station, we cannot repair any existing damage. This is why I want everyone focused on getting to the bottom of this so that we can resume normal operations."

"Sir?" says the first lieutenant who spoke. "Who's going to be completing the maintenance and repairs that the bots would normally perform?"

"Until the bots are back to work, we are on critical repairs only. There is a finite number of crew members who are trained to execute such repairs. However, in the event of the bots being disabled, that responsibility falls on the Space Force. I want any non-surveillance personnel fully EVA-ready as soon as possible. Until then, keep your eyes and ears open. I'll have new personnel orders out to all of you for your unit by eighteen hundred hours tomorrow."

He pauses and looks around, as if to make sure there are no more questions. "That is all."

Callaghan leaves, and the room erupts in an explosion of noise. Everyone is talking about the decommissioned bots. Without them, the colony can barely function, and postponing repairs on the exterior of the station leaves us all vulnerable.

I don't stick around to speculate what the attackers have up their sleeves. I head back to my pod and lock myself in my room. Queuing up my video feed, I lie back and lose myself in the videos of the attacks.

I've seen so much footage that I've become desensitized to it. The initial shock has worn off, and the destruction is starting to seem mundane. I've watched the same bot attack from multiple angles, but not once have I seen anyone who looks suspicious. There's no visible human controlling them from half a block away — no warning that the attack is about to commence.

One minute, the bots are patrolling Times Square as usual, their heads moving on a swivel to detect suspicious activity. The next, they're charging unsuspecting tourists and electrocuting them with their Tasers.

According to BlumBot's website, the bots are designed to parse footage and facial recognition from up to a hundred different sources at once. They screen a crowd for unusual activity: a pedestrian looking around nervously, the shape of a pistol tucked under a coat. Known criminals are identified from the National Crime Information Center database, and the bots are supposed to ping a human operator before moving in on a target.

In the case of the attacks, the bots were reprogrammed to attack autonomously. They used their "eyes" to read facial expressions and identify encroaching police officers. The technology allowed them to react to law enforcement with almost psychic precision.

I switch to a new video of a cop fighting a bot one on one. It's brutal. The bot seems to anticipate the cop's every move. He doesn't stand a chance.

Eventually, the officer succeeds in luring the bot off to the side. The video commentary says that the officers planned to deploy a concussive grenade to try to disrupt the bots' signal.

But a second later, the bot turns violent, and another officer jumps in to assist the first. One cop gets a kick to the sternum that sends him flying through a window. The other cop starts to back away, and the bot steps in with a three-sixty elbow that knocks him out cold.

My mouth falls open.

I know that move. It's the same exact elbow Maggie used on me — the one I showed her with the SPIDER.

Suddenly, I can't breathe. I can't even think.

I rewind the footage and play it again in slow motion, watching the bot's torso pivot as it drives an elbow into the cop's face. The bot executes the move perfectly and hits the officer dead on.

I see the light leave the cop's eyes, and a second later, his legs give out from under him. He hits the ground hard, and his head bounces off the concrete.

I shake my head. It can't be.

Anyone could have given the bot that move, I reason. I don't even remember where I learned it. But as I replay the entire sequence, I start to see things I never noticed before.

Everything about the bot's style is familiar, from the way it sets up its combos to the exact sequence of strikes that have worked for me again and again.

But this isn't a fair fight. These aren't human opponents of flesh and bone. These are robots designed to be rock hard and durable — unmatched in size or strength by any human alive.

Each fist and every elbow is a deadly weapon in motion.

My head is spinning. I think back to the last week's sparring sessions, running through all the combos I used when I was wearing the SPIDER. I ran through all my favorites. I didn't *need* anything new or fancy because they were guys I'd never sparred before.

I recorded my movements against five different opponents — five sergeants willing to go a few rounds in the gym. But I only shared those recorded neural pathways with one other person — the person who showed up on my doorstep before basic training.

I'M POSSESSED by rage as I storm across the pod to Maggie's room. My mind is racing with paranoia. I *knew* something was off about her, but I let it go. I was thinking with my dick instead of my brain, and it might have contributed to the deaths of dozens of people.

I pound on Maggie's door with my fist. At first, no one answers, but then the door slides open.

Adra appears, still in her sleep clothes. She's confused — and not very happy to see me.

"Where is she?" I growl, ready to kick down the door if Adra tries to cover for her.

"Who?"

"Jones. Who else?"

Confusion, suspicion, and anxiety flash through Adra's eyes, but I can't tell if she's nervous because she's covering for her room-mate or because she knows she's in trouble. "S-she isn't there."

Somehow I know she's telling the truth, but I throw the door open anyway. I storm inside, looking for Maggie, even though it's obvious that there's no one there.

"*Where — is — she?*" I growl.

"I-I don't know," Adra stammers.

But something isn't right. I know Maggie Jones isn't who she says she is. Now I just need proof.

"Which drawers are hers?"

Adra gives me a blank stare.

"Which — drawers?" I yell.

"Th-the bottom ones," Adra stammers.

I bend down and yank the bottom drawers open. There's nothing inside but sports bras and socks and plain Space Force–issue underwear.

It's a little fucked up — a male sergeant going through his female subordinate's underwear drawer — but I know the girl is up to something.

I can't get in her locker. Adra doesn't know the combination. But I cross over to her bunk and pull back the blankets to search between the sheets. I upend the mattress and run my hand along the lower springs, searching for evidence that doesn't exist.

My entire body is thrumming with rage. The fact that there's nothing here for me to find just reinforces my suspicions.

There's not a soldier alive — much less a civilian — who goes into space without any personal items. There are no photos, no makeup, and no civilian clothes. She's not a robot herself, so who the hell is she?

Ignoring the horrified look plastered across Adra's face, I storm out of their room and pound on Ping's door. It takes a moment for him to answer, but he looks wide awake and ready for action.

"What's up, sarge?" he asks, not at all put off by the late hour of my visit.

"I need you to find someone," I say in a rush, pushing past him into his room.

"Okaaay," says Ping, clearly wondering where this is going.

Davis is asleep in the top bunk, snoring like a chainsaw and dead to the world.

"Who, sir?"

"I need you to find Maggie."

"Sir?" Ping gives me a look as though he fears for my sanity. "Did you check her bunk?"

"Yeah . . . That's not what I meant." I take a deep breath. I have to tell Ping what's going on. "I need you to find her — the *real* her — online."

"Oh!" says Ping, looking relieved. "That's easy." He taps his Optix and runs a search. "All you have to do is go to the Elderon personnel database and —"

"I don't need you to find her personnel profile . . . I need you to find *her*."

Ping stops his search and gives me a blank look. "I'm not sure I'm following, sarge."

"I need you to find Maggie on the web . . . under whatever name she might be using. I need to know who she really is."

It seems to take a moment for this to sink in. Ping is staring at me as though he can't quite wrap his head around what I'm asking, but then his eyebrows shoot up, and his eyes grow wide. "Oh. Oh, wow. You don't think . . ."

I nod.

Ping's face falls, and he turns his attention to his Optix. I see him highlight Maggie's photo, and he mutters a command I can't quite hear.

His eyes flicker back and forth across the screen as he runs a search, and several windows pop up in front of him. Ping scans the images quickly, and then his face goes slack.

"Oh . . . Wow."

"What?"

He shakes his head. "You aren't gonna believe this, sarge."

"What did you find?"

Ping's feed disappears, and for the first time since I've known him, he actually looks upset.

"Are you sure you want to know?"

"Yes!"

"Because this isn't information you can ever un-know. Ya know?"

I roll my eyes. "What is it, Ping?"

"Maggie —" He breaks off, looking caught between his guilt over ratting her out and his sense of duty to me.

"Spill!" I say. "Whatever it is, she doesn't deserve your protection."

"It's just that Maggie . . ." He makes a face that tells me he's conflicted. "She isn't who she says she is."

My chest constricts, and it's hard to breathe. He just confirmed my worst fears. If my theory is correct, I just handed over all of my best moves to hackers bent on destruction. "Who is she?"

Ping touches his Optix and beams me a copy of his feed. I get a notification, and my Optix instantly populates with everything Ping found.

"Her real name *is* Maggie," he says. "But she's not an intelligence worker. She's a reporter for the *New York Daily Journal.*"

Maggie's smiling face jumps out at me from a photograph. In the picture, she's wearing glasses, and her hair is down in a low ponytail.

"Magnolia Barnes?"

"Here she goes by the name Layla Jones."

He scrolls down to another picture, and it pops up in the center of my screen. In this one, her hair is down. Wild blond curls fill the frame. She's beautiful, friendly — definitely the girl who came to my room.

"Listen to this," says Ping excitedly. "Layla Jones has been reporting on life on Elderon, but . . ."

"But *what*?" I groan. I'm desperate for information — greedy for it. And yet part of me doesn't want to know.

"There's no Layla Jones on the flight plan," says Ping, scanning a long list of names on Maverick Enterprises' letterhead. "There *is* a Magnolia Barnes. She's registered to the press corps." He looks at me. "Sarge . . . She's here in the colony."

28

MAGGIE

It's so late by the time I leave the newsroom that I wander back to my old suite by mistake.

I almost cry when I realize where I am. The corridor is illuminated only by the dim glow of emergency lighting, and it's too dark to see more than a few yards in front of me.

I'm too exhausted to walk all the way back to the barracks. I could almost fall asleep right here, but I know it's risky staying out all night. Adra will wonder where I am, and I don't think I'll be able to sell some other lame excuse.

Leaning against the wall, I close my eyes and tell myself that I only need to lie down for a few minutes. But I know that as soon as I sink into my comfy space bed and turn out the light, there's no way in hell I'm getting up for hours.

I let out a groan and force myself into an upright position. I just need to put on my fatigues and get back to the barracks. Then I can sleep as long as I want. Well, at least until I'm summoned for a briefing to find out what's going on.

But just before I reach my door, a low male voice echoes down the hallway behind me. "What are you doing here?"

Suddenly I'm wide awake. I know that voice. It's Jonah's, but there is absolutely no reason for Jonah to be here.

I turn slowly on the spot, my tired brain fumbling for a good excuse. Jonah is glaring at me with such animosity that I know he's discovered something he shouldn't have.

"Are you . . ." My voice comes out like a parched death choke. "Are you *spying* on me?"

It's too dark to see Jonah's expression. His shadow moves as he takes a step toward me, and suddenly I feel threatened and exposed.

"Interesting choice of words."

My heart is hammering against my chest. I can't quite manage a full breath, and I have the immediate impulse to run.

If Jonah is outside my suite, this can't be good news.

"What are *you* doing here?" I ask, fighting to keep my voice steady.

"Checking up on a lead."

I swallow, but I can't seem to wet my parched throat. All of my saliva is gone.

"I heard training was cancelled. I couldn't sleep . . . so I came down here to visit with a friend."

"Save it, Maggie. I know everything."

I freeze. Jonah is bluffing. There's no way in hell he knows. He couldn't — not unless he's drastically expanded his social circle.

When I don't respond, Jonah takes another half step toward me, and I start to wonder if there's another reason he'd be following me down a darkened hallway.

I didn't get a creepy stalker vibe from him during our training session, but my gut has been wrong before.

"Good night, sir," I say pointedly. "I'll see you tomorrow for the briefing."

I am done entertaining his creepiness. I turn to go and get a surge of horror when I feel his hand close around my wrist. I yank it back, but he holds on tight, pulling me around to face him.

He scans my face with his Optix, and I see the reverse image of my photo pop up. It's the weird mugshot from my fake ID, and I let out a slow breath of relief.

"Hmm," he says, his jaw tightening into a scowl. "That's funny . . ." He pulls up another two files on his Optix — the photo from my press credentials and my *Topfold* profile pic. "This person looks awfully similar to Maggie Barnes and Layla Jones."

I watch his face, which seems to have turned to stone. He releases my arm roughly, his eyes cold and unforgiving.

I take a deep breath, trying to summon some explanation that makes sense. I'm not sure which is worse — some made-up scenario or the truth — but either way, I don't think he'll believe me.

Jonah opens his mouth to speak. His voice is low and hoarse. "What you did . . . What you're doing . . . put *thousands* of people at risk."

I tear my eyes away. My breaths are coming sharp and fast, and my throat is burning with tears.

I don't know how that could possibly be true, but it still fills me with shame.

"The exercise we did the other day . . . those combinations that I shared with you . . ." Jonah drags in a ragged breath. "You are the *only* person I shared those with." A muscle in his jaw pops. His fists are clenched down at his sides. "The next thing I know . . . I see those same combinations being played out by hacked bots in Times Square."

A surge of horror rips through me, leaving a trail of heat in its wake. My brain is spinning. I don't know how that could possibly have happened, but if what Jonah is saying is true . . .

"That spinning elbow that you used on me?" He grits his teeth and sucks in an angry burst of air through his nose. "A bot knocked a cop out cold with that one. I don't know if he's even still alive."

That heat in my chest is expanding rapidly, choking me from the inside out. I keep breathing, but I can't seem to fill my lungs. A cop might be dead because of me, but I don't even know how it happened.

Jonah squeezes his eyes shut, waves of frustration pouring off him. "I had a bad feeling about you . . . My gut kept telling me that something was off, and I should have listened."

I stare down at my feet, willing myself not to cry.

"That one's on me, but this . . ." Jonah shudders. "That's on you."

"Jonah." I shake my head. "I didn't . . . I didn't share that data with anyone."

"Why should I believe you?" he yells.

I feel my shoulders folding in — trying to make me as small as possible — but I force myself to look him in the eye. "I wouldn't even know how."

He lets out a cold breath of laughter. I can only see his eyes. He's staring at a spot on the ceiling, as though he's so disgusted he can't even look at me. "Now that I've got you, you might as well come clean. Tell me, Maggie . . . Are you a spy or just a *liar*?"

That question knocks the wind out of me. Deep, boiling shame is seeping into my gut — poisoning me from the inside out.

I don't know why this is hitting me so hard. Somehow Jonah's anger makes the role I've been playing feel like a betrayal, but I know I only feel this way because I got caught.

"I'm a journalist," I murmur. "I was just doing my job."

"Doing your *job*?"

"I had a hunch," I say quickly.

"What hunch?" he growls.

"About the Space Force."

As soon as I start talking, it all pours out in a rush. "Maverick Enterprises couldn't stop bragging about the fact that they had built the first civilian space colony. But almost twenty percent of the personnel on board work for a private military group. Don't you think that's strange?"

Jonah doesn't say a word, so I keep on rolling.

"A third of the nonstructural budget for Elderon is dedicated to Space Force spending. Why would Maverick shell out that kind of money unless they *knew* they needed the manpower?"

"Where are you getting this information?"

I take a deep breath. Once I tell him, I can't take it back. Who knows what the consequences will be — for me or for Tripp. "Tripp Van de Graaf."

"He *told* you that?"

I shrug. "In a manner of speaking."

"Jesus," he hisses, turning away and kneading his temples. "Is there anyone you won't manipulate to get a story?"

That hurts more than I'd like to admit.

"You do realize that posing as a soldier and stealing all this information puts the entire colony at risk?"

"Oh, come on!" I cry. "The colony was built by Maverick Enterprises. The security is state of the art!"

"And you haven't sent this information to anyone on Earth?" he growls. "Not even your editor at that disgusting rag you write for?"

"No!" I say, feeling strangely insulted on behalf of my inferior alter ego. "Have you *watched* any of my stories at *Topfold*?

Because a story like this would never fly. I was brought here to create fluffy little videos to make space seem fun — not unravel a conspiracy that we're building a civilian army!"

"So you never transmitted any of your findings to Earth?"

"No."

He shakes his head. "I wish I could believe you, but right now I don't believe a word that comes out of your mouth!"

"Look," I say, horrified and furious that he's trying to pin this on me. "Nobody else knew about this. I mean, I did tell my editor, Alex Brennan, but she didn't even want me to do the story. All she cares about is getting to the bottom of these attacks."

Jonah takes a deep breath. I can tell from his expression that I'm dead to him, but he seems just as eager as I am to find out what the hell is going on. "What do you know?"

"Not much. I know Maverick received some threats."

"Threats from whom?"

"All the usual suspects. I talked to my friend at *The Tribune* after the first attack in Chicago. He says it looks like Russia or the Bureau for Chaos but that they wouldn't have the capabilities to reprogram the bots."

"What does that mean?"

"The technology is so refined that only someone with a working knowledge of BlumBot's technology would have been able to pull that off."

Jonah rolls his eyes. "I'm guessing you have a theory . . ."

"I have a couple."

"Care to share?"

I take a deep breath. "Either Russia is trying to put an end to US space development by bankrupting Maverick Enterprises, or the bot attacks came from the Bureau to remind the world that they're still at large. Or . . ."

"*Or?*"

"Or maybe the attacks were just a distraction."

"A distraction from what?"

"Something bigger. I don't know . . . While everyone is focused on the bots . . ."

"They're hacking the Pentagon."

"Or the treasury or a bullet train."

For a moment, it seems as though Jonah and I are on the same team. I can see his wheels turning and know that at least one of my theories is probably sound.

But then his expression changes, and it's as though he just remembered that he has to turn me in.

"You may not be a spy," he says. "But I still don't trust you. You put the entire colony at risk. Hell, you put the whole *world* at risk. And for what? A fucking story?"

I don't say a word. I don't know how the data could possibly have been transmitted from the SPIDER down to Earth, and I don't believe I had anything to do with it. But Jonah doesn't seem convinced.

"I didn't do this," I say. "I know you don't trust me, and I don't blame you. But please . . . Just give me a chance to get to the bottom of this."

"Why the hell would I do that?"

"Because I'm on your side."

He shakes his head, and a look I don't quite understand replaces his anger. "I don't believe you."

His voice is no longer trembling with fury. It's resigned, almost regretful. It's the voice of someone who's been betrayed, and I suddenly hate myself for lying.

"I think we should be looking at BlumBot," I say quickly. "The hackers have someone on the inside. It's the *only* way they could have stolen that SPIDER data and tampered with the bots."

Jonah just stares at me. With the shadows playing across his face, I can't tell exactly what he's thinking. But when he speaks, his voice cuts me straight to the core.

"There is no 'we,' Maggie. You need to turn yourself in to the captain, or I will."

29

MAGGIE

The feeling of having let Jonah down is even worse than the prospect of talking to the captain. I don't know why, but the look on his face when he learned what I had done made me feel worse than I have in a very long time.

And it's not *just* Jonah. Coming clean to the captain means that I'll be ousted from the Space Force. Alex will find out that my cover was blown, and I'll be on Layla Jones duty for the rest of my life.

That's the best-case scenario. Worst case, I'll be sent back to Earth and forced to forfeit my signing bonus, most of which I already sent to my parents. I'll miss the chance to report on the story of a lifetime and return to New York with no job, no money, and no decent bylines.

Because none of this can possibly get any worse, I head to the microgravity chamber in the middle of the colony before I'm fired, shunned, and deported.

The chamber is an enormous orb that spans all six wings of the colony. It has windows that wrap around the entire sphere, and, because the inner chamber acts as Elderon's immobile axis, it allows one to experience the effects of microgravity.

I leave my bag in one of the lockers outside. No loose items are allowed in the chamber.

I walk along the rotating catwalk in the outer tunnel, which shoots me into a side tunnel leading to the core of Elderon.

I feel my feet leave the ground, and immediately I'm floating in the dimly lit inner chamber listening to soothing New Age music. The low lights are all swirling in different colors, and I get the feeling that whoever designed this place did it to create a serene atmosphere for relaxation and meditation.

I could definitely use some of *that* in my life.

Somehow, I managed to take the opportunity of a lifetime and fuck it all up. Not only did I screw up the press corps job — I might have fucked my whole career.

I take a deep breath and try to give in to the relaxing float, but my mind is still reeling from Jonah's accusations.

What happened with the bots can't *really* be my fault. To start with, I never asked Jonah to share his motor memory with me. I didn't know what was happening until afterward, and I have no idea how the data from my SPIDER could possibly have fallen into the hands of hackers on Earth.

I don't know exactly how the technology works, but I'm sure Maverick encrypts all of its data and stores it in some super-secure server.

It does seem strange that both the bots and the SPIDER are BlumBot creations. If anything, it seems that the person responsible for the hacks has to be imbedded in the company.

Suddenly I see another floater coming up on my right. I twist my body just in time to avoid colliding with him, and when I turn back around to see who it was, I nearly groan aloud.

The man has a cloud of dark curly hair, the body of a pro soccer player, and a face that's undeniably handsome.

It's Tripp. He's wearing a pair of relaxed-fit jeans and a plain white T-shirt. He pivots at the torso when he sees me, and a wicked grin spreads across his face.

"You should watch where you're going," I call.

"My apologies," he says, still flashing that winning smile. "Well, well . . . Magnolia Barnes. What are you doing here so early?"

"Couldn't sleep."

Tripp lounges back and stretches his arms over his head so that his shirt rides up. I can see two rows of perfectly cut abs. "I could have helped you with that."

I roll my eyes. "Yeah, I'm sure."

"You know, a lesser man might be hurt and offended that you just stopped answering your messages . . . He might have assumed that you never wanted to hear from him again."

"A lesser man might take the hint," I say, thinking back to all the messages from Tripp that I'd studiously ignored.

It wasn't that I was purposely avoiding Tripp. I just couldn't risk being seen out with him and blowing my cover in the Space Force. As the CXO of Maverick Enterprises, Tripp doesn't exactly blend in.

"I'm sorry," I add. "I haven't been ignoring you on purpose."

Tripp's grin falters, but his eyes continue to twinkle. "I hope not."

"I've just been busy . . . with work."

"You know what they say about all work and no play," says Tripp. "I take it your story is panning out?"

"No. Not really."

"No?" Tripp looks vaguely surprised. "I would have

thought it would be an easy slam dunk. I pretty much gave you an all-access pass."

I stare at him for several seconds, and suddenly it hits me. He knows.

Tripp knows that I've been digging into the Space Force, because he sent me the documents and the uniform. It makes sense. Tripp of all people has the access. It would have been easy for him to get me into the Space Force under an assumed name.

"Thank you for that, by the way."

Tripp quirks an eyebrow, as though he's not quite sure what I'm alluding to. "Uh . . . You're welcome?" He shakes his head. "You've got some cojones, Ms. Barnes — I'll give you that."

I frown. I think his words are supposed to be a compliment, but his tone is less than flattering.

"Sorry I didn't say anything before," I mumble. "I honestly had no idea it was you."

Now Tripp looks really confused. "Wow."

"What?"

He lets out a dry, humorless chuckle. "Hey, this is nothing new. I've had plenty of company information stolen before. But I don't think anyone's ever *thanked* me for it."

"Thanked you for what?"

Tripp frowns. "Porter told me you were taking stills of the documents I had out on my desk. I assumed that you were writing some kind of story about me or my company."

I shake my head. Is *that* what he meant when he said I had an all-access pass? Is *that* what he thought I was thanking him for?

"*What*? No. I wasn't . . . I mean, yes, that was me. I did take pictures of the Elderon budget, but . . . There's nothing else that you've done for me lately?"

He waggles his eyebrows. "Is there something you'd *like* me to do for you?"

"Ew, no. That's not what I meant. I mean, there's nothing else you've done that might have helped me with my story?"

"I don't think so . . ." says Tripp, clearly confused. "I mean, I was the one who insisted that we hire you, but other than that . . ."

My stomach turns, and I get an unexpected kick of guilt. I'd almost forgotten that Tripp was the one who brought me to Natalie's attention. If it weren't for him, I wouldn't even be here. So far I've done a pretty poor job of repaying him.

"Unless you want to thank me for my persistence." He chuckles. "I have to say . . . I don't think I've ever actively pursued a girl who was using me to ruin my company."

"I'm not!" I say quickly. "I mean, I *am* working on a story, but I wasn't using you. And I don't have a vendetta against your company."

My brain is too busy putting the pieces together to feel the appropriate amount of shame. The truth is I *did* use Tripp to gain information, but there will be plenty of time to stew in my guilt when I'm on a shuttle back to Earth.

"Wait," I say. "So you *haven't* sent any mysterious packages to my suite lately?"

"No . . ."

I shake my head. It doesn't make sense. Who else could have had that kind of access?

"And Porter *knew* that I was taking shots of all those documents?"

"Trust me," says Tripp. "There's nothing that happens in our office that Porter doesn't know about."

I don't know what bothers me more: the fact that I didn't notice I'd been caught or the fact that Porter tattled on me to his boss.

"He didn't confront me about it," I say.

Tripp shrugs. "That's not really his style."

"But you knew I'd done it."

"Yeah. Porter's bad at keeping secrets when something's bothering him. He knew that I liked you, and he was trying to protect me."

There it is — that kick of guilt I've been avoiding. I really have been shitty to Tripp. He has all the trappings of a conceited pretty boy, but he's been nothing but nice to me.

He knew I'd stolen information from his office, but he didn't turn me in. He *let me* do it — even when he knew it could blow back on his company — and he continued to send me messages.

He doesn't deserve the way I've treated him, and I don't deserve Tripp. I need to cut him loose before this goes any further.

"Tripp, I —"

"Maggie, before you try to break up with me, remember that we've never gone on an actual date."

I open my mouth to speak, but no words come out.

"In fact," says Tripp, cracking that familiar roguish grin. "You did promise me a date, and you've never made good on that deal."

In that instant, it all clicks into place. I'm too shocked to respond, though I know I owe Tripp an apology.

Tripp has no idea what favor I was referring to. And if he's trying to get me on a date, why wouldn't he take credit for it? The only logical explanation is that Tripp doesn't know anything about the fake Space Force credentials. He doesn't know anything because he didn't send them.

But there was someone else who knew I was snooping — someone else with high-level access who might have the connections to get me a fake ID. I don't know how — I don't know why — but somehow I know that Porter is involved.

30

MAGGIE

My dramatic exit from the microgravity chamber is somewhat hampered by the fact that I have to half swim, half drift out of the area.

I leave Tripp even more confused than he was before and make a mental note to repay him for being such a good sport. I can't take back my shitty behavior, but I can do better in the future. Maybe I'll let him take me on that date.

I scan my face to unlock my locker and pull out my over-stuffed messenger bag. I dump the contents onto the table and rifle through the pile.

The messages and the package all came to me less than twenty-four hours after my initial conversation with Alex. She was the only other person who knew I was digging into Maverick to find out more about the Space Force, but she had no reason to conceal her identity if she had been my mysterious source.

Somebody must have been eavesdropping.

Tripp had no idea what I was talking about, which only leaves Porter. Porter knew that I was digging into the budget.

He knew I was a journalist. He must have thought that I was going to use the information against his company, so he decided to do some digging of his own.

He had to have found a way to listen in on my conversation with Alex, and I'd bet money it has to do with my bag. He took it from me when I went into Tripp's office, and he only brought it back after catching me taking pictures. He must have bugged me.

I pull out my coffee-stained notebook and inspect each one of my pens. There's nothing in my makeup bag or in the pockets of my sweater. I turn my bag inside out, combing the interior. I run my hand along the strap, and then . . . jackpot.

It's almost impossible to tell, but one of the rivets isn't like the others. Three out of the four holding the strap in place are scratched brass rivets designed to look vintage. The fourth is silver and looks almost brand new.

If I could bust this thing open with a hammer, I'd bet money it would reveal a tiny listening device registered to Maverick Enterprises.

Furious, I stuff all my notes and pens back into my bag and head straight for Maverick headquarters. Porter *must* have heard me tell Alex my hunch. Either he's working for the hackers and wanted to see how much I knew, or he's just a nosy little shit.

I burst through the spotless glass doors leading to Maverick HQ, resisting the urge to kick one of the decorative orange poufs clean across the lounge. It's barely oh six hundred, and there are only a few people milling around.

"Can I help you?"

I turn. The voice is high pitched, timid, and squeaky. Porter is nowhere in sight. I'm being flagged down by a disturbingly hip Korean girl with long silky black hair. She's wearing neon-yellow cropped pants, dizzying heels, and oversized orange specs that make her look like a cartoon.

"Porter around?" I huff, feeling extremely out of place.

"Do you have an appointment?" The girl is bending over backwards to keep her voice polite, but it still prompts an involuntary eye roll from me.

"I need an appointment for Tripp's *assistant*? Are you fucking kidding me?"

Orange Specs Girl blinks several times very fast. "I-if you'd like, I can leave him a message or —"

"Sure," I say, the electricity in my voice crackling in the air. I wouldn't be surprised if my mad-scientist curls were standing on end. "Why don't you tell him that I found his little listening device. Did you know that it's *illegal* to bug someone without their consent?"

Orange Specs Girl just stares.

"Did you know that I'm a reporter? How do you think it would make Maverick Enterprises look if I published a story about its long history of illegally wiretapping journalists and then using that information to blackmail them? Is that how you manage to kill the stories your bosses find unflattering?"

The whole thing is a bit of a stretch, but judging by the look on Orange Specs Girl's face, she isn't about to call my bluff.

"J-just a second," she says, practically falling out of her enormous heels as she staggers down the hall.

I sigh. It feels good to yell at somebody — even if that somebody isn't the appropriate target for my fury.

Two minutes later, Orange Specs Girl reappears with a very agitated Porter in tow. He's wearing nautical blue high-water pants, a white sweater, boat shoes, and the sort of preppy man scarf that makes me want to strangle him.

"You summoned?" he says, his voice barely a hiss.

"Yes," I say, bending down to wrestle the little rivet out of my bag. "I think this belongs to you."

His face turns, if possible, even paler. "I-I don't know what you mean."

"Oh, you don't?"

Now he looks nervous. "Shall we adjourn to my, er . . . desk?"

"No!" I cry. I'm not stupid. On the off chance that he is working for the Russians or the Bureau for Chaos, I'm not giving him the chance to get me alone. I want to know what the fuck is going on.

Porter glances around the room. Orange Specs Girl is still staring at us as though she might lose her job, but apart from her, we're alone.

He waves his hand in a kingly "leave us" gesture, and Orange Specs Girl scoots away. Porter must be head bitch around here.

I hold up the listening device. "Care to explain?"

The shrug that Porter fakes is so clearly a lie that I'm actually insulted. Does this kid think I was born yesterday? I know the little shit bugged me, and I know he's lying to my face.

"So you're saying that if I took this to an independent lab and had them dissect it, it *wouldn't* be registered to Maverick Enterprises?"

Porter opens his mouth and then closes it again.

"Yeah, I thought so," I spit. "*Explain* yourself."

"All right! All right! But . . . can we not do this here?"

I look around. I understand his desire not to be overheard, but I'm not about to let him lure me down some dark murder-y hallway.

"Fine," I growl. "Tripp's office. Now."

Porter marches back to the executive suites, and I make him leave the walls of Tripp's office unfrosted.

"Spill," I say as soon as we're behind closed doors.

Porter looks cagey. Beads of sweat are springing up all over his forehead, and he keeps wiping his palms on his designer capris.

He's not exactly spy material.

"Why — have you — been eavesdropping on me?"

Porter doesn't say a word.

"Are you working for the hackers?" I ask. "Was I getting too close?"

"No! No! Of course not." Porter takes a deep breath. "I saw you taking photographs of Mr. Van de Graaf's private documents, and I got suspicious. All right? It's not the first time we've had problems with leaks . . . I thought you might be spying for the competition or writing some trashy exposé."

Porter takes a deep breath. "Mr. Van de Graaf obviously liked you. I couldn't have him falling in love and then getting his heart broken when you turned out to be some evil skanky spy."

Evil? Skanky? I'm not sure which descriptor I find more offensive. "Why does *everyone* think I'm a spy?"

Porter takes a deep breath. "Anyway . . . I bugged you. I figured that whatever you were up to, I had to find out for sure. And Mr. Van de Graaf was too blinded by his infatuation to be objective. He's *always* had that problem. You think you're the first girl to try to get close to him for money or information?"

I recoil from the kick of guilt that rolls through me. At the time, I hadn't thought that I was *using* Tripp, but it certainly seems that way now.

"Any-hoo . . . I heard you talking to your editor." He glances away, and I know there are some things that he *hasn't* shared with Tripp. "For the record, I also thought it was odd that Maverick Enterprises brought up so many military personnel."

Aha! I feel strangely vindicated.

"So why didn't you just ask Tripp about it?"

"Because Mr. Van de Graaf doesn't know everything," says Porter, lowering his voice as though the mere statement is treason. "I'm sure you've heard about the growing chasm between Strom loyalists and those who have embraced the younger Mr. Van de Graaf."

I give him a blank look.

Porter rolls his eyes, as though he's annoyed by my naiveté. "Obviously, most people expect that the elder Mr. Van de Graaf will hand over the reins to his son when the time comes. But the construction of the colony has created some friction between them. The elder Mr. Van de Graaf has made a lot of decisions that the younger Mr. Van de Graaf doesn't agree with. But it's still his company, so . . ."

"Are you saying that sending a thousand Space Force personnel up to Elderon was Strom's idea?"

"It must have been." Porter shakes his head. "Apparently, Maverick received a few threats after it announced the colony. We were never able to prove where they'd come from, but they had the Bureau for Chaos written all over them. I don't think the younger Mr. Van de Graaf even *knew* about the threats. He doesn't concern himself with things like that. He was focused on designing a world-class space station. He has always been a visionary, which is why he has people to help him hammer out the details."

"And you are one of those people."

Porter dips his head in a display of fake modesty. "Mr. Van de Graaf pays me to know things so that he doesn't have to."

"So when you heard about my theory, you went and found Amelia McDermit."

He gives a reluctant nod.

"*You* sent me her personnel file and the fake ID."

Porter doesn't answer. He just swallows a few times, sweat beading up on his brow.

"How did you do it?" I ask. "Whoever sent me that ID *must* have hacked into the Space Force personnel database. That had to take some serious skills."

A muscle near Porter's left eye twitches, and I know it's killing him not to take credit.

"I work for the largest tech company in the world," he mutters. "I know a guy."

"Does Tripp know that you use his employees to hack into military databases and make tweaks when it suits you?"

"I am Mr. Van de Graaf's right-hand man," says Porter. "I am also the unofficial head of our internal security. It's my job."

"It's your job to spy on Maverick employees and journalists?"

"Spying is such a loaded term."

"I wonder what Tripp would call it if he found out you checked into all of his potential girlfriends and weeded out the ones you didn't like."

"It's not like that."

"Really? 'Cause that's sure what it sounds like."

Porter is clearly enamored with Tripp. There seems to be no end to the things he would do for his boss.

"Anyone Mr. Van de Graaf is connected to represents a potential threat to this company!" Porter snaps. "It's my job to make sure those liabilities are identified before they become a problem."

I hold back a satisfied grin. I knew Porter was on the verge of unraveling. The kid is putty in my hands.

"Too bad you didn't see the bot hack coming."

That, it seems, was the worst sort of insult I could have hurled at Porter. His face turns beet red, and he looks as though he wants to deck me.

"No one — and I mean *no one* — could have seen that coming," he says in a low angry voice.

I raise an eyebrow. Porter might be a sneaky little bastard, but it's looking less and less likely that he had anything to do with the bot hacks. His whole world is protecting Tripp. He wouldn't do anything to jeopardize Tripp's company.

"I can think of one person who saw it coming," I say. "Whoever stole the data from Jonah Wyatt's SPIDER and used it to reprogram the bots in New York. You know anything about that?"

Porter shakes his head, but I can tell he's holding back.

"Porter . . ."

"I don't!"

"Yes, you do!" I cry. "And if you don't come clean, eventually this is gonna blow back on the Space Force *and* Maverick Enterprises."

"No, really," says Porter. "If I knew who was responsible, I'd be promoted so fast my head would spin."

"What aren't you telling me?"

Porter glances toward the door behind me, as though he's planning his escape. "If I tell you, will you let the whole bugging thing go?" he asks. "Mr. Van de Graaf can't ever know . . ."

"I can't make any guarantees."

"Well, then I can't help you."

"Fine," I groan. "I won't tell Tripp. So what is it?"

Porter's expression turns deadly serious. "Magnolia Barnes, this information does *not* leave this room."

"Yeah, I got it."

"It's one hundred percent off the record."

"All right!"

Porter takes a deep breath. "We're not just looking for one person who's responsible."

I wait for him to elaborate, but Porter is sure taking his sweet-ass time.

"Hacking the bots is one thing, but stealing Sergeant Wyatt's neural data is a whole other ball of wax. That is *much* more alarming."

"More alarming than hacking a bunch of seven-foot-tall bulletproof bots?"

"Yes." Porter lowers his voice to barely above a whisper. "BlumBot's security is second to none — as close to unhackable as it gets. That's one of the reasons Mr. Van de Graaf wanted to acquire the company. We've even used some of their techniques to strengthen other entities under our umbrella."

"Including the Space Force?"

"Including the Space Force."

I turn that over in my head for a moment. "But if there was a double agent inside BlumBot . . . couldn't he or she have hacked the Space Force?"

"It doesn't work like that," says Porter. "The Space Force data is kept siloed on private servers that only high-ranking officers can access. Only someone inside the organization could have compromised its data."

"So what are you saying?"

Porter raises his eyebrows so high that they are in danger of disappearing into his hairline. "We're not just looking for one double agent," he whispers. "This was a coordinated effort between the Space Force and BlumBot International."

BY THE TIME I leave Tripp's office, I feel as though my brain is on the verge of a total meltdown.

I knew whatever Porter had to say was going to be juicy, but

I had no idea just *how* juicy. I recorded the entire conversation on my Optix, but suddenly I'm wondering if I should have.

Maverick Enterprises *invented* that technology. If someone on the inside is dirty, who knows what else they have access to?

One thing's for sure: I have to tell Jonah what I know. This piece of information won't change what he thinks of me, but I still want to tell him. I haven't known Jonah that long, but I feel as though I can trust him.

Jonah was shattered when he thought I might be working as a spy. You can't fake that kind of a letdown.

I also know that I can't hold on to this information. Sooner or later, someone outside the Space Force is going to figure out that I've been skating by on a fake identity. And if that someone is working for the hackers, it won't take them long to figure out why a journalist was posing as a member of the Space Force.

I don't have enough information to put all the pieces together, but that might not stop the double agent from thinking I'm too dangerous to keep around.

I'm so distracted by my conversation with Porter that I take a wrong turn on the way to the barracks. I went the back way to avoid running into Tripp. As terrible as I feel about blowing him off, I don't think I can stomach lying to him about what I know.

I turn down another hallway to zigzag over to Sector Q, but when I round the corner, a searing pain shoots through my scalp.

Someone has me by the hair.

I stumble back onto my heels and try to scream bloody murder, but my attacker jams something soft in my mouth.

I suck in a burst of air on instinct and inhale something sickly sweet. I gag, trying to expel whatever I just breathed in, but already my brain is swimming in fog.

I stumble. My limbs feel extremely heavy, and darkness is pressing in along the edges of my vision.

I have the fleeting thought that Porter will say something to Tripp before unconsciousness overtakes me and I float into the black abyss.

31

MAGGIE

When I come to, I'm lying on the cold hard ground. My body is bent at an awkward angle, and my head is resting on my right shoulder.

I straighten my torso and try to push myself into an upright position, but my hands are bound together.

I groan and try to move to my feet, but my ankles are bound, too. There's something wet and cottony in my mouth.

When I realize that I've been bound and gagged, my misery morphs into rapid panic. I'm lying in a dark room on cold black tile. I'm shivering so violently that my whole body aches, and I don't remember how I got here.

I try taking deep breaths to steady myself, but the gag just pulls tighter at the corners of my mouth. I can feel the saliva pooling in the back of my throat, and I have a fleeting worry that I might drown in my own spit.

Instead of succumbing to my fear, I look around and try to pick out some details that might tell me where I am. I don't recognize my surroundings. The walls are stark and untreated.

There's some heavy equipment that I don't recognize and

what look like odd geometric scaffoldings that span outward rather than up. At the moment they're collapsed like dried-up dead spiders, but I have a feeling they're used for exterior maintenance on the space station.

I can't see more than a few yards in any direction. The only light is emanating from a keypad to my right and a single emergency-exit sign. The keypad is positioned in front of an airlock. I can tell from the reflective tape stuck all around the door.

Scaffoldings, airlock . . . I must be in a staging zone for the maintenance bots.

Sure enough, when I twist my body around, I can just make out the outline of a dozen or so bots standing like statues along the wall behind me. They aren't made up to look like humans. Their bodies are mazes of metal fragments, and their eyes are empty sockets.

I have no idea how long I've been here — only that the place is deserted. The maintenance scheduled for oh two hundred was cancelled in light of the bot attacks. Who knows how long it will be before anyone wanders in.

The person who brought me here must have some high-level clearance. Otherwise he never would have been able to bypass security. Whoever it is must have wanted to keep me quiet — or at least keep me from telling Jonah.

Tilting my head onto my shoulder, I try to wake my Optix to see if I can get a ping out. Nothing happens. I try to activate it by command. Still nothing.

I groan around my gag. The bastard must have stolen my Optix so that I couldn't make contact.

I'm starting to panic in earnest. My heart is thumping so hard that I can hear the blood thumping in my temples, and it seems to require an enormous effort to breathe. I'm covered head to toe with goosebumps, and the numbness spreading through my extremities only adds to my distress.

That's when it hits me that no one knows where I am. I never returned to the barracks last night, I ran away from Tripp without so much as "goodbye," and Jonah probably thinks I'm preparing to turn myself in. Porter was the last person to see me alive, but he'd probably prefer never to see me again.

Forcing down a sudden kick of despair, I cast around for something I can use to saw through my zip ties. None of the scaffoldings have any sharp edges, and neither do the bots. I know there have to be tools nearby. I just need to find them before my captor returns.

Lying back on the cold ground, I plant my feet and push myself across the floor. I slide easily across the slick black tile, though I have no idea if I'm headed in the right direction.

I'm about halfway across the room when a low male voice crackles through the darkness.

"Don't bother. There's nowhere here for you to run."

I freeze, my heart performing a series of wild gymnastics as I cast around for the source of the voice. It's too dark to see much of anything, but the voice couldn't have been more than twenty feet away.

"Magnolia Barnes, New Jersey native, floundering young reporter . . ."

A sudden jolt of irritation manages to crowd out a little of my fear. I am not *floundering*, and I resent whoever's making that assessment.

"Usually writes under the pseudonym Layla Jones — the pretty little girl next door."

My blood is boiling. The stranger's voice isn't getting any louder, which means he's hiding somewhere in the shadows.

Coward. He isn't man enough to come say this crap to my face.

"Barnes, Barnes, Barnes . . ." he muses, as though my name

is a lyric that's escaping him. "Now that is a familiar name. Though, fortunately for you, also a very common one."

At those words, every muscle in my body tightens.

"Your father was a journalist, too — was he not? I'm rather surprised you use his name at all . . . I'm sure it must make finding work more difficult, being the daughter of a lunatic who went after one of the most powerful men in the country . . ."

I make an involuntary noise of protest, straining at my zip ties until the plastic cuts into my skin. If my hands were free, I'd choke the bastard.

"I remember reading about your father in *The Journal*," he muses. "Years ago. A one-hit wonder who wanted more. So he wrote another book, and the whole world found out what he was — a hack . . . a *fraud*."

I squirm and thrash against my restraints. I'm going to kill him.

"What's it like being the daughter of such a spectacular embarrassment?" he asks. "Is that why you're so *desperate* for a story? Why you won't mind your own goddamned business?"

I stop moving. This is exactly what he wants — to get me so worked up that I exhaust myself struggling. I need to conserve my strength and find a way to get the hell out of here.

"It must have made it that much worse when you realized that you would always be a failure, too. You'd never be able to atone for his mistakes."

I grit my teeth so hard that I think my molars might crack. He's baiting me. That's it.

Nobody knows what happened with my dad's second book — least of all me. My mother refuses to talk about it, but it's the book that pushed Dad over the edge.

He swears up and down that his reporting was accurate. To

TARAH BENNER

this day he insists that the politician paid to cover up his crimes.

I believe he thinks that. My dad isn't a liar, though paranoia can be a symptom of his disorder. I've spent my entire adult life convincing myself that he's not crazy, but it doesn't really matter to anyone but me.

"You're a journalist, Maggie," says the man. "It would be so easy for you to learn the truth. Why haven't you done it after all these years? You could have cleared your father's name."

I try to swallow, but the gag is making it impossible. I can hardly breathe.

"Instead you decided to go poking into places where you do not belong. If you'd just minded your own business, you wouldn't be here right now. You could have kept writing Layla Jones pieces for the rest of your life. Who knows? Maybe you could have become a *real* journalist."

I stop struggling and try to control my rapid breathing. He's getting around to why he captured me in the first place. Maybe I'll finally learn who this psycho is.

"But you had to go digging, didn't you? Just like Sergeant Wyatt."

I freeze.

"He has turned out to be *much* more trouble than he's worth. I'm the one who recruited him, you know. I saw the work he did while he was deployed. I knew I needed someone with his lethality to program the bots, so I had his old captain bring him in for the job."

My mind is racing. This guy has been watching us very closely. He must know that Jonah figured out that his data had been stolen. That means Jonah is in danger, too.

"I anticipated that Wyatt might cause a scene if he ever put two and two together. Well, it doesn't matter. He was discharged from the army for a personality disorder . . . I

286

figured he would be easy to discredit. But then he developed an interest in you, and I discovered that you were also pretending to be someone you were not."

He sighs. "I'd hoped I wouldn't have to kill you. It would have been so much easier just to send you back to Earth — a traitor without a platform to do any real damage. But then you had to go talk to that little rat, Porter, and I knew you'd learned too much."

At those words, my muscles seize. My lungs are burning from working so hard, and I feel as though my heart might beat its way out of my chest.

I'm going to die. He's going to kill me, and no one will ever know why.

"Now you won't just be a traitor . . . You'll be the one responsible for killing all those innocent people. Who's to say it wasn't you who stole all that motor-memory data? You infiltrated the Space Force, earned Sergeant Wyatt's trust, stole his SPIDER data to use on the bots, and then killed yourself. Clean and simple."

My heart is pounding. My lungs are burning. The window for me to escape is closing fast.

I look around. I can just barely make out a faint glimmer of white light fanning out from under the door. That must be the exit that connects this area to the rest of the colony. If I could only reach the door, I might have a chance to escape.

But my frantic train of thought is interrupted by the soft clunk of footsteps to my right. I turn.

It's still too dark to see his face, but I recognize the man's plain black boots. They're Space Force standard issue, and they're attached to a body in uniform.

I squint. He's got patches that say he's some kind of officer, but in my panicked haze, I can't remember what the insignias mean.

The top half of his face is hidden in shadow, but there's something about him that's vaguely familiar.

The next thing I know, his hands are on my ankles. I feel a sudden release of pressure as he cuts the zip ties holding them together.

A shiver of excitement shoots up my spine. I can move my legs. I'm only a few yards from the door. This might be my only chance.

The man hauls me to my feet, half marching, half dragging me across the room.

He can't be relocating me for any good reason. He's taking me somewhere to kill me.

I fake a stumble, and I feel the man's grip on my arm loosen. I yank it away in one rough motion and make a break for the door.

I propel myself forward as fast as my legs will carry me. It's awkward running with my hands bound in front of me, but I just head straight for the door. Deafening footsteps thunder behind me, and I know before it's over that I'm not going to make it.

The man seizes me roughly by the hair, and I choke on my gag as a few curls separate from my scalp. He gives my hair a violent tug, and I fall backward into his chest.

I struggle to right myself and squirm out of his grip, but he shoves me forward, and I hit the ground. I cry as my nose smacks into the tile, but I can't even hear myself scream.

A sudden burst of agony starfishes out from my ribcage — a boot. The bastard *kicked* me!

I moan in pain, and he kicks me again. This time, I feel a burst of heat somewhere in my kidney. It rolls out in a tidal wave of pain, and I have to fight the urge to throw up.

I can't move. I can't breathe. I can only fight through my hot angry tears of pain.

I recoil at the feeling of hands on my shoulders, but he tugs at my skin and flips me over. I groan. My eyes are still flooded with tears, but I blink them back. Lieutenant Buford swims into view.

His face is sweaty, and his hair is mussed, but it is definitely Buford. His eyes are shining with a kind of manic desperation, and his usually smooth friendly face is contorted with rage.

He bends down to bind my ankles, and I aim a kick at his horrible shiny face. I miss. He seizes my ankle, and I try another desperate kick.

At this point, Buford seems to lose all patience. He doesn't care if he hurts me. He wants to see me dead.

He throws his body over my knee to lock my leg in place, and I scream as all his weight slams down on the joint.

I jerk and thrash beneath his body, but Buford strikes me across the face with something hard and solid. The pain reverberates to the back of my skull, and the entire room shifts on its axis.

I blink. The room does not right itself. I can see the wavering outline of the bots — tall metal soldiers waiting in the wings. They look like the dead with their empty eye sockets, and I can feel myself slipping away.

I flail around in one last fight, thrashing like a headless fish. Buford wants me to roll over and die, but I will not go quietly.

I scream as loud as I can around the gag, but the sound disappears into the folds of cloth.

The last thing I remember is Buford hovering over me.

His face is shining with perspiration. He thinks he's won. And then everything goes dark.

32

MAGGIE

I come to with the feeling that I've been buried alive under an avalanche of rocks. My head is throbbing as if it has its own heartbeat, and my spine is bent at an awkward angle. I can taste dried blood in the corners of my mouth, and I'm sitting in near total darkness.

I shift to the right and bang my head against the wall. It's too dark to immediately tell where I am — only that the space is small and not well ventilated. It smells new.

Slowly, the events of the past couple hours come floating back to me. I was kidnapped on my way back to the barracks, and the man holding me hostage is Lieutenant Buford.

Buford.

Just thinking of him gives me a sickening jolt of rage. The man has been working above me in the Space Force for the past three weeks. He brought Jonah here to use as a pawn in his scheme, and he was involved in hacking the bots.

I'm still not sure how he's connected to all of this, but at the moment I have more pressing problems.

For one thing, I'm still gagged. The wad of fabric in my

mouth is soaked with spit, and my wrists and ankles are bound.

I shift onto my left side and feel along the wall. There's a strip of something slick beneath me that could be reflective tape.

Am I in a storage zone? Some compartment in the maintenance sector where they keep the bots? I can't tell.

Suddenly, I feel a whoosh of air on my face. Dim bluish light filters into the compartment, and I'm able to make out the dark shape of the bots to my left and the black-and-yellow tape around the doorway of my cell.

Buford's silhouette appears in front of me, and I see him fiddling with a keypad on the wall.

"I really am sorry about this," he says, not sounding remorseful at all. "If you would have just minded your own business, none of this ever would have happened."

My heart starts pounding again in my throat. It sounds as though he's preparing to execute his plan for my demise.

"Everything appears to be in order," he continues. "These bots were decommissioned like the rest of them. The scheduled maintenance was postponed, but I just overrode the system."

I let out a furious scream, but it just comes out sad and muted around the wad of fabric between my teeth.

"In twelve short hours, you will no longer be my problem."

I'm beginning to hyperventilate. This is it. Twelve hours. In twelve hours, I'll be dead.

"At twenty-one hundred, these doors will open, and you won't be able to tell anyone whatever it is you think you know."

At those words, the blood turns to ice in my veins. Buford isn't going to kill me himself — he's going to set me afloat in the endless vacuum of space.

"Not to worry," he says. "I'm told it's extremely quick —

not instantaneous as it is in the movies, but relatively fast. You'll only have about fifteen seconds before you pass out. Within a minute, the water and gas in your bloodstream will form bubbles in your veins, effectively stopping circulation. Soon after that, your body will cease to function."

I think I'm going to be sick. Hot scalding fear is rising up in my chest. I'm going to choke to death on my own vomit before the airlock even opens.

"I am sorry it had to end this way," he says. "But you should have minded your own business."

I've never considered myself a violent individual. I never thought I'd be able to kill someone . . . until this very moment.

I *want* to kill Buford. I want to tackle him to the ground and beat him with a crowbar. I want to hear him beg for mercy, and then I want to end his life.

"Ah, well," he says. "Enjoy your last few hours. I'm sorry that I couldn't make them more comfortable."

I hear a series of mechanical beeps. The airlock door slides shut between us, stopping the flow of air from the station to my horrible cramped death cell.

My panic intensifies. I pull and tug on my restraints, but they don't loosen one bit. I scream and cry around my gag, but it's no use. No one can hear me.

I'm trapped in a colony with five thousand other people, but I might as well be floating out in space. No one knows where I am. No one is coming to rescue me.

33

JONAH

The next morning, I'm running on pure unbridled fury. I didn't sleep more than a few hours. I'd lain awake stewing over Maggie and racking my brain to figure out how the hackers got their hands on my data.

When I get to the latrine, I make the water as hot as I can stand and try to rinse myself clean of everything that's happened. Last night I learned that Maggie had been lying the entire time. She's been lying to my face ever since I've known her, and I don't know whether I should believe her now.

I'm not working with my squad today, but the captain called us in for another emergency briefing. The only news is that there isn't any news. Representatives from the FBI, the NSA, and the Department of Homeland Security will be docking tomorrow, and they'll be combing our surveillance records and questioning everyone.

I'm not sure what it is they're hoping to find. Maverick Enterprises maintains that they have no idea how the bots were hacked. They're launching their own full-scale investigation, but if anyone at the company knows anything, they're keeping it awfully quiet.

I don't know why the FBI or Homeland Security would want to talk to the rest of us. It's not as though we have any contact with the people inside Maverick — unless they know about the SPIDER data.

Callaghan repeats what he said last night: we need to cooperate with the feds and bring anything suspicious to his attention.

That's exactly what I plan on doing, but I'm giving Maggie until the end of the day. After that, I'm gonna turn her in myself and let her worry about the consequences.

After the briefing, I ping Maggie's Optix. I want to tell her that she has until seventeen hundred to come clean, but the call doesn't go through. Either her device has been disabled, or it's completely dead.

Not being able to reach her gives me an uneasy feeling, but I put it out of my mind and head to the dining hall for breakfast. Maggie can avoid me all she wants, but there's nowhere on this space station for her to hide.

When I get to the dining hall, I see Ping sitting at a table with Kholi and Davis. He's wearing an Orlando Magic jersey and a pair of high-top sneakers.

He flags me down, but I shake my head.

Ping ignores my obvious "don't fuck with me" signals and calls out for me to join them anyway.

Reluctantly, I turn and head for their table. Ping grins broadly, but Davis and Kholi exchange uniform looks of dread. I can tell that they don't want to sit with me any more than I want to sit with them.

"Whassup, sarge?" says Ping brightly, standing up to offer me some weird secret handshake.

I clear my throat. "Not much."

I should write his ass up for what he's wearing. Guys aren't allowed to wear tank tops even when they're off duty.

"Have you seen Jones?" I ask.

"No," says Kholi with a scowl. "Why?"

There's an accusatory note in Kholi's voice, but it takes me a minute to understand what she's implying.

I clear my throat, trying to play it off. "No reason . . . I just thought she would be hanging out with you guys."

"I haven't seen her since training yesterday. She didn't come home last night."

"She didn't?"

My shock must have shown on my face, because Kholi seems to realize she's misread the situation. She shakes her head in a panic. "I'm not trying to get her in trouble. I bet she just fell asleep in the lounge."

"Jones isn't in trouble. I was just curious."

There's a long awkward silence, and I wish I hadn't asked.

"Ping," I say, shooting him a look. "Can I borrow you for a sec?"

Ping looks as though Christmas just came early. "Sure, boss. Only, aren't you gonna eat first?"

I shake my head. "I'm not hungry."

Just as the words leave my mouth, I realize that Ping isn't finished. But he jumps to his feet and dumps his tray without so much as a second thought.

As we're leaving, I see him turn around and shoot a double thumbs-up at Kholi and Davis, who look absolutely baffled. Clearly I don't have to worry about blurring the boundaries between me and the squad. I don't think any of them except Ping want anything to do with me.

"What's goin' on, sarge?" he asks, quickening his pace to follow me back to the barracks.

"I need your help with something."

"Cool."

"Can you . . . uh, can you keep this between us?"

"Sure thing."

I take a deep breath and lower my voice. "Can you locate someone by pinging their Optix?"

Ping looks taken aback, but his surprise passes quickly. "Uh, yeah. Yeah, you usually can . . . unless they have their location set to private."

"How?"

"Do you really want to know?"

I consider this for a second. "No, not really. So how can you tell if someone has their location set to private?"

"You can't . . . at least not until you try to ping it." He shoots me a knowing glance. "Who're you trying to locate?"

"Somebody on this station."

"A Space Force somebody?" he probes. Judging by his tone, he knows I'm trying to find Maggie.

"Maybe."

"Well, that's easy," says Ping. "As an officer, you should have access to every lower-ranking Space Force operative in Elderon."

"It's . . . It might be more complicated than that."

"Sarge?"

"You told me this'll stay between us."

"Yeah, of course."

"I need you to ping Maggie's Optix. It might not be registered to the Space Force. Remember?"

"Oh, right," says Ping, as if he'd totally forgotten about Maggie's secret double life. He stops at a T in the hallway. "We should probably do this from my room, then . . . unless you subscribe to a VPN."

"A what?"

"Virtual private network. If I'm going to color outside the lines, I'm not doing it on an unprotected connection."

"Okay . . ."

Whatever he's talking about sounds borderline illegal, but I don't care. I just can't shake this bad feeling about Maggie.

We turn down the hallway toward the privates' barracks, and Ping scans us into the room he shares with Davis. It's surprisingly tidy — spotless, actually. Everything seems to be a hundred percent regulation until I sit down at the end of his bunk.

The bottom of the upper bunk is covered in cutouts of naked girls. I get up and move to stand by the door.

"Should we be expecting Davis anytime soon?"

"Nah," says Ping. He switches on his desktop, which he has propped up on the chest of drawers. "You want to tell me what this is about?"

"What?"

"Well, yesterday I told you that Maggie Jones is really Maggie Barnes, and you just ran off like you had somewhere to be."

I don't respond. I know what he's asking, and I don't really feel like getting into it.

"You don't have to tell me," he says after a few seconds of strained silence.

"Okay."

More silence.

"I mean, it might be *nice* of you to tell me . . . since we're breaking the law together and all."

I roll my eyes. I should have known I wasn't going to get of that easily. Ping is a nosy son of a bitch.

"I think . . ." I take a deep breath. I don't know if I can him. I can't even bring myself to say it out loud.

"You think Maggie is a double agent who might be working for the hackers."

For some reason, having Ping guess it without me having to put it into words fills me with a sense of relief. "*Yeah.*"

I wait for him to start off on one of his long one-sided conversations, but he just shrugs.

"Well?" I say, surprised that I want to hear Ping's opinion.

"I don't see it."

I scowl. "You don't *see* it?"

"Yeah. I mean I just never got that vibe from her is all."

"You never got that *vibe* from her?" I repeat. "She's a liar . . . maybe a spy. You're not supposed to get that 'vibe' from a spy."

"You're dreaming," says Ping, stifling a laugh. "Maggie isn't a spy. Aren't spies supposed to blend in? And why would she plant herself at the lowest level of the Space Force? It doesn't make any sense."

I raise an eyebrow. Ping makes some good points. Maggie definitely doesn't blend in.

"I think she might have leaked some important data," I say quietly. "Data the hackers used in the bot attack in New York."

Ping stops what he's doing and turns to look at me. "What sort of data?"

I take a deep breath. I don't know why I'm hiding it from Ping. He's the only one I trust to help me with this.

I launch into everything I know about the SPIDER and tell him about the training session I had with Maggie. By the time I finish, Ping's brows have inched so high that they look in danger of permanently freezing in that position.

"Wow," he says.

"What?"

He shakes his head. "I mean, I'd heard that BlumBot was ʲeloping some sort of technology to enable rapid motor ing, but I had no idea that they had a working prototype!"

"You've heard of this?"

"How have you *not*?" he says incredulously. "It's, like, the holy grail of artificial intelligence."

"What do you mean?"

"Think about it!" he says. "This technology would change robotics forever. If bots could learn to do things the way we do them just by downloading the muscle-memory data . . . It would be a game changer."

Suddenly, my head is spinning. If Ping is right, then it isn't something BlumBot would want floating around. Applied to their bots, the technology would be worth billions. But in the hands of their competitors or a group of hackers . . .

"Who else knows about this?" he asks.

I shrug. "I don't know. You think Maverick gave the technology to the Space Force after it acquired BlumBot so that they could use our data?"

"Nah," says Ping. "Whatever data that thing collected on you would have been stored in one of our secure servers."

"Whoever reprogrammed those bots had to access my data somehow."

But Ping is already shaking his head. "Not unless that person had access to confidential Space Force data. All that stuff is siloed off. No way to access it unless you have pretty high-level security clearance."

"How high?"

He shrugs. "I'd say lieutenant or higher."

I let that idea float around in my head. If Ping is right, then this goes much higher than I thought.

"Maggie couldn't have done it," he says, finishing my thought. "Not unless she was working with an officer."

Just then, a black map with green outlines of the sectors overtakes the screen.

"Hmm . . ." says Ping. "That's weird."

"What is?"

"It's showing that Maggie's Optix is completely disabled. I can still see where her device went offline, but —"

"But what?"

"I'm not sure how accurate this is . . ." He zooms in on the sector where her Optix was last emitting a signal. "That can't be right."

"What?"

Ping shakes his head. "It's showing that her Optix was in a restricted area. That was at oh seven hundred this morning."

34

JONAH

We've been holed up in Ping's room for the past eleven hours. Upon finding out that Maggie's Optix was last emitting a signal from a restricted area, he's been doing everything he can to access the security feed.

Unfortunately, hacking a protected feed on Elderon isn't easy — even for a pro like Ping. The goal is to find out what Maggie's been up to and whether or not she's involved with the officer who stole my SPIDER data.

"Well, that's disappointing," says Ping, sitting back in a chair he lifted from the lounge.

"What is?"

He takes a swig from a can of Ener-G. There are already five empty cans scattered across his makeshift desk. "The area where Maggie's Optix went down is kind of a dead zone for cameras."

"You're kidding."

"Nope." He finishes the can and crushes it against his head.

"That can't be a coincidence."

"It would be a pretty lucky one if it was," he agrees.

"Shit."

Eleven hours in, and we've hit a dead end. I know what I have to do, but something inside me is resisting.

I should have turned Maggie into Callaghan hours ago. And the longer I wait, the more suspicious it looks. I feel as though I'm in too deep now. I need to find out *exactly* what she's been up to.

"I could pull the cameras from the area just outside the restricted zone," Ping offers.

"You can?"

"Sure." Ping reaches for another can of Ener-G and cracks it open with a hiss. "I'm already in the system."

"Do it."

Ping's fingers start to fly again, and he lands on a list of what appears to be camera locations throughout the space station. I had no idea that there were so many hidden cameras, but it seems as though there isn't a single hallway or public space that isn't heavily surveilled.

The restricted area where Maggie's Optix went dead is somewhere in Sector J. Ping locates the camera just outside the area and scrolls through the digital timeline. He stops the footage thirty minutes before she went offline and speeds up the video.

The camera is located in a hallway that doesn't get a lot of traffic. Not a single person traipses through the frame in the entire half hour we watch.

Then I see someone — or rather, two someones. One of them *is* Maggie, but she isn't moving on her own.

I can only tell it's her because of her long curly hair. She's slumped over a man's shoulder, and she doesn't appear to be conscious.

"Ho — ly shit," says Ping.

"Who is that?" I ask, pointing at the man. The camera is too far away to make out the man's face, but something is definitely wrong.

Ping zooms in, but the feed just gets grainier. The man's features are completely obscured, but I recognize his outfit. He's wearing Space Force fatigues.

"Can you go back?" I ask. "Retrace their steps?"

"Hang on."

Ping flips back to a map of the middle deck and pulls up the camera from the hallway in the next sector. Nothing. He tries the end of the hallway that connects Sector K to I, but there's no sign of Maggie or the man.

Finally, he locates the feed for the stairwell leading from the lower deck to the middle deck. The man is carrying Maggie up a flight of stairs, and she is most definitely unconscious.

"Shit."

Ping retraces Maggie's kidnapper's steps to a hallway just outside of coach housing in Sector O. One of the cameras seems to be down for maintenance, and I don't think it's a coincidence.

I can't believe this. Maggie didn't go offline because she was hiding. Her Optix shut off because she was kidnapped.

I can feel the bile rising up in my throat. After all the shit I gave her, Maggie wasn't a spy. She didn't steal my SPIDER data, and she certainly wasn't involved with the hacks.

I don't know why she's been kidnapped — only that she's in danger.

"Can you get me into the restricted area?" I say in a rush, trying to push back the horrible thoughts that are flooding through my brain.

"Uh . . . yeah," says Ping, shifting gears and pulling up another screen with dizzying lines of different-colored code. "It might take some time, though."

"She doesn't have time!"

I'm feeling desperate. For all I know, Maggie could be dead. It's been thirteen hours since she was snatched. Either she's already been killed, or she's in serious danger.

Waiting for Ping to hack Elderon's mainframe is pure torture. All I really want to do is storm the restricted area. Instead, I have to sit and wait while Ping's hands dash across the keys. I don't have clearance to access that part of the building, and I can't tell the higher-ups because I don't know whom I can trust.

Whoever kidnapped Maggie is part of the Space Force, which means I have to treat the entire organization as though it's been compromised. I'm furious that Maggie's kidnapper is one of us. He's been right under my nose the whole time.

"I'm in," says Ping after what seems like forever.

I breathe a heavy sigh of relief. I just hope that we're not too late.

"Take that, you fucking space fascists," says Ping around a yawn.

"I can go?"

"Not yet . . . I still need to go in here . . . upgrade your clearance . . ."

"Hurry!"

"I am. I am . . ." Ping's fingers start to fly. I spot my own name and a long alphanumeric code. This must be how the Space Force controls which parts of Elderon its operatives can access.

"And . . . done!" says Ping, breaking into a triumphant grin.

I don't even have time to thank him. As soon as he finishes, I bolt through the door.

I already grabbed a rifle and a pistol from the armory. It isn't *technically* allowed, but I'm breaking all kinds of rules, so I might as well go big.

It feels warranted under the circumstances. I have no idea

what I'm running into — only that I'm going head to head against someone who's trying to get Maggie out of the picture.

Luckily, the hallways are mostly deserted. Dinner ended almost an hour ago, and most people have already retreated to their pods.

I take the back stairwell three steps at a time and sprint through Sector J to the restricted area. I try to visualize the blinking dot where Maggie's Optix was shut off, but I don't even know if that's where she is.

I pass several "Top Level Personnel Only" signs as I fly down the hallway, and the warnings become more aggressive the farther in I go. There's no way to play this off in the event that I get caught, but I don't encounter a single living soul.

Finally, I reach a set of heavy double doors. They're locked. The restricted area requires three-way biometric authentication, and I just hope that Ping didn't screw this up.

I press my palm against the fingerprint pad while the scanner reads my face. My voice doesn't sound like my own when I speak my name for voice recognition, but miraculously, the light above the scanner turns green.

I pull open the door and hurry inside, glancing up at the camera pointing down from the ceiling.

I'm hoping Ping can do some hacker magic to make that footage disappear. I'd be in deep shit if anyone found out I was here.

Lights flicker on down the hallway. The walls around me are a plain slate gray, and everything has a sparse, utilitarian feel. There are no screens or frozen yogurt stands — just row after row of fluorescent lighting and two sets of dotted lines on the floor. I'm probably one of the few humans authorized to walk these halls.

As I approach the second set of doors and scan myself in, I get a faint tingle of paranoia on the back of my neck. I am totally and completely alone, but I can't shake the feeling that I'm being watched.

I walk down a long hallway toward a door with a large yellow sign warning me about autonomous bot activity going on inside. A room seldom used by humans seems like a good place to hide someone, so I chamber a round in my pistol and let myself in.

The door whooshes open without a sound, and I step inside the room. Light pools around me just inside the door, and I pivot at the hips to scan for threats. The place appears to be deserted.

The door closes behind me without a sound, and I'm thrust into total darkness. I flip on the light built into my Optix, and a tiny white beam pierces the shadows.

I take a step forward, and my footsteps echo loudly around me. I keep my pistol raised. My heart is pounding.

I turn to my left, and the light from my Optix pans up a pair of gleaming steel tibias connected to titanium joints operated by wires. Fanning out from those joints are a pair of solid steel femurs with metal wings that vaguely resemble something human.

I breathe a sigh of relief. It's a bot.

These are designed for performing maintenance on the exterior of the space station. Their breastbones are solid plates of metal, but I can see through their abdomens to wire innards and an ugly jumble of moving parts. Where the colony-facing bots all have moveable glass eyes, these just have dark pits where their eyes should be.

They look like the undead — zombie robots. It gives me the fucking creeps.

I want to call out for Maggie, but I know that isn't smart. Whoever dragged her here could still be in the room, and I don't want to give up my position.

I turn down my light and keep moving, eyes scraping the corners for any signs of life.

I comb every inch of the place, but I don't see Maggie anywhere. All I see are bots and scaffoldings, and there isn't any sign of a struggle.

She isn't here. I search every corner, even checking behind the stationary bots, but there's no sign of her or her kidnapper.

Finally, I come upon a set of airlock doors. There's only one place I haven't checked.

I hit a button beneath the keypad, but all I get is a beep of protest. The keypad flashes. I need a code.

I call Ping.

"Did you find her?" I can tell by his tone that he's just as worried.

"No. Not yet. I need you to open this airlock."

"She's in the airlock?"

I glance over my shoulder to make sure I'm still alone. "I don't know. It's the only place I haven't checked."

"Hang on."

I hear the clacking of keys in the background, and the faint prickle on the back of my neck intensifies. I whip around, ready to fight, but there's no one in the room but me.

"Shit," says Ping. "That airlock's closed until midnight."

"What?"

He shakes his head. "There's no maintenance scheduled for tonight, but that's the door they'd go through."

"The bots?"

My mind is racing. It doesn't make any sense.

"Can't you override it?" I ask.

"I'm trying, but . . ."

"But *what*?"

"They put safeguards in place to keep the inner door locked.

They won't let me unlock it when the outer door is about to open."

"When is the outer door going to open?"

"About five minutes."

"*What?*"

Blood rushes to my muscles. Maggie could be behind those doors. My first instinct is to kick my way through, but I know that that's impossible.

"Ping!" I shout. "Maggie could be inside the airlock! You need to figure out how to keep that outer door from opening."

"I can't," he says, a slight edge of panic to his voice. "Once it's set, it can't be changed without an administrator key code."

"Can't you get one of those?"

"There's no time."

"Then you have to open the inner door."

"But if the outer doors open while the inner doors are —"

"Don't tell me you can't!" I shout. "Find a way!"

I look around for something I could use to pry the doors open — a crowbar, a screwdriver — anything. Deep down I know it's useless, but my desperation is mounting by the second.

Ping's back. "I have an idea . . ."

"Better be a good one."

I check the clock. We've only got two minutes before those doors are set to open. If Maggie's in there, she'll be ripped out into the vacuum of space as soon as the airlock unseals.

"I'm cutting the power to that whole sector," says Ping. "Everything that's linked to the restricted section will shut off — servers, modems, the external exit systems . . . When I turn it back on, the system will reboot itself. Any scheduled missions should be scrubbed, and you should be able to open the doors."

"*Should* be scrubbed?" I repeat.

"It's just a theory . . ."

"Fine!" I say. At this point, we are out of options. "How long will that take?"

My clock says we have less than a minute.

"Ping . . ."

No answer.

"Ping!"

Just then, the keypad shuts off. The little blue light fizzles out, and silence fans out all over the room. The only light in the entire storeroom is coming from my Optix, and it's eerily quiet without the hum of electronics working behind the scenes.

All I can hear is the sound of my own breathing. Even Ping's feed has gone dark.

I wait. I don't hear the sound of the airlock opening, but I'm not sure if I *would* hear anything. Seconds go by, and my stomach twists into knots. If this didn't work . . . If Maggie was in there . . .

Suddenly, everything springs back to life. The storeroom is filled with the faint hum of electronics, and the keypad blinks blue. I feel a rush of cool air as the HVAC system kicks on, and the row of bots light up behind me.

When Ping said he rebooted the whole system, he really meant he rebooted the *whole* system.

I slam my hand down on the button under the keypad, and the airlock doors whoosh open. I'm relieved when I'm not immediately sucked into space, but my relief fizzles out when I see Maggie on the floor.

She's crumpled in a heap against the outer door, and she's got a wad of blue fabric shoved in her mouth. Her arms and legs are bound with zip ties, and she has a nasty bruise across the bridge of her nose.

"Maggie?" I croak, stowing my pistol in its holster.

She doesn't respond.

"Maggie!" I drop to my knees and turn her over. Her skin is

pale and cold as ice, and there are painful-looking scratches all over her wrists. I swallow down a wave of disgust. Whoever did this, they were brutal. But Maggie did not surrender.

I hurry to loosen Maggie's gag, and then her eyes crack open.

"Maggie!" I gasp, relief spilling through me.

Her gaze is slow to focus, and tears erupt in her blue-green eyes.

When I release her gag, she sucks in a deep shuddering breath. She lets out a little moan, and I pull out my knife to cut her zip ties.

"Jonah?"

"You're gonna be okay," I say, slicing the ties around her wrists.

"Jonah, it wasn't me . . ."

"I know," I growl, furious that I let it get this far.

"It's Buford," she croaks.

My insides freeze. Surely she didn't just say what I think she did.

"Who?"

"Buford," she repeats, her eyes slightly glassy and unfocused. She's been trapped in here for almost fourteen hours. She has to be teetering on the verge of shock.

I cut the ties around her ankles and grab her around the shoulders. She winces at my rough touch, and I immediately soften my grip. "Sorry."

She shakes her head.

"Maggie . . . Are you sure it was Buford?"

"Yes!"

"Why would he —"

"I don't know," she gasps, tears shining in her eyes. "We have to go . . ."

"We will, but —"

Suddenly, I hear a high-pitched whir behind me. Maggie's eyes widen in panic, and I wheel around just in time to see one of the bots flying toward me. It moves like a human propelled by springs, its empty eye sockets fixated on us.

"Shit!"

I scramble to my feet and take aim at the bot. I fire, but the bullet just ricochets off its chest.

Panicking, I grab Maggie by the arm and haul her out of the way just as the bot careens into the airlock. It moves like a person with superhuman speed, but it doesn't corner fast enough. The bot smashes into the outer door, but it rebounds immediately and pivots to face us.

My stomach turns. That did not just happen.

But the other bots are waking up, and they're all turning in our direction. I don't know what happened when Ping reset the system, but the bots are awake, and they're coming for us.

"Run!" I breathe.

Maggie doesn't hesitate.

We sprint across the room away from the bots, and I hear the groan of their joints as they move. Loud mechanical footfalls echo behind us, but I just focus on the door and pull Maggie along.

I sprint toward the door with Maggie in tow, and the bots seem to pick up speed. The door opens automatically, but it doesn't close fast enough. The bots spring through one after the other, and I push my legs harder.

Maggie is having a difficult time keeping up. The hallway ahead is long and straight. There is nowhere for us to hide.

I hit my Optix. "Ping!"

"You got her?" His voice is ecstatic.

"We've got a problem," I huff.

"What?"

I turn to look over my shoulder, panning my Optix over the

rogue maintenance bots.

"Oh, shit. Are they . . ."

"Yeah!" I growl. "You have to lock the doors behind us."

"No can do."

"Ping!"

"There's no time!"

"Just do it!"

My legs burn as I push them harder. Then Maggie stumbles, and I almost lose my grip.

I can feel her arm slipping through my fingers, but I manage to grab her at the last second.

I glance behind me. She looks as though she might pass out, but we're almost at the first set of doors leading out of the restricted area.

"Ping!"

"If I lock it, you won't be able to get through."

I let out a growl. I can't form real words. I need all my energy to get me and Maggie out of here alive.

I swipe us through the first set of doors, and the time it takes for them to open are precious seconds lost.

The bots are quickly gaining on us, and soon one's snapping at Maggie's heels. She screams, and the horrible thing seems to pick up speed.

It runs like a track star propelled by Satan. The bot reaches out with its cold dead hands, and Maggie lets out a scream of terror.

I jerk to a halt but don't let go. The bot has her by the neck, and it seems to be tightening its hold. Maggie kicks and thrashes, but it's no use. The bot is stronger than both of us.

I watch in horror as it straightens its torso. I can hear the hydraulics lifting it higher, and Maggie's feet leave the ground. Her face is turning an alarming shade of red. She's kicking at the air — completely petrified — and there is nothing I can do.

The bot could break her neck. It would be that easy — one simple jerk at a forty-five-degree angle — but it's going to strangle her instead.

Feeling desperate, I bring the butt of my rifle down on the bot's mechanical joint. The clang of metal pierces my ears, and I hit it again.

The bot doesn't release her, but its hold is weakened. I continue to beat the bot's joint with my rifle, huffing and hacking like a madman.

Maggie jerks her body desperately, and I grab her around the waist. She looks down. Our eyes lock. I know we're out of options. I tug her down as hard as I can, and somehow she slips free.

Everything that happens next is a horrible blur. I catch Maggie as she falls to the ground, deep painful gashes spewing blood from her neck. She gasps for air and chokes for dear life, but I just grab her hand and run.

I don't look back to see what the bot does next. I can hear the others gaining ground, but we make it through the next set of doors.

"Ping!" I yell.

"We lost some!"

"Not all of them!"

We're approaching the last set of doors separating the bots from the rest of the colony. The doors open automatically, and I hit the button to seal them before the bots come through.

"Come on, come on, come on," I mutter.

But the rest of the bots are just yards behind us, and the stupid doors won't move.

We're out of time.

Keeping hold of Maggie, I turn and run. There's nothing else I can do.

35

MAGGIE

My body gives out just when we reach the archway leading to the barracks. I feel my legs wobble beneath me, and Jonah lurches forward to catch me before I hit the ground.

He smells good — some bright citrusy notes from deodorant or cologne. It's clean and fresh and completely human, which I find comforting at the moment.

I allow myself to lean against him, and he keeps one arm locked around me as he pounds on a keypad mounted beside the archway. It must be some emergency lockdown protocol, because a second later, a door seems to unfold from the wall, sealing off Sector Q from the rest of the colony.

Jonah scoops me off my feet, and I feel a surge of embarrassment that I need to be carried. Jonah doesn't speak or even pant. It's as though I weigh nothing at all.

He walks me down to his room, scans himself in, and deposits me on his bed. His blanket is folded in a perfect rectangle, but he shakes it out and drapes it over my shoulders.

Then he disappears, and I take the chance to study the picture above his bed.

It's the only personal item he has in the room, so it must be important to him. It shows a pretty woman with long dark hair and two boys that look like her sons.

The youngest is probably around ten years old. He's got big blue eyes and a reluctant smile that tells me he *has* to be Jonah. The other is a teenager — maybe seventeen or eighteen. He looks like Jonah, but there's something about him that's very different.

A second later, the real Jonah reappears with two bottles of water. I tear my eyes away from the picture. He sits down next to me, opens a bottle, and orders me to drink.

I don't need telling twice. I am absolutely parched.

Jonah watches me for a moment with a concerned expression. He's thinking about the killer bots. I know he needs to report them.

Then there's Buford. He left me in that airlock to die, which is problematic for so many reasons. For one thing, it's our word against his. For another, we don't know whom we can trust.

There's also the tiny problem of us being in a restricted area in the first place. I'm not exactly worried about my standing with the Space Force, but this is Jonah's career. There's a lot at stake for him, and going up against his commanding officer could have far-reaching consequences.

He gets to his feet and touches his Optix to make a call. He starts to pace back and forth, and a second later, he rolls his eyes.

"The emergency dispatch is an *answering service*. Can you believe that?"

He lets out a groan of frustration, but I'm still in too much shock to respond. I can't believe how close I came to death by space vacuum *and* death by killer robots.

"Sergeant Jonah Wyatt, number 85-6827. I'd like to report a dozen rogue maintenance bots originating from Sector J." There's a pause as he listens to some automated message, and he hangs up with a grunt of frustration.

He tries another number, and this time he reaches a dispatcher in hospitality. That's when it goes from bad to worse.

"This isn't a *prank*. Are you stupid? There are ten or twelve bots that just tried to kill me roaming around the station."

Pause.

Jonah's brows knit together into a tighter and tighter line, and I realize that he's actually kind of cute when he's mad — when that anger isn't directed at me.

"Check the cameras, you stupid fuck, or I'll call Captain Callaghan and tell him how incompetent —" Another scowl. "No, I can't 'hold.' Are you —"

He scowls. He hangs up and tries to ping someone else, but he just ends the call with a furious growl. He must have gotten another automated service.

"They didn't believe you?" I ask, my voice raspy from dehydration and very near death.

"They said all the bots were shut down." He shakes his head. "At least they've been warned. As soon as they get off their asses and check the cameras, the whole station'll be on lockdown."

He sends out another quick ping and then reaches under the bed for something. It's a first-aid kit, and it occurs to me that he's responsible for taking care of his squad in the event of an emergency.

He passes me the second bottle of water without a word, sits down, and lifts the hair off my shoulders to examine my neck. It feels strange to catch him in such a human gesture. By now the deep gashes have started to clot, and the blood has taken on a tacky texture. My neck is unbelievably sore. I can already feel it swelling.

Jonah handles me with a surprising amount of care, but I still shudder when he swabs the blood away.

"Sorry. Does that hurt?"

"No." I shake my head, thinking back to the bot that grabbed me. "It's just . . . Those things . . ."

"I know."

"What happened?" I ask. "I thought they disabled them."

"They did," says Jonah grimly, dabbing at my cuts with an antiseptic wipe.

I savor the harsh sting that sizzles in my wounds. It means I'm not dead.

"Ping had to shut off the power to that sector to open the airlock. When he rebooted the system, I guess it reset the computer that controls the bots and allowed the malware to take hold."

"Ping shut off the power?" Ping is the *last* person I expected to be involved.

Jonah shrugs. "He's the one who helped me find you. If it weren't for him, you'd be dead."

I turn that thought over in my head. A day ago, Jonah called me a liability to his squad and then accused me of being a spy. He was going to turn me in to Captain Callaghan, and yet he came to my rescue.

"I know you weren't the one who stole that data," he says in a low voice.

I don't dare say anything. I can't tell if he still hates my guts or if this whole ordeal was some kind of weird bonding experience. If it was, I don't want to ruin it.

"I shouldn't have accused you," he continues, his voice slow and unsure as if he hasn't had much practice apologizing.

"It's all right," I say. "I did lie about who I was. But I swear I never meant to put anyone in danger."

"I know."

We fall into awkward silence, and Jonah wraps a clean bandage around my neck.

"I found out who sent me the fake ID," I murmur.

"*Who?*"

His tone is so severe that it makes me question our newfound camaraderie.

I take a deep breath. "Tripp Van de Graaf's assistant, Porter."

"Why?"

"He also thought it was weird that Maverick brought a thousand private military personnel onto a civilian space station. I guess he figured sending me in would get him the information he needed."

Jonah raises both eyebrows. "You think he's capable of hacking the bots?"

I take another swig of water. "No. He has the connections to make it happen, but it wasn't him."

Jonah shoots me a dubious look.

"I'm telling you . . . That man's whole life is taking care of Tripp. He would never do anything to put Maverick in jeopardy."

"Wow," he says, averting his gaze. "You're on a first-name basis with the guy?"

I don't know how to respond to that.

Luckily, I don't have to. There's a frantic knock at the door. I jump, but Jonah lays a hand on my knee.

"It's just Ping," he says. "I told him to meet us here."

He takes his hand away and gets up to let Ping in, and I let out a slow breath. Jonah checks the peephole first and throws the door wide open.

"Get in," he says, casting a furtive glance into the pod.

Ping squeezes into the small space, looking as though he just got dressed. His boots are untied, and his shirt is half-tucked.

"What the hell is going on out there?" asks Jonah.

"The silent alarms are going off everywhere," says Ping. "And I got a message from the captain that we should prepare for emergency defense protocol."

"It's the bots," says Jonah. "I had to report them."

"Shit."

"I know."

Ping turns and suddenly notices that I'm in the room. "Hey! She lives!" he cries, coming over to give me a hug.

I offer Ping a weak smile and lean into his one-armed embrace. "I hear I have you to thank for that."

"Ah, it was no biggie," says Ping, though I can tell he's secretly glowing.

"Maggie says she knows who sent her the fake ID."

"Porter Guffrey," I say. "Assistant to Tripp Van de Graaf. But he's not the one who's responsible for the hacks."

"So who kidnapped you?" asks Ping.

I glance at Jonah, wondering if I should tell him. Jonah nods. "Lieutenant Buford."

"You're *kidding*."

"I wish I was. I think he hacked my Optix somehow . . . maybe yours, too. He knew that you'd figured out that I was a journalist, and he knew I'd been to see Porter."

"It makes sense," says Jonah. "He's the one who showed me the SPIDER in the first place. That data could only have been stolen by someone with access to the private Space Force servers."

"That still doesn't explain who's been helping him," I say. "Porter said that hacking the bots had to be an inside job. But whoever did it must not care what happens to BlumBot. This hack is going to *decimate* the company."

"His accomplice could be anyone who's ever worked for BlumBot," says Jonah.

"Any idea why he kidnapped you?" asks Ping.

I take a deep breath. "He kept saying that I should have minded my own business . . . that I knew too much."

"After you talked to Porter?"

"Yeah."

"He said he was going to pin it on me . . . try to make it look like I was the one who stole that data."

"Does he know you escaped?" asks Ping.

"I don't think so."

"We need to get to Callaghan before Buford does," says Jonah.

Ping and I exchange a look.

"We have to get ahead of this. And Callaghan needs to know what we're up against."

"Agreed," says Ping.

The last thing I want to do is leave this room. I feel as though all the life's been sucked out of me, and there are killer robots on the loose. Still, Jonah's right. We don't have a choice.

"Are you okay?" Jonah asks. "Because you don't have to come if you don't feel up to it."

"I'm coming," I say, getting to my feet and trying not to wobble. Like I'm gonna stay here alone.

Jonah turns to Ping. "Where's your rifle?"

"My rifle?"

"The maintenance bots are supposed to be bulletproof like the security models, but I used mine to clobber the bot that got hold of Maggie."

"Yeah. I can get Davis's, too," says Ping. "I know his combination."

Ping grabs the rifles from the lockers and hands Davis's to me. The M500 feels heavy and foreign. We've only had about a week of practice with rifles in training, but the feel of cold aluminum and steel between my fingers still has a steadying effect.

We keep a tight formation as we leave the room and move down the hallway toward the captain's suite. Luckily, no one is out to raise the alarm, but I'm sure we'd scare anyone watching from the security cameras.

We reach the captain's quarters and knock, but no one answers. There's no sound from inside the room and no light coming from under the door.

"He must still be in meetings," Jonah mutters. "Let's check the war room."

I hold back a shudder. I'm not sure what freaks me out more: the fact that there are still murderous bots roaming around the space station, or the prospect of coming face to face with Buford again.

Ping moves down the hallway in a low defensive stance, and Jonah gives my shoulder a squeeze. I look up. He moves ahead and averts his gaze, but I still catch that quick bracing look.

We move silently down the hallway toward Sector R. I didn't even know that there *was* such thing as a war room on board, and instantly my brain populates with half a dozen story ideas.

I push them out of my brain and refocus on the mission. Get to Callaghan. Tell him about the bots. Throw Buford under the bus.

Part of me worries that Callaghan won't believe us. He never seemed like a very nice guy in the few brief interactions I had with him. The other part of me is terrified that he will and that I'll have to confront the man who's responsible.

Fortunately, I don't have time to overthink things. We reach the main hall within minutes, and Jonah glances over his shoulder to make sure we weren't followed.

It's nearly twenty-two hundred, and the place is deserted. Our footsteps echo loudly in the empty hallway, and I can see our reflection in the shiny white tile. The cleaning bots must have gotten to this sector before they were powered down.

We stop outside an unmarked door near the end, and Jonah knocks three times.

Nothing.

Ping glances back at me, and I start to feel anxious.

Jonah knocks again. Still no response.

"Maybe he's on his Optix?" Ping suggests.

Jonah knocks one last time, pounding so hard that he rattles the door.

"I'm goin' in," he mutters, touching a button to wake the scanner.

"Are you sure that's a good idea?" asks Ping. "What if he's in an important meeting, or —"

"This is more important."

I can't argue with that. Nothing screams urgent like a handful of murderous bots.

The scanner reads Jonah's face, and a second later, the door clicks to unlock. He pushes it open and walks right in, but I freeze where I'm standing and stare through the doorway.

Just inside the war room is a sleek silver cart. It's loaded with a carafe of coffee and all the fixings for a late-night refreshment. Shards of white ceramic are scattered over the floor, intermingling with flecks of ruby-red blood.

A woman is lying facedown on the floor, her legs splayed out behind her at an awkward angle. She's wearing a crisp white collared dress, and she's got long black hair as sleek as a doll's. The jaunty blue scarf is a dead giveaway — she's one of the hostesses.

My eyes follow the bright trail of blood to a broken chair, scattered papers, and another broken coffee cup.

There's a long smear of blood where the struggle took place, leading to a pair of heavy black boots. Captain Callaghan is slumped in the corner, his face as pale and white as a ghost's.

His eyes are drooping, but he's still alive. He's propped up against a set of built-in cabinets, clutching his abdomen with shaking hands. On the floor beside him is a large metal frame — some certificate of commendation.

By the looks of things, the frame was ripped clean off the wall, and the corner is scratched. It definitely struck something solid.

"Captain —" Jonah croaks, stopping dead in his tracks.

Callaghan's eyes bulge, and his breathing grows more rapid. He raises his hand to point at the woman, and I see that his palms are bloody. A dark pool of blood is spreading from his abdomen, and more blood is spilling out by the second.

"Call the emergency line at the infirmary," Jonah growls, bending down to tend to the captain. "Hurry!"

I don't have my Optix, but Ping springs into action. I stumble blindly into the room, narrowly avoiding the trail of blood.

My mind goes blank as I survey the carnage. It feels like watching a bad slasher movie.

My brain detects a shiny silver knife with a blade that's covered in blood, and I survey the room to piece together the struggle.

Jonah's voice calls me back to the present. He lays the captain flat on his back and rips off his own overshirt.

"Help me!" he chokes.

My body seems to move without consulting my brain. I

stagger forward in a horrified daze, carefully avoiding the captain's eyes. His shirt and pants are soaked with blood, and there's a sizable puddle beneath him.

Still, I follow Jonah's directions and peel up the captain's shirt. The ripped fabric sticks in his wound, and I hold back a gag as the slash is exposed. It's clean and surgical. It looks like a knife wound.

Blood is bubbling out at a terrifying rate. The knife must have pierced something major. Jonah shoves a wad of fabric into the wound and applies pressure with both his hands.

I just stare. I don't know what to do next.

"Check for a pulse," Jonah huffs, jerking his head back at the woman in white.

I nod. I'd almost forgotten about her. I scoot back on my heels and slide on the blood. It's everywhere, and now it's on me.

I take a deep breath and turn to the woman, whose mop of dark hair is obscuring her face. Her royal blue scarf is still crisp and perfect. The sight is unnerving, to say the least.

Hands shaking, I lift up her hair just as Jonah did for me. But the instant the side of her face is exposed, I yank back my hand and stifle a scream.

"What is it?" Jonah yells.

I shake my head. I can't move. I can't speak.

I stare at the woman and continue to shake, eyes traveling over the curve of her shoulder and the neat French manicure on her cold dead hand.

"Maggie!" Jonah yells, still trying to staunch the flow of blood.

I look behind me and wish I hadn't. The captain's face is as white as a bone. His eyes are closed, and the blood is still seeping through Jonah's blue shirt. He isn't going to make it.

I lift the woman's hair again to expose the wreckage underneath. By the looks of things, her head was completely bashed in, but there's not a drop of blood or even the hint of bone.

Everything about her is perfectly human — from the cracks in her lipstick to the mole on her neck. I can see the wispy hairs just beneath her ear, but nothing about her is remotely real.

A fine curl of ivory flesh has been violently torn, revealing a dense metal structure laced with wires and screws. I meet Jonah's horrified gaze, and a second later, Ping walks in.

He looks from Callaghan to the woman and freezes on the spot. He sees what I see, but he can't believe his eyes.

This woman isn't a hostess — not a real one, anyway. She's a BlumBot creation unlike any I've ever seen.

She isn't like the bots in the dining hall or the ones that tried to kill me. She doesn't have weird doll eyes or silicone skin that feels like rubber to the touch.

Her flesh is silky smooth and dotted with fine white hairs. I can see the hint of a vein beneath the surface and a patch of pink near her elbow where the skin starts to crinkle.

Everything about her looks and feels real. She's the next generation of artificial life, and she is indistinguishable from a human.

AUTHOR'S NOTE

Thank you for reading *Colony One*. I hope you enjoyed the book. This series is a slight step outside my wheelhouse of gloom and doom, and I had a ton of fun writing it.

Of course, I can't seem to write a story that doesn't threaten the survival of humanity, but hey, it's robots in space! What could *possibly* be better?

I knew that it would take quite a bit of research to create a believable space colony, but I never imagined the amazing discoveries and advancements that I would uncover. Moreover, this is one of those times where the research had a massive impact on the story itself, so if you haven't looked into any of this before, I would highly recommend setting aside an evening to go down a Google rabbit hole.

I chose the rotating design of Elderon to offset the health problems and logistical issues caused by microgravity. Long-term weightlessness causes muscle atrophy and a deterioration of your skeleton, and it puts astronauts at risk for kidney stones and bone fractures. Space travel can also lead to diminished cardiac function, and increased radiation exposure during long missions can put astronauts at a greater risk of cancer.

The current and most cost-effective solution to the problems posed by microgravity is to have astronauts work out for several hours a day while in space. They run on a treadmill with bungee cords holding them to the machine and lift weights to maintain muscle mass.

To reduce the health problems — and the need to pee into a tube — I designed a colony that rotated and used centripetal force to simulate the effects of 1G. In my research, I learned that the concept of a rotating "donut" colony like Elderon was entirely possible — just prohibitively expensive.

The colony would have to be constructed in space, and apparently, it costs roughly $1 million per pound just to lift something into low orbit. To spin that large of a donut fast enough to simulate 1G would take an enormous amount of fuel, but I'm convinced that the rapidly plummeting costs of space travel and technological advancements would make this plausible if not practical.

As I was thinking about what the colonists would eat, I got so excited that I just *had* to give you a peek behind the curtain. The scene where Maggie goes into the food-science lab was written after I learned about some of the incredible advancements in cultured meat.

So far scientists have produced a $300,000 burger that tastes almost exactly like the real thing, and startup Memphis Meats has created a meatball for roughly $1,000.

Despite some critics' beliefs that cultured meat is a PR stunt that can't possibly live up to the hype, the scientists who are working on it say that cultured meat could help feed the world and meet the growing demand for animal products that are contributing to greenhouse gas emissions.

Many vegetarians and vegans have even thrown their

support behind the development of "clean meat." (Though as of this book's publication, the process for cultivating meat requires a nutrient serum derived from sugar, amino acids, and real animal blood.)

The real question is whether consumers would want to eat meat that's been grown in a lab — even if it's cheaper and tastes identical to meat from a natural-born cow. Would you?

And speaking of freaky technology, what about those robots? A brief foray into the robotics industry of 2018 is both wickedly cool and terrifying. Imagine what it's going to be like in 2075.

My first iteration of robots in the book were loosely based off some models that are currently in production. As of this book's publication, California-based Knightscope, Inc. has four different robot models designed to help prevent crime in parking lots, malls, sporting arenas, and airports.

Their most well-known model, the 400-pound K5, stands five feet tall and is shaped like a bullet — or a cone-headed version of R2-D2. It tops out at three miles per hour, has four cameras, and can read up to 300 license plates per minute. It costs about $6 per hour to rent.

The robots have already come under scrutiny after one hit a toddler in a mall parking lot and another was hired by a San Francisco animal shelter to cut down on crime allegedly emanating from a nearby homeless camp.

Another company called Starship Technologies has launched a fleet of food delivery robots in Washington, DC, and Redwood City, California. These are glorified coolers on wheels equipped with GPS, cameras, and sensors that allow them to navigate city sidewalks at a normal walking pace.

Then there's Eve — one of twenty-five robots roaming the halls of UCSF Medical Center in San Francisco delivering meals, picking up dirty trays, and transporting medications and lab samples throughout the hospital. Think of Eve as a refrigerator-sized flatbed truck that knows the hospital's floor plan.

But while the robots working in hospitals and parking lots are about as threatening as C-3PO, there was one robot that stood out from them all and legitimately gave me the creeps. Her name is Sophia, and she was designed by a Hong Kong–based firm, Hanson Robotics.

Sophia is different because her "face" looks almost human. She's designed to resemble Audrey Hepburn, and she's equipped with cameras that allow her to track faces, maintain eye contact, and mimic up to sixty different human expressions. She can even hold conversations on her own.

Saudi Arabia made Sophia its first robot citizen, but Sophia is not the only lifelike humanoid robot. There's also Erica, created by Professor Hiroshi Ishiguro at Osaka University, and Jai Jai, the interactive "robot goddess" created by a team at the University of Science and Technology in China led by Chen Xiaoping.

This one can hold simple conversations and says things like "You're a handsome man" and "Don't come too close to me when you are taking a picture. It will make my face look fat."

Did I mention she refers to her male creator as "my lord"? Barf.

The fate of these supersmart cyborgs? To perform "a range of menial tasks in Chinese restaurants, nursing homes, hospitals, and households." You know — lady things.

Believe it or not, the rampant sexism in the fields of AI and robotics almost bugs me more than the fact that these robots exist at all.

Today, most robots are created *by men* to look and talk like idealized versions of *women*. They're designed to be charming, polite, and ultimately subservient to their creators — basically walking, talking Barbie dolls. (Though Sophia did once throw shade on Elon Musk. Bad robot.)

When designing his robot Erica, Hiroshi Ishiguro combined thirty photos of real women to create what he says is the "most beautiful robot in the world." These robots' creators dress them up like demure ladies in classic skirts, button-up shirts, and gloves — except when Sophia is rented out. Then her wardrobe is dictated by the client.

The cold truth is that, whether they're aware of it or not, these men want to create robots who are beautiful, helpful, smiley, and obedient — just as the patriarchy demanded real women behave before that became a societal no-no.

Even our seemingly innocuous AI assistants Siri, Alexa, and Microsoft's Cortana all have female names. Google specified that it didn't want to give its AI a gender, though its default voice is female.

Samsung named its virtual assistant Bixby — assumedly an attempt at gender neutrality — but Samsung also sets the default voice on its devices to female. (Even more infuriating is the differing descriptions Samsung lists for the speaking styles of its virtual assistant: "chipper" and "cheerful" for the female Bixby and "confident" and "assertive" for the male.)

I think it's clear that our treatment of robots and voice assistants says a lot about our unconscious biases. No piece of technology is created without a shadow of humanity's greatest faults, and none is immune to corruption.

Pay close attention to the quote at the beginning of this book. It was first uttered in 2065 by Benjamin Blum — the father of modern robotics and Ziva Blum's dad. (Is it weird to reference fictional quotes from the future-past?)

It's not that I believe robots are evil. It's that they are created by humans, who, by nature, are less than perfect.

Many of the hacks carried out by the Bureau for Chaos are

based on real events — or controlled cyberattacks conducted by researchers in an academic setting.

In 2015, a German steel mill was hacked. The hackers went after the control systems, which prevented a blast furnace from being shut down and caused massive damage to the plant's equipment.

That same year, a security hole in Uconnect software allowed hackers to crash a Jeep into a ditch by cutting the engine and the brakes. University researchers have shown that Tesla's autopilot sensors can be tampered with to perceive objects where they don't exist or make objects "invisible."

As I was editing this book, a woman was struck and killed by a self-driving car crossing the street in Tempe, Arizona. As of this book's publication, we still don't know exactly why neither the car nor its human safety driver attempted to stop.

It's not that humans are inherently careless or that the people who work in artificial intelligence are evil. It's that humans care about profits and easy living.

This is one reason why as many as thirty-eight percent of US jobs are at risk of being overtaken by automation by 2030. (Compare that to thirty percent of jobs in the UK, thirty-five percent in Germany, and twenty-one percent in Japan.)

I feel profoundly lucky that my husband is even deeper in the tin-foil-hat camp than I am. On a recent vacation to Arizona, a worker at McDonald's actually refused to take our order. She pointed us toward the self-serve kiosk in the middle of the restaurant, and my husband asked me if we could leave. (We walked next door to Carl's Jr., where a human took our order and fried our chicken tenders by hand.)

Automation doesn't just threaten jobs in manufacturing, hospitality, health care, and food service. Journalists, narrators, and even authors may soon find their livelihoods threatened.

In just one year, *The Washington Post* produced 850 news

articles using its own automated storytelling technology known as Heliograf. This huge swath of articles included 500 stories centered around the election and around 300 reports about the Rio Olympics. It's important to note that *The Post* was bought by Amazon's Jeff Bezos back in 2013, but it isn't the only news outlet utilizing AI in some way.

Reuters uses an application called News Tracer to "extract insights from social media" to give reporters a head start in churning out breaking news stories. Basically, it identifies clusters of Twitter users talking about the same thing, rates an event's "newsworthiness," and attempts to vet the source to determine whether or not the information is factual.

The New York Times has developed Editor to apply relevant tags to news articles, group meta data, and categorize article elements such as pull quotes and key points. The goal is to simplify research and fact-checking.

The Times is also experimenting with AI for moderating comments with a tool from Google's parent company, Alphabet. The tool sorts comments based on a sliding scale of "toxicity" and allows readers to self-select comments that are more or less inflammatory.

ViralGauge, the tool used in the book to predict just how "viral" a news story will go is loosely based on HitPredictor — a real-life tool owned by iHeartMedia to predict which songs will be hits.

In his book *Hit Makers*, Derek Thompson writes about HitPredictor and its UK cousin, SoundOut. According to Thompson, each song is given a numeric rating based on "catchiness," with sixty-five being the threshold that predicts a potential viral hit. (Justin Bieber's "Sorry" scored a seventy-seven, while Adele's "Hello" scored 105.)

Artificial intelligence is even being used to create fiction. In 2017, Botnik Studios released an AI-generated *Harry Potter* story using two predictive keyboards. The story is called "Harry Potter and the Portrait of what Looked Like a Large Pile of Ash," and it is hilariously bad. It features a tap-dancing Ron who eats Hermione's family, a ghost called Mr. Staircase, and Death Eaters who enjoy ironic T-shirts.

AI may soon be reaching into the audiobook space, too. Amazon Polly is a new service that turns text into more lifelike speech. The tool has fifty-two different voices and is available in twenty-five languages. Already the service has spawned new endeavors to turn books into podcast-length chapters narrated by these computerized voices, and it's only a matter of time before they are applied to full-length audiobooks. (Google claims that its text-to-speech system, Tacotron 2, is indistinguishable from a human voice.)

Proponents of AI technology insist that these products and services aren't designed to *replace* humans. Rather, they say, they're intended to "free up" humans to do more high-value work.

But to anyone with even an ounce of common sense, it's clear that as these technologies get better and better, they're going to allow media companies and publishers to produce nearly infinite amounts of content on the cheap, and human creators are going to suffer.

Even worse than the dystopian hellscape run by robots we'll all soon be living in is the highly surveilled police state that we consumers are funding with our own hard-earned money.

Not sure what I'm talking about? Go ask Alexa.

The proliferation of home assistant devices made by Google, Amazon, Apple, and Microsoft are all doing what seemed crazy and terrifying in the context of *Nineteen Eighty-Four* and *The Handmaid's Tale*: normalizing widespread surveillance.

Of course, Amazon's device is designed to listen locally (meaning on the device itself) and only starts recording once you say the "wake word." After that, data from your request is housed in Amazon's servers — waiting to be used to improve the service, market things to you, or be sold to third-party developers.

But what devices are designed to do and what they're capable of doing are two very different things. One British researcher has already proven that the device can be hacked with just a few minutes of physical access.

By installing his own software, he was able to stream audio from the device to a remote server — essentially transforming the helpful home assistant into a stylish bug.

The FBI can neither confirm nor deny wiretapping Amazon home devices, and Amazon Echo data has already been involved in a 2015 murder case. (Amazon did push back against investigators' requests, and the defendant willingly relinquished his data.)

Any freedom-loving person should be alarmed by the sheer *possibility* of a home device listening to your conversations (and your arguments, political discussions, love-making, vacation plans, etc.), but the truth is that too many people are willing to subject themselves to these kinds of intrusions for the promise of greater convenience.

Ah, convenience — the root of all evil. Convenience is what prompts us to install so-called "smart locks" in our homes, get our meals delivered by robot, and tell Alexa everything from what music we want to hear to what kind of toilet paper to order. It may save us five seconds or five minutes in the short run, but in the long run it's costing us jobs, money, and privacy.

Let me be clear: I'm not hating on Amazon. I love Amazon, both as a customer and as a book vendor. But I am reexamining the slow bleed of personal information that companies like Amazon, Facebook, Google, and Apple are siphoning from us on a daily basis. I want to limit the amount of data I'm putting out in the world, but at the moment I'm still struggling to find a balance between using the services I need and maintaining my privacy.

I'm also fighting back against the rapid concentration of wealth and power among a few corporate monoliths. I am making an effort to support local businesses — and the humans who work there — whenever I can.

You can do your part by supporting this human (me) in my creative endeavors. You can show your love for my books by leaving a review. Reviews help readers discover indie authors like myself, and I really appreciate them.

And don't forget to sign up for my Reader Army. Members get awesome sneak peeks and extras. It ensures that I can still get in touch with you and organize the revolution following a robot apocalypse.

Just visit www.tarahbenner.com to join. And stay human, my friends. Stay human.

Looking for your next great read?
Check out more books by Tarah Benner:

Recon
Exposure
Outbreak
Lockdown
Annihilation
Lawless
Lifeless
Ruthless
Dauntless
Bound in Blood
The Defectors
Enemy Inside
The Last Uprising

Follow on Twitter @TarahBenner.
"Like" the books on Facebook.
Connect at www.tarahbenner.com.

89352710R00207

Made in the USA
Lexington, KY
26 May 2018